BLAC

The Aleph Null Chronicles: Book One

A Dark Fantasy Novel

DEAN FRANK LAPPI

"Chaos and absolute power collide with the awakening of the Aleph Null, true wielder of Black Numbers."

– *from* **The Black Numbers** *manuscript*

REVISED EDITION

Copyright © 2013 by DEAN FRANK LAPPI

All rights reserved

Print edition

Except as permitted under the U.S. Copyright Act of 1976, no part of this publication may be reproduced, distributed or transmitted in any form or by any means, or stored in a database or retrieval system without the prior written permission of the publisher.

This is a work of fiction. Names, characters, places and incidents are products of the author's imagination or are used fictitiously and are not to be construed as real. Any resemblance to actual events, locales, organizations, or persons, living or deceased, is entirely coincidental

Original cover artwork by Sellingpix, royalty free and licensed from Dreamstime.com.

ISBN-13: 978-0-9891726-0-8

Published by DEAN FRANK LAPPI

Cover Design by Dean Frank Lappi

Dedication

To my editor, Erica Anderson – thank you for the amazing edit you performed on this book and for offering such fantastic ideas when I run my myriad book questions by you. Your insight and knowledge was helpful in so many ways.

To Pam and Wayne, who suffered through the early drafts of the manuscript and provided wonderful feedback that improved the book greatly.

To Lisa Danforth for her amazing ability to find continuity issues no one else can.

To all of my good friends at Myrrdin Publishing Group – thank you for your support, in-depth conversations about everything relating to books, and your friendships over the years.

And finally to my mom and dad, who always told me that I could be successful at anything in life if I worked hard enough.

Other books by DEAN FRANK LAPPI

BLOOD NUMBERS

The Aleph Null Chronicles: Book Two (Now Available)

BROKEN NUMBERS

The Aleph Null Chronicles: Book Three (Coming 2014)

BEYOND NUMBERS

The Aleph Null Chronicles: Book Four (Coming 2015)

Visit **http://www.deanlappi.com** for the latest news and updates on books and news by Dean Frank Lappi

A Note From The Author

Sometimes a new author, filled with the excitement of getting their first book published, releases it to the public before it is fully ready, and that is what happened when I first released *Black Numbers* in 2011. I have since fully revised the book.

The mathematics in this series were intentionally described without going into any mathematical depth. I wrote it this way because I wanted the math to be conceptual as a way to explain magic, for it to be more visually spectacular than mathematically precise. I did this because I felt the story transcended the math, and also because I imagine most readers are not mathematicians. My apologies to any true mathematicians who may read this and be disappointed. But I also hope that the story itself pulls you in and that the visual way that I describe the math is just as rewarding and enjoyable.

Audience

While Black Numbers is a traditional fantasy novel in most ways, it has adult-oriented themes not suitable for children under the age of 17, including a few scenes of sexual-based violence. Parental review is recommended before letting your teenager read it.

CONTENTS

Prologue | 1 | 2 | 3 | 4 | 5 | 6 | 7 | 8 | 9 | 10 | 11 | 12 | 13 | 14 | 15 | 16 | 17 | 18 | 19 | 20 | 21 | 22 | 23 | 24 | 25 | 26 | 27 | 28 | 29 | 30 | 31 | 32 | 33 | 34 | 35 | 36 | 37 | 38 | 39 | 40 | 41 | 42 | 43 | 44 | 45 | 46 | 47 | 48 | Epilogue | About the Author

See what's next for Sid in
Blood Numbers:
The Aleph Null Chronicles: Book Two

Prologue

The Korpor glided across the snow-covered ground of the dark forest, making no sound as it moved from tree to tree, sniffing constantly as it progressed toward its goal.

The early spring air in the forest was sweet and warm even for so late at night, but it was not the sweetness of the forest the Korpor was interested in. It paused and caught just a whiff of the boy's power of numbers and anxiously turned toward the direction where the scent was strongest, following it as easily as a physical trail.

It paused and listened, and from a distance it heard the soft footfalls of a deer. Blood lust filled it, but the Korpor pushed its hunger aside and continued on, for it had something more important to do than to feed.

The Korpor's massive body was heavily muscled and covered in white fur, and it moved through the woods silently and almost invisibly against the snowy ground. It leapt over a large, fallen Miq tree and as it landed on the other side it looked up at an even larger Miq tree, its base at least ten times larger than the trees surrounding it. On the branches not far up the tree, the Korpor saw a platform made from wood. It knew the boy had created it, his scent still lingering on the wood.

It walked around the tree and on the other side it came upon a giant Cassikan bear, carnivorous and easily the most aggressive of all bears, with long fangs that could deliver a poisonous bite that would kill its prey in just a matter of moments. It had black fur with a deep red stripe running down its back, and massive paws tipped with long, sharp claws. It was feasting on a badger that it had recently killed, burying its snout into the carcass and ripping out bloody flesh. It didn't notice the Korpor's presence at first, and the Korpor curiously studied the huge animal, having only seen a few of them before.

Suddenly, the bear must have smelled the Korpor, for the animal swung around with a snarl, rising up on its hind legs. It roared savagely, moving its long-clawed paws up and down in a rage.

The Korpor rose up to its full height, almost as tall as the bear, and growled deeply in its throat, then fully opened its huge eyes and glared at the animal.

The mighty bear whimpered and dropped to all four legs, backing away and lowering its head to the ground in submission and pain.

Finally, it swung around and loped away, crashing through the brush as fast as it could.

The Korpor smiled, then turned and continued on its way, already forgetting the encounter.

It soon stopped at the edge of a clearing and peered from around a large oak tree at a small house that stood on the other side. It could see everything as clearly as if it were day through its huge blue eyes, eyes that covered almost the entire top half of its head.

It blinked its left eye, followed by its right as it stared at the house. It smiled again, its sharp teeth gleaming in the meager moonlight.

The Korpor, without realizing it, slowly raked its long claws along the bark of the tree, cutting into the hard wood as easily as flesh. It inhaled deeply and shuddered at the intoxicating scent of the unawakened power simmering inside of the boy who slept in his bedroom not more than thirty paces away.

The Korpor knew that the boy was too young to Proof right now at just eight years old, but the time would come soon, perhaps in as few as seven or eight years, when he would be ready for the Proofing. The Korpor would know then if he was truly the Aleph Null, the one destined to awaken the incredible power of Black Numbers. But even now, at such a young age, the Korpor felt the astounding potential in the boy, and knew that he could very well be the one it had searched for so many thousands of seasons.

The Korpor trembled in anticipation of their next encounter, and exhaled harshly to push the sexual tension from its body. It needed to see what the boy looked like, to smell him from as close as possible, so it stepped from the treeline and moved quickly across the small clearing, angling over until it approached the house from the back. Two small windows were cut through the wall, covered with thick deer hides to keep the cold out. The Korpor followed the scent of the numbers to the window on the right and pressed its face right up to the stiff hide and inhaled deeply.

It reached up with one claw and sliced a small opening in the hide and peered through the cut. The Korpor could see in the darkest shadows of the room, its vision making everything glow in a blue light, and it immediately turned its head toward a narrow cot sitting against the wall to its right. It saw the form of the boy huddled underneath two thick woolen blankets, his head resting on a bundled-up coat.

The boy shivered as if feeling the cold air streaming through the small slit in the window covering, or perhaps he shivered because he subconsciously felt the presence of the Korpor. He lifted an arm up and pulled the blankets higher around his head until just a tuft of brown hair was visible.

The Korpor started to tremble again from its need to have the boy, and it stayed where it was until the moon was almost to the horizon and the sky began to grow lighter.

Then it slowly blinked its left eye, followed by its right eye, and backed away from the window, crossed the clearing, and faded into the darkness of the woods.

* * *

Sid grinned as he slid down the small hill to the main road that led into town, balancing on both feet and coming precariously to a stop at the bottom. It was sunny and warm enough that he didn't have to wear his wool jacket, the first nice weather to come after a particularly cold winter. The sun reflected brilliantly off of the snow crystals as they melted, the constant dripping of water underneath the hard crust a sure sign that spring was going to arrive soon. Sid took in a deep breath and smiled fully. The air even smelled differently, both damp and pleasant with just a hint of wet dirt. After more than five months of breathing sterile winter air, it seemed—alive to him.

His father, Danicu, had woken him up early to walk to the village of Orm-Mina for some supplies. The village was small, with no more than 300 people living in or near it. Like most small villages, it had a small tobacco store that sold not only tobacco leaf, but also tea, coffee, flour, spices, and other dried goods that folks either didn't grow themselves or were running short of after a long winter.

Sid was quite proud of the fact that, at eight years old, his father now considered him old enough to travel to town on his own.

He ran most of the way, his young body not tiring at all, and arrived at the tobacco store only slightly winded. He carefully opened the old wooden door to the shop and peeked inside. He immediately smelled the leaf tobacco and tea, a mixture that brought a grin to his face.

Old Mrs. Wessmank was reaching up to place a large tin of tea onto a tall shelf and turned toward him, motioning him into the store. "Close the door Sidoro. What do you think it is, summer? You'll let all of the heat out of the room."

Sid quickly stepped into the room and shut the door behind him. The room wasn't large, maybe fifteen paces wide by thirty paces long, with two tall and narrow windows facing the street. Mrs. Wessmank usually kept the curtains closed because she said the light damaged the tobacco and tea leaves, so the shop was often filled with deep shadows that flickered from the many candles burning in the room. Today the sun was bright outside, so the curtains were drawn tightly shut, and Sid had to wait a few moments for his eyes to fully adjust to the darkened interior of the room.

"Come on boy, I don't have all morning, what do you need?" Mrs. Wessmank bustled over to him, wiping her hands on her blue apron.

Sid handed her the small burlap sack that he had brought from home. "Um, I need some black tea, a measure of salt, three scoops of rice, and one piece of red licorice please." He finished saying the last bit with a lowered voice, hoping that it sounded like part of the list.

Mrs. Wessmank glared down at him. "Hmm... a piece of licorice is it? Your father has never spent his hard-earned coin on licorice. Did he say you could buy a piece?"

Sid lowered his eyes, unable to meet her fierce gaze. He couldn't lie to her; he never had been able to. "No, Mrs. Wessmank, he didn't."

Mrs. Wessmank made a noise at the back of her throat, a sound she often made when she was proven right in something. She took the burlap sack and moved about the store. She reached into a wooden barrel and pulled out a handful of black tea and wrapped it in a piece of cloth. Then she removed a tight lid from a small barrel, grunting as she pulled it up, and used a small wooden scoop to get a full measure of salt, which she poured slowly into the salt box Sid's father had sent inside of the sack. She then opened a third barrel, this one much larger, and scooped out rice three times into another piece of cloth and tied it up before carefully placing it into the burlap sack, which she set on the floor by Sid. "That will be three copper pieces."

Sid dug into his pocket and counted out three coins from the five that his father had given him, and handed them to her. She bent down to put the copper pieces into a box under the counter and when she stood up, she held a small piece of red licorice out for Sid. "Next time, do not try to fool me Sidoro."

Sid eyed the licorice hungrily, but then lowered his head and mumbled, "I can't accept that."

When Mrs. Wessmank didn't respond, he raised his head and was surprised to see that her eyes were damp.

She took his hand and set the piece of licorice into his palm and closed his fingers around it. "You are a special boy, Sidoro. Don't ever change." She briskly turned and waddled over to the stove, lifted a pot of boiling water, and poured it into two cups on the table, the steam rising around her face before setting the pot back on the stove.

Sid opened his fingers and looked at the shiny red candy, then carefully put it into his trouser pocket. It was a treasure that he didn't deserve, but his mouth watered when he thought of the tart sweetness. He had never before asked his father to buy him a piece of licorice, and he wasn't sure what made him ask for it this morning. Maybe it was because he was alone for the first time. He heard a small cough and turned, hurrying to the table where a plate of date cookies sat next to his steaming cup.

Mrs. Wessmank sat down in her chair very slowly, making small pained sounds.

Having tea and cookies was Sid's favorite part of the trip into town. Mrs. Wessmank always offered tea and cookies to he and his father when they came for supplies. His father rarely accepted the invitation to stay, although he did on a few occasions when Sid begged him. But the visits were always short and uncomfortably silent, as if his father couldn't stand to be in the same room as the old woman. Most times Mrs. Wessmank would simply hand Sid two or three cookies as he and his father were leaving. They were usually simple sugar cookies, crispy yet sweet, but on rare occasions she made date cookies, which were his favorite.

Sid quickly picked up a date cookie and took a large bite, chewing with relish. He had watched her make them once when he had wandered into her store while waiting for his father to attend to other business in town, and had been enthralled with the way she so quickly moved her hands as she prepared them. She rolled out cookie dough until it was flat and thin, then she used an up-side-down glass to punch round holes in the dough, doing it so precisely that there were very few scraps left. Then she placed a dollop of minced dates in the middle of each and folded the cookie dough over, making each one look like a half moon. She had finished by pressing the edges together with a fork to seal the dates inside. When she had taken them out of the small wood-fired oven, the edges of the cookies were brown and crispy; but that was what made them so delicious because the crunchy cookie mixed with the soft dates inside, a perfect combination.

He swallowed his first bite and put the rest of the cookie into his mouth, chewing loudly.

Mrs. Wessmank smiled, looking pleased at the way he ate her cookies with such abandon. She leaned over to him conspiratorially and said, "Do you want to hear the story of the Korpor?"

Sid stopped chewing briefly, then nodded eagerly. Some crumbs stuck to the corners of his lips as he smiled.

She chuckled. "I thought you would like this one."

She situated herself, making more soft, pained sounds as she got herself comfortable. She finally stopped moving around and stared at Sid for a few moments.

Sid didn't move. There was no way he was going to give her any reason not to tell the tale. He loved her stories almost as much as her cookies and tea.

Mrs. Wessmank narrowed her eyes, then began speaking in a hushed voice, moving her wrinkled hands to emphasize the story. She told of how she had grown up in a rich household, on the edge of a large city with her father, mother, and twin sister, and of how she had a normal childhood. They had lived good lives until one dark night. Mrs. Wessmank paused here, drawing out the suspense until Sid was practically falling off the chair leaning toward her.

She smiled and continued very quietly. "There are stories of an ancient and powerful creature called the Korpor, stories often told by the flickering light of a fire. It is said that it roams the land, looking to take people from their homes. No one knows why, but some think that it searches for a person who has a special kind of magic."

She stopped speaking briefly to raise the suspense, before continuing. "I never believed in the stories, but that one night, many, many years ago, when I was only a handful of years older than you are now, my sister and I caught a glimpse of the Korpor."

Sid gasped. "You actually saw it?"

Mrs. Wessmank chuckled. "We sure did. We both had peeked out of our bedroom window one night, although I don't even remember what had awakened us. My sister and I looked fearfully through our white curtains and in the moonlight, we saw it glide from tree to tree. My sister immediately wanted to go outside to get a better look at it. I was afraid, but I wouldn't let my sister go out alone, so I followed her. We walked barefoot through the woods in our nightgowns, peering at every shadow."

Sid stared, wide-eyed. "Didn't you even take a knife with you for protection?"

She laughed softly. "No Sidoro, we didn't even think of it. We were just little girls."

Sid scoffed. "I never go anywhere without my knife, and I'm younger than you were then."

Mrs. Wessmank narrowed her eyes. "Don't get smart, boy. Do you want me to continue?"

Sid nodded. "I'm sorry. Yes, please."

Mrs. Wessmank smiled kindly at him again, but then turned serious. "We walked only a short ways into the woods when all of a sudden the creature peered around a tree right in front of us. It looked at us with huge blue eyes, eyes so large that they covered almost half of its face. Blinding pain shot through our minds and we both screamed and fell to our knees. Eventually, the pain faded away and when we finally dared to open our eyes, the creature was gone." She puffed her hands outward with the last word.

Mrs. Wessmank sat quietly for a few moments before continuing. "My sister and I never saw it again. But I'll never forget the pain."

She stared directly into Sid's eyes, studying him as if searching for something.

He stared back, frightened but enjoying the story.

As if satisfied by his reaction, she laughed lightly, her eyes brightening.

Sid sat in the chair, the remaining half a cookie forgotten on his plate. It was the best story he had ever heard.

Mrs. Wessmank smiled and motioned toward the door. "Now you had better finish that cookie and be getting back home with your supplies or your father will come looking for you."

Sid stuffed the last piece of cookie into his mouth and chewed it quickly, then took a long drink of the cooled tea, wiping his mouth with his sleeve. He jumped down from the chair, grabbed the sack and ran for the door. Before he opened it though, he stopped and turned back to Mrs. Wessmank. "Do you think the Korpor will come for me one day?"

Mrs. Wessmank studied him for a moment, a look of sadness on her face. "I hope not Sidoro. But if it does, you need to be brave, for it will mean you are special. Now go on, I'm just an old woman telling stories that I shouldn't be telling to a boy your age. Forget about it and bring your father the supplies."

Sid eyed her carefully. He knew she was not telling him everything, but he didn't know what she was leaving out. He then thought of the Korpor and his imagination started going wild. What if he had a special kind of magic and the Korpor came for him? He would be a hero to the people with the Korpor by his side. He happily waved goodbye to Mrs. Wessmank and opened the door, already forgetting her look of concern as he shut it behind him and took off at a full run up the street.

When he got home he set the sack on the floor, dropped the two remaining copper coins on the table, then ran outside again to play in the woods. He was halfway across the yard when he heard his father yell for him. He turned and saw his father shutting the door to the chicken coup, a chicken struggling in his large hand.

Sid sighed and walked over, worried that he was going to have to do more chores.

His father spoke calmly as he held the chicken against an old tree stump, the wood cut and gouged from many years of slaughtering animals on it. "Did you get the supplies?"

"Yes Father. They're in the house."

His father nodded without looking at him, pulling an axe free from the wood. "Good, did you feed the pigs?"

Sid nodded. "I did before I left for town. Can I go play in the woods now?"

Danicu looked up at Sid, then nodded as he brought the axe blade down on the neck of the chicken. Blood spurted and the chicken jerked briefly before it stopped moving. He spoke quietly as he threw the head into a bucket, "Be home before dark."

Sid nodded. "Of course, father." He turned and ran across the yard, entering the treeline and disappearing from view.

Danicu watched his boy enter the woods, then looked back down and began tearing the feathers out of the chicken's body, whistling while he worked.

Sid ran for a ways, then slowed and started walking quietly, moving from tree to tree pretending he was the Korpor. No one would see him, but if they did, he would inflict them with blinding pain for daring to look at him. He liked that.

He smiled as he lifted a branch out of his way. He wasn't scared of the woods and he decided to explore further than he had ever gone from his home. He was a Korpor after all and he had the new knife his father had made for him. It was very sharp and he marked his trail through the woods by cutting the tips off of large ferns every hundred steps.

He walked through the woods until the sun was high overhead. He had made small trails all over the woods where he lived, but making a new one this far from home was exciting. He heard the loud honking of geese and looked up in time to see them flying past just over the tops of the trees, the air whooshing from their wings. He took a step, his neck still craned upward and stumbled on a root, falling hard to the ground. He pushed himself back to his feet, brushing snow from his trousers and realized he was getting a little tired, so he decided to head back home.

But not far away he saw a thick clump of bushes and he thought he could see something man-made through them. He crept forward and pushed through them and gasped softly when he looked out at a small field with a hut at the other end. The hut was small and leaned slightly as if ready to fall down at any moment. It looked deserted at first, but then he saw a thin wisp of smoke curl up from a small pipe in the roof.

He saw junk thrown haphazardly and piled high in places. Sticking up from the last of the snow cover by the hut, he saw a strange, colorful shape, but he couldn't tell what it was from so far away. Over toward the back of the hut, Sid caught sight of a muddy pen that held a few pigs.

He sat at the edge of the field, partly hidden by the bushes, his heart racing.

This must be Rugger's place. No one knew where the man lived, or even if he really existed at all. But as Sid looked around, he was sure of it. No one lived out here that he knew of. There were no roads or trails leading to or from here; it was so isolated that it could only be Rugger's home.

The kids in town had all heard the stories that Rugger would catch you at night if you weren't careful. Sid had heard it from Tris, his only friend, one night the previous summer while they lay under the stars in the field behind his house. Tris always said things to scare Sid, to make him feel inferior, and Sid put up with it because Tris was the only person who ever talked to him. But that night Sid had vowed to some day prove he was as brave as Tris.

Kneeling on the edge of the field now, remembering that night, Sid felt cold and scared. But he wasn't going to run home. He was a Korpor after all and the Korpor wasn't scared of anybody.

Sid saw a massive, dead tree standing on the other side of the field, only a short way from the old hut. It was gray and had no bark, the top blackened and split. It looked like a pitchfork pointing up to the sky. It would be a good tree to hide behind and get a better look at the hut. He took a deep breath and released it to steady his nerves, then made his way across the field, crouching low and placing each step carefully, the soft crunching of snow under his feet sounding loud in the quiet field.

By the time he got to the old tree, he was shaking with fear from being out in the open for so long. He leaned his head back, then turned and pressed his face against the cold, dry wood. Soon his breathing and heartbeat slowed.

He took a deep breath and almost gagged.

A rotten smell filled the air. It wasn't the pigs. He had pigs of his own and they didn't smell this bad. He took a tentative sniff of the air and immediately put his hand to his mouth to keep from throwing up. It smelled like rotting meat and it was then that he noticed a massive mound of bones behind the house. He crept over to it, pinching his nose tightly against the smell and saw a rusted barrel sitting next to the bones, filled to the top with a blackened soup of guts and blood.

Sid backed away, feeling sick to his stomach, and turned to study the hut. It didn't have any windows and the siding was made of warped boards, blackened from dried pitch. There was no door. It must be on the other side.

He listened closely but couldn't hear anything except the soft grunting of the pigs. He wanted to turn around and run back the way he had come, but he thought of Tris and knew he had to find something to prove that not only was Rugger's place real, but that Sid was brave enough to come out here by himself.

Taking a shallow breath, Sid moved to the side of the hut, putting his back to the wall. He could feel his heart beating heavily in his chest. He inched slowly along the wall and when he came to the corner, he put his cheek to the rough wood and took in a few deep breaths to try and stop his teeth from chattering. He saw the colorful object that he had seen from across the field and his blood ran cold when he realized it was a red shirt sticking up from a huge pile of rotting clothing half-buried in ice and snow.

He had to get the shirt. He could take Tris out here later and the shirt would prove he had gotten this close to the hut. He took two deep breaths then stepped around the corner of the shack, but before he could take a step, he felt a hand grab his collar and spin him around, lifting him until he was dangling above the ground. Sid struggled and was thrown backward, landing hard on the ground. He looked up in a panic at a man standing two paces from him.

The man wore stained coveralls smeared with fresh blood and he had a long, white beard that hung to his waist.

The man chuckled, then spoke in a high, singsong voice. "I've never had a child come to me before. How convenient."

Sid slowly tilted his head back and began shaking uncontrollably when he looked at the man's face. The nose was unlike anything he had ever seen. It was merely two narrow slits that sucked open and closed like the gills of a fish; but it was the man's eyes, partly hidden behind long stringy hair, that made Sid sharply draw in his breath. He cried out and scrambled to his feet, but before he could take a step, the man lunged forward and struck him in the temple. Sid hit the ground hard and watched in a bleary daze as muddy boots stepped close to his face.

Then blackness crept over his vision and he saw nothing more.

* * *

Sid felt himself returning to consciousness. He was sitting on a hard wooden chair, his feet not touching the floor, his chin resting on his chest.

He didn't open his eyes, afraid to see the man again, hoping this was all a dream. He sat still and slowly became aware of a sound. He wasn't sure what it was at first, and when he tried to concentrate, it faded away completely.

After a short while, he dreamed of his father eating a slab of beef steak. His father picked up the meat and took huge bites, tearing gristle, fat, and flesh from the bone. Then he started to gnaw the bone itself, sucking the marrow noisily out of it. Juice dripped down his chin and Sid wanted to yell at him to stop. 'Why was his father eating this way?' Then his father's jaws opened impossibly wide, his mouth stretching until it looked like it would split his face in two. He stuffed the whole bone into his mouth and chewed with his back teeth in a steady crunching rhythm.

Sid couldn't stop himself from crying, his small chest heaving with each sob. Slowly, the image faded away and a quiet darkness descended upon him. He realized, with a final sob of relief, that it had just been a bad a dream.

Then he heard the crunch of bones again, the sound real and close by. He tried to move his arms but realized they were tied behind his back to the chair. A chill ran through him and his breathing came in short gasps. In trepidation, he opened his eyes a crack and through his eyelashes, he looked to see where the sound was coming from. It was to his left but the blurred image made no sense to him. He opened his eyes a little wider and when the image became clear, he immediately squeezed them tightly shut again and whimpered.

Rugger isn't real. He can't be real.

Sid heard a chair creak and then slow, heavy footsteps approached him. He jerked when he felt Rugger pinch his left eyelid with two fingers and lift it up. Sid didn't dare move as he watched the man lean down until they were face-to-face, his breath reeking of rotten meat. "Do not shut your eyes boy. If you do, I will scoop them out. Do you understand?"

The man's high voice would have been beautiful if it weren't for the words themselves.

The fingers left his eyelid, and Sid blinked rapidly to keep back the tears, then opened both eyes. He shivered as he watched Rugger walk back to his chair and sit down, picking at his teeth with a black fingernail and staring at Sid with a bored expression.

The man was tall, his head just about touching the ceiling even though he was slightly stooped at the shoulders. He appeared to be middle-aged, and his clothing was ragged and full of holes. Sid focused his gaze on Rugger's beard because even though it had pieces of bloody meat knotted within the hair, it was better than looking into the man's eyes again.

Rugger spoke sharply in his high voice. "Look at me boy!"

Sid shook his head. He couldn't.

The man's voice softened. "You will obey me boy."

The soft, high voice frightened Sid because it was so different from the man's visage. He looked slowly up to Rugger's eyes and before he could stop himself, he voided his bowels.

The stench filled the room and Rugger took a deep breath and laughed.

Sid didn't care. He couldn't take his gaze from Rugger's eyes now. Although partly hidden by long dirty hair, they were the deepest black that he had ever seen and were so large that they took up almost the entire top portion of the man's face.

Rugger smiled. It was a beautiful smile and Sid relaxed slightly, until the man raised his hand and took a large bite from the front leg of a deer, the hide still on it.

Rugger pulled hard with his teeth, ripping away flesh, sinew, and hide. He chewed slowly, blood dripping down to his beard. He reached two fingers into his mouth and pulled out a wad of hair and tossed it over his shoulder, then swallowed the flesh.

Sid noticed that the man's teeth were yellow and very sharp. He closed his eyes, unable to watch anymore.

The chair creaked. Sid heard the leg of the deer fall to the floor with a thud and heavy footsteps approached him again. Tears squeezed from his closed eyes and ran down his cheeks as he trembled uncontrollably. The stench of rotting flesh was so strong that he wanted to vomit. But he also caught a faint scent of freshly baked bread. The two smells together were nauseating.

He felt a hand on his head again, but this time the fingers slowly caressed his hair and then traced lightly down his forehead. The fingers rested on Sid's eyes and he stopped breathing, too terrified to move. But they started moving again down Sid's cheek and to his mouth, sliding along his upper lip and then down to his lower lip.

Then the hands were gone from his face and Sid felt the rope being untied from his wrists. A flare of hope surged through him. He was going to be let go. He felt a rush of relief and he almost cried. But before he could even bring his hands around to his front, Rugger grabbed him by the shoulders and lifted him from the chair.

Sid screamed and struggled, but the grip on his shoulders was too tight as he was lifted clear of the chair. He opened his eyes and looked wildly around. The man carried him at arm's length, like a parent carried a peeing baby, over to a pile of hay in the corner of the room.

Sid looked at the hay for a moment, not comprehending what was happening, and was thrown roughly down onto his stomach. Straw poked his face, hurting him. Before he could move, Rugger grabbed Sid's trousers and yanked them off. Sid tried crawling away, but the man put a foot on his back and pushed him down. Sid flailed his hands, throwing hay everywhere, but it was no use. He was pinned securely by Rugger's heavy foot.

He gasped for air and turned his head to look behind him.

Rugger stood quietly for a moment looking down at him. Then, slowly, with one hand, the man pushed down his own dirty trousers.

Sid looked away, terrified by the hardness sticking up from between the man's legs.

The pressure of the foot left his back, and Sid heard hay crunch behind him. He didn't know what was happening but he was so scared he couldn't think straight. He scrambled forward on all fours and looked back wildly when he got to the wall. The monster of a man smiled at him as he grabbed Sid's foot and dragged him back to the bed of hay. Sid kicked and screamed, and actually connected with Rugger's shin.

In a rage, Rugger leaned down and punched Sid hard across the temple again.

Sid fell onto his stomach and through a haze, he briefly heard the hay crunch and hard calloused hands grabbed his waist. He then felt a new pain flare inside of him before darkness descended.

But the darkness faded quickly away.

Sid opened his eyes. He still lay on his stomach in the straw. He shifted slightly and a sharp jab of pain hit him. It felt like there was a knife buried in him. He tried to shift over to his side, but pain flared again sharply and he cried out. He panted as he laid half on his stomach and half on his side.

From across the room he heard a chuckle. Its high pitch made him shudder.

"Hurts, don't it boy?"

Sid shifted again and tried to roll over onto his back. The pain was intense, but his desire to get away was more important to him. He gritted his teeth and finally managed to get onto his back. After a short while, the pain faded slightly, so he put his hands down on the straw and tried pushing himself up. It took two tries, but he finally managed to sit up. His head spun and he threw up.

Another chuckle came from the corner of the room.

Anger flared in Sid and he spit toward the man. "I hope you die!"

Rugger looked quizzically at Sid, tilting his head a little to the side. Sid felt a pressure against his mind and he instinctively blocked it as if he were putting his hands up to protect his face from a strong wind.

Rugger's eyes rose in surprise, and jumping to his feet, he crossed the room and shook Sid by the shoulders. "What did you just do?"

Sid had no idea what the man was talking about, but the anger never left him. He felt more pressure against his brain, and he blocked it just as easily as the first time.

With a start, he realized he could see numbers in his mind as if they were solid objects. He had used mathematics for as long as he could remember and had often pictured numbers in his head as he added and subtracted, but now the felt alive, full of some kind of power, almost as if they were physically inside of him. It made him flush as he felt them simmering under the surface of his mind.

Rugger's voice sounded distant. "I've done this to a lot of children over the years, hoping they were the Aleph Null; praying that I could find the one before the Korpor did, to ruin the beast's chances of taking him or her like it took my father and killed him." The man blinked back tears and angrily wiped them away. "But none of the children showed any sign of numbers inside of them, so I killed each one. I had to, or I would've been hunted and killed myself. But you, you are different. I can feel the numbers in you even now."

Sid heard him from far away, but wasn't really listening to him. He was concentrating on his numbers. He could feel them bubbling from spaces within his mind that he never knew existed. He absently heard the man say, "I want you to kill that creature. Your numbers should physically awaken in a few years." But Sid ignored him. The power in the numbers filled him with joy, but also with a feeling he didn't understand.

Rugger slapped him across the face, leaned down to him, and whispered angrily. "Listen to me. Master the numbers. Master the numbers and kill the Korpor!"

Sid looked away, coming back to the real world fully, his cheek burning where he had been slapped. Then he felt a warm liquid oozing down his thighs and became light-headed when he saw the straw underneath him soaked with blood.

The man stood up, crossed the room, and sat back down. "Get your trousers back on and get out of here." He narrowed his eyes. "If you ever speak about me to anyone, I will know. I will be watching you carefully and will kill everyone you love if you even mention my name out loud. Do I make myself clear?"

Sid shivered, knowing that Rugger would not hesitate to do as he threatened. The thought of him hurting Mrs. Wessmank or his father was terrifying. He nodded, then forced himself to concentrate on what he had to do. He reached over, grabbed his trousers, and pulled them on, moving slowly to avoid more pain. They were torn, and when he slid the trousers to his waist, they fell open on his right side where the man had ripped them. But he also felt the knife and sheath still strapped to the inside of them. A thrill of hope filled him.

He stood up slowly and fastened his trousers closed, and as he did, pain flared in him again and he cried out, putting a hand to his backside. When he brought it back around, his fingers were red with blood.

Rugger looked at Sid's bloody hand and his face filled with emotion, his eyes flashing from anger to anguish to anger and back to anguish so quickly that Sid couldn't even see the changes happen. Finally, Rugger let out a soft sob and hung his head, his long, stringy hair almost touching the floor.

Sid held his breath, afraid to move. The room was silent except for the soft squeak of a mouse coming from the darkened corner behind him. The man remained still until, without knowing that he did it, Sid stepped backward and the floor board creaked, sounding loud inside the small room.

A chuckle came from Rugger, low and soft. He slowly raised his head and pushed the hair away from his face. His eyes glinted and he grinned, although there was no humor within the smile.

Sid backed up another step when Rugger stood up, the creak of the chair sending new shivers coursing through Sid.

Rugger moved toward him with a grotesque smile on his face.

"I think I'll have one more go at you before you leave. If you are the Aleph Null, then fucking you twice will only double the chances of your numbers awakening."

Sid was not going to let that happen. A cold anger welled up and he stopped shivering. As Rugger walked toward him, time seemed to slow down. Sid closed his eyes and saw his numbers floating in front of him again, but they were different now. They seemed to pulse with power and were drawn to a point in front of him. Numbers came from all over, more numbers than he had ever known existed. He pulled them from his mind and they flew toward him quicker than ever before, forming a solid wall in front of him. He felt a flush of warmth and power, like he could do anything.

Through the numbers, Sid heard a grunt and a loud impact in front of him, like a fist hitting a solid wall. The numbers bent back a little, but they held. He heard a howl of frustration, then a barrage of loud hammering. The numbers in his mind bounced around with each thud, like water in a pot when he banged the side with a metal spoon. But they didn't dissipate. Instinctively, Sid knew that the numbers were protecting him from the man. He risked opening his eyes. Rugger was only inches from him, his face mottled in rage as he struck at Sid. But his fists hit some kind of wall.

Sid was untouched.

The pounding stopped and Rugger closed his eyes.

Sid felt a new kind of pressure on him, and he saw his numbers start to bend, like they were being pushed and pulled at the same time. He found it more difficult to hold his numbers in place. Some of them slipped away, floating off into the distance. Then more of them followed in little clusters. He knew that he couldn't hold the numbers for much longer, so he did the only thing he could think of, he sent a cluster of his numbers toward Rugger with as much force as he could muster.

Rugger screamed in pain and put his hands to his head. The pressure against Sid's wall of numbers immediately ceased, although the scream continued for longer than Sid thought possible until the man slumped down to his knees, hanging his head.

Without pausing, Sid put his hand inside his trousers and touched his knife. With a deep breath, he released his numbers and they went flying away. At the same time he drew his knife and struck down at Rugger's head, but instead of penetrating his skull, the knife glanced sideways.

Rugger roared and stood up, his eyes flashing murderously.

Sid backed up, panting and holding the knife awkwardly in front of him. Rugger charged and Sid frantically tried to pull the numbers back in front of him like before, but he wasn't able to get them all there in time.

Rugger slammed violently into him, but the numbers that he had been able to call were enough to deflect the man off to the side, sending Sid to the floor in the opposite direction.

Rugger fell to the floor with a whoosh of breath and immediately struggled to his hands and knees.

Sid got up and without hesitating, he jumped on top of Rugger and plunged the knife into the middle of the man's back with a scream, the blade crunching through bone and sinking all the way to the hilt, so powerful was his rage.

Rugger fell hard to his stomach, his arms splayed out, gasping for breath.

Sid climbed off of the man and backed warily away, staring down at the figure lying on the floor. After a few moments, when Rugger didn't move, he carefully crept forward. Rugger's face was turned away, so Sid edged his way around until he was on the other side of him.

Rugger turned his massive eyes up at Sid and thick tears streamed down his face. Drool leaked out of his mouth and pooled on the floor.

Sid knelt down hesitantly.

A bubble of spittle formed between Rugger's lips and he moved his mouth soundlessly.

Sid leaned down lower and Rugger whispered softly, more breath than sound, "Kill the Korpor… please."

A soft bubbly sigh escaped Rugger's lips and he didn't take another breath. The monster of a man looked peaceful, almost innocent and child-like in death.

Sid looked at him for a few moments, then relief flooded through him and he started to shake. He looked down at his trembling hands. He couldn't believe it was over. He had killed the monster.

Bile rose in his throat and he threw up again, but there was no longer anything left in his stomach, so he dry heaved, his body convulsing hard.

When he was able to, he wiped at his mouth and stripped off his trousers, red and soaked with blood. As he did, the small piece of red licorice that Mrs. Wessmank had given to him fell to the floor. He bent down and picked up the shiny red candy with trembling fingers and just looked at it for a few moments, turning it in the meager light. Then, with a cry of anger, he flung it across the room with all his might.

He reached down and pulled at the hilt of the knife that he had buried in the man's back, but it wouldn't come out. The blade was stuck in bone. Hesitantly, he climbed onto the man's back and with both hands pulled as hard as he could. At first it didn't budge, so he pulled harder. Pain flared in his backside and he was about to give up when the knife slid out with a crunching sound.

Sid fell backward, holding the bloody knife, and sat hard on the dead man's legs. His vision swam, and he felt more blood run down his own legs. He sat there, gasping, until the pain faded away to a manageable throbbing.

Sid stood up on wobbly legs. He held the knife in his hand and stared at the almost black blood that dripped from it. He looked at the dead man one last time and then left the hut in a daze.

The sunlight blinded him after being in the dim interior of the hut for so long. He looked down at himself and was surprised to see how much blood covered him. He didn't know a person could have that much blood in their body. He stripped off his shirt and stepped over to the pile of clothing and dug into the snow until he found a shirt and trousers that were almost identical to his own and about the same size. They were dirty and wet from being buried in the snow and mud.

He felt ill at seeing the dozens of pieces of clothing buried in the snow, all that was left of the many children that Rugger had raped and murdered over the years.

Sid walked naked, except for his boots, around the hut toward the pigpen.

As he had hoped, there was a wooden barrel filled with rain water. He dropped the knife on the ground and dunked his head in the barrel. The water was ice cold, but he didn't care as he scrubbed his hair and face. It felt wonderful. He lifted his dripping head and then dipped his arms in the barrel and scrubbed them hard, paying extra attention to his fingers which were caked with blood. He then looked down at his bloody legs. Taking a deep breath, he slipped off his boots and climbed into the barrel. Water sloshed over the sides as he slid in up to his chest. It was so cold that he couldn't breathe, so he quickly reached down and scrubbed his bloody buttocks, private parts and legs. Thankfully, the cold water numbed him.

He climbed out of the barrel and stood shivering. Even though he had scrubbed the blood away, he still felt dirty and ashamed. The sunlight was warm and the water dried quickly on his skin. He dunked the dirty clothes he had found into the water and scrubbed at them. He then wrung them hard and held them up. They were about as clean as they were going to get. He put on the wet trousers and shirt and looked down at his bloody boots. He picked up some snow and scrubbed at them until they were relatively clean, then put them back on and stood up, stretching his back like a cat.

He picked up his knife and cleaned it in the barrel of water. The water was now red, but it still got the knife clean. When he finished, he tried to slip the knife into his trousers but realized that these new trousers didn't have the special sheath tied to the inside. So he went back to the door of the hut.

He hesitated, not wanting to go inside again. *What if Rugger really wasn't dead?* Angrily, he pushed his fear aside, shoved the door open and marched purposefully into the hut.

He saw his old trousers lying in the straw. He edged around the dead man without looking at him, reached down, untied the sheath from inside his torn trousers, and tied it inside his new trousers. He then slipped the knife into the sheath with a soft thunk. It was a comforting sound and it felt good to have the knife pushing against his thigh.

Sid quickly left the hut and looked up at the sun. He was surprised to see that it was already halfway toward the horizon.

Anger welled up inside as he thought of what Rugger had done to him. It was so blinding that he was tempted to go back inside and attack the man again, even though he was already dead. He fantasized about cutting off Rugger's penis, of scooping out his large black eyes and puncturing them with his knife. He wanted to kick him, stomp on his head, plunge his knife into him over and over and over.

Sid screamed up at the sky and fell to his knees, shaking uncontrollably. He then fell to his side and curled up as tightly as he could, rocking back and forth. Tears came and he cried violently. He stayed like this for a long time until the tears dried up and his crying subsided to an occasional hiccup. Finally he opened his eyes and looked at the snow and mud that stretched out in front of him.

He angrily wiped his eyes and sat up. He was not a baby!

He scowled as he stood up and promised himself he would never cry again. He turned and marched across the yard toward the field, walking awkwardly from the constant throbbing pain. His mind was filled with images of what had happened, bits and pieces flashing randomly. The pain, the blood, and the fear all vied for supremacy but all merged together into a burning anger. Tears sprang from his eyes again and he angrily wiped them away.

He would not cry, and he would never tell anyone what had happened, especially not his father.

Sid came to the old dead tree but didn't stop. When he got to the other side of the field and entered the woods, he turned and looked back at the hut. Smoke still spiraled from the small pipe in the roof, and it looked just like it had before.

Sid smiled to himself, a smile that wouldn't have looked right on a normal eight-year-old's face if someone were there to see it. It was flat and expressionless and his brown eyes were partially-lidded.

He had gone to the hut to get proof that he wasn't scared of Rugger, but instead he had battled the monster and won. He took comfort in that thought. Tris would never know about this place, nor would anyone else.

Sid entered the woods and followed his own trail signs for the rest of the afternoon until he reached the familiar trees and hills around his home. As the sun was setting, he stepped from the woods and saw his house across the yard. A think trail of smoke rose from the chimney and he could smell the distinctive aroma of cooked chicken. He turned back to the woods, already hidden in shadows.

He remembered being frightened of the woods at night. His father had once told him that there was nothing in the woods that would hurt him.

Sid now knew his father was a liar.

Real monsters existed.

Chapter 1

The Black Robe sat high up in the Oblate chamber on a stone platform built out from the wall. A gleaming black door, cut directly from the stone, stood open behind him. He folded his hands together and rested them on his beautifully crafted Miq desk. The wave-patterned grain of the wood from the rare and giant tree reflected the flickering light of the torches in the chamber. As always, his two Haissen bodyguards stood calmly behind him, radiating a deadly presence in their stillness.

He gazed down at the fourteen other members who made up the Oblate.

Thirteen Blue Robes sat facing him on hard chairs set in a semi-circle. Thick hoods concealed their faces and most hid their hands inside of thick sleeves.

He shifted his eyes down to his Red Robe. As the Fractionally Ascended, she sat just below him and to his left.

The silence stretched uncomfortably until the Black Robe finally spoke, his voice quivering as he forced himself to be heard. His lungs had wasted away at an alarming rate over the past few years, making it increasingly difficult for him to be heard from the top of the platform. "We need to wait another year before we Proof Danicu's boy. He is not ready."

The Red Robe briskly shook her head. "No, we cannot wait. As planned, Danicu has been teaching his son advanced mathematics, and he is confident that his boy could be the Aleph Null." She raised her voice. "You of all people know that we've been Proofing every potential Aleph Null for a thousand years, and every Proof has failed. Every... single... one! If there is even a chance that this boy is the Aleph Null, then we cannot let him slip through our fingers. We need to Proof him now!"

The Black Robe sighed. "No, it is too soon. Our chance for a successful Proofing will only increase as the boy matures."

The Red Robe raised her hands wide. "And what happens if some young whore spreads her legs for him? What then? You know that if he is the Aleph Null and he has his virginity taken by anything but the Korpor, his power of numbers will only partially awaken in him and he could be forever ruined—just a shell of what he would be as the Aleph Null. We cannot risk that!" The Red Robe turned her hidden face toward the Blue Robes. "In fact, I say we should have the Korpor *Ring* the boy."

Shocked whispers came from the Blue Robes, but the dark void inside of the Red Robe's hood made each Blue Robe lower their head uncomfortably. She lowered her voice to an ominous rasp. "It has been prophesied that a *Ringed* Aleph Null will have the power to expand the power of Black Numbers exponentially. We must take that chance, for with that harnessed power, we will no longer have to control from behind the scenes." She slammed her hand on her chair. "We can finally take power for ourselves!"

Murmurs of agreement rose until the Black Robe lifted an arm for silence, his wrinkled hand covered with blue veins. "Enough!" A cough wracked him. His chest rattled and he had to put his head down until it subsided. He breathed shallowly, unable to fully expand his lungs to get enough air. It had been getting worse over the past few months and he knew he did not have much time left. After taking a more few shallow breaths, he continued.

"You all know prophecy is inherently difficult to trust. While it is true, it states that one so *Ringed* will control Black Numbers exponentially. It also says, rather emphatically I must add, that the *Ringed* Aleph Null could lose his or her mind in the process." He looked slowly at each Blue Robe before staring straight down at his Red Robe. "What good is that to us? And the gods only help us if he or she loses control of that power." He slammed his own hand down on his desk. "We cannot take that chance!"

The Blue Robes jumped slightly in their chairs, for the Black Robe rarely displayed that kind of anger.

The Black Robe sat back in his chair. He gasped for air, glad that his face was hidden in his hood so his Robes couldn't see him. In between shallow breaths, he continued. "We will wait... a year... before Proofing... Danicu's boy."

The Red Robe spat and waved an agitated arm. "It is just like you to passively wait for events to unfold." She turned her covered head up to the Black Robe and hissed. "You are pathetic!"

The Black Robe sat back, stunned, and listened to the murmurs around the room. A Red Robe had not spoken to a Black Robe like that in hundreds of years. He gazed down at his Red Robe; even for her such a display of insolence was unprecedented. He remembered when he was first a Blue Robe, and then the Fractionally Ascended Red Robe long ago. He had always treated the Black Robe with respect and honor. Maybe he was getting too old. Maybe it was time to pass the robe to her.

At this thought though, he clenched his fists inside his thick sleeves. No, they were close this time. He could feel it. The Aleph Null was going to be found. Maybe it was even Danicu's boy. He would not hand over power just yet. He glanced down at the Red Robe and squeezed his fists harder; especially with her as the Fractionally Ascended.

He took a ragged breath and rasped, "You will show your Black Robe respect!"

The Red Robe glared at him from inside of her hood. "Oh shut up. You are past your usefulness old man."

The Black Robe stood up. He had not stood up in months, for his Haissen carried him everywhere. He raised his right hand and pointed a trembling finger at her. "Silence!"

Standing up herself, the Red Robe raised her head proudly. "I will not be silenced!"

The gasp of thirteen Blue Robes filled the room.

The Red Robe stood still and quiet for many moments and the Black Robe was about to order his Haissen to take her from the chamber when he saw numbers appear in front of her, popping into existence in small clusters. They glowed white as she manipulated them. With a small flick of her hand, they began to slowly rotate on an axis, spinning faster and faster until they were an undulating ring of light.

The Black Robe realized with shock that his Red Robe had just initiated the Challenge of Ascension. He should have seen it coming, but a challenge had not happened in hundreds of years and he never dreamed it would happen to him. He immediately started to pull his own numbers in defense, but was unprepared for the power he felt in the Red Robe's numbers.

He put that thought out of his mind as he hastily built an array of numbers to use as a wall to protect himself from her initial attack. While he was old, he was the most powerful mathematician in the past eighty years, and despite his age, he was confident he could crush his Red Robe's challenge. But as he gathered his numbers, he became light-headed and struggled to take in ragged gasps of air.

He realized that he had made a mistake in standing up; it had weakened him and his lungs wouldn't give him enough oxygen. Struggling for air, he couldn't concentrate enough to hold his numbers in place, and when he felt the Red Robe hurl her numbers at him, he was unable to keep his array intact. Her ring of numbers struck his numeric wall, the sound similar to a slap to the face, and he screamed in frustration as his own numbers burst apart in all directions.

Her numbers twisted and turned like maggots as they burrowed into his chest and he was defenseless as he felt his lungs begin to burn, the pain beyond anything he could have ever conceived of. He clutched his chest and fell to his knees, his vision already beginning to dim.

The Red Robe hissed between breaths. "For too long you have weakened the Oblate with your reliance on passive politics." She managed a strained laugh and theatrically raised her hands and made a circular motion with them.

The Black Robe let out a hoarse whisper of air as he felt her circle of numbers spin faster and contract fully around his lungs. He threw his head back, the pain unbearable, causing the hood to fall from his head, showing his long white hair to the Robes below for the first time. He sadly closed his pale blue eyes, knowing that he had failed.

The Red Robe grunted as she collapsed the circle of numbers around his lungs. She whispered through clenched teeth. "It is time... for full ascension... now!"

The Black Robe felt his lungs burst from the heat. He coughed, and was momentarily surprised when he saw dust puff from his mouth. He tried to take one final breath, but his lungs were gone. He glared at the Red Robe, then fell forward, seeing nothing more.

The two Haissen had not moved the entire time and didn't even bother to look down when the Black Robe collapsed at their feet.

* * *

Silence filled the room. The Red Robe sighed as she brought her spinning numbers to a stop. Then, with one final release of energy, she made them disappear. She shook with the effort that she had just expended. With trembling hands, she sat down in her chair.

She had done it. She was the Black Robe and now ruled the Oblate!

To the outside world, the Oblate didn't exist. It was nothing more than a myth whispered around the fireplaces of local pubs. But secretly, behind the veneers of the noble houses, the Oblate exerted influence to control almost all kingdoms of the land, whether through finance or politics. Within the Oblate, the Robes held the highest power. They were all failed Proofings from the search for the Aleph Null and while none of them had passed the Proofing, they were all adept mathematicians. But only a few in a generation became strong enough to manifest numbers into the physical world, and they were the ones who ascended.

The Red Robe had spent the first ten years working her way up the ranks within the Oblate to her current position, but for the next seventy years she bristled at being second in command.

Now, she was the Black Robe.

She stood and looked up longingly at the Black Robe's platform. No stairs led up to it from where she stood, so she carefully descended the eight marble steps from the Red Robe dais and exited the chamber.

She strode confidently to the Black Robe's chambers and the Haissan that stood guard by the door stepped aside and let her in without a word. She made her way to the back of the room and pushed at a stone that looked no different from the others. As she did, the wall clicked and a hidden door opened on well-oiled hinges. She had known about it for years.

A narrow and damp hallway led into darkness, but she didn't hesitate as she strode forward, and she very quickly came to another door. It opened before she could push against it and two Haissen stood in front of her. At first she thought they were going to block her way, but then they half-bowed and stepped aside. Without hesitating, she climbed twenty-four steps and stood at the top in exultation.

Before her was an opening in the smoothly polished stone wall and just beyond, the Black Robe platform.

She stepped through and looked down at the dead Black Robe crumpled at her feet, his body lying face-down between the chair and Miq desk. She bent down and pulled the robe from his body, rolling him over in the process. His dead, pale-blue eyes stared up at her. She was surprised by how frail he looked. His chest was sunken in and the skin that hung from his arms and legs was bruised black and blue and looked like it was made of semi-transparent parchment. Using her foot, she grunted softly as she rolled his body off of the platform. It landed with a soft thud and she looked away, already forgetting him.

She faced the thirteen Blue Robes below and held up the black robe. "The Red Robe has fully Ascended!"

The Blue Robes stood as one and bowed, keeping their heads down.

The woman turned away from them and removed her red robe, dropping it without a thought, then slipped the black robe over her shoulders. It was snug, but she would have her servant fit it to her size. She slowly pulled the deep hood over her face and turned to face her Blue Robes below. The robe hid her every feature.

"Look upon your new Black Robe!"

All thirteen Blue Robes gazed up at her. This was an event that had not taken place in over seventy years.

A thrill of adrenaline coursed through her. Then she wrinkled her nose. The robe smelled of old man and sickness. She ignored the stink and focused on the Blue Robes below her. "We will meet in one week and a new Red Robe will Fractionally Ascend at that time."

The Blue Robes bowed again and sat down.

She knew that now would begin an intense period of scheming between them. Since only one of the Blue Robes could ascend to Red Robe, they would make their case with her. Give her gifts. Promise favors. Denounce the others. They would do almost anything to be considered for the Red Robe position.

The new Black Robe gazed around the room. "Now, to business. We will indeed send out the Korpor to Proof Danicu's boy."

She let the silence extend for a few moments before she continued in a whisper. "And the Korpor will *Ring* him."

The Black Robe waited for any dissent, but the Blue Robes sat perfectly still and silent. Elated that they completely accepted her as Black Robe, she stood and nodded. "I will contact the Korpor tonight. After it *Rings* the boy, it will bring him to Father Mansico, who will bring him to us. We are beginning a new era in the Oblate and one day soon, we will be able to remove our robes and rule the land for all to see."

The Blue Robes nodded but stayed silent.

The Black Robe smiled inside her hood. She had instilled fear in them and now gave them hope for a better future. They were sheep. Worthless. But soon she would have no use for them. Once she controlled the Aleph Null and his Black Numbers, she would rule the land herself, and everyone would know who she was. Her smile grew wider. It would be soon. But first she needed to rest. The challenge had completely exhausted all of her energy reserves.

The Black Robe spread her hands. "This meeting is finished." She turned and stepped through the dark opening in the wall and descended the steps.

One Haissan walked in front of her, the other behind her.

As soon as the Black Robe was gone, the thirteen Blue Robes rose as one and silently filed out of the room. Even though they were excited that one of them would ascend to Red Robe, they didn't envy what the Black Robe had to do this evening. Just thinking of the Korpor sent shivers down their spines.

Except for one of them. He kept silent as he shuffled out of the chamber, but he couldn't keep from sneering inside of his blue hood. A voice chuckled in his head.

"*She gave quite a performance.*"

The Blue Robe smiled. He knew the Korpor had been listening to what had just transpired through him. "*Indeed she did. You know what to do?*"

The chuckle stopped. "*Yes. They will all think I am under their control, just like we planned.*"

The Blue Robe nodded, even though the voice was in his head. "*Excellent. After you Proof Sid, bring him directly to me. Oh, and the new Black Robe was correct, I want you to* Ring *him.*" He paused and even through the telepathic link, his voice lowered to an ominous whisper. "*And when you* Ring *him, make sure the pain is... exquisite.*"

The Korpor's voice became silky smooth. "*Of course... Master.*"

Chapter 2

Sid cursed his father under his breath as he swung the axe down hard on the chunk of wet wood, hitting it with such force that the wood not only split, but the axe head sunk deeply into the old and scarred Miq tree block. The handle still vibrated slightly as he let it go and angrily picked up the two pieces of wood and stalked into the house.

At sixteen years old, he hated the fact that his father still treated him like a child, making him do chores when he could have been down by the river fishing for their meal tonight. He thrust first one, then the second piece of wood into the bin, but as he pulled his hand out, a long splinter slid under the skin of his palm. He jerked his hand up and grabbed his wrist with his other hand, his face turning red as he squeezed his eyes shut. When he opened them, they were wild and unfocused.

With a trembling hand, he slowly slid the splinter out of his palm and more pain flared in him. He dropped the small sliver of wood with a scream of anger and viciously kicked the wood bin, causing his brown hair to flop over his eyes. He was thin, but working on a farm made him strong and the bin shuddered violently. It was made of thick oak panels and withstood the kick, but a large piece of wood tumbled from the top and fell onto his shin, peeling skin and flesh. Intense pain shot through his foot.

In a blinding flash of rage he picked up the piece of wood, spun violently around and hurled it with a scream against the wall. It smashed into a framed drawing, which shattered and fell to the floor.

The anger left him as quickly as it had come, anger that always seemed to make him break things.

He stared at the broken picture frame. It had held a charcoal drawing of his mother, but now the frame was shattered into four pieces and the drawing was torn in the middle. Sid closed his eyes and hung his head, feeling sick to his stomach.

He opened his eyes and looked again at the piece of parchment lying on the floor. He crossed the room and fell to his knees, picking it up with shaking hands. It was very rare to have a drawing, as parchment was incredibly expensive. His father had drawn the portrait from memory and it was very detailed. Sid saw a young woman with long hair and thin unsmiling lips. Her eyes were large and he felt sadness emanate from them. It was the only image that he held of his mother. All other memories of her were dim in his mind.

He looked down at the torn and crumpled drawing, then pushed his fingers against the paper, trying to smooth it back out, but the paper was too badly damaged and he smeared the charcoal across his mother's face and through her left eye.

Sid looked at his blackened fingers and imagined the lack of emotion that he would see in his father's eyes at the sight of the damaged picture. His father rarely showed any kind of emotion, neither anger, nor joy. He seemed to be a man who merely existed in life. The only time his father became even slightly animated was when he taught Sid mathematics. He would spend part of each day with Sid discussing the merits of this equation over that equation.

Sid enjoyed learning and using math just because it was the only thing he and his father had in common. He had long ago stopped caring about what his father thought of him, but he missed his mother greatly. She had died when he was six and he didn't remember much about her. The only thing he knew was that he had felt warm and safe back then.

He focused again on the smudged portrait of his mother and then down at the broken picture frame. He put down the ruined drawing and picked up two of the broken pieces of picture frame, then took a deep breath and slowly let the air hiss out in a controlled release.

He had taught himself to do this as a way to get over the anger that always seemed to be waiting to jump out of him. His mind cleared and he saw the jagged edges of the two pieces of wood. They were shaped like a rough "W," one end fitting inside of the other. Sid closed his eyes and pulled them apart, then slowly felt the pointed end with his fingers. In his mind he could see the jagged points, the grain of the wood.

Soon numbers appeared in his mind, hovering above the image. He breathed deeply. The numbers always brought him a sense of peace.

He had always seen numbers in his mind. They were always there, whether he was stacking firewood, cutting wheat with his dad or just sleeping.

Sid's father, Danicu, had taught him mathematics for as long as he could remember. Where Danicu learned mathematics he never told his son. He was a quiet man who never talked about his past. He taught Sid simple arithmetic at first, how to count his fingers and toes. As Sid got older, Danicu taught him more complex mathematics, such as advanced theoretical equations and complex formulas that stretched Sid's understanding of that which made up the every day items around him.

Danicu taught him to visualize these numbers in his mind, to pretend they were written in the dirt and then to move them around and perform the mathematical procedures as if they were real numbers.

By doing this, Sid was able to memorize every number he saw, no matter how many digits were involved. It was hard work, but his father taught him to do this because paper was very expensive and difficult to come by and actually writing in the dirt was like cheating. Sid pushed himself continually to see the numbers in his mind and keep them straight as he manipulated them.

As far as Sid knew, no one in Orm-Mina even knew what math was, beyond counting bales of hay or the number of copper pieces needed to purchase things like cloth, food, and other goods. People rarely had a need to count beyond the number ten. But now, at age sixteen, Sid knew there were numbers and equations that couldn't even be imagined.

Mathematics were cold and sterile, but they were all Sid had in common with his father, which made Sid angrier and angrier the older he got.

He scowled at these memories and his heartbeat quickened. The anger bubbled to the surface again as he looked at the numbers that floated above the piece of wood in his mind. They were bright white on a black background. With cold precision, he mentally started spinning the numbers in a clockwise motion, then stopped them. He then pushed half of the numbers away until they were almost too small to see, while he brought the other half of the numbers forward until they were almost too large to focus on. He then made the numbers switch places, zooming back and forth, mixing them up until everything seemed like chaos.

Sid realized he was just angrily throwing the numbers around, so he brought them back to the same plane in his mind, then made them disappear entirely. He calmed himself, letting all thought fade away. His mind was now dark except for the piece of wood that slowly rotated as it floated.

He studied the broken end, at the way the jagged edge on one side made a "W" shape. The three pointed ends were not equally long. He could see that the right point was 0.7 times longer than the middle point, which was .04 times shorter than the left point.

He made his numbers appear again, placing them above each jagged point. Then he moved them into space above the piece of wood. An equation appeared in his mind and variables appeared next to the numbers. He carefully moved the letters and numbers into their proper positions. As he placed the final variable, the equation snapped together. The simple equation was right.

He got an idea. With his eyes still closed, he used his fingers to feel along the end of the second piece of wood, touching the jagged edges. He visualized the second piece of wood in his mind and it appeared next to the first one, both pieces slowly rotating in space. He could see every detail of the second piece. The grains of wood, the pulpy consistency of the broken ends and the dark brown stain that had been brushed on long ago.

He made it stop rotating and studied the jagged points and valleys of this piece and he pushed the correct numbers and variables next to it, using these numbers to create a second equation. He instinctively knew where they went. One last number floated apart and Sid nudged it to the end of the equation, where it snapped into place. It was almost a physical sound and he felt a flush of excitement. He felt sweat bead on his forehead and his breathing quickened.

He stared at the two equations that floated above the pieces of wood in his mind. He knew there was a way to take these two equations and make them into one large equation. He brought them together, but they wouldn't snap into place. It felt like two magnets pushing against each other. He knew that would have been too easy.

He rotated one of the equations and looked at the numbers upside down. He rotated the second equation the same way, then twisted them into a circle so the numbers of one equation met the other. But they still pushed against each other so he let them swing back.

He frowned as he stared at the numbers. There had to be a way to solve this but he instinctively knew that he was missing a third equation that was needed to bridge these two. How could he invent numbers from nothing? It was impossible.

These two equations were easy because they were formed from the two pieces of wood, which were real. He realized he was trying to solve something he had never seen before. This was beyond anything his father had taught him. He didn't even know if it was real math he was trying to do. But somehow, Sid knew he could do this.

He abruptly felt very tired and the numbers in the equations started to get blurry. He always got a little tired when manipulating numbers in his mind, but right now he felt like he was going to fall over if he didn't let the equations go. He had never felt this exhausted before.

He sighed. He knew that the equations were burned in his memory and that he could recall them at anytime. So he took a long, deep breath and mentally erased them, letting calm blackness cover his mind. He took another breath and exhaled. He opened his eyes and as they focused, he saw his father sitting in a chair, watching him. Sid hadn't been aware that he had even entered the room.

* * *

Danicu stared at his son as he sat on the floor. The boy had grown over the winter. His brown hair hung to his shoulders and his face had filled out. Where last summer he had been just a boy, now he was a young man. Although his son's chin was rounded and weak looking, when Sid looked up at him, Danicu was amazed again by the depth of his son's brown eyes. They were constantly in turmoil, a mixture of pain and anger that not only made Sid look older than his sixteen years, but sometimes caused Danicu to look away. They frightened him, almost like the boy could see what he was thinking.

Danicu looked down at the two pieces of the picture frame. He had watched as the jagged pieces of wood slowly smoothed over, almost like they were growing together. He had never seen anything like it before and he looked at his son with sudden excitement. Maybe he was Aleph Null. He had trained Sid and made him study mathematics, but he had never dreamed that his son could develop physical mastery over numbers at such a young age.

It was definitely time for the Proofing.

Danicu suppressed his excitement and kept his face expressionless. "You were doing something new weren't you?"

When Sid looked up at him with a puzzled expression, he glanced down at the two pieces of wood and then back to Sid with a questioning expression.

Sid studied the two pieces of wood in his hands. He was holding them together, broken end to broken end, and when he tried to pull at them, they seemed reluctant to part. He pulled harder and they made a sucking sound, like pulling a boot from deep mud. The "W"-shaped ends were still there, but they were smooth, almost like they had been sanded so they would fit together. He pushed the two ends together and they fit so perfectly that the seam became invisible. He furrowed his eyebrows in thought as he stared at the pieces. How could they be so smooth?

His father remained silent, giving him time to think it through.

Sid looked up at his father and opened his mouth to speak, but his father held up a hand, stopping him. "Don't try and explain it now. You are tired and will make mistakes. Go take a nap and later we can talk about it."

Sid slowly stood up, the effort causing him to sway a little. He bent down to pick up the other two pieces of wood, along with the charcoal drawing of his mother and walked into his bedroom.

Outside of Sid's room, Danicu sat down at the table and put his head into his hands. A deep ache started at the back of his skull and grew.

The Korpor was close and tonight it would Proof his son.

Sid was the Aleph Null. He knew it now, deep in his heart. If the Proof was completed successfully, the Korpor would sexually consummate the union and take Sid to the Oblate with full control of his power of numbers.

Danicu would not see his son again, but still smiled through the pain in his head.

The Oblate had waited a thousand years for his boy and he couldn't wait to give Sid to them.

Chapter 3

Sid opened his eyes and stared at the cracked ceiling. Light from the moon came through the window opening and cast a silver square right above him. He listened to the light wind rustling the trees. Otherwise it was quiet. No frogs croaked and no crickets chirped.

He lay in bed lazily, wondering what had awakened him. He couldn't believe that he had slept straight through the afternoon and into the night. He stared at the moonlight on the ceiling, half in a dream state, enjoying the cool breeze on his face. He closed his eyes and started to drift back to sleep when he heard another sound outside. He quickly opened his eyes and saw the moonlight on the ceiling disappear for a moment, as if someone had walked past the window.

Sid was immediately wide awake. He didn't move as he stared at his window. It was too quiet outside. He knew his father wouldn't be outdoors in the middle of the night, but he was certain that he saw something pass by his window. He strained to listen, but it was completely silent outside. Even the breeze had died down. He wondered if he were imagining things. Night had always held his darkest fears.

The sound of tearing flesh startled him, coming from just outside the window, followed immediately by a sickening scream that made goose bumps stand up on his arms. The scream rose in volume and then slowly faded away, ending with a lingering bubbling sigh.

Sid sad up in bed, his heart pounding. The soft white moonlight was no longer a comfort to him.

A thumping started, slow and methodical. He closed his eyes and pushed his knuckles into them until pain and stars erupted. He then opened them and looked at the window. He gripped the coarse wool blanket without even thinking about it. A breeze came in through the window again and its coolness felt good on his face, but also carried with it a smell that Sid couldn't comprehend. He sniffed and covered his nose. It was a combination of freshly baked bread, blood and animal feces.

With that smell, memories came back to him that made him tremble with trepidation as he pushed back his blanket and swung his legs over the edge of the bed, the cool breeze feeling very cold on his feet. Wearing only a pair of trousers, he shuffled slowly to the window.

The thumping continued, although now Sid could also hear wet splashes after each thump.

He stopped a single pace from the window, not sure if he wanted to see what was out there. He took a deep breath and let it out slowly, then took the final step to the window and leaned his head through the opening.

In the moonlight, he focused quickly on a dead deer that lay a short distance from the house, its head smashed to pulp with blood and brain matter scattered in every direction. The stomach was ripped open and the guts were scattered around the ground. Sid saw the entire image in a few moments, but his gaze was immediately drawn to the creature that stared at him with eyes that were dark blue and so large they covered the top half of its face.

Sid started to shiver uncontrollably as memories of Rugger flooded back; of his massive black eyes, of the pain as he thrust into him, of his anguished plea for Sid to kill the Korpor. Then he remembered the story that Mrs. Wessmank had told him of the Korpor on that same day, of how it might come for him some day like it came for her and her sister. He recalled how Mrs. Wessmank and her sister had fallen to their knees in intense pain as they looked upon the Korpor and Sid pulled back slightly from the window, expecting the pain to hit him. But instead, pleasure filled him from deep within, a pleasure so intense that he felt his penis grow and pulse with it, so instantly hard that it hurt as it pushed against his trousers.

Sid stared at the creature outside of his window in awe and fear. The eyes froze him in place, eyes that were almost the same as those of Rugger, except this creature's eyes were a deep blue. It was half again as tall as Sid, its body completely covered in white fur that glowed in the moonlight. Muscles flexed and undulated beneath the fur, the movements showing that the creature was unbelievably strong. Its gray-skinned face was hairless and beautiful, with red lips curved into a slight frown, like that of a sad woman. Where its nose should have been, it had slits that flared slightly with each breath, almost like gills.

Sid shivered as he gazed upon the Korpor. It was real and standing in front of him. For eight years he had both dreamed of and dreaded this moment, for despite his hatred of Rugger for what the man had done to him, he somehow knew that Rugger had spoken the truth about the Korpor, that it was evil. He felt his anger come back full force.

The creature stared at Sid, its head tilted slightly to the left and it huffed softly, the sound faint and sensual. The anger left Sid as quickly as it had come and he didn't feel the cold anymore, nor could he hear anything, almost like he was under the warm water of his monthly bath.

The Korpor took five strides toward Sid, moving so quickly that he didn't even have time to take a breath before it came to a stop a few paces from the window. Sid sneezed quickly, three times, and when he opened his eyes, the Korpor had taken the last few steps, its face almost touching his own.

Sid was unable to move.

The creature slowly blinked its left eye followed by its right eye.

Sid stared, captivated. He wasn't frightened or angry anymore. The Korpor moved its lips, almost like a smile. It exhaled and Sid felt its breath on his face, smelling like freshly baked bread. Sid wanted to pull his head back, but he couldn't move.

The Korpor blinked that odd staggered blink again, and Sid now noticed small blue hairs growing from the eyeballs themselves. That is where the blue came from, he realized. The creature was so beautiful! It wasn't anything like the man with the black eyes he had killed in the hut.

The Korpor leaned forward a little more until they lightly touched faces.

Sid held his breath.

It opened its mouth and pressed its lips to Sid's mouth. The kiss was slow, long, and soft. The lips felt warm and dry. He felt himself grow even harder in his trousers as he released his breath into the mouth of the Korpor.

Sid flushed but he didn't pull away. The creature kissed him harder, forcing its tongue between his lips. He opened his mouth slightly and when their tongues touched, his penis felt like it was going to burst. His breathing quickened and he couldn't think of anything but the kiss.

He didn't want it to end.

But somewhere deep within his mind he knew that it was wrong, that he needed to fight it.

He closed his eyes and tried to fight the sexual pleasure that coursed through him. An orgasm was imminent, building deeply within him. Sid wanted it more than anything he had ever wanted before.

A soft voice whispered in his head. *"Crawl through the window Sidoro. Come to me and this pleasure will never end."*

Still kissing the Korpor, Sid immediately put his hands to the window ledge and as he did, the impending orgasm throbbed harder within him. He lifted one knee to the ledge and was about to pull himself through the window and into the Korpor's embrace when an image of Mrs. Wessmank flashed into his mind.

He hesitated.

The voice of the Korpor spoke more forcefully in his head and the promised orgasm pulsed closer to release. *"Come to me Sidoro. Now."*

This all seemed so wrong to him. Sid held on to the image of Mrs. Wessmank and he felt the coming orgasm subside a little bit. Other images began to flash through his mind randomly, fighting with the intense sexual pleasure that pulsed harder within him. He saw his father staring at him blankly as they ate dinner. His friend Tris racing him to their fishing hole, always beating him no matter how hard Sid ran. He saw Mrs. Wessmank again, pouring tea into his cup, the steam rising over her face. Then he saw the hut across the snowy field. It rushed toward him and then he was inside and the black-eyed man was thrusting into him and he felt the tearing inside of him, the pain shooting through him.

He cried out and instantly the pleasure disappeared and his erection subsided.

The Korpor pulled its lips away from him, its tongue the last to slip from his mouth. It glared at him, looking very dangerous and hideous. Its blue eyes grew even larger, looking astonished at first, then changing to darkly angry, an anger that promised deadly violence.

Sid was afraid to move. In a panic he felt for his numbers and they instantly appeared in his mind. He pulled them as quickly as he could to form a wall in front of him, just like he had done in the hut.

He heard a howl of rage inside his mind and felt his numbers being forced away. He pulled harder to hold them in place, but no matter how hard he tried, some of the numbers tumbled away, end-over-end into darkness. The Korpor was incredibly strong, so much more powerful than the man in the hut. Sid started to sweat as he concentrated on keeping the remaining numbers in place, but the Korpor relentlessly peeled them away, layer after layer.

Sid grunted with effort. In his mind, the numbers looked like apple peelings as the Korpor pulled at them. Frantically, he brought more numbers to replace them, but as fast as he added them, the Korpor yanked them away.

They fought each other for what felt like eternity. Sid's body shook with the effort and sweat ran into his eyes. He didn't know for how much longer he could pull in numbers. They seemed to respond sluggishly now.

Then the pressure was gone.

Sid opened his eyes and saw the creature standing over the deer carcass, its shoulders slumped in exhaustion.

For the first time Sid noticed that the creature's arms ended in paws that had three claws, each one as long again as the paw. Blood dripped from them in thick black drops. It opened one paw and Sid saw that it held the deer's heart. It slowly crushed it, then dropped it to the ground.

Sid shivered and his legs felt numb. He locked his knees to keep from falling.

Never taking its eyes from his, the Korpor slowly stepped inside the deer carcass and squished its feet around like a little barefoot boy in a mud puddle. It then jumped up and down, stomping the deer guts.

Sid now knew where the wet sucking and thumping sounds had come from. Blood sprayed out in a starburst-pattern every time the creature's feet came down inside of the deer. Sid had no idea why the Korpor was doing this.

The Korpor stopped and stepped out of the deer carcass. It casually bent over and picked it up, slinging it over a shoulder.

It smiled crookedly at Sid, then whispered again in his head, its voice dark and seductive and tinged with exhaustion. "*I will be back for you Sidoro. You are mine.*"

And then it turned and loped into the woods, the smashed deer head flopping up and down on the Korpor's back.

Sid stood at the window, staring out into the moonlit darkness. Without even thinking, he let his numbers spin away. He rubbed his eyes and looked at the ground below. The blood looked slick and black in the moonlight and he could see crushed organs scattered about.

Sid felt sick to his stomach and stumbled back to his bed and crawled under the covers. He lay there shivering, so cold he couldn't stop his teeth from chattering. It felt like a nightmare, but he knew that it had all been real. He instinctively knew he had just battled for his life with the Korpor. He lay awake in his bed, thinking about what had just happened, unable to sleep. Finally, the morning sunshine peeked through his window and he heard his father begin moving around the house.

Chapter 4

The Korpor initiated contact with the Black Robe and when she accepted the connection, she immediately asked, *"Is it done?"*

"No, not yet, but soon, Black Robe."

"Why not? I told you to Proof and Ring him tonight."

The Korpor paused, having to force its voice to sound respectful, even though it wanted nothing more than to tear the old woman's face off. *"There were... complications. But do not worry, it will get done soon."*

The Black Robe snarled at him, *"Do not fail me."*

The Korpor gritted its teeth. *"Of course... Master."* Without waiting for a response, the Korpor broke the connection and immediately opened a connection with Father Mansico, a man it truly despised.

"Yes?"

"Danicu's boy is the Aleph Null, but the Proofing was not fully completed."

"Why not?" The anger in Father Mansico's voice irritated the Korpor so it replied curtly, *"It is of no concern, it will be done soon."* The Korpor broke the connection before Father Mansico could respond, and with a sigh it opened the final connection to its true master.

The Blue Robe spoke softly, *"Tell me what happened."*

The Korpor sighed, suddenly a little afraid. Nothing in this world frightened it except for this man.

"The boy is indeed the Aleph Null. He fought me and won... this time."

The Blue Robe's voice was silent for some time, until he said, *"That should not have happened. Sid should not have been able to match you, his true power of numbers should have been dormant."*

"Yes, but that is not the case. His numbers are awakened, at least partially."

The Blue Robe was silent for some time, as if digesting the information, until he spoke firmly to the Korpor. *"Interesting... all right, I want you to contact Danicu in the morning and have him send Sid away from his home. Tell him to send Sid to Father Mansico. I then want you to follow the boy for a few nights and take him when he is most vulnerable, but before Mansico can take him."*

"Of course Master."

The Blue Robe was silent for some time, but the Korpor didn't dare break the connection yet. After a few more moments, the man's voice hissed darkly, *"Next time, do not play any games. Just take the boy forcefully and quickly. Do you understand?"*

The Korpor grimaced. *"Yes, it will be done as you wish."*

"Good."

The connection between them was severed and the Korpor slumped its shoulders, more tired that it had been in hundreds of years. Its mental battle with the Aleph Null had drained its energy reserves more than it had let on to its master. It quickly found a patch of soft grass and laid down, and was instantly asleep.

Chapter 5

The sunlight felt warm on Sid's face. And welcome. He got out of bed and pulled on his tunic, then walked into the small, shared room and went straight to the shelf and grabbed his tea mug.

His father's voice shook slightly, "Sidoro, we have to talk!"

Sid filled his mug with hot water from the pot that hung over the fire and added a small amount of tea leaves. The bitter smell calmed him a bit. He wanted to tell his father about the Korpor, but when he turned to look at his father, he hesitated, suddenly not sure that he should. He looked down into his tea and blew on it to cool it down a bit. "About what father?"

His father had a strange look on his face. "I... saw the Korpor last night."

Sid looked at his father in alarm. "You did?"

His father shrugged, his face suddenly haggard and tired. "Yes, I saw it running into the treeline."

This was the last thing Sid had expected to hear from his father, that he knew what the Korpor was. The realization hit him like a physical blow.

His father leaned forward and hissed, his gaze deep and piercing. "Did you feel blinding pain at the sight of it?"

Confused by the question, Sid answered honestly. "No, there was no pain at all." He hesitated but didn't say anything more. He wasn't about to tell his father that he had kissed the Korpor, much less that he had gotten sexually excited by the creature.

Danicu held Sid's gaze with his own, and the intensity in his eyes frightened Sid. He felt tears come to his eyes and he quickly wiped them away, angry and embarrassed by them.

Danicu spoke forcefully, "Sidoro, you must leave. Today. Now." He stood up and walked over to Sid, placing a hand on his shoulder.

Sid looked up at him and he could tell that his father was lying about something, but he was too shocked to give it more thought.

Danicu let his face go slack again. "You are not safe here. The Korpor will be back and I can't protect you." He stared blankly at Sid.

Leave? Sid was unsure of what was happening. Why would he leave, it was safer in the house than outside. He looked questioningly at his father. "How do you know about the Korpor?"

Danicu turned away as he spoke. "We don't have time for this discussion Sidoro. Now stop asking questions and get yourself ready to leave."

Sid wanted to ask more questions, but he knew that once his father spoke like this, there was no way he was going to say anything more. "But where should I go? We don't really know anyone else in the village."

Danicu held his son's gaze. "You will be going much farther than town this time son."

What his father didn't say spoke more to Sid than anything. His father knew exactly what was going on. Sid stood and stumbled back, suddenly feeling very young and unprepared to handle what was happening.

As if not caring about his son's fear, Danicu turned away and started collecting items for Sid to take with him.

This was all happening too quickly. Sid's head spun in confusion. He was leaving? Just like that? He sat down and watched his father gather his pack and start putting items into it. He did it methodically and with little emotion. Then, as if a door slammed shut inside of his mind, a sense of calm washed over him and he realized that he didn't care if he left his home and his father. There was nothing for him here. He was sick and tired of seeing the complete lack of emotion in his father's eyes. The anger came back full force and Sid hardened himself. So be it. He would leave and never come back.

In a handful of moments, Sid stood in the small room holding his pack, ready to go, everything he owned or had cared about in his sixteen years inside of it. His father stood in front of him. "I've packed you three loaves of bread, some dried deer meat, a large chunk of white cheese, some apples and onions, a tinder box and flint, ten copper pieces, a heavy coat, a winter shirt and trousers, a heavy blanket, a thirty foot rope, and a heavy pair of boots. Even though it's spring, the weather could quickly turn cold again."

Numbed, Sid just nodded. His father had thought of everything it seemed, except for the most important item of all. Sid stepped into his room, rolled up the torn drawing of his mother, tied it with a piece of string and slid it safely into a waterproof pocket of his pack. He didn't know if he would ever return here, and the portrait of his mother was the only thing he treasured.

As he was fitting the pack straps more comfortably on his back, his father left the room. Sid thought maybe he wasn't even going to say goodbye. He took a look around the small main room which had a simple fireplace, a small table, two chairs, two cupboards, and a cutting block. All were made by his father and even though they were simple in design, they were beautifully crafted.

His small room was off to the left of the table and his father's room was to the right. It wasn't much of a home, but it was all he had ever known. Even though he did not have many good memories, Sid felt fear of the unknown outside of that door. He had no idea where he was going to go.

A scratch of a boot in dirt brought Sid back and he turned to see his father standing next to him. He was holding a large knife in a sturdy leather sheath. He held his hand out. "Take this, son."

Sid took the knife and sheath, turning it in his hands. He had never seen it before. He looked up questioningly at his father.

"It is a very special Rissen blade."

Sid didn't know what a Rissen blade was, so he merely nodded. He unsnapped the strap and slid the blade out of the sheath. The handle was made from the bone of some animal that he couldn't identify. The blade was as long as his forearm, almost twice as long as the knife he had carried since he was eight. The steel was thick and heavy and inside of the steel there were beautiful wave patterns. He stared at it, transfixed. There were no pits in it and the weight said all that needed to be said about the quality. It was a knife used for killing.

Sid lightly dragged his thumb horizontally across the blade to test the sharpness like he always did when he sharpened his own knife; but this time, even though he only lightly touched the edge, he jerked his thumb away with a yelp and sucked at it. He took it out of his mouth and looked at it. The blade had shaved a thin layer of skin from his thumb, like one would do to cold butter when scraping a knife against it. He looked up at his father and saw a smile on his face. He couldn't remember the last time he had seen his father smile.

Danicu put a hand on his son's arm and chuckled. "I take it that will be the last time you touch that blade with your fingers." His chuckle left him as quickly as it came, and his eyes became serious.

"This blade was made a long time ago by a master bladesman in a land far to the north. While it is similar to other Rissen blades, this one is... unique. Care for it with your life. I recommend not showing it to anyone. It has... it is dangerous to let others see wealth, which you know. And this knife is beyond valuable."

Sid looked down at the knife again. He carefully slid it back into the sheath, then glanced up at his father and nodded.

His father smiled a sad smile, then motioned him over to the table. He reached into his shirt and pulled out a blank piece of parchment.

Sid stared at it. "Where did you get that?"

His father waved the question away and pressed a non-descript corner of the wall. A panel opened with a snick. He reached inside and removed a bottle of ink and a quill.

Sid never knew of anyone who had writing parchment and ink, let alone his father. "Have you always had that?" he asked incredulously.

His father nodded absently as he removed the stopper of the bottle and dipped the quill into it.

Danicu looked up at his son and motioned for him to stand next to him. He began drawing, his strokes smooth and practiced. Sid watched him with awe. He never knew his father had such things.

Danicu spoke as he drew. "Head north along the road through town. Follow it for a day to Oiro." He looked up briefly at Sid. "You and I have been there before. Not far outside of Oiro you will come to a split." He drew a line for the road and smoothly marked the split. "Take the east split and continue along that road for another three days and you will come to the city of Yisk. Don't stop for anything. Once in Yisk, go straight to the House of Healing and ask for Father Mansico. Show him the Rissen blade and tell him you are my son. He will help you. If you can't find the House of Healing, ask a patrol member and they will lead you there. Father Mansico will take you the rest of the way to Undaluag."

Sid stopped his father. "Why must I go to Undaluag? Father, what's going on?"

Danicu looked blankly at Sid. "Don't ask questions, boy. You will do as you are told."

Sid looked away. He was angry but he kept silent.

Danicu stared at his son for a few moments, then continued. "Father Mansico will take you east to Undaluag. If, for some reason you can't find Father Mansico, travel on to Undaluag yourself and enter the city via the west gate. Find the Undaluag House of Healing and tell them you are my son. They will take you to a large building. It will have no markings but a single door. Again, show the Rissen blade to the man who answers the door. He will recognize it and bring you inside."

Sid twisted the knife in his hands. "What is this thing? Why do I have to show it to these people?"

Danicu sat back to let the ink dry on the map. His voice softened. "Son, sit down. Please."

Sid reluctantly sat down opposite his father at the table. "Could you just tell me the truth, for once, without making everything so cryptic?"

Danicu merely stared at him.

Sid wiped his hand through his hair. "Can you at least tell me why I should go to this place?"

Danicu tested the ink on the map with a finger and finding it dry, folded the paper into four precise folds. He reached into the hidden panel and removed a small leather pouch and opened the drawstrings. He placed the folded map inside and closed it tightly. He looked at his son as he slid it across the table.

"The Rissen blade will be proof that you are my son. The people who will protect you will know who you are when you give this to them."

"What people are you talking about? Why will they protect me?"

Danicu shook his head. "I can't tell you very much at this time. You will just have to trust me. But I can tell you this. You are going to a special place that no one knows about. It is called the Oblate. It consists of a group of people who are unknown to the outside world, yet they exist in every layer of government throughout the land. They are very powerful, and they work for the good of all humanity. Son, the Oblate is the only place where you will be safe."

His father paused for a long time before speaking. "We will likely not see each other again, but the Oblate will be your new family." He reached into his jacket and brought out a piece of cloth, blew his nose loudly, then folded it and put it back in his jacket pocket.

Sid looked at his father as a stranger. "How do you know about the Oblate, then?"

Danicu merely shook his head. "That is not important right now."

The breeze picked up outside and blew through the window, tossing Sid's hair a bit. It was a warm, cloudless morning. The pigs outside were noisily shuffling around and grunting, anxious for their morning food.

"For how long will I have to stay there?"

Danicu smiled blankly. "Until you are safe."

Sid shivered. "What if I choose not to go to this Oblate?"

"Son, it is the only way. Please trust me."

Sid shook his head. "But what if I go stay with Mrs. Wessmank? No one will know that I'm there."

Danicu roared at him. "You will do as I say!"

Sid almost dropped over backward in his chair and pressed his hands to the table to catch himself. He remained silent for a few moments. He had never heard his father raise his voice before, much less yell at him.

His father glared at him. "I don't want you seeing that woman again, do you hear me?"

Sid felt the familiar anger rise inside of him and he glared back at his father. "She is my friend, and I will see her if I want to."

They stared at each other, a test of wills that Sidoro would have lost at any other time, but the anger within him gave him strength, and he just glared at his father.

Danicu finally sighed. "You are a handful, Sidoro. You must do what you think is right. That is all I can ask. I hope you know, though, that I would never put you in harm's way. The Oblate is a good place, and it is the only place where you will be safe from the Korpor. I trust you to make the right decisions when the time comes. Now, you must go. It is already mid-morning."

They both stood up and looked at each other, neither one making a move. Finally Danicu put a hand on Sid's shoulder and squeezed. "I know you have saved up some copper pieces, but I want you to take these too." He reached into the hidden panel again and brought out a small leather pouch and handed it to Sid. "There are ten silver pieces in here. You can make change at any town market. But do not let anyone see you flashing this kind of coin."

Sid felt the weight of the bag. He had never felt this much coin in his life, and he wondered where his father had gotten silver. He could get one hundred copper pieces for each silver piece. He started to hand it back, but his father put a hand up.

"No, you take that. I have no need for it anymore."

Sid reluctantly started to take his pack off to put it inside.

"No, not in your pack, son." His father took the pouch and opened up Sid's shirt and tied the pouch around his belt. He then closed the shirt and pulled it over the belt to hide the pouch.

"A person can lose their pack. This way the coin is always on your person."

Sid felt unprepared for traveling in the world. He had rarely been off his land. Even the village was rarely visited. How was he going to get by when he didn't even know how to protect coin?

His father seemed to sense his trepidation, and he placed a comforting hand on his shoulder.

"Son, listen. You will do well. You are smart and you know how to live off the land. You don't have any experience with outsiders, but you have your brain. Use that," he tapped Sid's forehead, "and you will be fine. Listen to your instincts and think situations through before you do something. And most importantly, trust no one until you get to Father Mansico."

Sid nodded to his father, unable to speak. He was overwhelmed. Too much had happened too quickly. Despite how little he cared for it and his bravado from a little earlier, everything he knew in his life was here in this house. Now he was leaving it. In the space of a morning he had learned more about his father than he had in all of his sixteen years. He felt cheated that he was only now learning all of this. Anger welled up again and he set his face in a blank look, just like his father always did.

He tightened his pack straps one last time and without another word, he walked through the door of his home and into the clear cool spring morning. The pigs started squealing when they saw him, thinking they were about to be fed. Sid stopped by the pen and put his hand through the opening. All six pigs rushed over to him, grunting hello. He smiled and scratched behind an ear of each pig. They leaned into his hand, closing their eyes in pleasure. "Good bye my friends."

Standing up, Sid turned to the house and saw his father standing in the doorway, who raised a hand to Sid. Sid raised his own hand briefly in farewell and turned away, walking across the grass and dirt-packed yard to the treeline where the Korpor had disappeared the previous night. He found the trail to the main road without thinking about it. His mind was filled with thoughts of the Oblate, maps, and the Korpor.

Birds twittered in the branches and two squirrels chased each other up a tree, circling around it as they went. The ground was damp and spongy. As Sid pushed a branch out of his way, he heard his father's voice but couldn't make out the words. He turned his head and looked back at the house through the trees.

His father still stood in the doorway. He was talking, but Sid couldn't hear what he was saying. His father saw him looking, raised his arm and slowly waved. Sid gave a short wave, then turned and let the branch snap back before starting down the trail.

Chapter 6

Danicu watched Sid enter the woods as he stood in the doorway. When his son was out of sight, he continued speaking. "I sent him away like you asked, but why didn't you take Sidoro last night? Why didn't you *Ring* him?"

A rumbling voice echoed in Danicu's head. "*He fought me.*"

Wild pain coursed through Danicu as he turned and shut the door. It was intense, almost debilitating. Standing in the corner of the room the Korpor stared back at him, its huge blue eyes blinking the strange staggered blink.

Danicu strode to the table and sat down. The pain coursed through him, burning the blood in his veins. But he didn't stop looking at the Korpor. "I know he fought you, and apparently defeated you. I don't know what is happening. Sidoro should not have been able to do that. Something is wrong."

The voice floated inside Danicu's head. "*He is the Aleph Null.*"

Danicu slammed his hand down on the table. "Even so, he should not have been able to resist you. His full power of numbers is not awakened yet!"

The voice cooed in his mind, "*The blood from the deer awakened my need. I almost had him. Oh how I wanted to Ring him.*"

Danicu glared at the Korpor. "I willingly give my son to you. Don't be vulgar."

The Korpor stared at Danicu, the slow, staggered blinking of its blue eyes making him breathe a little harder. Danicu remembered his own Proofing with the Korpor; the intense pain he had felt at that stare and the shame he felt at failing the test. He had not been the Aleph Null. But his son was.

The voice whispered in his mind. "*Yes, you were almost the Aleph Null. I would have enjoyed you.*" The Korpor smiled. "*The boy's numbers are awakened.*"

Danicu looked directly at the Korpor. The pain grew stronger. "That is impossible. Only you can awaken them by consummating a sexual act during the Proofing."

The voice cooed. "*Someone else did it. Was it you?*"

Danicu stood and took a menacing step forward then fell to the floor. His head felt like it was going to collapse.

The Korpor's huge eyes became hooded. "*Don't forget who you are dealing with.*"

Danicu managed to stand back up, holding his head. "I did not touch my boy in that way, and if you ever suggest it again, I will kill you or die trying."

The Korpor's lips formed what may have been a smile. "*I understand. And you would not have fully awakened his numbers anyway. It has to be done by me for that to happen.*" It stopped and cocked its head, thinking. It scowled as realization hit it, and it whispered. "*It must have been my son who did it!*"

"Your son? What are you talking about?"

For the first time, the Korpor looked uncomfortable.

Danicu raised his voice. "What son?"

"*A failed Proofing from many years ago. I let my lust get the better of me and I took the young man anyway. I managed to get him hard even through his intense pain and his seed filled me even as he died from that pain. It was... a mistake.*"

Danicu shook his head. "A mistake? A mistake? All of our plans could be at risk and you say you made a mistake?"

The Korpor blinked but held its temper. "*Yes, I gave birth to a son, and it was a mistake to let my son live, a mistake that I won't make with your son if he is ruined. I will kill him without hesitating.*"

Danicu heard the threat but actually fully agreed with the creature. If Sidoro wasn't the Aleph Null, then he was of no use to anyone. He nodded to the Korpor. "If that time comes, then yes, you should kill Sidoro. Now what does your son have to do with Sidoro?"

The Korpor smiled slightly at the dedication of this man, then said, "*My... son lived not far from here, until eight years ago when I found him dead. Only he could have possibly awakened your son's numbers enough to fight me, although not as fully as I will do it. He likely raped your boy to get back at me for giving him life. It is the only explanation for how your boy resisted me.*"

Danicu's eyes filled with rage. "Your son raped my boy when he was eight years old?"

"*Probably.*"

Danicu was angrier than he had ever been. Not at the fact that his son had been raped, but because that rape had prematurely awakened his son's numbers. An unknown variable had been entered into the equation. His plan, the Oblate's plan for Sidoro, now needed to change. They couldn't *Ring* Sidoro, like the Black Robe wanted. It would likely destroy Sidoro's mind and it could bring forth unknown powers that would be uncontrollable. They couldn't risk that, not if they wanted to control the Aleph Null.

Danicu forced himself to look directly at the Korpor. The pain was excruciating. "You must not *Ring* Sidoro now! It is too dangerous. You must just Proof him and consummate the union to bind him to you."

The Korpor smiled, its teeth gleaming in the dimmed light. Its voice cooed in Danicu's head, "*I was ordered to* Ring *the boy. That is what I will do.*"

Danicu swept the two tea mugs from the table. They shattered against the wall. "Then you better make sure you have full control of his mind first! Your idea to send him away from here so he will be weakened and filled with fear at being alone is a good plan, but you must take him unaware and swiftly."

The voice grew stronger in Danicu's mind, "*Oh I will.*"

Danicu spoke as in an afterthought, "And when you take him, look in his pouch. I have given back the ten silver pieces and the Rissen blade that were paid to me sixteen years ago by the Oblate. I've produced a son like they asked and paid for, but I don't want the payment. The fact that my son may be the Aleph Null is payment enough. Take the coins and Rissen blade to Mansico."

The Korpor chuckled in Danicu's mind as it moved silently across the room and disappeared into Sid's room. "*A believer and a patriot. How nice.*" The voice faded away, but was still low and rumbling, "*By the way, your son tasted... sweet.*"

Danicu clenched his fists in anger, but as he walked into Sidoro's room and looked at the open window where the Korpor had just exited, the anger faded away and he exulted at his success.

His boy was the Aleph Null.

Chapter 7

Sid made his way down the trail, not really noticing the familiar landmarks as he absently placed each foot in front of the next. He avoided the half-buried rock that he had tripped over one day while running down the trail. He lifted a heavy oak branch that hung over the trail, a branch that had slapped him hard in the face one evening because his friend Tris had not held it long enough as they raced each other. And Sid didn't even notice the small moss-covered cave entrance that he had always used for a hideout when he was a little boy playing the warrior on lookout for the evil Trogurs, his wooden sword notched and worn from fighting dead tree trunks.

Sid knew every corner of these little woods that surrounded his home. His favorite area was the large stand of birch trees to the south of his house, where he would sit quietly, pretending the tall and narrow white trees were sentinels watching over him, protecting him.

But none of these memories were on Sid's mind this morning. He was thinking about the Oblate. Why was his father sending him there? Sure, to be safe from the Korpor, he said. But why there? It was just like his father not to give him the information he wanted. He always made Sid work out the answers for himself. Even on the most complicated mathematical equations, his father would tell him to work it out one step at a time.

That was what he had to do now. It was no good thinking about what the Oblate was, or what he would do when he got there. He had to concentrate on how he was going to get there, and that started with these first steps down the trail.

Sid focused his eyes on his surroundings for the first time since he had left his house. He knew where he was right away and turned his head to the right. He immediately saw the giant Miq tree through the brush and smaller trees, standing tall and majestic above every other tree in the area.

He narrowed his eyes and looked up through the branches until he finally picked out the deer stand sitting on a single but wide Miq branch, a platform that he had built one summer when he had been seven years old which he sat on, waiting for deer to wander within range. He had killed many deer for food during the first two winters after he had built it, using a bow and set of arrows that his father had carved for him. But he soon outgrew the platform and never built another one. He realized with a start that he had forgotten his bow at the house and considered going back for it, but he decided not to. He would probably not need it, as he was going directly to the city and he was carrying enough food to get him there.

Without thinking, Sid stepped off of the trail. He pushed prickly brush and small, low-hanging branches out of his way until he came to a large fallen Miq tree, the sister to the one standing so tall in front of him.

He crawled under the old, decomposed tree. The base of the tree had been pulled out of the ground whole as it had fallen. Its twisted roots looked like a woman's skirt flared out in a perfect circle. Sid stood up on the other side of the fallen tree, brushed dirt from his knees and looked up at the giant Miq. It was so tall that when Sid craned his head up, he could just barely see the top. Its needles were long and blue, each one the length of Sid's arm. Most of the thick branches grew on the sun-facing side of the tree, almost like it was trying to reach for the life-giving warmth. It was Sid's favorite tree.

He tilted his head up. His deer stand was just a small wooden platform tied to a large branch high above the needle-covered ground. Sid's father told him to never drive metal into a tree because it would kill it. So Sid had worked for a full day trying to secure the platform to the branch using only rope. It was difficult, but using an equation that he created in his mind and visualizing the system he would need to make the platform stable, Sid was able to run rope to the upper and lower branches from each corner of the platform, tying complex knots that slipped and tightened when he put his weight on any corner of the platform.

The deer stand had been very stable, and Sid remembered how proud he had been when he brought his father down from the house to see it, holding his hand as he pointed up at the platform.

Danicu had taken in the complicated rope system and ruffled his son's hair. Sid remembered looking up at his father and seeing one of his rare smiles, his teeth crooked and discolored and the hair in his nose tangled like the brush he had just walked through. Sid had loved his father at that moment and felt nothing but pride. His father hadn't said anything though, and his smile had disappeared as quickly as it had come. He had ruffled Sid's hair again, then turned and walked back to the house. Sid had listened to the crunching of his father's fading footfalls and the swishing of brush until it had become silent in the woods once again.

Thinking of that day now, Sid smiled sadly to himself as he ran his hand lightly over the rough bark of the tree and looked up at the platform.

He saw that the ropes were frayed and rotting. The platform was tilted at an angle, and he noticed one corner was no longer tied. A length of rope twisted slightly in the breeze as it dangled from the platform. The tree swayed and the wooden platform creaked as it rubbed against the branch. It was a lonely sound.

Suddenly a Rypper gurgled from a branch above the deer stand. Sid noticed for the first time a large nest built on a thick branch, sticks and leaves woven intricately and securely fastened to the branch, almost as if mocking his deer stand below it.

A large red-feathered head with green eyes peeked over the nest and looked directly at him. The two long red beaks of the Rypper were hooked sharply at the ends for tearing flesh. They moved up and down like scissors as it gurgled again. It wasn't smart to be around a Rypper when it had a nest. They were known to attack the face and eyeballs of unwary people who didn't heed the gurgled warning.

Sid turned and walked slowly back toward the trail, his head down. The Rypper gurgled softly one last time, but it didn't leave the nest. In a few moments he was back at the trail. He took the Rypper as a sign. There was no turning back now. He was on his and he had a long way to go.

He quickly came to the small hill above the road and he slid on his feet down the two well worn ruts that he had made over the years, and without pausing at the bottom, turned right and started toward town.

The road was large enough for two wagons to pass each other. It was a little muddy, but walking was easy. Sid enjoyed the sunlight on his face, and the warmth was comforting. He listened to songbirds twittering in the branches of trees that were just starting to bud with new leaves. He made good speed and was soon in town.

He angled directly over to the tobacco store. He wanted to visit old Mrs. Wessmank one more time, despite his father warning him not to see her.

He pushed open the old wooden door, the squeak a familiar sound to him, and stood in the entryway with his eyes closed. He inhaled the sweet smell of good tobacco and tea. Releasing his breath slowly, he opened his eyes and saw Mrs. Wessmank, her back to the door, bent over a large brown sack on the floor.

With fumbling fingers she was trying to tie the ends of the sack together, but it kept coming loose before she could finish tying the knot. The old woman's head tilted slightly at the sound of the door squeak, but she didn't look up or turn around.

"You're just in time Sidoro. Come here and help me."

Sid took a few steps forward and knelt down next to her. "You can't tie a cord around a bag of tobacco any more Mrs. Wessmank? You're getting old!"

The old woman glanced at Sid with one raised eyebrow. "You watch your mouth boy! And for your information, my hands hurt quite badly today."

Sid smiled. Mrs. Wessmank always complained about her aches and pains. In fact, she had a new ache every time Sid saw her, it seemed. But Sid loved the old woman.

Mrs. Wessmank pulled the cord tight and Sid put his finger against it as she tied a knot. When she was finished, the old woman stood slowly, groaning the whole time while holding her back with one hand. "I think it is time for a cup of tea."

She shuffled over to the well-cared-for stove in the corner and lifted a steaming pot from the hot surface. She ambled over to a small wooden table covered with a bright blue tablecloth and with practiced ease, poured boiling water into two clay cups that were already set on the table. The trickle of water was a comforting sound and the slightly bitter aroma that wafted to him was unique. He wasn't sure what tea it was, although he thought he knew every type of tea that she carried.

Sid smiled. Mrs. Wessmank always seemed to know when he would show up. He couldn't remember a time when she didn't have two cups of tea sitting on the table and water boiling on the stove. How she did it, he didn't know, but he smiled to himself and gratefully took a seat at the table and watched her put the kettle back on the stove, her bright blue apron swaying as she slowly walked. He had never seen her without that blue apron around her waist.

She was a small woman, although round and healthy looking. She had long, red, frizzy hair, and a face so wrinkled that Sid had one time reached out and touched it to see what it felt like. He had pulled his hand back immediately, horrified that he had done such a rude thing. But Mrs. Wessmank had taken his hand and put it back against her face. "Feel it boy, feel what time does to a person." Sid had been nervous, but he was surprised by how soft her skin was. The wrinkles were pleasant to the touch. He remembered smiling up at her. From that moment forward, Sid had felt closer to her than anyone in his life.

As long as Sid had known her, she had always been an old woman. He had no idea how old she was, she had always just been old Mrs. Wessmank to him. He looked at her wrinkled face and as always, he couldn't help looking at the two large moles above each of her eyes. They gave her the appearance of having four eyes. He remembered being scared of the moles when he was a child, but over the years he found himself comforted by her strange appearance.

Sid took a small sip of tea, trying not to burn his lips, yet eager to figure out what flavor it was. It wasn't often that Mrs. Wessmank got new tea in. He let the liquid sit in his mouth for a few moments, swishing it slightly. It was sweet and had a strange lingering taste, one that he couldn't quite place, kind of like a mixture of wild flowers and honey.

Mrs. Wessmank shuffled over and, putting one hand on the table and the other on the back of the chair, lowered herself with a sigh. She spent a couple of moments adjusting herself to get more comfortable, making little sounds the whole time.

Sid sat quietly waiting for her to finish. It was a ritual that he knew well. Mrs. Wessmank never just sat down. She made a large production of it.

"You know, I thought I knew every tea you carried, but there is something about this one that I just can't place. It has a sweetness, but there is... I don't know, I can't place it. It's almost like a floral sweetness, but I've never tasted anything like it before."

Mrs. Wessmank looked up at Sid and smiled a beautiful smile, one that usually never failed to put Sid into a good mood. But today nothing could make him feel better. He smiled back, but it was slightly strained.

Mrs. Wessmank noticed and her smile slowly faded. Her eyes turned hard, the pupils dilating. "It's jasmine my boy. It is from far away and I paid the seller dearly for it. So, that father of yours is sending you to the Oblate, isn't he?" She said this last part with ice in her voice and Sid's throat went dry.

She sat perfectly still across from him, her face hard. "Well?"

Sid was so shocked that he couldn't say anything. He just nodded slightly.

Mrs. Wessmank shook her head and smacked her hand on the table, the loud slap jarring him. "I always suspected but I never could prove it." She looked up fiercely at him. "You must not go there!"

"What are you talking about? How do you know about the Oblate?"

Mrs. Wessmank continued, almost as if she hadn't heard his question, "The Korpor has come for you, hasn't it?"

Sid's face turned pale and sweat beaded on his forehead. He nodded again and whispered, "Last night."

Mrs. Wessmank closed her eyes. "Did you feel pain?"

Sid shook his head, but realized she couldn't see him. So he said in a quiet voice, "No. None at all." He couldn't tell her about the pleasure he felt.

Mrs. Wessmank looked up at Sid, her mouth twisted slightly, and her eyes hard. "Did you have sex with it?"

Sid started to speak but was cut off.

"And tell the truth Sidoro, no matter what."

Sid swallowed and looked down. He couldn't tell her. He was about to lie, but the look in her eyes stopped him. He swallowed again. "No. I didn't."

Mrs. Wessmank's eyes widened. "You didn't?"

Sid shook his head and his face turned red. "I wanted to at first."

"But?"

"I made it stop."

Mrs. Wessmank's eyes widened even more. "You stopped it? I said don't lie to me Sidoro!"

Sid's eyes flashed in anger. "I'm telling the truth!"

Mrs. Wessmank glared at him for a few moments then let out her breath, and Sid thought he heard her whisper, "Aleph Null," but it was so quiet he couldn't be sure. The old woman looked shaken, but her voice came out steady. "I'm sorry. I am just an old woman who can't control her anger sometimes." She folded her hands together on the table, wringing them together in agitation.

Sid looked into her eyes. Where just moments before they were hard and piercing, they were now moist with tears. He relaxed and reached across the table to take her hands in his. "What is going on? I don't understand anything that is happening."

Mrs. Wessmank took her left hand from under his and wiped a tear from her eye. She smiled sadly at him. "I had hoped that this day wouldn't come. I knew you were special, but I had hoped it would pass you over." She dabbed at a tear again, and then straightened up, her voice gaining strength. "But that is neither here nor there. You must not trust your father."

Sid started to protest, but she cut him off. "I am sorry Sidoro, but look deep inside yourself. You know that to be true."

Sid sat back. He thought back to everything his father has told him today. Then he thought back further and couldn't remember one time when he had truly felt that his father loved him. He had always felt like a stranger. Deep in his heart, he knew that Mrs. Wessmank was right.

It hurt.

He put his head into his hands and let out a short sob.

Mrs. Wessmank touched his face. "I know it hurts Sidoro. But you must be strong now. You are in danger, and you have to bottle that pain away."

Sid looked up, his eyes red and wet. He knew that she was right. If that day in the hut had taught him anything, it was that he was alone in this world and he could take care of himself. He angrily wiped the tears from his eyes and sat up straight. His eyes became hard, and he nodded to her. "Tell me what to do."

Mrs. Wessmank stared at Sid for a few moments, looking worried about him, then sat up straight herself. "You must stay away from the Oblate. As much as it hurts me to say this, your father is an agent for them. For a thousand years the Oblate has been waiting for you Sidoro."

Sid raised his eyes in surprise. "What are you talking about? I'm ordinary."

Mrs. Wessmank chuckled. "Oh Sidoro, you are far from ordinary."

Sid scoffed.

Mrs. Wessmank glared at him until he stopped making derisive noises. When he was silent and she had his attention, she continued, "Sidoro, you are the one the Oblate has been searching for and they will have you anyway they can. The Korpor was sent to consummate the union, to awaken your numbers and control your mind. It was then to bring you to the Oblate where they would use your powers for their own ends." She looked at him quizzically. "But somehow, you have prevented the creature from taking you."

She narrowed her eyes briefly. "Some day you will have to tell me how you did it. But now you must leave quickly. You haven't much time."

Sid openly stared at Mrs. Wessmank in disbelief. "How do you know all of this?"

Mrs. Wessmank took his hand again. "Trust me Sidoro, and don't ask any more questions. Time is of the essence. You must leave."

Sid pulled his hands away again, anger filling his eyes. "I'm sick and tired of everyone telling me to trust them! How can I believe you over my father? He told me the Oblate was the only safe place for me. Now you tell me to ignore everything he said!" He rubbed his hand through his hair.

She spoke softly. "Sidoro, you've known me your entire life. Have I ever frightened you?"

He shook his head no immediately.

"And have I ever asked you to do anything you didn't want to do?"

Again, he shook his head no.

"So please trust me now, Sidoro."

Sid put his head in his hands, not thinking about anything at first. But after a short while, he thought about his father, of his blank stares and bored expressions. Then he thought of Mrs. Wessmank and he felt nothing but love for her. She was the only person in his life whom he had ever felt close to. He knew, deep down, that she was telling the truth. A deep sense of loss filled him at realizing that his father was a liar. He felt out of control, unsure of who he was.

Sid raised his head to look at Mrs. Wessmank and saw her eyes were wet and red. He whispered, "So what do I do now?"

Mrs. Wessmank let out her breath as if she had not been aware she had been holding it. "I'm sorry, Sidoro. More sorry than you will ever know." She composed herself. "There are some people who can help you. I would take you to them, but I am an old woman now and will only slow you down when speed is of the essence. You will have to travel on your own, as much as that pains me. But it must be done."

Sid nodded. "I understand. Where must I go?"

"Undaluag. There you will find..."

Before she could continue, Sid hissed and leaned back in his chair.

Mrs. Wessmank looked at him in alarm. "What is it?"

Sid's heart started beating quickly, loud in his head. He looked at Mrs. Wessmank and saw that she was genuinely confused. He took a deep breath. "Undaluag is where my father sent me, to the Oblate."

Mrs. Wessmank's eyes widened and she whispered. "So that is where it is located. I never knew." She looked back at Sid. "Many people have died looking for that place." She composed herself, shifting on the chair. "Unfortunately, that is also where the Anderom is located. What bad luck," she whispered.

"The Anderom? What is that?"

"The Anderom is a group of people who can help you."

Sid leaned forward. "How do you know?"

She looked at him intensely. "Because I am their leader."

Sid's eyes widened. His head began to hurt. Too much was happening too quickly.

Mrs. Wessmank leaned forward. "We oppose the Oblate in every way. You must go to the Anderom, and you must stay away from the Houses of Healing and the patrols. They are not safe anymore."

Sid shook his head. "But how do I find this Anderom? I've never even been more than a day's travel from Orm-Mina before."

Mrs. Wessmank patted her forehead with her blue apron to wipe a bead of sweat off, then looked at it in her hand and her face turned white. She put her finger to her mouth in a quiet gesture and then untied the apron and walked into the back room. In a little while she came back without it.

Sid looked up at her questioningly.

"The apron is a way for the Oblate to spy on me, it has been for decades. Unfortunately, I am so used to wearing it that I completely forgot about it until just now. That means that they may now know that you are aware of them and it will make things harder for you. I'm sorry, Sidoro. I have put you in more danger with my forgetfulness."

"Don't worry, I don't think it's going to make much difference."

"Just the same, it makes it a more difficult road for you. When you get to Undaluag, go through the east gate. You will see a tobacco shop immediately inside the gate called Leaf Or Be Gone. The owner's name is Mr. Rubion. Tell him I sent you. He will know what to do."

She looked lost in thought for a moment and whispered to herself, "There was something else I was going to tell you..." and then she sat up straight and gasped, "How could I forget?" Looking directly into Sid's eyes, she spoke quickly, "I am getting old and almost forgot about the Fahrin Druin."

Sid looked irritated. "Fahrin Druin? Let me guess, more people who want to capture me, right?"

Mrs. Wessmank slowly shook her head no. "I wish that were the case, but it is not. The Fahrin Druin murder anyone and everyone who have even just the potential to be the Aleph Null."

Sid shook his own head. "Great. This day just keeps getting better and better."

"I know and I'm sorry."

"So how do I spot these Fahrin Druin and avoid them?"

"You will know them as traveling wizards, although it is merely a cover that lets them search every village and city for young men and women who show even a hint of mathematical ability."

"I guess I'm lucky that they never found me."

"Oh, it wasn't luck, Sidoro. I've made sure they never found you up until now."

Sid was going to ask her how she managed to do that, but she leaned back and patted his hands as if to stop him from asking any questions. "I think I have prepared you as best I can in the short time we have had right now. I wish I had told you more before now, but I didn't know about your father, or that you truly were the Aleph Null. It makes things harder for you, but we have had this brief chat, which helps. You had best be going, for every moment that you spend here puts you in more danger. Stay the night in Oiro at a place called Riana's Tavern. Mistress Riana is a good person. She will take care of you. Travel quickly and trust no one. Remember, always stay indoors at night. If you find you cannot make it to a village or town for the night, stay awake and keep the Korpor out of your mind."

Sid sat at the table, taking in everything Mrs. Wessmank told him, committing it to memory. Twice in one day he had his world change on him. But instead of feeling sorry for himself, he felt anxious to get going. He looked at Mrs. Wessmank sitting across from him and realized how much he loved her. She was the one person who had been there for him his whole life.

He touched her wrinkled cheek. "I will miss you Mrs. Wessmank." It was a simple statement, but he realized that he really meant it. He felt he was truly leaving home.

She let Sid caress her cheek for a few moments then took his hand. "Please, call me Elenora."

Sid's eyes widened. He had never known her first name before. He mouthed it, but the name sounded strange to him. She would always be Mrs. Wessmank to him.

She lifted her teacup and held it out to him. Sid lifted his, and they lightly touched cups before they each took a sip. They both sighed this time. The tea was the best Sid had ever had. They sat in silence, both enjoying the quiet and company. The whole time they sipped their tea, Mrs. Wessmank stared down at the table.

When Sid finally set his empty cup carefully on the table, Mrs. Wessmank quickly stood up. She looked down at him for a moment and then turned and went through the doorway into the back room, talking as she went. "I don't want you going hungry. You need your energy. Let's see, some hard bread, some cheese, a little salt, a packet of dried deer meat. What else, oh yes, can't forget the vegetables. A boy needs his vegetables. Ah, here they are. Some carrots, onions... and potatoes, yes those are good and filling."

Sid listened to her moving boxes around, talking to herself the whole time. He raised his voice so she could hear him, "No, you don't have to give me any food. I've got plenty."

She was always trying to feed him. Food was love to Mrs. Wessmank and Sid always left the store with a satisfied belly. Sometimes it was cake and tea. Other times she served him meats, cheeses and bread. Every time it was something different, but delicious.

Sid couldn't make out her response but he could hear her muttering as she moved about. Sid stood up to give her a hand, but before he could step into the back room, she appeared in the doorway with a small sack that bulged.

"Well don't just stand there my boy, help an old woman with this heavy sack."

He reached out and took it from her. "Thank you, Mrs. Wessmank, but I really don't need," but he didn't finish his sentence because she bustled past him, opened the door to the outside, and sunlight spilled into the room. Sid followed her through the door and stepped out into the bright sunlight.

Mrs. Wessmank held her hand up to shield her eyes from the sun. "No boy should be on his own, but at least you won't be hungry."

Sid stood in front of her, suddenly not wanting to leave.

"Come now, give this old woman a hug good bye and be on your way. Daylight is wasting away."

Before he could move, the old woman took two steps forward and wrapped her arms around him tightly. She pushed herself onto her toes and reached her mouth up to his ear and whispered softly. "You be careful, Sidoro. Don't let the Korpor into your dreams." Her voice cracked and her breath was warm on his ear, "And you come back to me, you hear me?"

Sid squeezed her tightly back. "I promise." His mouth was dry, and the last word came out as a rasp.

Mrs. Wessmank squeezed him back and then let him go. They stood apart, looking at each other. She reached up and touched his cheek, then turned and shuffled slowly through the doorway without turning back.

Sid stuffed her sack of food into his pack, threw it over his back, tied it around his chest and stomach, then stood in the sunlight taking in the sight of the small village. He deeply inhaled the sweet tobacco smell that wafted from the open doorway and let it out with a rush. He turned and walked purposefully down the narrow street. It was muddy, so he angled over to the edge where it was a little dryer. In only a few moments he was through the village and on the main road, heading north.

Chapter 8

The road curved around low-rolling hills and over bubbling streams, and was slightly muddy and rutted from wagons and horses. Sid knew this area just north of Orm-Mina very well.

As the road turned up ahead, Sid smiled when he came upon the small dirt trail that led to the house where his best friend Tris lived. He stopped and gazed down the trail with sadness. Tris had mysteriously left town the previous month with no farewell.

Sid turned away and started down the main road again. He would miss his friend. Aside from Mrs. Wessmank, Tris had been the only person with whom Sid spent time. They had known each other for most of their lives, played together as children, and talked about their dreams as young men.

Tris was two years older than Sid, but it didn't seem to matter to their friendship. Sid had always been amazed they had even become friends. Tris was tall and perfect looking, with blond hair, eyes that were almost black, and a full mouth the girls in the village adored. He was strong-willed and a born leader. Even most of the adults in the village fawned over him. The women, many of whom were two and three times his age, looked at him with longing eyes and intakes of breath. And most of the men treated him with respect, even when he had been a child. Tris quite simply could get people to do what he wanted. Every kid in the village would do as he asked and would follow him around like a pack of dogs, but it was Sid who he had chosen as his best friend.

The fact that Tris had left Orm-Mina a month earlier without even saying goodbye hurt Sid deeply, especially now when he really needed his friend. He would have given anything to have Tris go with him on this journey. He just felt safe with Tris. Sid thought even the Korpor might have hesitated to bother Tris.

As the morning turned to afternoon, Sid thought about all that had happened since the previous evening. Everything that he thought was real in his life had been turned inside out. His father's betrayal hurt the worst though. Even if they weren't close, his father was the only family he had.

Sid looked ahead. The dirt road stretched in front of him. He had no idea what was in store for him, but he didn't really care. He would deal with whatever happened in the future. He was alone and he preferred it that way.

The sun was actually hot, a complete change from even a few weeks earlier when the snowed had piled up to his knees in an early spring snowstorm, the kind where the snow was heavy but began melting almost immediately. Now, he was sweating. That was one of the things Sid loved about the seasons, how quickly they changed.

Bugs lazily buzzed around his head as he came upon Oiro just after dark. He waved them away as he took in the town just ahead of him. It was quite a bit larger than Orm-Mina, with more commerce, which gave it an air of a small city rather than a large town. Sid had only been here twice before in his life and then only as a small child with is father, so everything felt unfamiliar to him as he gazed at the grand houses that lined the road leading into Oiro. They seemed huge, at least in Sid's eyes compared to his own tiny house, and they actually had glass covering the windows. Oh, how nice it would be to not have mosquitoes buzzing around his head every night in the summer and actually having sunlight in the house during winter months instead of boarding up all of the windows like he and his father had to do.

He soon came to the entrance of Oiro and the houses gave way to store fronts, most of which were already darkened. Only a few people were about and they all hurried about their business, trying to get their errands finished for the evening. The shadows were dark in the corners of the buildings and none of the people whom he passed met his eyes.

The night was warm. At any other time, Sid would have preferred sleeping under the stars, but after last night's encounter with the Korpor, he decided to take Mrs. Wessmank's advice to heart and find Riana's Tavern.

Three taverns stood out on the street, as they all had bright light spilling from their windows and doorways. He looked at the names as he walked down the street. The Flying Goat was the largest one and also the loudest. Music came from inside, along with raucous laughter. The second tavern was called The Ale House. 'A very basic name,' he thought to himself. It wasn't as large as The Flying Goat, but it was just as boisterous inside. Sid walked further down the middle of the street until he came to the last tavern at the end. It was fairly small and much quieter. The outside was painted red and green, very colorful compared to the other two taverns, which were unpainted. Sid looked at the sign and saw it simply read Riana's Tavern. He hoped that Mistress Riana was working tonight.

He had never been in a tavern before, so he was nervous as he crossed the street and stood outside the door. Through a small window, he could see that the place was well lit and filled with people sitting at small round tables eating, drinking ale, and laughing.

Sid straightened his shirt and trousers, adjusted his pack, and opened the door. He was instantly assaulted by noise and he shrank back a little. Steeling himself, he stepped inside and let the door shut. Smoke filled the air and he inhaled deeply. He could tell it wasn't as good quality as the tobacco that Mrs. Wessmank sold, but it brought thoughts of home. He lifted his head high and walked purposefully into the room.

No one took notice of him as he stepped to the bar, which ran the length of a wall. A pretty woman worked behind it, so Sid stood at the end, waiting for her to notice him, hoping that she was mistress Riana. She placed a glass underneath a long metal spout that reached to the bottom of the glass and began pulling a wooden handle back and forth. Sid watched in amazement as ale swirled in the bottom of the glass, a dark brown mixed with what looked like cream. Each pull of the handle pumped more ale into the glass until just a small amount of froth spilled over the top and she stopped. She carefully set the glass of ale in front of the man with a smile on her face. When she turned to walk away, the man reached over the bar and squeezed her butt, laughing as he did it. She saw Sid and rolled her eyes.

Sid swallowed twice as she came up to him with a raised eyebrow. She was very beautiful.

"You are a young one." She said, looking him up and down.

Sid blushed slightly. He didn't talk to women very often and had no idea what to say to her.

She noticed his embarrassment and her lips curved upward in a kind smile. "I see you are not like the rest. Please forgive me." She put her arm on the bar in front of Sid and leaned toward him. "So what can I do for you young man?"

Sid smiled politely. "I am looking for mistress Riana. Do you know where I might find her?"

She looked him up and down again, then she smiled brightly. "In the flesh. And how is my name known to you, if you don't mind my asking?"

Sid leaned forward and spoke quietly. "My name is Sidoro and my friend Mrs. Wessmank told me that you might provide me a small room for the evening." Embarrassed, he quickly added, "If it is not too much trouble, I mean."

He stood there, looking down, feeling like nothing more than a kid from the country. He had no idea of the proper process a person went through to get a room for a night, or even how much coin it would cost. But the woman behind the bar quickly nodded. "Of course, it will be three coppers a night."

Sid relaxed and removed his coin pouch. He dug three copper pieces out and placed them on the bar.

She didn't pick them up as she raised an eyebrow at him. She looked calmly around the room and spoke quietly. "Put those coins away lad. You don't pay up front and you don't put money on the table like that. You will be robbed before you know it."

Sid quickly slid the coins off the bar and put them in his pocket. He was really confused and the woman noticed. "You poor boy. Go around back and up the stairs. Take the third room on the right. I'll have some sausage and potatoes sent up in a short while, along with some ale. Come see me in the morning. Now go on."

Sid thanked her and walked out of the tavern. The night was cool and refreshing after being in the warm smoky room. He walked around to the back of the building and saw the stairs leading up into darkness. He studied the darkness, not liking it, but he didn't sense anyone hiding there, so he stepped into the shadows and climbed the creaky steps. He soon came to a small landing and a narrow door. He opened it, the squeak very loud in the night, and entered a short hallway lit by a single candle on a table. He found the third door on the right and knocked lightly. No one answered, so he turned the handle and opened the door.

Inside was a small, dark room lit by the shaft of light from the hallway candle. He could see a straw bed and a single table with an unlit candle in an iron candleholder, as well as two old chairs. Sid shrugged out of his pack and set it softly on the floor, then picked up the candleholder and carried it into the hall to light it from the already burning candle. He returned to his room, quietly shut the door, then set the candleholder onto the small table. He collapsed into one of the chairs with a sigh. He rolled his shoulders up and down and it helped to relieve some of the pain in them. He wasn't used to carrying such a heavy pack for such a long time.

He looked around the room. The walls were simple, unpainted wood planks with cracks between that were large enough to see light from the rooms next door to him, although at the moment they were dark, so the rooms must either have been empty or the people in them asleep. The lack of privacy didn't make him feel very safe, but he was tired and just wanted to eat and sleep.

He took his boots off and had just set them next to the table when there was a soft knock at the door. He warily stood up and opened it.

A plain-looking, young girl stood in the hall holding a tray of food. She smiled shyly at him and murmured quietly, "Hello, sir. Your food and ale." She coyly looked him up and down. She couldn't have been more than fourteen years old.

Sid reached out and took the tray from her hands. "Thank you very much."

He took a sniff and when he realized the food smelled delicious he told her so. She smiled up at him and thanked him for the compliment. She kept standing there and Sid was at a loss as to what he should do next. When he didn't do anything for a few moments, she scowled and turned quickly. As she walked away, he heard her mumbling under her breath.

Sid had no idea what he had done wrong, so he stuck his head out the door and watched her walk down the hall and turn the corner. He sighed and backed up until he could swing the door shut with his foot. He didn't understand what had just happened, but he was too hungry and tired to care. He never was able to understand girls.

He carried the tray to the small table and set it down. There was a large sausage, a steaming potato, and a pile of carrots. He sat down and started eating quickly, hardly chewing his food. It was delicious. He took a large swallow of ale after the first few mouthfuls of food. It was warm, but very tasty.

Growing up in the country like he had, Sid and his father drank spring water, or on the rare occasion when they didn't use all of their goat's milk for making cheese, they would share a small cup of warm milk. It was slightly bitter and a real treat. But he knew that in town, people drank mostly ales because clean water was hard to come by and could make them sick. Sid had never gotten a taste for ale, but now it tasted wonderful and smooth. He took another large swallow and then finished off the food on the plate. With a satisfied sigh, he downed the last of the ale and sat back. His stomach was full for the first time since the previous day.

His eyes started to droop from the food and alcohol, so he got up and flopped down on the bed. Within moments he was asleep, snoring loudly.

* * *

The door to Sid's room squeaked open during the night and the serving girl poked her head inside. She saw him sleeping on the bed and quietly entered the room. She knew he had coin on him and after he refused to tip her she was going to take what was hers and more. She hated country folk and anytime she could take their money, she felt no remorse. They were ignorant and rude.

She reached his pack and untied the flap. Inside she found nothing but food and clothing. She didn't expect to find any coin in it, but she thought maybe he didn't know better. Her opinion of him rose slightly. She crept over to where he was laying on the straw bed, snoring loudly. He was on his stomach, his hands at his sides and his face turned toward her. She lightly felt his pockets but found nothing. His coin pouch must be underneath him. Just her bad luck. She was about to give up and leave, but then she decided that he was probably so deeply asleep that she could flip him over without waking him.

She stood there, looking down at him, trying to decide if she should take the chance. She noticed that he was kind of cute. He was skinny but had defined muscles on his arms. He was a boy used to doing hard work.

She knelt down next to him and studied his face. He was young, but even in sleep she saw that he looked angry. His mouth was set hard and his eyes danced behind his lids. She leaned down to look closer at him, when he suddenly opened his eyes and stared at her. She yelped and stumbled back, bumping into the chair.

His eyes were a solid dark blue as he sat up, looking slightly confused and still in a semi-sleep state.

She turned and fled from the room, although she shut the door lightly behind her. Despite her fear, she didn't want to wake Mistress Riana. She slowed to a walk as she descended the stairs. She couldn't stop thinking about those eyes. They were not that color when she brought the food to him. He had brown eyes, she was sure of it. She shook her head and hurried a little faster. She wanted nothing to do with that boy.

* * *

Sid slowly focused on the room as he sat in the straw bed. His eyes changed back to their normal brown color, but he wasn't aware of it. At first he wasn't sure where he was, but then he remembered he was in the tavern. Something had woken him up. He seemed to remember seeing the serving girl in his room, but he knew that must have just been a dream. Probably because she was the last person he had seen before he had fallen asleep. He lay back down on the bed and closed his eyes. He was sound asleep again in moments.

When the morning sun sliced through the cracks in the wall, Sid smiled to himself as he woke up. He enjoyed the sunlight on his closed eyelids. It was chilly in the room and his nose was cold. He didn't hear the pigs, which was strange. They were spoiled and usually started grunting for food right at sunrise. He reached down and scratched his groin, then sat up and stretched his arms over his head. He opened his eyes and stared uncomprehendingly at the small room. Then he was instantly awake and remembered where he was.

With a rush, he swung his legs over the edge of the straw bed and stood up. He was still fully dressed, which surprised him. He must have been really tired last night. But now he felt refreshed and ready to start the day.

He used the chamber pot and washed his face with the bowl of water on the table. He then pulled on his boots and gathered his pack, looking around the room to make sure he had everything. He opened the door, looked to his right and saw the stairwell just down the hall. He didn't know if the tavern mistress was awake yet, but he figured he might as well find out. He walked quietly down the stairs. They were narrow and dark, but the boards didn't creak under his feet. At the bottom he saw a large kitchen to his right and a storage room to his left. Just ahead of him was a curtained doorway, so he pushed his way through and found himself in the main tavern.

The room was empty except for one old man sitting at a table by himself. His back was straight and he wore a plain brown long coat. As Sid walked toward him, the man smiled a toothless grin and lifted his mug of ale in greeting. He then took a careful sip and put the mug down. There were already four empty mugs next to him. Sid smiled hesitantly back and walked quickly past him to the bar.

He stood there, unsure what to do next. Did he clear his throat or say hello, hoping the tavern mistress would hear him? Before he could do anything, she pushed through the curtained doorway and smiled at him when she saw him standing by the bar.

She was dressed in a bright yellow and green dress that fell just past her knees and it was cut low down the front, showing more cleavage than Sid had ever before seen on a woman.

"Good morning, Sidoro!" she said, beaming at him.

She was struggling with a large box, so Sid hurried over and took it from her.

She smiled brightly at him and motioned as she spoke. "You are very kind, thank you. Please, put the box on the bar over there."

Sid did as he was told. It was heavy and clinked as he walked. He was astonished when he realized it was a box of new glass mugs. They must have cost a fortune. He carefully set the box on the bar.

The tavern owner walked behind the bar, wiping her hands on a towel. "That was very nice of you to do. Please sit, I'll have some food brought out right away."

Sid thanked her and sat at the nearest table, his back straight and hands in his lap. The old man, a few tables away, turned to Sid and raised his glass with a silly smile and took another drink. He was already drunk and Sid wondered what kind of life he had that he started drinking this early in the morning. He looked well-to-do. Maybe he was just bored.

Sid had only to wait a few moments before the serving girl from the previous night entered the room with a tray loaded with food. She didn't meet his eyes or say hello as she set it on the table in front of him, and she left before he could even say thank you. Sid thought that was strange. He must have really angered her last night, but he still didn't know what he had done wrong.

The smell of eggs and potatoes brought his attention to the tray on the table. He saw four eggs sitting on top of a large pile of cubed potatoes. On the side was another large sausage that was the length of the plate itself and very thick. Another glass of ale, frothy at the top, was the only thing to drink. Sid picked up the wooden fork and started eating, barely pausing between bites. It was delicious food, just like the previous evening, and before he knew it, he had taken his last bite. He sat back with a small belch, took a small swallow of the ale but put it down, not really liking the taste this morning.

He heard a soft laugh and looked over to the bar. Mistress Riana smiled at him. "That was impressive. Thank you for the compliment."

Sid turned red in the face and looked down. He couldn't believe he had eaten that way in public, much less in front of such a beautiful woman. "I'm so sorry for my poor manners."

Mistress Riana smiled again. She did that a lot, Sid imagined. Her face seemed to light up when she did. "Sidoro, you are a breath of fresh air. No need to apologize to me." She pushed a long strand of hair from her eyes. "I take it as a compliment that you appreciate my simple food."

She spun around with a swish of her skirt and walked around the bar to his table. She sat down and looked him directly in the eyes. She was so close to him that Sid could smell her skin, a soft fragrance like fresh flowers.

He sat up a little straighter in his chair. Mistress Riana took his hands in hers. "So tell me Sidoro, are you going to stay a few nights?"

Sid stopped breathing at the touch of her hands. They were cool and dry, while his were hot and sweaty. He swallowed and looked down. "I'm leaving right now actually, as soon as I settle my bill with you."

She playfully squeezed his hand. "So where are you going in such a hurry?"

Sid thought of Mrs. Wessmank and her comment that he could trust Mistress Riana. He wanted to impress her, so he leaned forward and spoke quietly. "To the Anderom."

He blushed again as he looked at her beautiful face.

She smiled down at him, although her eyes narrowed. "Your bill is ready. It is a beautiful morning for traveling. It is a bit chilly out this morning though, so you may need your coat." She motioned her eyes toward the man sitting next to them and shook her head slightly.

Sid looked over at the old man drinking at the table next to them. 'Why was she worried about him?' But as he thought this, Sid saw that the man was no longer drinking and was sitting very still.

The old man turned and looked at them, his eyes clear and intense. He smiled that toothless smile, but now it was curved down in condescension. "Oh don't worry about me, go ahead, keep talking. You left off at the Anderom, I believe."

When neither Sid nor Mistress Riana said anything, the man chuckled. "Why so quiet all of a sudden?"

The old man stood up and removed his jacket with a grand flourish and twirled it in a flash before putting it back on. Sid gasped as shifting colors danced in his eyes and a slight tinkling sound came from inside.

The old man folded his arms and leaned against the edge of the table. "You're another one for the Proofing aren't you? And someone that the Anderom is interested in. How curious."

Mistress Riana glared at him and hissed. "Fahrin Druin!"

The old man half-bowed. "In the flesh, mistress. Don't worry, I will leave soon. After I kill the boy, that is."

"Over my dead body, assassin. This boy will live. You and your order have killed thousands of potentials in your sick goal of trying to prevent the Aleph Null from coming into existence." She stood up and pulled a small knife from her hair as she glared at the wizard. "But you will not kill this boy."

Sid stood up also and placed his hand on the hilt of the Rissen blade in his pants, ready to pull it out at any moment. When he heard Mistress Riana hiss 'Fahrin Druin,' his body began to tremble. He never expected to actually run into one of the assassins so soon after leaving Orm-Mina, but he would defend himself if attacked and he would protect Mistress Riana.

The Fahrin Druin just laughed. "Oh you two are very dramatic." He clapped his hands slowly, then shrugged and put his hands into his coat pockets. "Unfortunately, you have it wrong. I am not an assassin. I am a protector of our world. I am saving it from destruction at the hands of the Aleph Null. If I have to kill a few hundred innocents, well that is not my problem. It isn't my choice. We can't take any chances, even with such a scrawny little boy such as this one." He smiled again and pulling his hands from his pockets, he spread his arms dramatically. "I am really a hero and while I think that you should be thanking me for saving the world, I understand that since the boy has to die in the process, he probably feels a little unhappy about all of this. But believe me, I don't enjoy killing... much."

Without warning, he threw his hands out and powder flew into both of their faces. Sid was immediately blinded and his eyes started to burn. He screamed as he frantically rubbed them, but it only made the burning more intense. He heard footsteps come toward him, combined with the tinkling sound, and a low chuckle came from the man. Sid reached frantically for the Rissen blade, but the pain in his eyes was too much and he dropped to his knees, moaning. He heard Mistress Riana fall next to him, but he couldn't concentrate on anything else.

Sid heard a gasp, followed by a body hitting the floor close by. He pictured Mistress Riana lying dead next to him and rage built in him. He felt his numbers in his mind, but the pain in his eyes made them jump around chaotically. He couldn't focus on them or control them. In frustration, he rubbed his eyes harder, trying to clear the burning powder from them.

Miraculously, Sid heard Mistress Riana's calm voice. "Thank you, Lori. Please fetch a pail of water."

"Yes, mistress."

Sid heard light footsteps fade away, then Mistress Riana spoke next to him.

"Sidoro, are you all right?"

"Yes, I'm fine. How about you?"

"Oh, thank the gods. Hold tight, Lori will be back with some water soon and we can wash this powder from our eyes. No matter how much you may want to rub at your eyes, do not do it. That will only make the powder burn more. Water will neutralize it."

Sid nodded as he heard Lori's light footsteps approach, along with sloshing liquid. The pain was intense in his eyes, but he obeyed Mistress Riana and didn't rub them. The burning sensation kept getting worse and he was about to scream in frustration when he felt Lori shyly touch the back of his head.

She spoke quietly, yet professionally, "Bend your head down and splash water into your eyes. Keep doing it until I tell you to stop."

Sid complied, cupped his hands in the water and splashed his eyes. The cold water instantly made the pain dissipate and soon Lori placed a towel against his eyes. He dabbed at them and when he took the towel away, he blinked rapidly. The pain was mostly gone and he could see Mistress Riana also dabbing her eyes with a towel, with Lori standing not far away, concern in her eyes.

When she saw Sid look at her, she quickly turned away.

Sid nodded to her. "Thank you for your help." She only nodded in return, looking anywhere but at him. Sid blinked his eyes a few more times, then noticed the old wizard lying face down on the floor in front of him, a knife buried in his neck. Only he was no longer a toothless old man, but a handsome young man with blond hair and a clean-shaven face. Sid widened his eyes and looked at Mistress Riana.

She daintily dabbed the towel at her eyes and motioned down at the dead man. "Fahrin Druin are sometimes adept at illusion, making us see what isn't really there. It isn't magic, it is more like hypnosis. But don't be too sad about his death, it was either him or us Sidoro." She looked up at Lori. "You have earned yourself a nice raise in pay, young woman."

Lori curtsied.

"Now, go and get a shovel and dig a hole in the back deep enough to bury this... garbage. Go on, hurry."

Lori bent down and pulled her knife from the man's neck, wiping it on his coat before returning it to a sheath hidden in her blouse. Then she bent down and dragged the wizard through the curtained doorway.

'She was certainly very strong,' Sid thought in wonder. He wasn't even sure he could have dragged the dead body that easily.

Mistress Riana stood up, so Sid hastily got to his feet as well. She nodded at the trail of blood on the floor. "You will have to be very careful what you say in public from now on. There are people like him who want you captured or dead. Trust no one."

She was the third person who told him that now. But after what had just happened, it seemed like good advice. He nodded at her, unable to speak.

Mistress Riana touched his shoulder. "How are your eyes? Will you be able to travel?"

Sid's eyes felt raw, but there was no longer any pain. "They are fine. Just a little sore."

"Good. You should leave quickly. Elenora told you how to find the Anderom safe house in Undaluag, right?"

Sid nodded. He wasn't surprised that she not only knew Elenora, but was an agent of the Anderom herself.

"Good, please get there as quickly as possible. There are worse than the Fahrin Druin in this world, and for Elenora to tell you about the Anderom means that you must be very special."

Sid didn't know what to say. He wasn't special in any way. He had no idea why so many people were taking such an interest in him and it made him uncomfortable. So he only nodded and picked up his pack.

With a swirl of her skirt, Mistress Riana went through the curtains and soon came back into the room with Lori following. "We need to clean up this blood right away. I don't want any customers to see it. We don't need anyone nosing about."

Lori curtsied and retrieved a bucket and washcloth and started scrubbing the bloody floor.

Sid immediately knelt to help her. This was all his fault anyway. It was the least he could do. But she looked up at him then at Mistress Riana with confusion in her eyes.

"Sid, please, let Lori do it. You are our guest." She laughed lightly. "Plus, I think you make young Lori nervous."

Sid stood up and shook his head. No girl was interested in him. And he sure wasn't interested in the serving girl. For some reason, she bothered him almost as much as he apparently bothered her. He raised his eyes to Mistress Riana and gazed at her beautiful face, at how her long, red hair hung over her face, still wet from when she washed her eyes. He felt his breath leave him and he stammered, "I guess I'm just used to doing my own work."

He looked into Mistress Riana's eyes and noticed they were a sparkling green that, along with her red hair, made her look mysterious and alluring. He glanced down at her cleavage and felt himself stir in his pants. He wondered what it would be like to put his hand inside her shirt, how soft her skin must be. With a start he realized he was staring and lifted his eyes guiltily up to Mistress Riana's eyes.

She merely smiled again and turned, apparently used to men looking at her that way. "Lori, please get three of our juiciest apples for Sidoro."

Lori stood and curtsied slightly. "Yes, mistress." She turned and quickly disappeared into the back room, wiping her hands on her apron.

Apples this time of year were very expensive, so Sid stammered. "No, please, you don't have to do that Mistress Riana. I've got plenty of food."

"Nonsense Sidoro, it is my gift to you for your fine company this morning."

Lori came back through the curtain carrying three large green apples and set them down on the bar carefully. She immediately started to clean the bloody floor again.

Mistress Riana polished the apples with a clean towel she took from under the bar and handed them one at a time to Sid. He bent down and lifted his pack flap and gently set them inside. There wasn't much room, but he made sure they all fit. It was a generous gift. He didn't know how she kept them so fresh.

When he stood back up, Mistress Riana put her arms on the bar. "Now, I supposed we should take care of the unpleasant part. Your bill."

Sid immediately took out his coin pouch. "Three copper pieces right? And how much for the meals?"

Mistress Riana smiled. "I think a copper piece is sufficient."

Sid frowned at her. She had said three copper pieces last night for the room and that didn't begin to cover all the headaches his stay had caused.

He began to protest, but Mistress Riana put up her hand to stop him from talking. "No protests, please. I've enjoyed your company, and you are a friend of Elenora. One copper piece is enough."

Sid was quiet for a few moments, but realized he couldn't argue with her. He placed a copper piece on the bar. He remembered her admonishment last night for doing that, so he quickly picked it up and placed it in her outstretched hand.

"You are learning, Sidoro." She quickly placed the copper piece in a box under the bar. "Now, you best be on your way. I've kept you long enough to myself."

Sid looked at Lori as she wrung the bloody rag into the bucket and impulsively leaned down and handed her the other two copper pieces. She looked at the coins in his hand, then up at Mistress Riana, who nodded with a smile on her face. Lori carefully took the two coins and said thank you without meeting his eyes.

Sid stood back up and retied his coin pouch to his belt. He picked up his pack and slung it over his shoulder and looked at Mistress Riana. "Thank you very much for... everything." He didn't know what else to say.

Mistress Riana waved him away. "You stay safe out there. Keep your eyes open and remember, trust no one." Mistress Riana softly touched his cheek. "Such a young man..."

Sid flushed. Just her touch made him shiver with pleasure. He backed away to cover his embarrassment. "Thank you. I look forward to seeing you again." He turned and left the room, stepping out into bright sunlight.

It was another beautiful morning, even warmer than the previous one. The sun was well above the horizon and the birds chirped loudly in the trees lining the street. Sid stood in the doorway and took a deep breath of fresh air. He turned to his right and started walking along the side of the road, heading north.

From this moment forward he was now further from home than he had ever been in his life. He walked slowly at first, picking his way along the street. It wasn't long before he left Oiro behind him. The road stretched out in front of him and he quickened his pace, taking long strides, his head up and back straight.

Chapter 9

Not far outside of Oiro, Sid came to the fork in the road his father had told him about. One led west and one led east. He took the east fork and made his way at a comfortable pace. He didn't need to take out his map. While his plans had changed, he still needed to get to Undaluag. The road was wide and fairly dry, so he was able to keep up a comfortable pace without effort.

The breeze was warm and he raised his face to the sun, enjoying the heat. He looked at the trees along the road. The leaves had opened quickly over the past few days. The countryside was turning a light green everywhere he looked and when he came to an opening in the trees, he saw a small glen surrounded by tall narrow birch trees. It reminded him of the little woods by his home and he got a lump in his throat. He would miss them greatly.

He continued on and as he walked, he thought of Mistress Riana. She was older than him by quite a few years, but she was the most beautiful woman he had ever met. He thought of her red hair, the freckles on her neck and her cleavage. Oh, that cleavage. He pictured her turning and the swishing of her dress, the view of her legs as the material twirled up. He had no idea what was hidden under the dress, but his breath shortened when he thought of it.

Sid was so deep in thought that he didn't notice the man sitting on the side of the road until he was almost upon him. He immediately stopped and stared at the man distrustfully.

The man sat cross-legged on a large flat rock. He took a large bite from a loaf of black bread and watched Sid through eyes hidden partially by long black hair that hung halfway down his back.

He was the biggest man Sid had ever seen. Even sitting down like he was, he was still taller than Sid. He was young, perhaps only a few years older than Sid. Crumbs from the bread collected in the wispy hair that grew from the man's upper lip and chin. He took another large bite and chewed it slowly, watching Sid with a bemused expression on his face.

Sid didn't know what to do. He wasn't comfortable passing so closely by the man and thought it would be rude to cross to the other side of the road and pass. He didn't want to anger such a large man.

Finally realizing he was being rude just standing there, Sid took a few hesitant steps forward and the man didn't move. With growing confidence, he picked up his pace. In a few strides, Sid was even with the man and then he was past him. The man turned his head to watch Sid as he passed by, slowly chewing a mouthful of bread.

Sid kept his face neutral, glancing at the man as he passed.

The man smiled widely with bread sticking to his white teeth.

Sid picked up his pace until he was almost jogging down the road. After a bit, he turned his head and looked back. The large man was still sitting on the rock, eating his bread, head turned, watching him.

Sid quickly looked away and after a short while came to a slight corner in the road. After he went around it, he turned and could no longer see the man. He breathed a sigh of relief. He didn't want to tangle with him. He was so large, he probably could have crushed Sid's head with one hand.

He couldn't trust anyone.

Sid walked until the sun was straight above him. It was mid-day and he realized he was hungry. Up ahead he saw a clearing off from the road under a small Miq tree. He took that as a good sign and quickly left the road, pushing brush out of his way until he was standing under the tree. It was only about half the size of the Miq tree from his woods, but it was still grand. The needle-covered ground underneath the tree was soft and dry as he sat against the bark and stretched out his legs.

He pulled the flask from his hip and took a short drink of water. He put the cork back in to seal it. He then dug in his pack and took out one of the large green apples. He took a small bite. The sweet juice ran down his chin. The apple was the sweetest he had ever tasted. He chewed and swallowed the first bite and took an even larger bite. Before he knew it, he had popped the last piece of core in his mouth, sucking the juice from his fingers.

He then dug in his pack and took out a chunk of bread and cheese. He ate these quickly, too. When he was finished, he leaned his head against the rough bark of the tree and looked up through the branches to the sky. A few white puffy clouds floated by and the branches swayed slightly in the breeze. Sid thought of home and his deer stand and of the times he had played in the giant Miq tree. Soon his eyes drooped and he started snoring slightly.

*　*　*

The two men had seen the thin young man leave the road as they came around the corner. They stopped and listened and they heard the man pushing through brush. The crunching sound soon ceased so they figured the man had stopped close to the Miq tree up ahead.

They looked at each other and smiled. They were rough-looking men. Their hair was long and stringy and they wore scuffed, stained leather over their tunics. The taller of the two had a nose that bent to the side of his face and a scar ran from his mouth across his cheek. He had an ugly, nicked-up sword hanging from his hip. The other man was shorter but was as wide as he was tall. He was just as rough-looking as his friend, but where his friend had a dull look in his eyes, this man's eyes were hard. He carried a large axe over his shoulder, the handle sticking up past his head.

The shorter man pointed to his left and whispered, "We'll go in here and come at him from the north." It was a statement, not a question. The taller man didn't reply, staring into the trees. The short man nudged him in the side. "Trouq, you imbecile, are you listening to me?"

Trouq looked slowly down at his friend and nodded. "Yes, Gib."

They turned and waded into the brush, being very careful to make as little noise as possible. They took their time and made a large circle so they could come upon the Miq tree from the north. The tree stood taller than all the other trees around it, so it was easy to plan their route.

Gib put up his hand and they came to a stop. He reached out and slowly pushed a bush out of the way. Through the opening, he could see the young man sleeping against the Miq tree, a large bulge in his trousers. 'What a fool,' he thought to himself, shaking his head in amazement, looking at the boy's crotch. The stupid lad was dreaming of some woman. 'Oh well, at least he will die dreaming happy thoughts.'

He smiled up to his partner, and the man grinned stupidly back at him. With a nod of his head, they both stepped through the last of the brush into the clearing. They walked toward the young man, not caring about making noise now. He was a lamb for the slaughter.

Gib reached back and removed his large axe. Trouq saw him and took out his sword, the ring of steel loud in the clearing.

* * *

Sid gazed upon the beauty of Mistress Riana. She was kissing him, her breasts pushed against him, her hands caressing his backside. Sid felt her soft, wet tongue inside his mouth and he was very hard. She pulled back from the kiss and her eyes were dark blue with hairs growing from them. She reached down and cupped his groin, smiling at him. He saw sharp teeth in her mouth. It was strange, but he didn't care. She slowly pulled his trousers down and gave a throaty laugh. He saw blood on her hands and he stumbled back from her. She held up her hands and she was holding a crushed heart, blood seeping from between her fingers.

Before he could scream, he heard the hiss of steel being pulled from a scabbard. Mistress Riana slowly faded away and Sid realized he had been dreaming. He took a deep breath and he heard footsteps approach him. He quickly opened his eyes and saw two large, ugly men stop not far from him. One was short and held the largest axe Sid had ever seen. The other was very tall and held a sword. They both wore fierce grins on their faces. When they saw that Sid was awake, they smirked.

The short one lifted one bushy eyebrow. "Having a nice dream, I see." He motioned with his eyes to Sid's crotch and Sid looked down. He saw that he was still hard. He put his hands to his groin and quickly stood up.

The men laughed and slowly advanced toward him. They knew the boy had nowhere to go, so they took their time, their eyes showing that they enjoyed the fear in his eyes.

Sid reached inside his trousers, pulled out the large knife his father had given him and held it up defensively.

When the short man saw the blade, his eyes widened. He nudged his friend. "I can't believe it. I think that be a Rissen blade." He stared in awe at the knife in Sid's hand and his eyes glinted with greed.

The large man nodded his head in agreement and said in a low voice, "Gib, what's a Rissen blade?"

Gib shook his head. "No need to worry about that. All you need to know is that it is going to be mine."

Trouq agreed dumbly. "Of course Gib, just let me kill him first. I want to kill him."

Gib grinned evilly up at the large man and motioned him forward with a sweeping gesture. "By all means, please do."

Sid knew he was going to die. There was no way he was going to stop these two. Why did he pull his father's knife? He was told how valuable it was and he didn't even know how to use it in a fight. Now he was going to pay the price. He looked quickly over his shoulder. His only option was to try and run for it.

The two men sensed his decision and rushed him with a yell.

But before Sid could move he was pushed roughly to the ground. He landed on his back and a rush of breath exploded from his lungs. Above him stood the large man he had seen sitting on the rock along side of the road. He was holding a sword that was longer than Sid was tall.

The man looked quickly down at Sid and grinned broadly, then winked. "Now for some fun!"

The two charging men slid to a sudden stop and held their weapons in front of them, warily eyeing the giant man. They didn't seem to like their odds, but then the shorter man looked at the Rissen blade in the boy's hands and his eyes filled with greed again. He nudged his taller friend in the arm. "We can take him. You go left and I'll go right. Let's take the giant down like a tree."

His partner smiled broadly, most of his teeth missing in the front.

They both charged, screaming as they ran.

The tall man stood calmly, tossing his sword from hand to hand like a toy. He grinned down at Sid again.

The taller of the two men swung his sword hard at the giant man's head, while the short one swung his axe at the man's legs. Before the blades could connect though, they were slapped out of their hands by the man's long sword. He had flicked it so quickly that the sword was nothing but a blur. Both men yelped and held their wrists, their weapons lying on the ground at their feet.

The giant of a man raised one eyebrow. "That wasn't very fun, even a bit disappointing when you think about it. Come my friends," he motioned down to their weapons lying on the ground, "give it another try. That one didn't count."

The two men hesitantly bent down and picked up their weapons, then backed up a couple of steps. The shorter one's face was filled with anger, while the taller one just stood there, waiting to be told what to do.

A glint filled the shorter man's eyes and he gave his partner a hand signal and they slowly circled around the giant of man who was protecting Sid. The short man tripped on a root and fell to the ground, then stood up slowly.

The giant man just stood next to Sid, grinning in anticipation and holding his sword almost casually.

The short man gave the slightest nod to his partner and they both attacked the man. But instead of swinging his axe, he threw a handful of dirt and needles at the giant man's face.

It hit the man directly in the eyes and he put his hand up reflexively. As he did, the two men swung their weapons as hard as they could at his midsection. They connected with a loud thunk, but instead of their blades sinking into flesh, they bounced off of the man. His clothing was cut where the blades had struck, but there was only a slight trickle of blood where the axe and sword should have been buried in flesh. It looked like the man had no more than scratched himself on a branch.

The tall man rubbed at his eyes until he could see. "Very good, my friends. I've seen that dirty trick before, but honestly didn't think you two were smart enough to try it." He then looked down at the cuts in his clothing on each side of his waist where the blades had struck him. "Great, this was my favorite tunic too. Now I have to get it repaired."

The two men looked at each other, down at their blades, then at the man they had both struck with all their might. He wasn't wearing armor. He should have been cut in two from their powerful blows, yet he was talking about the cuts in his tunic like it was only an irritation to him. Then the shorter one's eyes filled with fear and he backed up slowly, his face blotchy. He whispered "Trith," over and over, his voice trembling. His partner looked at his friend in confusion.

The giant of a man stood calmly in front of the two smaller men, looking to all the world like he was just hanging out waiting for them to make up their minds. He suddenly leaned forward and said, "Boo!" to the men. It was too much for the shorter one, who turned and ran away as fast as he could into the woods. The taller one watched his friend run away, his eyes showing confusion, as if he had never seen his friend run from a fight. He took one final look at the giant man in front of him, then shrugged slightly, turned and ran after his friend.

Sid listened to the crashing of branches and brush, which quickly faded to silence. The two men must have run as hard as they could. Finally Sid looked up at the giant man, still stunned by what he had witnessed. He saw the bloody cuts on either side of the man's tunic and was astonished to see that the blood had already stopped flowing. The giant man reached a hand down to him and Sid reached up to grip it. He was hauled to his feet as easily as if he were a sack of tobacco.

The man smiled down at him and winked again. "Well, that was fun, although now I have to repair my tunic, which slightly negates my total enjoyment of the affair. But thank you for allowing me to have a little fun today. It had been a bit dull up until now."

Sid's head spun. Everything had happened so quickly that he was still trying to make sense of the events that had just transpired. Yet the man in front of him was chatting like he just had the best time of his life. He looked up into the man's eyes and noticed they were dancing with merriment.

Sid relaxed a bit. "Thank you for your help. I guess I owe you a debt of gratitude."

The giant man looked surprised, as if he had never been spoken to so respectfully before. He smiled broadly. "No worries, my friend. It was fun. But I don't think you should sleep out in the open like that when you are by yourself. It can be somewhat dangerous for a little man such as you." He raised his sword and swung it over his shoulder, sliding it with practiced ease into a scabbard tied to his back. He then sat cross-legged on the ground and sniffed the air. "That wouldn't be an apple I smell now, would it?"

Sid stared curiously at the man. He acted like nothing had just happened. What a strange person. Sid wanted to like the man, but he had only just met him and Mrs. Wessmank's warning not to trust anyone came back to him. Strangely, Sid felt no sense of danger from the giant man but he was still wary. He walked over to his pack, pulled out one of the green apples and tossed it to the man, who caught it easily in a hand so large that the apple looked about the size of a plum by comparison.

The man twisted it around in his hand. "Now that is a beautiful apple. Not a bruise on it." He sniffed it and smiled hugely. "And it smells fresh." He took a small bite. Juice ran down his chin and dripped from the small patch of hair hanging from it. He closed his eyes and chewed with complete satisfaction. When he had swallowed, he opened his eyes. "That, my friend, is the finest apple I have ever tasted." He quickly finished it off, enjoying every bite.

Sid leaned against the tree and studied the man. He had never met anyone like him before. The man was almost twice Sid's height, thin but muscular. His long, black hair swished around when he talked, almost like it was used to emphasize what he said. He was wearing a white tunic and black trousers made out of some kind of cloth that Sid had never seen before. It was light and flowed easily in the breeze. The man wore black boots with short heels. Sid had never seen a man wear boots that had a heel. He once saw a woman wear shoes with a short heel, but men usually wore flat-bottomed boots.

The man wiped his hands on the needle-covered ground and stood up. He held his hand out with a smile. "My name is Crowdal."

Sid stepped forward to shake it. "I'm Sidoro, but people usually call me Sid."

The man's hand was three times the size of Sid's, so it was like shaking hands with large bear. But Crowdal's grip was light and dry.

"Sid, my friend, it is a pleasure." He winked at Sid then looked up at the sun. "Well I am heading east. I saw you pass by a ways back. We can travel together for a bit if you like. I would enjoy the company."

Sid didn't really want to travel with this man, but in all honesty, he was nervous that those two men might try following him and attack him again. The naked lust in the short man's eyes when he had looked at Sid's knife sent shivers through him. He studied Crowdal for a few more moments, then decided that it would be all right to walk for a ways with him. Sid put the Rissen blade into the sheath in his trousers, promising himself to never take the knife out unless he was alone.

Crowdal noticed the knife and nodded toward it. "I would keep that hidden if I were you from now on. As you've seen, men will kill for that blade."

Sid looked up at Crowdal and smiled sheepishly. "You sound just like my father when he gave it to me."

Crowdal laughed lightly. "Then your father is a wise man."

Sid scowled. "Yeah, sure."

He put his pack on his back and adjusted the straps to make it more comfortable.

Crowdal straightened his tunic and walked a bit away. He bent down and retrieved his own pack. It was large enough that Sid could have probably crawled inside of it if he had wanted to. He motioned Sid. "Come, my tiny friend, let's see if we can avoid being attacked for a while."

Anger flashed through Sid and he glared at Crowdal, who put up his hands defensively. "I'm sorry, that was rude wasn't it? I guess I'm not used to being tactful. Just the same, while for me it was just a bit of fun with those criminals, it's probably best that you stay away from those types of men."

Sid felt foolish. He owed this man a debt of gratitude, not his anger. "I'm sorry. I'm just a little on edge. Thank you for saving my life." He spoke honestly, but he wanted Crowdal to know they weren't friends.

Crowdal reached down and put a hand on Sid's shoulder and smiled. "No debt incurred, my friend. You let me have a bit of fun, so really I owe you. I have been bored for a long time, so this bit of excitement was a welcome change. But, if you feel you must repay me, I would take another apple if you have one, which, by the apple smell coming from you pack, I'm betting you do."

Sid chuckled and shrugged off his pack. He opened the flap, took out the last apple and handed it to Crowdal. "This is my last one, but it is yours. I wish I had more for you."

Crowdal took the apple with glee. "I'll tell you what, I'll give you half."

Sid shook his head no as he closed his pack and put in on his back again. The apple was nothing more than a small snack for Crowdal, and Sid just wanted to get moving again.

Crowdal put the apple into a pocket. "I will save it for later." He spread his hand out toward the road, "Well my friend, after you."

Sid pushed through the brush and they were soon back on the road. They turned and fell into step side-by-side. Sid noticed that Crowdal purposely walked with very slow steps because his strides were so much longer than his own. The two of them would have looked comical to anyone watching them, with Sid's head barely topping Crowdal's waist.

He looked up at Crowdal from the corner of his eyes. He wanted to ask Crowdal why he didn't have any wounds from the attack and how he had found Sid just in time to save him from those men, but he wasn't sure how to bring it up. He had just met this man and while he seemed like a nice enough fellow, Sid didn't trust him. He already screwed up by pulling his knife on those two men and he almost got killed because of it. So he put his head down and ignored the big man, and walked in silence. It was already starting to get warm out, so Sid took off his coat and stuffed it in his pack as he walked.

Crowdal hummed tunelessly next to him as if he didn't have a care in the world.

Sid envied him, wishing his life was as simple as Crowdal's.

Chapter 10

The Black Robe rode her horse hard, the beast's mouth frothing whitely as it labored to breath around the hard metal bit in its mouth.

She knew that the horse would die from the run, but she needed to make all the speed that she could as she rode to the House of Healing in Yisk. The Fractional Ascension was happening very soon and she couldn't miss it, but she also had to spend some time with Father Mansico to ensure all was going according to plan.

She thought again of Danicu's boy. After her last communication with the Korpor, she was now certain that the boy was the Aleph Null. As she rode, she could barely contain her excitement. Of all the Black Robes throughout the millennia, she was the one who had found the Aleph Null. It was her destiny, just as she had always dreamed.

She turned her head and spit in anger. If only she didn't still need Father Mansico, then she wouldn't have to keep spending time at the House of Healing, hiding her identity, pretending that she cared about him. Over the years she had insinuated herself into his life, even though she was secretly his superior. That was the problem with the Oblate. Secrecy. No one knew the real identity of the Robes of Power. But she had anticipated the coming of the Aleph Null, and knew that the plan had always been for Father Mansico, as the top agent of the Oblate, to bring the Aleph Null securely to them. Father Mansico had, through the subtle power of the Oblate, developed a vast network of spies and lesser agents across the land, creating a net large enough to quickly take delivery of the Aleph Null no matter where he or she would be found, and safely bring the prize to the Oblate.

But she didn't trust Father Mansico to hand over the Aleph Null when the time came, so she needed to be as close to him as possible to ensure the transfer. He had no idea that she was not only one of the Robes of Power, but now the Black Robe. To him, she was just a low-level agent and sister to Elenora, the leader of the Anderom. She was looking forward to the day when the Oblate didn't need to rely on anyone to do their work for them, and more importantly, when she could reveal her true identity to the Father and see the look of fear in his eyes as she killed him.

She shivered. It was cold out tonight, it could even snow in the next few days. The horse pounded along the road and the wind blew her hood straight back. But the power of the horse was intoxicating and she felt at one with her destiny.

The Korpor was stalking the boy even at this moment. When the time was right, it would *Ring* the boy and consummate the union, thereby awakening the full power of the Black Numbers. It was going mostly according to her plans, plans that she had been maneuvering to make happen for more than seventy years. It was a long time to wait and at times over the past decades she had wondered if it would be worth it. But as she rode now, she laughed out loud into the strong wind that buffeted her. She continued to laugh for a long time, and if anyone had heard her, they would have shivered in fear at her madness.

* * *

The candle flickered, making shadows dance on the low ceiling. Father Mansico leaned back in his wooden chair and closed his eyes with a sigh. The laugh lines on his face were tense as he squinted his eyes tightly and pinched the bridge of his nose with two fingers. A slight throbbing in the back of his head irritated him.

He sat forward and opened his eyes, staring at the open manuscript on the table in front of him.

A soft snore came from under the table and Father Mansico felt the warmth of his Tulgin sleeping against his feet. He reached under the table and scratched the three-legged beast behind his ears. A low rumbling came from the beast as he slept and one of his legs started moving in a scratching motion. Father Mansico smiled. He had worked hard to first break and then train the Tulgin. It was a beast he trusted completely.

He straightened back up, propped his elbows on the table and rested his chin on folded hands. He stared at the manuscript for another few moments and realized he was too tired to concentrate, so he carefully closed it and secured the metal clasp. The musty smell of the parchment was wonderful.

He sat staring at the title for a long time.

"Black Numbers"

The title alone sent a thrill of excitement through him. He finally had the Black Numbers manuscript. After ten years of searching, it was finally his and he wasn't about to tell the Black Robe that he had it in his possession. The Robes of the Oblate were of no use to him anymore.

He stroked the book. It was his, only he couldn't understand any of it. He could read the first three pages only. Starting on the fourth page, there were only random numbers covering the pages... thousands of them. In frustration he unclasped the metal hook and re-opened the manuscript to the first page. Maybe if he read the first three pages again, he would catch something that he had missed the first time. Page one only had six words.

Black Numbers
Power Exponential Black Mathematics

An incredible waste of expensive and rare parchment and indicative of the wealth of the author.

With great care, Father Mansico turned the brittle page. The soft crinkle as it settled made him nervous that he would damage it before he had the Aleph Null, who was the only one who would understand it.

The second page was simple also. Just one poem. Father Mansico read it again.

Beyond sight, below sound, inside taction
Doors into light, windows into darkness
Numbers float randomly, lifeless, sterile
Until a variable unknown
makes black from white
A true Power Rule

He re-read the poem. The theory of Black Numbers was postulated by the Oblate long ago, but it had always remained theory. For a millennium, no mathematician in the Oblate had been able to prove the existence of Black Numbers and every Proof the Oblate had performed on the thousands of children had failed. Where this manuscript had come from, no one knew, but it was the key and held knowledge that only the Aleph Null could comprehend and use, and now the Aleph Null had been found.

He turned to the third page and concentrated.

What is not visible in this world rules supreme. Chaos and absolute power collide with the awakening of the Aleph Null, true wielder of Black Numbers, bringing that which doesn't exist into existence, or erasing existence for all.

A union of the Aleph Null and the beast, of claws and youth, binding a ring of bloody flesh to burst forth the seed of life. A birth, spawning numbers unknown, here yet there, a worm alive at both ends twisting the world upon itself until only power expands, bringing darkness upon the world. The Aleph Null, falls to infinity holding the Black Numbers in a mind's eye, twisting on an axis.

He sat back and digested the words. It foretold the *Ringing* of the Aleph Null, yet he had heard from the Korpor earlier in the evening. It had not *Ringed* or consummated the union with Danicu's boy, but the boy was indeed the Aleph Null, verified by the Korpor itself.

Frustrated, he closed the manuscript and slid the chair back, the scratch of wood on stone loud in the room. He pushed himself up with sudden force and paced the chamber.

The Tulgin raised his head and twitched his ears, looking out from under the table.

Father Mansico slid his hands into the opposite sleeves of his robe and put his head down as he walked. He had to have faith in the Korpor. It would *Ring* the boy and bring him here. He thought of all the years that he had been scheming, planning for this moment in time. While he was a good mathematician, he could not manipulate numbers and as such, had never been accepted as a Robe in the Oblate. So he had become an agent. The agents did not wield power within the Oblate, they worked for the Oblate.

Ironically, it was with the help of the Oblate that he had created his own power base outside of the Oblate. As Father of the House of Healing, he was one of the most powerful people in the land, but he wanted more. The Korpor was to deliver the Aleph Null to him and he was supposed to bring the boy to the Black Robe of the Oblate. But he had long ago decided to not deliver the Aleph Null to the Oblate. He would keep the Aleph Null and he would crush the Oblate and everyone else who opposed him. He would rule the land.

He chided himself, chuckling softly, realizing that he sounded like a power-mad lunatic. He didn't want to rule the land just to rule it. He wanted to change the power structure, to get rid of the Royal houses and the Oblate who ruled behind the houses. He wanted to give every person a chance to rise above their birth station. And he would be the one to rule to ensure that things stayed this way. Of course, they would all bow down to him as absolute ruler, but that was as it should be. If people had to die, then so be it. That was the way of the world.

A soft knock sounded at the door. Father Mansico tilted his head slightly.

"Come."

The door immediately opened and a woman glided in, the light from the hallway casting her face in shadow briefly as she turned to push the door shut behind her. She stood still for a few moments, then turned and walked lightly into the room and slowly knelt down on one knee in front of Father Mansico. "I am here as requested Father."

Father Mansico reached down and tilted her chin up until she was looking at him. He gazed down at her deeply wrinkled face, sunken eyes and white hair. "Ailinora, please rise."

Ailinora rose slowly and stood, a proud old woman. "Thank you,

Father."

Father Mansico cupped her cheek in his hand and smiled at her. "You are as beautiful as ever."

"Thank you Father, but I am an old woman so don't try your charms on me. They won't work." But she smiled despite her words. "I've received news."

Father Mansico gestured to a chair as he walked back to his desk and sat down.

Ailinora sat down with a long sigh, shifting back and forth as she got comfortable. "Thank you. This damp weather plays games with my joints."

"Oh stop it, you're not that old," Father Mansico rumbled.

Ailinora cocked her head slightly. "Really? I could have sworn that I passed the century mark already. Maybe my memory is failing with my old age."

Father Mansico laughed. It was pure and light, and filled the room with warmth.

Ailinora nodded. "It has been a long time since I have heard you laugh like that. You have been under too much stress lately."

Father Mansico closed and slid the manuscript around so Ailinora could read the title.

She gasped and leaned forward, reaching out with a trembling hand to touch it, but he pulled it away. "Now, now, I didn't say you could touch it."

Ailinora leaned back in her chair, her eyes bright. "You found the Black Numbers manuscript. When? How?"

Father Mansico held up a finger. "We will get to that. But first, you came here to tell me some news."

"Yes, of course." She looked at him with bright eyes. "My sister has verified the boy's abilities." She paused and then spoke quietly. "She has also warned the boy about his father and the Oblate. She has sent him to the Anderom instead."

Father Mansico slammed his hand down on the table, making the Tulgin scamper out from under it, nails sliding on the stone floor as he spun around to face them. The Tulgin stood a few paces away, trembling. Father Mansico chuckled and patted his leg. "I'm sorry boy. I didn't mean to scare you." He put his hand out. "Come here."

The Tulgin walked back to him in its odd three-legged gate, and stuck its muzzle into his open hand.

Father Mansico scratched behind the Tulgin's ear and ruffled his head, then slapped the Tulgin hard on the muzzle. "I've told you if you were skittish around me again, that you would suffer."

The Tulgin whimpered softly and hung its tail between its legs as it crawled back under the table and rested its head on Father Mansico's foot.

Ailinora chuckled. "Why is the Tulgin so jumpy?"

Father Mansico looked up at her and waved his hand. "He was beaten as a pup and gets skittish around loud noises, something I've been trying to break him of doing."

Ailinora frowned slightly. "I thought you were the only one who raised the animal?"

Father Mansico looked directly at her. "I was."

Ailinora nodded and quickly looked away. "Of course."

Father Mansico toyed with the manuscript, pushing it back and forth with one finger. "So, Elenora has finally put the pieces together. Good for her. It will be a pity to finally kill her. She has been very useful to us. We've learned a lot about young Sidoro through their conversations." He sighed. "Oh well..."

Ailinora nodded again. "I will be glad to finally get rid of her. Will you send the Haissen tonight to kill her?"

"Of course. No reason to wait." He looked at Ailinora with a small smile. "Did you want to go with them to say goodbye to your sister?"

Ailinora sat still for a few moments but finally shook her head. "If I were still young and able to travel I would go, but I am too old."

Lifting his finger, Father Mansico spoke quietly. "I can have them bring her here if you like."

Ailinora looked at him, then got a gleam in her eyes and smiled. "Yes. I would like that. A proper goodbye after all of these years is only appropriate." She chuckled softly. "Maybe I will take back that blue apron and tell her what it really is. The look on her face will be delicious." Ailinora tilted her head slightly as she looked at him. "You will be rewarded well tonight Father."

Father Mansico's own eyes gleamed briefly, but then turned immediately hard and narrow. "Now, to our other business." He slid the manuscript back toward her.

Ailinora hesitantly reached over and grazed her fingers over the ancient leather. Her voice trembled, but not from age. "I can't believe it is here in front of us. All of these years we've searched for it." She looked up at Father Mansico. "Where did you find it?"

"My spies heard it was in the possession of a Captain of the patrol. Apparently his father had been a scholar who had found it decades before. What is important is that we have it. Now we just need to add the final variable of the equation. The Korpor will take young Sidoro in the next few nights and *Ring* him."

Ailinora gasped lightly. "*Ring* him? That is dangerous. Has the Oblate approved this?"

Father Mansico's eyes blazed. "They are no longer of use to me. I approved this."

Ailinora cringed back slightly. "I'm sorry, Father."

Father Mansico opened a small wooden box that sat to his right and lifted out a beautiful black pipe. He then lifted out a pouch and opened it, inhaling deeply with his eyes closed. The lines on his face smoothed out and he opened his eyes to look at Ailinora. She really was a beautiful woman, even in her old age. He slowly packed his pipe with Uragon leaf, the most expensive and rare leaf available, then lifted the candle and stuck the flame above the pipe. He sucked in with small pulls, his lips smacking lightly on the pipe stem. The orange flame from the candle pulled downward into the tobacco as if alive. Finally he put the candle back down and breathed out a cloud of blue smoke with a sigh.

Calm once more, he continued. "As you know, the risk is something we have to take. I want the full power of Black Numbers, and the only way to awaken them exponentially is to have the Korpor *Ring* him. The possibility that his powers will irrationalize is just a chance we will have to take. The Korpor will not let us down."

Ailinora closed her eyes and seemed to sink into the chair. "We will do what we have to. The Aleph Null is all that matters."

Father Mansico sat up straight, sensing her discomfort. When it came down to it, she was really nothing but a weak woman. But she was useful in her own pathetic way, plus she had talents that he quite enjoyed. He smiled suggestively and said in a low voice, "It is late." He raised an eyebrow at her.

Ailinora grinned and leaned forward. She pushed the manuscript back toward him and stood up, then slowly walked around the table until she stood next to him.

He turned toward her, anticipation making him cough slightly on the smoke as he sucked on his pipe.

Ailinora untied the sash of her robe and let it hang open. Her breasts were partially visible, still quite firm and youthful. Father Mansico let his eyes trail down her stomach and settle on the patch of white hair between her legs.

Father Mansico leaned forward to tap out his pipe against a piece of marble on his desk, then turned back to Ailinora. He slid his hands up her stomach and cupped her breasts underneath the robe. He then pulled her toward him and slid the robe from her shoulders. She stood in front of him, unashamed of her body. He rose from the chair and led her to his large bed.

Ailinora untied his robe and chuckled throatily. "I see the manuscript has inspired you." She cooed as she ran her hands along his hardness, then lifted her head and kissed him softly.

He responded hungrily and pushed her onto the bed. He straddled her and kissed her harder. After a few moments he pulled back and studied her. Her wispy white hair splayed out in all directions and her deeply wrinkled face was intoxicating in its complexity and beauty. Even though she was almost twice his age, he couldn't get enough of her. He leaned back down and kissed her, tenderly this time.

She locked her legs around his waist and soon the bed was moving rhythmically against the stone wall.

The Tulgin stared from under the table, his dark eyes gleaming as he watched the bed. He had a lot to report to his mother. He whined softly as he thought of her blue apron. He missed her so.

Chapter 11

The road ahead of Sid and Crowdal was well-maintained and the sun warmed them as they walked. The trees started to thin out, in fact Sid hadn't seen a Miq tree since they left the place where he had been attacked. Now the woods along the road were filled mostly with thin, black trees that had branches covered with long thorns, each one the length of Sid's fingers. They pointed randomly in every direction, almost daring someone to come close enough so they could prick them. On the tips of each branch, leaves were already in full bloom.

Sid walked over and looked closely at the leaves. They were thin and purple and covered with a soft gray fuzz. He had never seen this type of tree before.

Crowdal nodded toward the tree and said, "They're called Wilden trees." He picked one of the purple leaves carefully from the branch and popped it into his mouth and chewed happily. "Delicious. They're very earthy tasting. If you add a few of these to a stew, it adds a nice, almost nutty flavor. But you have to leave them whole, otherwise they lose their flavor. Mmm... stew." He trailed off, a look of wistfulness on his face.

Even though Sid was only a day or so away from home, he had never seen this type of tree before. It made him realize just how isolated he had been in his little village. He turned away from the tree and kicked a rock as he started down the road again. It skipped, clacking against other rocks until it came to a halt. He glanced behind him and saw Crowdal following, whistling and enjoying himself. Noticing Sid turn and look at him, he waved and smiled, a purely happy expression on his face. Sid turned away and tried to ignore the large man. He heard thunder rumble faintly to the north and looked up. The sky was clear, except for a few clouds. A breeze had picked up and it felt good, drying the sweat that was beading on his forehead. But he was worried. When thunder boomed in a clear blue sky, it usually meant trouble. He had seen enough spring storms to know they could be nasty.

They walked for a few hundred more paces when Sid noticed the birds were no longer singing, in fact he couldn't hear any animal sounds at all, which was very strange. He heard thunder rumble again in the distance, although it sounded a little closer this time.

Sid picked up his pace and was sweating by the time he stopped next to a small river that crossed the road. The river wasn't very wide, maybe thirty paces at the most. A small stone bridge spanned it.

Sid studied the bridge. It was a beautiful piece of construction and solidly built. Five stone overhangs were built out from the bridge, spaced evenly all the way across. Suspended from these overhangs were ropes. Sid leaned sideways and gasped. Bodies swayed from every rope, some recently dead, some rotting and half eaten by birds. With a start, he realized this was a hanging bridge.

Sid shivered. He had heard of them before, but never actually seen one. He walked onto the bridge, stepped out onto one of the overhangs and looked down at the water below the hanging bodies. It was clear and gurgled over multicolored rocks. He could see fish swimming lazily against the current, some of them fairly large. They would have made a nice lunch, if he had his pole, that is.

Sid looked upstream and saw trees growing thickly along the tops of the banks on both sides of the river, but the banks themselves were too steep for anything to grow except scraggily brush. The river curved out of sight only a short ways upstream. Thunder boomed again.

Sid heard Crowdal come up behind him, but ignored him as he stopped beside Sid and looked down at the water. "You know what, I need a bath."

Crowdal walked to the other side of the bridge and dropped his pack on the ground. He took off his clothes and folded them neatly on top of the pack to keep them clean. Sid watched him with his mouth open.

Crowdal walked around the edge of the bridge and slid down the embankment, coming to a stop by the water's edge. He dipped his toe into the water and pulled it quickly out. "That's cold." He then steeled himself and walked into the water until he was in the middle of the river. It barely came up to his waist. He smiled up at Sid on the bridge. "Ah, now that feels nice. A little cold, but refreshing."

Sid saw Crowdal's penis and blushed. It was so large that Sid couldn't take his eyes away from it. It reminded him of a stud horse he saw in town one time. As he stared, he saw it sway back and forth as Crowdal turned and started splashing toward a pool of water upstream where it turned the corner and he blushed, turning his eyes away slightly.

Crowdal yelled back without turning his head. "Are you coming in? It isn't bad really, once you get used to it."

Sid turned his eyes back and saw Crowdal lower himself into the pool, gasping as the water rose to his chest. The large man vigorously scrubbed his arms, legs and chest before dunking his head under the water and scrubbing his hair. He came up spitting water and laughing, looking up at Sid. "This is wonderful. You're missing out, my friend. Come on in."

Sid was still uncomfortable with the large man, but a bath would actually feel good. He slowly stood up and walked to the end of the bridge. But before he could do anything else, he heard a series of loud cracks of thunder, this time so close that the hair on his arms stood up. Then a strange change in air pressure occurred and he looked around, trying to figure out what was happening.

His ears popped and he opened his mouth wide, trying to equalize the pressure in his head.

Then he heard it. A distant rushing sound. Instinctively he turned and looked upstream. The water was jumping as if a person was tapping the bottom of a pan of water. He looked down and saw the water level quickly dropping until only the middle part of the stream still had water. He turned and yelled as loudly as he could. "Crowdal, get out of the water, now!"

Crowdal looked up at him, smiling. Sid waved his arms violently and yelled again. "Get out of the water. Come on."

Crowdal's smile faded, and he looked down to see that the pool of water he had been sitting in was now only half as deep. He stood up, water dripping from his naked body. He looked upstream, realizing he was in trouble. He started to run toward the bridge, but had only taken two strides before a wall of water burst around the corner behind him. Within moments it hit Crowdal in the back, completely swallowing him.

Sid saw Crowdal get hit by the wall of water and disappear. Then he saw arms and legs tumbling in the now mud and debris-filled water, coming fast toward the bridge. He only had a few moments until Crowdal would be to the bridge, so without thinking, he pulled his pack off and pulled out the rope. He quickly tied it to the overhang and then around himself. He looked down and saw that Crowdal was almost directly below him, so he jumped without thinking.

He landed with a splash right on top of Crowdal. He wrapped his arms around his waist and hung on as hard as he could. They floated in the tumbling rush of water for a few moments before the rope yanked tight. Crowdal kept going and Sid's arms slid down his body. He knew he was not going to be able to hold Crowdal against the current for more than a few more moments.

Sid felt his arms sliding over Crowdal's legs when he felt Crowdal grip his own legs tightly. They hung there, pressed against each other gripping one another's legs, suspended from the rope in the rushing current. Water pushed into Sid's nose. He wasn't going to be able to hold his breath for much longer. Something hard hit him in the head, then bounced down his back. It felt like he was being punched over and over. His lungs burned so badly that he started seeing stars against his closed eyelids, and his strength was almost gone. He felt his grip on Crowdal's legs loosen.

Suddenly Sid felt Crowdal underneath him hit the bottom of the stream. In a moment, the water was only hitting Sid's face, and then his chin, and then his head was completely free of water. He took a huge gasp of air, then another and another. The water dropped so quickly that Sid found himself on top of Crowdal, who was lying on the riverbed, the water only knee-deep now.

Sid released Crowdal's legs and tried to roll off of him, but Crowdal was still gripping his own legs. "Crowdal." He coughed out some water and took another gasp of air. "Crowdal, let go."

Crowdal didn't move, and Sid was able to turn his head and look behind him. Crowdal was on his back, and the water was still rushing over his face.

Sid pushed himself up by the arms and kicked his legs as hard as he could until he broke free from Crowdal's grasp. He rolled off of Crowdal into the water and let himself float around until he was next to Crowdal's head. He dug his heels into the rocky river bottom and reached down to pull Crowdal's head from the water, only to find he couldn't lift it from the awkward angle he was in.

Sid pushed himself up and stood on wobbly legs, then quickly bent down and lifted Crowdal's head from the water. His mouth was full of liquid and he wasn't breathing.

Sid strained as hard as he could but couldn't lift Crowdal any further, so he slid behind Crowdal's head and sat down, the water rushing by his waist. But with Crowdal's head in his lap, he was able to keep him above the water level and he didn't have to strain himself lifting.

Sid reached down and opened Crowdal's mouth fully and turned his head to the side. The water drained out, but not all of it. Sid grunted as he tried to turn Crowdal on his side, but he couldn't budge him.

Sid wasn't going to give up, so he took a deep breath and pulled at Crowdal's shoulder as hard as he could. He strained, feeling his muscles trembling with the effort, and with the added buoyancy of the water, he felt the large man's body begin to turn over to his side. Sid immediately started hammering on Crowdal's back as hard as he could. Nothing happened for a few moments, and then Crowdal coughed out a rush of water and breathed in air with a gasp. He rolled back until his head was again resting in Sid's lap.

Sid sighed in relief and put his hands down, leaning back in the water. Crowdal looked up at Sid and smiled faintly. He tried to talk, but couldn't, so he just lay there.

Sid remembered the flash flood and looked upstream in a panic. There could be another one at any moment. They had to get out of the water now. He took his arms from the water and sat up straight. "Crowdal, can you understand me?"

Crowdal nodded.

Sid leaned his head down to Crowdal. "Listen. We have to get out of this water. It could flood again at any time."

Crowdal nodded again weakly and pushed himself into a sitting position. He coughed again and spit out a little more water. "I'm fine now," he gasped. He stood up and swayed slightly.

Sid got to his feet also and tried to untie the rope around his waist. He fumbled with it, but his fingers were so cold, and the rope was so wet and tight, that he couldn't get the knot undone. As he fumbled with it, he felt the air pressure pop again, and the river started to dry up even further. He started to panic and fumbled even harder with the rope. He heard the rush of air and water and looked upstream in a panic.

Crowdal recognized the danger and came out of his daze in a snap. He saw that Sid was still tied to the rope. There was no time to try and untie it so he just picked Sid up and ran with him until they were directly below the bridge where the rope was tied.

Crowdal yelled hoarsely to be heard above the roar of water coming toward them, "Grab the bridge when I throw you. Now!"

Crowdal heaved Sid upward so hard that Sid actually landed on the surface of the bridge. The wind rushed out of his lungs when he hit, but he immediately jumped up and looked over the side. Crowdal was running for the embankment. Sid looked up and saw another wall of water rushing toward them. He screamed at Crowdal to run harder, but there was no way he could be heard above the rushing sound.

Crowdal leapt at the embankment, covering at least three of Sid's strides in one bound. He scrambled up the muddy hill, slipping in the muck as he struggled upward. He was half way up when the wall of water roared by just below him. The mud started to give way at Crowdal's feet, so he scrambled even faster. The wind from the rushing water tugged at his hair and he looked like a wild man, naked and covered in mud, trying to avoid the rushing water just below him.

In a few moments, the water subsided a little and Crowdal collapsed on the muddy hill, his face half buried as he took giant gasps of air. Finally, he pushed himself up on his hands and slowly started to climb the embankment. The slower he moved, the easier it was for him to climb, and soon he pulled himself over the top and collapsed on the dry ground.

When he saw that Crowdal was safe, Sid reached down to take the rope from the outcropping of rock instead of untying it from his waist. Then he realized he had his knife in his sheath and smacked himself in the head for being so stupid and panicking. It almost cost them both their lives. He pulled his knife out and sliced through the rope easily, then put the knife back in the sheath and ran over to Crowdal.

Crowdal opened his eyes and smiled. "So, that was fun."

Sid laughed in relief and sat down by his side. "I wouldn't say that, but I'm glad you enjoyed yourself."

Crowdal sat up, pushing thick mud from his chest and flinging it away. "Now this is disgusting. I hate being dirty." He flicked his hands, trying to get the mud off, and a gooey chuck of it flew onto Sid's cheek.

Sid wiped it away with his wet sleeve. "Thanks Crowdal, I appreciate that."

The sky darkened and both Sid and Crowdal looked up. A green wall cloud was rushing toward them, boiling and roiling as it came. Lightning flashed and was immediately followed by a loud crack of thunder. The hairs on his arms stood up again and he smelled a burning stench.

They quickly got up and gathered their packs. Crowdal scooped up his clothes and stuffed them into his rain-proof pack. He pulled his boots on as they looked around for some kind of shelter. There was nowhere to hide. The wall cloud was almost upon them so they ran down the road, trying to find a place where they could be safe.

Crowdal immediately outdistanced Sid, one of his strides equal to three of his much shorter companion's.

Sid ran as hard as he could behind Crowdal. As he ran, he looked at the big man's back and thought it would be a comical sight if they weren't running for their lives. Crowdal was completely naked, covered in mud, hair sticking out all over the place, wearing only black-heeled boots as he ran down the road holding his pack.

Crowdal swerved to the right and ran into the sparse woods. Sid soon got to the place where Crowdal left the road and turned, running after him through the brush. The woods were a dark green color as the clouds overtook them, casting eerie shadows everywhere. As Sid ran, the wind died down and everything was abruptly quiet. Up ahead, through a green haze, Sid saw Crowdal stop by a small hut. After a few more strides, Sid stopped beside him, hands on his knees gasping for air.

The hut looked like it was almost ready to fall down, but it had a roof on it. Crowdal opened the door and shoved Sid inside. He followed him immediately and shut the door. It was pitch dark inside, but Sid heard Crowdal open his pack and take something out. In a few moments, he struck flint together and started a small fire from some tinder on the floor. Crowdal lightly blew on it, cupping it with his hand. The flame grew and Crowdal added some dry kindling from his pack. Soon, a small fire was burning on the dirt floor of the hut.

In the flickering firelight, Sid looked around. The hut was barely large enough for the two of them and the fire, but it was dry. There was nothing inside, not even a bench to sit on. Outside, the quiet bothered Sid more than anything. They sat quietly, crouching over the fire. As quickly as it had gone quiet outside, the wind picked up again, only this time it blew so hard that the hut started to creak and moan. The flames of the fire danced violently as the wind came through the cracks in the door. Just when Sid thought the wind couldn't blow any harder, he heard a distant roar that grew in volume, coming right toward them.

The roar intensified and the hut shook so loudly that Sid thought it was going to collapse. The fire went out and it was pitch black again inside the hut. They both put their hands over their heads and crouched down as low as they could go. Sid could hear Crowdal screaming, even over the noise of the storm.

The roar was now so loud that Sid jammed his fingers in his ears. He didn't think he could take it anymore. There was a loud wrenching sound and the roof of the hut was ripped off and disappeared into the sky. The walls shook back and forth now that they didn't have the roof for support. Rain and hailstones pelted them. Some of the hailstones were the size of Sid's fist. One hit him in the back of the head and he fell down, then another hit him in the shoulder, then the arm, then another in the head. Sid blacked out.

He awoke to the sound of Crowdal's voice and a hand on his shoulder gently shaking him. Sid opened his eyes. He was lying on the floor of the hut. It was gently raining, but there was no wind. The quiet was almost deafening. Sid sat up, putting one hand on the ground for support and raised his other hand to his head. He felt two large lumps where the hail had hit him. He looked at his fingers but didn't see any blood. He then looked over at Crowdal who was sitting with his hand to his nose, blood running from between his fingers.

He held up a chunk of ice the size of Sid's open hand. "Caught this sucker right on the nose. I've been punched harder than this though," he said with a smile.

Sid stood up and opened the door of the hut. As he did, the hut groaned and all four walls fell outward with a slow-motion crash. Sid turned around and looked at Crowdal with a scowl. Crowdal looked at him seriously and then he erupted in laughter. Sid tried to hold back, but he couldn't help himself. He started laughing with Crowdal, tears coming from their eyes.

Sid gestured at the walls lying on the ground all around them. "They don't build them like that anymore, do they?"

Crowdal laughed harder, standing up at the same time. Their laughter soon lowered to a chuckle and then they were silent. They had just survived two events that should have killed them both. The joy of surviving was replaced by that somber fact.

The temperature had dropped after the storm had passed. The rain was light but very cold. It rinsed the mud off of Crowdal and it ran down his body in black streams. He looked like a crazy man and was so cold he was trembling, so he dug in his pack and put on his clothes. It was difficult putting dry clothes on wet skin, but he soon finished and looked a little warmer, although he still trembled from the cold.

Sid dug in his pack and found his blanket. He handed it to Crowdal, who took it with a nod. The blanket barely covered his shoulders and back and got wet almost immediately, but it was better than nothing. Sid dug in his pack again and dug out his winter coat. He wrapped it around himself.

Soon Crowdal stopped trembling and closed his eyes. He started to snore lightly.

Sid sat with his arms wrapped around his knees. He was wet, but fairly warm inside of his winter coat. The shock of what had just recently happened kept him awake. He closed his eyes and remembered the rush of water, of being unable to breath, and then the roar of the storm, the green light that made the world seem it was about to end. The light rain was soothing and the false dark from the storm gave way to a cold, dim, gray afternoon. Rain dripped through the branches, and birds started singing again. Sid's eyes drooped and his breathing slowed down. It had been a long day and he quickly fell asleep.

* * *

In the near darkness, from behind a tree not far away from the destroyed hut, a pair of dark blue eyes came into view. They were very large. The left eye blinked slowly, followed by the right eye.

Sid moaned in his sleep and twisted his head, his breathing coming in short gasps, but he did not wake up. The eyes watched him for a long time, then disappeared. Sid immediately stopped moaning and his breathing slowed down. Soon he slept peacefully.

Crowdal kept his eyes shut to mere slits and continued to stare at the tree where the blue eyes had peeked around. His head pounded with a headache worse than any he had ever had before. What he had just seen confused him, as he had never encountered a creature like that. And the way the eyes stared at Sid's sleeping form made Crowdal uncomfortable. At one point when the eyes had focused on Crowdal, they had narrowed slightly as if angry, and the pain had increased inside Crowdal's head, but he hadn't looked away.

The rain continued to fall and Crowdal shivered. He was not sure what he had gotten himself mixed up in, but there was something about the boy that made him feel protective. His headache eventually faded completely away and he fell into a deep sleep, more exhausted than he had been in a long time. The last thing he remembered before sleep fully took him was that he thought he smelled freshly baked bread.

Chapter 12

It was late in the evening three days after Sid had left Orm-Mina. A thunderstorm had moved through the previous day, and Mrs. Wessmank hoped that Sid hadn't gotten stuck out in the open during the extreme storm. After the storm had passed, the temperature had dropped and it had continued to rain lightly until this evening when it turned to sleet.

She moved a pot of boiling water to a cooler section of the stove and cocked her head at the creak of the door. A cold breeze and the smell of horse made her nose twitch. She smiled sadly to herself, not surprised that her vision had been correct. And unfortunately, they were right on time.

Smoothing her hands over her blue apron, she turned around. The door was open and just inside the room stood three brown-robed figures. Hoods covered their faces and they waited quietly, patiently, as if they knew she wouldn't present a problem to them.

Mrs. Wessmank smiled kindly and motioned the Haissen further into the room. "Would you like a cup of tea before you take me to Father Mansico?"

One of the Haissen shut the door and they immediately strode forward and sat down at the table where four cups were sitting, each with a perfect portion of Jasmine tea leaves inside a small, round, metal tea strainer.

Mrs. Wessmank picked up the full pot of hot water and filled each cup. Jasmine-scented steam rose up and the three Haissen each bent down to inhale deeply. Mrs. Wessmank put the now empty pot on the stove, adjusting it fondly and letting her hand linger on the handle before she turned and sat down at the table next to the fourth cup. She put her hands on each side to warm them and looked at the Haissen. She could see a hint of their faces inside the hoods. "Please, at this table it is polite to remove your hoods when you have tea."

Each Haissan reached up and pushed its hoods back.

Mrs. Wessmank didn't react in any way, other than to nod to each of them a kind greeting. "Thank you." She raised her tea cup. "To warm nights and easy travel."

The three Haissen nodded back and raised their own cups. One of them spoke in a deep whisper. "Thank you, Elenora."

She wasn't surprised they knew her name. The four of them lightly clinked their cups and sipped the hot tea. They each sat in silence, enjoying the sweet brew until finally the same Haissan who had spoken set his empty cup down. The other two immediately did the same. The lead Haissan whispered to her in its strange voice. "It is time. Gather your things. You will not return."

Mrs. Wessmank stood up and the three Haissen stood with her, showing respect. She bent down and lifted a traveling pack from under the table. "I am ready. Can you carry this for me? I am an old woman."

The lead Haissan took the pack and handed it to one of the others, then put out his arm. Mrs. Wessmank took it and they made their way slowly across the room. By the door she lifted her heavy rainproof leather coat from the hook and put it on. She didn't look back as she stepped outside. She heard one of the Haissan softly close the door to her tobacco store, the shop that she and her husband had built eighty years earlier.

Four gray horses stood quietly in the sleet, heads up and proud, making no sound, with just a puff of air curling out through their nostrils.

The Haissan led her to a beautiful gray stallion with a black spot between his eyes. She reached up and stroked the wet hair between his eyes. "Hello my friend. Will you let me ride you this journey?"

The stallion's large black eyes stared at Mrs. Wessmank, unblinking. Then it lowered its front legs for her until she could easily step into the saddle. She patted his neck affectionately. "Thank you, my friend." The stallion stood back up and waited patiently as the other Haissen swung onto their own bare-backed stallions.

In the light sleet, the four riders trotted down the street and left town on the north road. One shuttered window was open slightly. It quickly shut as the riders went by. Even though the road was muddy, the horses were sure-footed and they made good time.

Mrs. Wessmank knew she would likely die in the next few days. But if she died, she knew she was doing what she had to do. For more than eighty years she had been planning for this time. She and her sister had both been Proofed as young women, but both had failed. Since that time, their paths had split forever. After the Proofing, they had both been visited in the night by an agent of the Oblate.

Her sister had been enthralled with what the agent had to say. The Oblate was going to change the world, rid it of the royal houses, create one government. Mrs. Wessmank, on the other hand, had deep reservations and did not agree with the agent's propaganda.

Ailinora had left that night with the agent and Mrs. Wessmank had not seen her sister since then.

Mrs. Wessmank looked down at her blue apron. She had worn it for more than forty years. It had arrived as an anonymous gift. She studied it that entire first night, meditating over it until she began to sense her sister's presence. It felt cool yet comforting. It was then that she knew it was a spying mechanism. The best she could figure was that her sister had infused it with part of her own self and used it as a link to see and hear what her twin sister was doing at any particular moment. How her sister got such powers, Mrs. Wessmank didn't know.

Mrs. Wessmank had kept it and worn it every single day since. She mended it when she needed to, but never replaced it. She figured it was best to let her sister think she was unaware of the link. An opponent held close was better than an opponent unknown.

The idea of spying made her smile and she thought about her Tulgin. She had found the Tulgin one day a few years earlier while she was picking raspberries. She had heard a soft cry in her mind and had stepped around a raspberry bush to see the small creature whimpering as it lay by its dead mother. Mrs. Wessmank had immediately seen that the mother had been killed violently by something large, probably a bear. How the pup had survived she didn't know, but as she had approached him, the little Tulgin had looked up at her and immediately stopped crying. She had heard a small voice in her head, a voice full of fear and pain whispering one word as a question: "Mother?" Through tears, she had scooped up the baby Tulgin and held him tightly as he snuggled against her neck for warmth. She had whispered back that he was safe now. She had never seen a Tulgin before and from that day forward, they had shared a telepathic bond of mother and son. She had named him Maelon.

Mrs. Wessmank smiled now at the thought of him. They had spoken long into the nights those first three months, his intelligence equal to or exceeding that of humans. When he had learned about the Oblate and Father Mansico, he had insisted that he be sent to the man as a spy.

It had been the most painful thing she had ever done, but she had agreed.

Maelon had traveled to Yisk by himself, even though he was only three months old and still very small. He made sure that Father Mansico had found him, and as they had planned, he was soon the man's pet.

"Yes Mother, he still thinks that. But I am yours and always will be."

The voice was soft in her mind and Mrs. Wessmank caressed Maelon with a gentle thought. *"And I am yours. I will never forgive myself for the beatings you have taken at the hands of that monster."*

The soft voice whispered back. *"I have told you, it was a sacrifice I was and am still willing to make. Father Mansico and your sister are waiting for the Korpor to capture Sidoro. And mother... they have the Black Numbers manuscript."*

"What? Are you sure?"

"Yes mother, I have seen it. Father Mansico is planning to betray the Oblate."

"The Black Numbers manuscript, I can't believe it. Events are moving along quickly now. Gods, I can only pray that Sidoro stays safe. Thankfully I sent him to the Anderom with as much knowledge as I could give him. We must hope that he stays strong and travels quickly. Thank you Maelon, you have done well."

"Mother?"

"Yes?"

"I can't wait to see you."

"And I you, my son."

A tear ran down Mrs. Wessmank's already cold, wet cheek and she wiped it away.

A deep whisper came from the darkness. "Are you feeling chilled?"

Mrs. Wessmank looked over at the Haissan and nodded yes. "I thought this coat would be enough, but I guess I was wrong."

The Haissan angled its horse closer to her, pulled a blanket out of its side pack and spread it over her shoulders.

She patted the creature's hand. "Thank you."

The Haissan angled back away without a word and continued riding as if nothing had happened, completely ignoring the sleet that pelted its face.

'They certainly are a quiet race,' she thought. She held no ill will toward any race. It was individuals whom she held responsible for their own actions. While she didn't know much about the Haissen, not even where they came from, she knew these three were merely doing their job. Why the Haissen did the bidding of the Oblate, she didn't know, but she could not sense any evil within them. She pulled the blanket tighter around her shoulders and let the stallion lead the way unguided.

The night became darker as thicker clouds moved in. A cold wind rustled the grass around her, the sound comforting, although she knew even colder weather was coming in the morning.

Her horse jerked to a sudden stop and she quickly came out of her thoughts as a group of figures melted out of the sleet-filled shadows and blocked the road in front of them. The Haissen sat perfectly still on their horses.

One of the shadows loped forward on all fours. Mrs. Wessmank gasped softly when she realized it was an Omthagrod. She never knew they were in the woods so close to Orm-Mina. If she had known, she would have put steel shutters on her doors and windows. They were a violent and wild race of creatures, vicious and cunning, and greatly feared throughout the land. But sightings were so rare that they were more legend than anything.

Mrs. Wessmank leaned forward to get a closer look as the lead Omthagrod stopped a few paces in front of the horses. Huge muscles worked beneath its fur and a rank smell assaulted her nose.

It leaned forward and then pushed itself upright and stood unsteadily on two legs in front of them. It wore no clothes and was covered in thick red and black fur that shed the sleet pellets easily. Its face as it looked at the four of them on the horses, was almost human, at least it might have been human in the distant past. Covered in thick hair, it had human eyes and a snout similar to a wolf although shorter and not as angular, and a mouth filled with long sharp teeth. It had a large, black nose that constantly sniffed the air, the sound deep and wet. It was large, rising up to the shoulder of the Haissan in the lead, even though the Haissan was sitting on a large stallion.

Mrs. Wessmank estimated the Omthagrod weighed almost as much as the horse. She sat up straight in her saddle. She had not seen this particular event through any vision and felt a thrill at the unknown. If the creatures attacked, she would likely be killed. She didn't think even the mysterious Haissen had a chance against a pack of Omthagrod. It was too bad. She would have liked to have seen her Tulgin again, as well as her sister. But what would be would be.

The Omthagrod sniffed toward the lead Haissan. It twitched its head slightly left, then right. The Haissen neither moved, nor spoke, merely sitting calmly on their horses as if they were waiting for nothing more than a squirrel to get out of their way.

Mrs. Wessmank heard soft footfalls, and she looked around. The remaining Omthagrod had circled them, all six of the massive creatures flanking her left and right. Being so close to them, she could tell that the source of the rank smell was a mixture of old feces, urine, and wet fur.

The lead Omthagrod sat on its haunches and cocked its head slightly, seemingly confused, as if it had never run across a meal that didn't show fear. Mrs. Wessmank suspected that the only reason they hadn't been attacked yet is that they hadn't run away in a panic.

The lead Omthagrod growled deeply and its six packmates moved in closer. The Omthagrod surprised her when it leaned forward and spoke in a thick voice, more guttural than speech. "Why do you not run from us?"

The Haissan in the front merely looked down at the Omthagrod out of curiosity. It then slid off of its horse, took one step forward, and answered, "We run from nothing."

The hackles rose on the lead Omthagrod and saliva dripped from its teeth as its eyes widened, as if in shock at being challenged. His packmates sensed his outrage and started to growl and move closer.

The remaining two Haissen slid off of their horses, one to each side, and stood calmly facing three Omthagrod each.

The lead Omthagrod's pupils dilated and long claws slid out of its paws, each wickedly hooked and glinting sharply in the moonlight. With a deep roar, it leapt at the lead Haissan, its arms spread wide, and viciously slashed with its claws in fury, a strike that no man could have survived.

But it didn't face a man. It faced a Haissan.

The Omthagrod's claws swished through empty air and it landed off balance. It tried to spin around to strike again, but couldn't move its legs. Confused, the Omthagrod turned its large head and looked at its legs dangling from a few bloody strands of tissue, not comprehending what was wrong. It heard the soft footsteps of the Haissan and immediately turned its head forward, growling, saliva dripping from its long teeth.

The Haissan calmly walked up to the creature, even as the Omthagrod bared its teeth and snapped at it. Without hesitating and without anger, the Haissan decapitated the Omthagrod with a single blow, its sword cutting through the thick bone and muscle so precisely that the head stayed on the neck for a few moments before sliding to the ground. Blood spurted high into the air and the Haissan casually stepped back to avoid it. The Omthagrod's body tipped to the side and twitched for a few moments before lying still in the mud. The whole event had only lasted a few moments and Mrs. Wessmank could only stare, her mouth open in horror and wonder.

The other six Omthagrod stood in silence, as if not comprehending what had just happened. The other two Haissen leapt forward and in a blur, two of the creatures were decapitated as cleanly as the first Omthagrod had been, blood spurting in hot steaming geysers into the cold air.

The four remaining Omthagrod jumped backward and circled around, swinging their heads back and forth as if unsure whether to attack or run away, a decision they had probably never had to make before. The two Haissen joined their leader and the three of them calmly faced the giant creatures, not seeming to care if the Omthagrod attacked or ran away. Such lack of fear from the Haissen seemed to be enough to make the remaining Omthagrod turn and lope into the woods.

The three Haissen smoothly flicked their swords into their sheaths and mounted their horses as if nothing had happened. The leader immediately started them forward.

Mrs. Wessmank had watched the entire event unfold and was unable to believe that she was still alive. What had just happened was impossible for her to comprehend. The three Haissen had just killed three Omthagrod as easily as men slaughtered pigs. No one for as long as she could remember, which was more than 100 years, had ever killed an Omthagrod. Yet these Haissen had calmly cut them down and remounted their horses like nothing had happened. She turned in her saddle and looked back at the three dead creatures lying on the road, almost invisible in the darkness as they rode away. She knew that some farmer or traveler would come across the bodies in the morning covered with bloody sleet and a new legend would be born of the men who had killed three Omthagrod.

With shaking hands, she chuckled softly to herself, for they would be very wrong. The Haissen were not even remotely human.

The four of them traveled the dark muddy road. The sleet never let up as they passed through Oiro in the middle of the night, and continued on. They crossed a bridge and even in the dark they could see that a Niyrreeben had just recently passed through. Trees were blown down like kindling along a path that stretched away into darkness. They had to pick their way around fallen trees and branches for a brief distance until they could continue on more easily.

By the time daylight came, they were amid farm fields for as far as she could see. It was a dim gray morning. The sleet was turning to snow as they stopped by a small stand of trees and the lead Haissan helped her down from her horse. She was so stiff she could barely stand, so the Haissan gently led her to the tree and helped her to sit down.

"Thank you, you are kind to an old woman." She stretched out her legs and winced at the pain in her joints. She stretched her back and then her neck. She didn't know if she would be able to stand up again later on. But at this moment she didn't care.

One of the other Haissen walked over and handed her a chunk of hard black bread, along with a hunk of white cheese. She took it gratefully and started to eat. The food was delicious, even if it was simple.

Soon it was time to mount up again and Mrs. Wessmank reluctantly stood up, grimacing at the pain that flared through her back. The Haissen stood by their stallions in the gray, snowy morning, waiting patiently for her. The lead Haissan brushed the slushy snow from her saddle and then helped her up onto the horse. They were soon on their way.

The ride was peaceful in the snowy morning, but the temperature kept dropping and Mrs. Wessmank's breath puffed white with every exhale. On the horse, covered with a blanket, she actually enjoyed watching the passing countryside. Despite the snow, it was a beautiful time of year, where the leaves turned green and the fields were being prepared for planting. She was able to rest and prepare herself for Yisk, letting the horse do all of the work. She needed to have her wits about her when they arrived.

Mrs. Wessmank hadn't seen another person on the road all the previous night, or this morning until, through the snow, she saw a wagon being pulled by a horse with a man walking beside it. As they came up to the wagon, she looked down and saw with surprise that the man walking beside the wagon was a Trith! She hadn't seen a Trith in decades and instantly became a little nervous.

But the Trith merely looked up at the group as they passed. He was handsome and young, but looked close to exhaustion. The Trith smiled slightly to her as their eyes met and she smiled back.

Then she was past the wagon.

She pulled her coat and blanket tighter around her shoulders and hid her hands inside of her sleeves to try and keep them warm. She looked to her right and saw that the Haissen rode wearing just their robes, completely disregarding the snow.

Mrs. Wessmank wrapped the blanket around her head, leaving only a small opening for her eyes as she put her head down and just concentrated on staying warm. Her bones ached so badly that she started to wonder if she would be able to stand again. After a while, she looked up through the small opening in the blanket and was surprised to see people on the road, most of them slogging through the wet snow. She saw oxen and donkeys struggling to pull wagons through the almost frozen mud, their drivers whipping them constantly to keep them moving. The wagons were filled with hay, textiles, food goods and clothing, everything that a large city like Yisk needed.

She saw a group of families traveling together. The children ran and played in the snow while the elders plodded tiredly along.

Then she heard a tinkling sound carry through the snowy wind and her blood ran cold. She looked ahead and saw a colorfully-dressed wizard barely visible through the snow, walking toward Yisk. She watched the wizard carefully as she came up behind the figure.

"Fahrin Druin." she hissed inside of her blanket. She had protected Sid from their visits over the years, making sure they never saw him. She knew their order and she despised them. As she passed the Fahrin Druin, Mrs. Wessmank was surprised to see that it was a woman. The Fahrin Druin looked up and smiled brilliantly, snow sticking to her eyebrows and face. She was young and beautiful, and combined with the mystique of the traveling wizard persona, she probably had village men in her bed every night. Mrs. Wessmank heard the tinkling very clearly now, coming from somewhere within the Fahrin Druin's clothing. Some day she would like to find out the secret behind that sound.

Mrs. Wessmank turned in her saddle and saw that the wizard had stopped to watch them pass. Most people moved quickly out of their way, but the woman had a calculating smirk on her face and even gave a happy wave to the last Haissan that passed her. The Haissan never acknowledged the wizard and the tinkling sound faded to silence as their horses carried them down the middle of the road.

Soon they crested a hill and she saw the city of Yisk spread out below her, the buildings covered in snow. Her breath quickened. It was the end of her life-long journey. She gazed across the snow-covered, red clay roofs of homes, businesses and even the castle on the far hill. She picked out the large domed roof of the house of healing far in the distance. Smoke rose lazily into the cold sky from chimneys. It was so beautiful she couldn't stop staring. It had been too long since she had been here.

They descended the long hill and entered the city without slowing down for the large groups of people on the street. Everyone managed to get out of the way until they came to the first cross street, when two young boys who were chasing each other ran in front of them on the slippery street. One boy was able to stop just shy of them, but the other slid off balance underneath the lead Haissan's horse.

The Haissen didn't attempt to stop or turn out of the way. As the boy fell, Mrs. Wessmank saw the whites of his eyes as he disappeared from view. The lead horse walked over him, killing the boy instantly as its back hooves crushed his head. The other little boy stood in the mud and stared at his dead friend with an ashen face.

No one said anything, but as they rode away, Mrs. Wessmank heard a woman wail for her dead son, the anguish in her voice making bumps rise on Mrs. Wessmank's arms.

She yelled to the lead Haissan. "Stop right now! We have to help that little boy!" But the lead Haissan didn't acknowledge her. The group just kept moving forward. She attempted to pull her stallion to a stop, but it would not obey her. In fury, she turned to look at the group of people who surrounded the crushed little boy, but their rage-filled faces caused her to turn away and hunch down in her saddle.

They continued on for a short while longer. Even on this cold spring day, the streets were filled with stalls selling every kind of item, from food to clothing to weapons. People filled the street. Most were regular people, but she saw a few rich ladies on Kritle, a covered chair sitting on two long poles, being carried by four large men. But even they moved out of the way immediately. Soon the street became wider and to the right it opened up to a courtyard filled with trees and bushes. Toward the back of the courtyard, Mrs. Wessmank saw a tall building, at least four stories tall with a round roof. Two huge doors marked the entrance, which was guarded by two more Haissen. The House of Healing.

They came to a stop and the Haissen immediately slid off of their mounts, landing lightly on the snow-covered ground. The lead Haissan walked over and helped her down.

Her joints ached and her legs felt like frozen logs. As her feet touched the ground, she started to collapse, but the Haissan held her and whistled loudly.

The two doors of the building immediately opened and another Haissan came quickly out carrying a chair and set it down by them. The Haissan gently lowered her to the chair. She was grateful, but after the incident in the street, she couldn't thank the Haissan. The two other Haissen from their group picked up the chair and they entered the building. The two huge doors shut quietly behind her, the sound dully echoing through the large room.

Chapter 13

Crowdal opened his eyes to a cold and drizzly gray morning. He looked over and saw Sid sleeping on his side next to him. He scanned his surroundings and saw the four walls lying on the ground where they had fallen after the storm. Beyond where the hut had stood, a path of fallen trees ran into the distance, looking like a child had wandered through a wheat field leaving a trail of broken stalks. There must have been a Niyrreeben. They were rare, but when they did strike, the power of the twisting wind destroyed everything in its path. 'They had been very lucky,' he thought.

Crowdal then remembered the creature with the huge blue eyes that had watched them throughout the night and he swung his head around to where he last remembered seeing it. He immediately saw the tree from which the creature had watched them. He didn't know what kind of creature it was, but he knew it wasn't human and he knew it wasn't there for him. It had wanted Sid. He didn't know how he knew that, but he was sure of it. He got slowly to his feet, his knees creaking. The drizzle had not let up and he was cold and wet, but he wanted to have a look around that tree.

Crowdal bent down and examined the tree. At first he didn't find anything, but as he stood up he saw something out of the corner of his eye. He bent back down and ran his fingers along the bark around the tree. There it was. With huge fingers he pulled out a small tuft of white fur. He lifted it to his nose and sniffed. He grunted in surprise. It smelled like freshly baked bread. But there was something else, too. He took another sniff. He could smell something faint. He inhaled deeply and then recognized the smell. It was blood. Very faint, but it was there.

Crowdal put the patch of fur into his pocket as he made his way around the perimeter of the hut. He found another patch of white fur half-buried in the mud, even closer to where they had slept. The creature had circled around them during the night and Crowdal hadn't heard it. He shook his head in disgust at himself.

After making a full circle of the hut, Crowdal was satisfied and returned to where Sid was sleeping. He wasn't going to get a fire going today, so he bent down and nudged Sid awake. "Sid, it's time to get up."

Sid opened his eyes and sat up swinging his fists in anger.

Crowdal caught Sid's arm as it flew out at him. "No need to do that, my friend."

Sid's eyes focused on Crowdal and he smiled weakly. "Sorry about that. I thought you were my father."

Crowdal raised his eyebrow. "I take it you don't like your father, then."

Sid sat up and rubbed his eyes to get the sleep out of them. "I just don't think about him much, is all." He ran his hands through his hair and yelped, then gingerly probed his scalp.

Crowdal nodded. "You took a couple of good hits during that hail storm."

Sid looked at his fingers for blood and when he didn't see any, he put his fingers back to his head and winced as he probed. "I've never seen hail that large before." He looked around and his eyes widened when he saw the destruction all about him.

Crowdal nodded as he also took another look about the woods. Looking at the path of destruction, Crowdal knew that it had narrowly missed them. He saw that Sid had come to the same conclusion because the boy started to shake, realizing just how close they had come to dying in that storm.

Crowdal put his hand on Sid's shoulder and squeezed lightly. They sat like this for a few moments in silence, each absorbed in their own thoughts about the storm.

* * *

Death didn't frighten Sid. But he was frightened by the idea that there was nothing he could have done to stay safe from the storm, much like what happened to him at the hut when he was eight. Sid thought back, remembering how the first few months after that day in Rugger's hut he had had the same dream every night: of blinding pain, crushing fear, of stabbing a bloody knife over and over and over, blood flying everywhere. He would wake up gasping for air, sweating, most times looking down at himself to see if he were covered in blood.

After a few months, he started seeking out the dream when he closed his eyes at night, but he changed it, becoming the hunter, stealthily making his way into the hut, seeing Rugger turn to him, baring his teeth, his huge black eyes dancing angrily. The man would charge and Sid would slide between his legs and stab him viciously in the groin as he went past. The man would fall to his knees and Sid would walk calmly up behind him, tilt his head back and slowly slide the knife across his neck, feeling the hot blood run across his hand. Sometimes he altered the dream, coming up with new ways to kill Rugger and bring him as much pain as possible. He always killed the man and he had come to enjoy it. The idea of death became comforting to him, saving him from going over the edge of insanity.

So now, sitting in the destroyed hut with Crowdal, Sid thought of those memories and drew strength from them. He had survived death three times now and come out alive.

He realized that he felt starved, so he undid the flap of his pack and felt around inside. Thankfully, it had stayed dry. He pulled out a chunk of dried meat and bread and broke them into two pieces, handing one each to Crowdal.

Crowdal put up his hand to the meat but took the bread. "Sorry, I don't eat meat. I'll have the bread, though." He took a large bite of bread and smiled at Sid, showing teeth with bread stuck to them.

He apparently liked to do that, Sid thought. Sid lifted the piece of dried meat to Crowdal. "You don't eat meat? I've never heard of such a thing. What do you eat then?"

Crowdal lifted the piece of bread. "Oh, bread is one of my favorites," he said. "Fruit, when it is in season. Lots of vegetables. Carrots and rutabagas are excellent. Beans are one of my staples. They can be carried dry and when cooked, they take care of my rather large appetite quite well, although I tend to pass a lot of gas which is annoying even to me."

Sid chuckled, then shook his head as he took a bite of the dried meat. Not eating meat was one of the strangest things he had ever heard. Who wouldn't want to eat meat? He swallowed and took a drink from his flask of water, swishing his mouth before speaking. "Did you ever eat meat?"

Crowdal nodded as he chewed a mouthful of bread. He was silent for a long time and Sid didn't think he was going to answer. But eventually he swallowed and spoke in a quiet voice, "Until a few years ago, I did. But on my fight day, the day I became a man in my circle, I killed my opponent, a good friend of mine."

He saw Sid's confused look. "In my circle, or village as you think of them, a boy becomes a man only by fighting a fellow boy. I had the bad luck of having to fight one of the only boys I got along with. During the fight, I got caught up in the battle lust and lost control of myself for a brief moment." He was quiet, his eyes looking far into distance. "But that one moment was all it had taken and I stabbed my friend through the neck." His voice cracked slightly. "I watched him die, his blood hot as it spurted into my face. I cried as I held his head in my lap and listened to the jeers of my circlemates. While deaths didn't happen often during fight day, there had been precedence. You see, it was the fact that I cried that was considered shameful. Consequently, I was considered weak and un-Trith-like by the Circle Lead and sent away. They didn't tell me where to go. I was just to travel. In reality, I suspect I am not wanted back home."

Crowdal paused for a few moments, his brow crinkled as if he were deeply in thought, then he continued, "On the road, I had a lot of time to think and realized that I no longer had to follow my circle laws, I could do whatever I wanted for the first time in my life. It was a revelation and a relief of proportions I can't describe. One day while hunting for breakfast, I caught a rabbit in a trap. As I removed its foot from the rope and held it up, I stared into its large, black eyes. It hung there, twisting slightly, but didn't kick or fight me. It just looked at me as it chewed a mouthful of clover. I put it gently down and it hopped a short ways away, then started eating more clover like nothing had happened. It wasn't scared of me in the slightest. I realized that I couldn't kill it."

Crowdal looked at the expression of disbelief on Sid's face as if not expecting Sid to understand. He sighed. "So that's that. I can see you think I am a bit strange."

Sid had looked into Crowdal's eyes as he told the story. He had heard the compassion and pain in Crowdal's voice and knew he was sincere. Sid didn't understand what a circle was or why two boys would be made to fight. It added to the mystery that was Crowdal, a mystery that made Sid want to find out even more about his new travel companion. But looking at the large man and at the pain on his face, he didn't want to ask him anything more personal. It wasn't his place because he didn't know him well enough yet.

As far as not eating meat, Sid could understand Crowdal's reasoning, even if it sounded a bit flawed. Killing someone was one thing, but killing animals was no big deal. They were food, plain and simple. But he supposed a person had a right to eat what they wanted. Crowdal sure didn't look like he was wasting away from hunger. "Don't you miss it, though? I know I could never give up meat."

Crowdal laughed. "No, I don't miss eating meat. In fact, I feel healthier and stronger than I ever have before."

Sid snorted. "Sounds to me like you miss it."

Crowdal finished off the piece of bread and rooted around in his pack, finally bringing out a strange-looking item. Sid looked at it questioningly. It looked like a pile of manure. Crowdal broke off a large piece and put it in his mouth. He chewed with satisfaction, smiling when he saw Sid's expression.

The right side of Sid's lip rose in disgust. "What is that?"

"It's Liret. Want some?" He broke off a piece and handed it to Sid.

Sid brought it to his nose, sniffed and was surprised it didn't smell bad. He took a small nibble from the corner and immediately made a face as he swallowed it. It tasted like green grass and lemons. "That's disgusting."

Crowdal chuckled. "Oh come on. It's good for you."

Sid handed back the Liret and brushed his hands on his trousers as if they were dirty. Crowdal was a strange man. But Sid also realized he liked him. After what they had gone through yesterday, Sid knew he could now trust Crowdal with his life. He looked at the large man's face, studying it. He was a good-looking man and even though he laughed a lot, he had a seriousness just under the surface.

Crowdal reclined on his back, one hand behind his head as he slowly chewed the last of his Liret, his eyes closed. Even after everything that happened to them, Crowdal seemed calm. Aside from the dried blood in his nose and the light rain beading on his face, he looked like he had just spent the day lying in the sun, not fighting for his life... twice. Sid didn't know how he remained so unaffected. He seemed to treat life like a game.

Crowdal swallowed the last of his Liret and sighed. He lay there for a few moments, enjoying the light rain hitting his face, then opened his eyes and stared at the gray sky, a peaceful look on his face. Finally he shifted his gaze to Sid and saw him staring. "Can I help you?"

Sid shrugged. "No, sorry. I was just... I wanted to thank you."

"For what?"

Sid shrugged. "For fighting off those men. For trusting me in the water. For saving my life."

Crowdal looked at Sid, suddenly very serious. For once he didn't have a joke or flippant comment. "You're welcome. I owe you, too, for risking your life to save me in the flood. That was amazing. You're an interesting fellow. You know, when I first saw you on the road, when you passed by me, I thought you were too young to be travelling alone."

Sid was about to speak but Crowdal held up his hand. "Please, let me finish. I have since seen your courage. Not many people would have jumped into a raging river to try and save someone whom they had just met. But you did Sid. So thank you from the bottom of my heart. You are a man worth knowing." He bowed his head to Sid briefly.

Sid turned away. He didn't like compliments. They always sounded fake. But Crowdal seemed sincere, which made him feel uncomfortable. "Well, we should get going. It's not doing us any good just sitting here in the rain."

He stood up and put his pack on his back, looking around at the destruction, at the hut's walls lying on the ground. The rain was turning to a thick mist, which was actually colder. He tightened his coat around himself and stamped his feet in the soft wet ground.

Crowdal stood up and handed the blanket to Sid. Since the blanket was soaking wet, Sid tied it around his shoulders like a cape. It wasn't going to do any good to put it in his pack.

Crowdal put his own pack on his back and looked at Sid. "Well, let's hope we can find a warm dry place to sleep tonight. I'm tired of the rain already."

Sid nodded and walked past Crowdal as he spoke. "We will find something. I'm sure of it. But we won't if we stand around here all day talking like old ladies."

Crowdal laughed, but it sounded subdued in the thick, misty rain.

They made their way back to the road and started east again. Branches and small trees covered the road, and they had to pick their way carefully through the debris as they went. It was slow going at first, but they found that the damage grew less severe the further they got from the destroyed hut and soon there was no indication that a storm had even passed. The misty rain continued and they made their way in silence, their boots sloshing in the mud.

By midday, the mist had given way to cold rain and the wind picked up from the north. They put their heads down against the driving rain as they walked. The mud had grown thick and soupy, making walking treacherous. They were tired and hungry, but neither one of them felt like stopping to eat.

As the afternoon wore on, the temperature continued to fall, making their breath plume out in white puffs. Their wet clothing caused them to shiver as they walked.

Sid stared miserably down at his feet as he pulled each foot out of the mud, over and over. His teeth chattered and his fingers were numb. He squinted up against the rain at Crowdal walking beside him. He was just a shadow in the dim gray light. He had his hood over his head, so the water ran down his shoulders. Sid couldn't see his face but he assumed Crowdal was feeling just as miserable.

For the entire day they had not come across a small village or even a farmhouse in which to get out of the soggy weather. They did not talk much. They just kept their heads down.

By the time the light started to fade from the sky, Sid was barely able to put one foot after the other.

Crowdal still looked strong as he walked, as if he was not affected by the bad weather and the effort he was expending.

Sid wanted nothing more than to stop for the night, but as it became fully dark, they still had not come across any sign of civilization and the rain started to change over to sleet. They could hear it hitting the ground with a constant hiss. There was nothing for them to do but keep slogging along the muddy road, each lost in his own thoughts.

Chapter 14

The Korpor stopped and knelt in the mud alongside the small footprint. The viscous ground had been filling in the footprints all day, but now that the rain had turned to sleet and the day had given in to full night, it was cold enough that the imprints didn't disappear as quickly.

The Korpor slowly ran a sharp claw around the edges of the small boot mark. It lifted the claw and sniffed with its flat gill-like nose. Even though the boot mark was partially frozen in mud, the scent intoxicated the Korpor. It had been tracking the boy since he had left his home, staying just out of sight and enjoying the hunt. It was in no hurry. It could have the boy at any time.

The Korpor flexed its leg muscles and stood back up, its white fur gleaming in the falling sleet. It sniffed the air. The boy was not far away. The road was bathed in a luminescent blue light as the Korpor scanned it with its large dark blue eyes. It turned and ran silently through the grass along the road and into the treeline where it turned and ran on all fours through the trees, parallel to the road. The Korpor breathed easily as it ran, never tiring. Then its ears twitched toward the road as it picked up the sound of footsteps. The humans were so noisy that it didn't have to even concentrate to know exactly where they were now.

The Korpor angled back toward the road until it was at the very edge of the treeline. It peered around a tree and watched two figures, one very tall and one much smaller, move slowly past. A purple glow from their presence lagged behind them a short ways. The Korpor narrowed its eyes and focused on the smaller figure. It could hear the boy's heart beat, slow and deep. The boy was almost asleep on his feet. The Korpor smiled and a vibration started deep inside its chest, and a deep warmth flushed through its body.

It couldn't wait any longer to take the boy.

It moved from tree to tree carefully as it paced the two walking figures. As the Korpor crept along, it glanced at the taller figure and frowned. The tall one could be a problem.

The Korpor thought back to the previous night, of how the tall one had known that the Korpor was watching them from the darkness of the trees. The man had not moved and had also never stopped staring in the Korpor's direction. Few creatures made the Korpor uneasy, but this tall man did. The pain that the Korpor was able to inflict with its eyes should have made anyone fall to the ground unconscious, but this tall one had just stared at it. He was formidable.

The Korpor stepped around a raccoon without the small animal detecting its presence until the animal caught an unnatural movement of air and a strange smell. The raccoon looked around but didn't see anything, so it continued digging into a tree trunk to get at the insects living inside.

The Korpor got ahead of the two figures on the road and hunkered down behind a large Wilden tree to think. It didn't want to deal with the large man if it didn't have to. But it also couldn't wait to take the boy. It raised a paw and scratched behind its shoulder with a long claw, sighing in pleasure as it watched the road.

The Korpor's sharp teeth gleamed in the darkness. It would take advantage of the boy's exhaustion and lure it into the woods. If it was lucky, the large man wouldn't even know the boy was gone for a short while, after which it would be too late.

The Korpor cast out its thoughts to the boy. It projected calmness, a sense of tranquility. As the boy trudged past, the Korpor whispered the boy's name. It saw the boy look toward the trees, but knew the boy couldn't see anything through the sleet. The Korpor smiled and paced the boy, moving from tree to tree.

After a short while, the Korpor reached into the boy's mind and softly whispered his name again, projecting safety and warmth at the same time. It saw the boy falter, so the Korpor continued whispering his name, beckoning him to come into the trees. The boy slowed down, falling behind the tall man. The Korpor stepped out from the treeline and called urgently to the boy. The boy stopped and turned toward him fully.

The Korpor called again.

Chapter 15

As Sid pushed himself on, he heard his name whispered. He looked toward the treeline but didn't see anything but trees highlighted against blackness. He walked on.

A few moments later he heard his name again, only this time he realized it was directly in his mind. He felt very sleepy, barely able to keep his eyes open. The voice continued to whisper his name. He didn't feel cold anymore and fell further behind Crowdal.

Then, from the darkness to his right, he heard his name called more urgently. He sluggishly lifted his head and looked into the treeline and saw a white shadow standing next to a tree not far away. He heard his name again, whispering softly to him. He felt sleepier. He couldn't go on, so he turned and staggered into the woods. It would be warm in there, and dry. The sleet and snow continued to batter his face, but he no longer felt it.

Sid entered the darkness of the trees. He was so warm now. A promise of release waited for him in the shadows. A soft white light glowed behind the trees just in front of him. He felt like he was floating above the ground. A part of him resisted, pulled back from the edge he was about to plunge over, knowing he was in trouble. But then he heard his name called again, so sweet and soft, like he dreamed his mother's voice would be.

He let go.

He moved through the treeline and the world changed. The trees disappeared. He was blind. Panicked, he tried shutting his eyes, but he couldn't tell if he had. Darkness. Pure darkness all around him. He felt himself floating up. His stomach felt queasy. Then he saw a pinpoint of light appear. It looked like it was far away, but it calmed him. He wasn't alone.

The light slowly grew, expanding. His eyes hurt but he couldn't shut them. It continued to grow until he realized the darkness had receded and through falling snow he saw himself lying in a circle of light in a clearing in the woods. He was far above his body, looking down. He looked to his left and saw tree branches. Above him he saw snow falling straight down, mesmerizing him. Dizzy, he looked back down to the ground. His body was still lying there and his eyes were closed.

Sid heard his name again in a whisper so soft he had to strain to hear it. He looked around but didn't see anyone.

He heard it again, this time much closer. He floated above his own body, but he was aware. He didn't know what was happening, but he didn't doubt it was real.

The voice came again and Sid realized that it wasn't a human voice. It was raspy and deep, almost like it wasn't speech at all, but rather sounds that only resembled speech by accident. From the trees he saw a brighter glow moving toward the clearing, lighting up the trees in the immediate vicinity as it moved toward him. Light filled the clearing as the glow reached the edge of the trees. Sid couldn't see what caused the glow.

Then it moved toward Sid's body and he realized it was the Korpor. He stared, fascinated. He tried to move, but he was floating and could do nothing. He could only watch as the Korpor stopped beside his body.

Sid could see the pure white body and the long claws on the ends of its paws. It looked exactly like he remembered from his bedroom window. The Korpor looked down at his body, then slowly up directly at him. The huge blue eyes stared right at him.

The Korpor smiled. Where before Sid thought it was the mouth of a beautiful woman, now it was hideous, especially all of the blood around its mouth. They stared at each other for a long time. Then the Korpor slowly blinked its left eye, followed by its right eye. It turned its head back down to Sid's body, then knelt down and touched Sid's face with a paw, the long claws caressing his eyes, then his cheek and mouth.

The Korpor slid its claws down Sid's chest and continued moving. It unfastened Sid's trousers, pulling them down around his ankles. Sid saw that his penis was soft, but the Korpor touched it lightly with two claws, slowly sliding them up and down, and Sid watched, horrified, as his penis grew hard. He felt nothing as he floated above, but he remembered that night when the Korpor had kissed him, how sexually excited he had been, the pure pleasure that had coursed through his body. He felt disgusted and wanted to shut his eyes. But he couldn't do anything but watch.

The Korpor bent further down and ran a long, black tongue along the length of Sid's penis, and Sid watched as his body arched its back. The Korpor then looked up at Sid and smiled grotesquely. Sid felt blinding pain in his head and he screamed. He saw his body below open its mouth and scream in response.

The Korpor looked back down and grabbed Sid's penis in one massive paw, then extended a single, sharp claw of its other paw to slice lightly around the base. Sid saw blood well up as the claw cut into the skin. He couldn't move or do anything to stop this creature from mutilating him.

The Korpor then slowly slid the skin from his penis. Sid saw blood well up as the Korpor held the sheath of skin up to him. He screamed and his body below screamed in response.

The Korpor smiled, then ran its paw up and down Sid's skinned penis, spreading the blood all over.

It straddled Sid's body and slowly lowered itself until it was sitting fully on him. Then it started moving up and down. Sid realized in horror that the Korpor must be female. Blood ran freely down his thighs as the Korpor moved back and forth, faster and faster, until Sid's body started arching and convulsing. The Korpor instantly stopped and just sat on him. Sid's body twitched a few times and eventually stopped moving. When it was still, the Korpor lifted itself from him. It looked at his bloody member, then bent down and licked it. When it was done, it slid the sheath of skin back over the bloody penis. Then, to Sid's horror, it bent down and took the whole thing in its mouth. When it lifted its head, Sid saw his penis was whole again and there was a clean circular scar at the base. It looked completely healed.

The Korpor looked up at Sid again and in a throaty whisper spoke in his head, "*You are Ringed now. You are mine.*"

Pain flared through Sid, worse than any pain he had ever felt before. He screamed for what felt like days, unable to move, to get away from the agony that ripped through him, begging the Korpor to end it, to let him breath again. Then, suddenly, the pain left him completely.

Sid looked down in confusion and saw Crowdal calmly walking toward the Korpor, his long sword in his hand. He wanted to yell at Crowdal to get away, but he couldn't do anything. He watched the Korpor turn toward Crowdal, who immediately fell to his knees screaming, his sword falling to the ground.

Sid cried out in frustration and fear.

The Korpor advanced on Crowdal and Sid wanted to turn away, to not see his friend die. But as the Korpor swung its deadly claws at Crowdal's face, his friend miraculously rolled out of the way just in time.

The Korpor howled in rage and ran at him. Crowdal picked up his sword as he rolled and came to his feet facing away from the Korpor. Sid knew there wasn't going to be time for Crowdal to spin around and stab with the sword but he watched in amazement as Crowdal kicked out backward with a long powerful leg, connecting with the Korpor directly in its chest. The Korpor flew back and slammed into a tree, sliding down to the ground unconscious. Sid wanted to cheer, but he couldn't. He saw Crowdal put his sword away and pick up Sid's body, throw him over his shoulder, and run into the woods.

Sid felt himself being pulled along toward where Crowdal ran into the woods. He wanted to yell with joy. But then he saw the Korpor look up at him and leer while leaning against the tree. Sid's forward motion jerked to a stop and he started to move back toward the Korpor.

It felt like he was being pulled in two directions at once.

Pain coursed through him, yet he also felt an incredible sexual pleasure infuse him. The pain grew as Crowdal moved further away, and the sexual pleasure grew as the Korpor stood up. Pleasure and agony filled him. He hovered, not moving in either direction.

Looking down into the Korpor's huge blue eyes, Sid felt warmth building up in his groin area, even though he didn't have a body. He wanted nothing more than to stay here in the clearing with the Korpor. Then pain flared up again and Sid looked over to where Crowdal had run.

Sid didn't know how long he could go on like this. He was going to be ripped apart. He was going to die. It was so much easier to move toward the pleasure and away from the pain. He started floating slowly down toward the Korpor. The intense warmth grew and the pain faded away. The Korpor's eyes were warm and loving. The creature's beautiful face smiled and Sid longed to be enveloped in its arms. He floated down until he was right above the Korpor. He was almost there. He groaned in pleasure. He felt he was going to explode, right on the edge of orgasm.

Then, from a distance he heard his name being called. At least he thought it was his name. The impending orgasm pulled back slightly. He looked at the Korpor and the intense sexual pleasure pulsed in him harder, and he started to move toward orgasm again.

He heard his name, this time a little louder. Who was calling to him? Someone was pleading with him to come back. Back where? He didn't want this pleasure to end. He was so close. The Korpor looked at him with such longing that he ached to be in its arms.

The voice came again. This time it yelled at him to come back. He looked down at the Korpor and he saw anger in its eyes. It snarled and was suddenly ugly to Sid. Pain shot through him, intense pain, causing the pleasure to disappear instantly.

With sudden clarity, Sid realized he was being called by Crowdal. He remembered everything that had happened. Crowdal had saved him from the Korpor and carried his body from the clearing, but Sid was caught between them somehow. He needed to break away from the Korpor's hold. Sid thought about his new friendship with Crowdal. He remembered Crowdal saving him from those two mercenaries, his quick and easy laugh afterward putting Sid at ease. For some strange reason they had instantly connected with each other as if they had known each other their whole lives. Crowdal was not only his friend, he was like a brother.

Sid started to rise up and away from the Korpor. The creature reached out for him with a howl of frustration but Sid moved away with quickening speed. The trees whipped by in a blur. The soft, white glow of the clearing faded away. Soon the light was a dot in the distance that finally winked out.

Sid looked down and saw Crowdal bent over his body on the road. He hovered above them and felt a well of love for Crowdal, who was covered in sleet and caressing Sid's forehead gently.

He floated down and felt sleet on his face and Crowdal's hand on his forehead. He took a breath and it felt wonderful. Instantly the darkness returned. He couldn't see anymore. But he could hear the outside world, and that was enough for him.

As he lay there, taking in the sensations of the physical world, he felt like he was finally safe. But then, in a deep part of his mind, he could hear the distant whisper of the Korpor.

"You cannot get away. You are Ringed now. You are mine."

He felt his consciousness being pulled again, faint, but insistent. It grew until he felt like his mind was going to burst. Pain flared and he cried out. As quickly as the pain hit him, it faded to a numbness, which slowly moved from his head down through his body, finally ending with his feet. He tried pushing it away, but when he breathed he found it difficult, almost like he couldn't get his lungs to work. He couldn't move and cried in frustration.

Sid felt himself being picked up and then he was bouncing around. He couldn't open his eyes. Panic took hold of him and he wanted to scream. What was happening?

Chapter 16

Crowdal knew he didn't have much time as he ran, holding Sid over his shoulder like a sack of grain. He assumed he had only stunned the creature with his kick and didn't know if he would get so lucky again. Sid's pack was still on his back, which made it a little more difficult to hold him, but Crowdal didn't stop to get a better grip.

He ran back the way he thought he had come, branches whipping him in the face. It was so dark he could only see a few paces in front of him and when one large, low-hanging branch appeared in front of him, he didn't have time to dodge it. He slammed into it, his head snapping backward and pain flaring in his skull. He stumbled and almost dropped Sid, but he quickly got his balance and shook his head to clear the pain, then continued running, doing his best to dodge trees that appeared as shadows in front of him. He didn't hear any pursuit as he came out of the treeline and saw the road in front of him.

Crowdal slowed to a trot and continued on down the road. He wanted to save his strength so he could keep up a pace like this all night. The pain in his head was gone, he realized. Well, at least the pain from the creature was gone. His head still hurt from smacking it into the branch, but that was a normal pain, nothing like what the creature was somehow able to inflict. He could think clearly again. He looked behind and to his right often, but he saw no sign of the creature.

He had no idea what kind of creature it was but he was scared witless of it. He had never been worried for his life. No man frightened him. But this... thing, was altogether different. It was massively muscled and exuded a deadly energy. Crowdal never wanted to see it again, but he knew that he would if he stayed with Sid. For some reason the boy and the creature were connected.

After a while he looked over and saw Sid was not breathing well, so he stopped and lay him down. He pulled Sid's trousers fully up and fastened them securely. Sid breathed in quick short gasps, his face was white and his skin felt cold. Sid's eyes raced behind his eyelids, and his mouth looked slack, his skin seeming to hang from his face. Crowdal didn't know how he knew it, but Sid was losing some kind of fight with the creature.

Crowdal bent his head and spoke directly into Sid's ears, "Sid. Wake up. Come on, my friend."

He slapped Sid's face softly. Nothing happened, so he slapped him harder. "Sid, fight it. Come back. Come back."

Sid cried out and arched his back so high that Crowdal thought it would snap. He thrashed, hitting his head on the ground. Crowdal held him down by the shoulders. "It's all right, Sid, you are safe now. I've got you."

Sid's cry faded into a raspy cough. He stopped thrashing around and lay on the ground, his chest heaving. He didn't open his eyes, but it looked like he was breathing a little better, although his breaths were still shallow. His skin was still cold. The sleet collected on his cheeks and Crowdal wiped it away.

Whatever had happened, it seemed to be over. Crowdal looked into the woods, afraid the creature was coming for them. He didn't want Sid to face it again, especially in his condition.

He wrapped Sid in the blanket and his heavy coat, then put him gently over his shoulder and started jogging down the road, trying to keep from bouncing him about too badly.

Thoughts of the creature kept him going at a steady pace. He ran like this for the whole night, sweat running down his back even though sleet collected on his hood. He ached for the light of morning. Somehow the darkness of this night seemed thicker and the shadows pushed in on him.

He would not stop this night.

Chapter 17

The Black Robe sat in the chair and looked down at her Blue Robes. They sat silently, looking up at her.

"It is time for the Fractional Ascension. Rise now."

All of the Blue Robes stood as one. The room was perfectly silent.

The Black Robe raised her arms and held out a red robe. "This red robe signifies the rank of the Fractionally Ascended. It is a position of high responsibility. It is a position of power!"

Low murmuring came from below.

The Black Robe scanned the group. Over the past week, she had spoken with thirteen of the fourteen Blue Robes, heard their cases, their promises, their dedication to her. But the fourteenth Blue Robe hadn't come to see her. He didn't have to. They both knew he would be the new Red Robe, for he was her great-grandson.

She had a daughter very soon after coming to the Oblate, and her daughter had another daughter by the time she was seventeen years old. She was excited when her granddaughter showed great promise with mathematics, so by the time she was seventeen, they had arranged for her to get married and move to Orm-Mina to spy on Elenora and her daughter Lorielle.

It was there that her great-grandson Tris had been born. Even as an infant, he had shown incredible promise in mathematics. She had suspected he very well might be the Aleph Null, but Elenora's daughter Lorielle had also given birth to Sidoro who showed great promise, as well. So she had instructed Tris to become close with Sidoro. He was a natural leader and had performed admirably, giving her valuable information over the years. Unfortunately, Tris had not passed the Proofing. It grated on her nerves that Sidoro had passed it, which also made things more difficult now. But her great-grandson was almost as powerful as the Aleph Null and her plans would proceed.

She looked at the group of Blue Robes and spread her hands wide. "The Fractionally Ascended has been chosen."

The murmur grew louder.

"Silence!"

The room instantly became quiet.

"The next one who makes a sound, even a sneeze, I will have silenced forever." She watched them all from within her black hood.

She handed the red robe to the Haissan behind her, who took it and descended the stairs at the back of her platform.

She raised her hands and concentrated on her numbers. It took a supreme effort to make them appear in her mind. But she had to push even harder. She had to make them appear in the physical world. It required equations of such complexity that she had been preparing for the past week. The proper equation was required to bridge the gap from the psychic to the physical. She started to sweat as she moved variables, integers, derivatives and anti-derivatives of functions around into the proper equation. She had practiced it in her quarters for days until she could create the equation quickly. And she didn't fail now.

The equation complete, she saw the air in front of her turn blue as her numbers became visible. She rejoiced inside. Performing the Fractional Ascension ceremony was the main show of power a Black Robe had to display. If the Black Robe could perform the ceremony, no one would challenge for the position, for such power was beyond 99.99% of all people, even in the Oblate. Theoretically.

She started spinning the numbers, making the light grow brighter until it was a solid blue circle. She heard a gasp from the Blue Robes. Many of them were not old enough to have witnessed this before. The last time was seventy years ago. She concentrated, then sent the spinning circle of light out and away from her. She had to concentrate to keep it spinning. The inside of her robe became wet with sweat and her hands started to shake lightly from the effort she expended. She knew she could only keep this up for a short while longer. She must finish it quickly.

She sent the spinning blue circle of light out over the Blue Robes. It passed in front of each person, stopping briefly before moving on to the next. Some of the Blue Robes who were passed by put their hood-covered heads into their hands and sobbed, but most just sat quietly, accepting their fate. The light moved to and passed the thirteenth Blue Robe before coming to a stop in front of the fourteenth. The Black Robe changed two of the variables in the equation and the blue circle changed to red. She made the circle spin horizontally and lifted it over the Blue Robe's head before lowering it. The red circle of light sunk over his head and she expanded the circle so it could fall over his shoulders, down his body and to his feet. Where the red circle passed over, his body glowed red for a few brief moments.

"Step forward, Fractionally Ascended."

The man took a calm step forward.

"You have been chosen. Ascend the steps now."

The Blue Robe slowly walked forward and climbed the steps to the Red Robe platform, which was much lower than the Black Robe platform and accessible via steps from the chamber floor, but it was still above the Blue Robes. The Haissan was standing there already, holding the red robe.

The Blue Robe reached out and took the red robe. The Haissan immediately bowed and stepped back.

The Black Robe used the last of her energy to make the man glow bright red as he turned toward her, his back to the other Blue Robes, and pulled his robe over his head. She saw her great-grandson's face for the first time in a long time. Even though she knew he was nineteen years old, he somehow looked older than she expected. He was beyond handsome, with a mouth that probably melted girl's hearts. He handed his blue robe to the Haissan, then pulled the red robe over his body and adjusted the heavy hood so it was comfortable on his head. He stared up at the Black Robe, waiting for permission.

The Black Robe nodded.

Her great-grandson turned to face the Blue Robes.

The Black Robe added one final variable and the red circle of light pulsed up and down over the man's body, growing brighter as it did. With the last of her reserves she gasped, "The Red Robe has Fractionally Ascended. All bow to the Red Robe."

As one, the Blue Robes turned and bowed to the Red Robe.

The Red Robe raised his hands and spoke, "All bow to the Black Robe."

As one, the Blue Robes shifted and bowed to the Black Robe.

The ceremony was complete and the Black Robe let the equation collapse and the red light instantly disappeared. She had to remain strong in front of everyone, so she stood tall with her back straight.

"You are all witness to the Fractional Ascension. From this point forward, the Red Robe's word is law within this chamber. The time of the Aleph Null grows ever nearer. Each and every one of you has already received your orders. Leave immediately and report back to me in the agreed-upon intervals."

The Blue Robes nodded respectfully, and as they turned to leave the chamber the Black Robe spoke one last time. "Do not fail me."

All of the Blue Robes shuffled out of the room, the scrape of their feet on the stone floor the only sound in the chamber. When the door shut behind the last one, the Black Robe sat hard in her chair and took a deep breath. It was done.

The Red Robe craned his neck up toward her. "So what is my first task, great-grandmother?"

The Black Robe opened her eyes and glared down at him. "Do not ever call me that again, do you hear me?"

Tris nodded slightly, but she couldn't tell if he was contrite or mocking her. She continued, "As you know, we gather here twice a year to take care of business, but today was a special gathering for you."

Tris bowed. "We both know that this is just as we planned."

The Black Robe narrowed her eyes. "Be that as it may, don't you dare think that you are special in any way. You are merely a pawn, and don't you forget it. Now, until our next meeting, I want you to continue preparing the mathematical array that will imprison the Aleph Null. Do you think you can handle that?"

Tris nodded, although he looked to be barely controlling his anger. "Of course. I believe I am close to solving the mathematical equations that will confine him. It will be done in time."

The Black Robe eyed him briefly, not liking his lack of respect. She would likely have to kill him after she took control of the Aleph Null. For now, she nodded curtly. "Good. Now leave me."

Tris backed down the stairs from the Red Robe platform, then turned and left the room.

The Black Robe pulled her hood from her head. It was very hot inside of the hoods and her sweaty white hair plastered her face. But she didn't care.

She smiled, her skin cooling in the air.

Things were going according to plan. She would leave here tonight to visit Father Mansico in Yisk for the final time, to be there when he took possession of the Aleph Null. She wanted to ensure he did not betray her. The normal three-day journey would take less than a day because she had three horses staged along the route, and she would ride them each to their deaths to get there so quickly.

She didn't have the luxury of time on her side, as things were coming together very quickly now.

She could hardly wait to have her sister's grandson in her custody.

Oh the nasty things she had planned for him.

Chapter 18

The dim light of dawn started to creep over the horizon directly in front of Crowdal. It was a welcome sight. He could now see the road clearly in front of him. The sleet had not let up all night and was coming down even harder in the dawn light. He didn't know how much longer he could run, so he slowed to a fast walk. The creature had not attacked him again and with the day starting, Crowdal felt safer for some reason.

When it was fully light out, Crowdal stopped and carefully set Sid down on the ground. His eyes were still closed and his face was pale. His breathing came in shallow breaths.

Crowdal bent down next to his face. "Sid? Sid, can you hear me?"

He shook Sid's shoulders lightly as he talked but Sid didn't awaken. Crowdal sat back on his heels with a concerned sigh. He didn't know what to do. If he kept going, Sid could die. He didn't even know what was wrong with him. But he couldn't stay here, either. Crowdal stood up, rubbed his eyes and looked around the countryside. The Wilden trees that had lined the road were now gone, replaced by large fields. They had come into farm country during the night. They must be getting close to Yisk so there should be farmhouses around here somewhere. But all he saw were empty fields, still unplowed in the early spring. Most of them were filled with slushy water from the long night of falling sleet.

Crowdal took his flask of water out and knelt down beside Sid. He tilted the boy's head up and poured a small amount into his mouth, but it just trickled out the sides. He took a long drink himself, put the stopper back on the flask, and tied it on his belt. The sleet was starting to turn to snow and the temperature was still dropping. Crowdal knew spring weather was unpredictable, but he never remembered a Niyrreeben occurring one day and then having snow the next. Very strange. They were both soaking wet and the temperature was now below freezing. He had to find them shelter soon.

Crowdal picked Sid back up and slung him over his shoulder. He adjusted him a little until he was in a comfortable position, then started jogging again down the road. The farmland around them was barren. There were no trees except for a few wind breaks, and these trees were twisted as if they were old and tired. He saw a large flock of birds fly across the field to his left, heading north. It was a sign of spring, but today sure didn't feel like it. The ditches that ran along the road were filled with black water.

The sleet soon turned completely over to snow and the flakes that fell were thick and wet, covering Crowdal and Sid completely. But Crowdal didn't slow down or try and shake it away.

The snow began to build up on the ground, mixing with the mud on the road, which made running very difficult.

A sharp corner in the road came up, lined with bushes, and Crowdal slid to a stop as he rounded the corner when he saw a horse and cart turn onto the road from a connecting trail up ahead. Crowdal started running again as hard as he could, and soon caught up to the cart. He yelled hoarsely, out of breath. The driver turned his head and pulled on the reins to stop the cart. The horse stood calmly as if it didn't care whether it walked or not.

The driver turned stiffly in his seat to look back at Crowdal. He was very old, his skin wrinkled and sagging. He was wearing basic brown trousers and a heavy wool coat. A farmer, Crowdal thought.

Crowdal looked down at the old man even though he was standing on the ground and the man was sitting in the cart.

The man eyed Crowdal, looking him up and down, then at Sid slung over his shoulder. He spit a large glob of tobacco over the side of his cart and grunted, a sound that could have been a question or a statement.

Crowdal smiled his most charming smile. "Good day, sir." He bowed awkwardly with Sid on his shoulder. "As you can see, I have a sick friend. Where are you traveling?"

The man eyed Crowdal with a hard glare. His wrinkled eyes squinted as if he were used to glaring into the sun all day. He moved the chew around in his mouth and grunted what sounded like, 'Yisk.'

Motioning down the road, Crowdal asked, "You are going all the way to Yisk?"

The man nodded slightly, looking anxious to get moving again.

Crowdal smiled again, hoping to put him at ease. "I'd be grateful if you let my friend ride in the back of your hay wagon to Yisk. I'll pay you."

The old farmer chewed slowly, then spit over the side of the cart again. "Ten copper pieces. Put him in the back. But just him. You walk."

Crowdal knew that was an exorbitant amount, almost robbery. But Sid needed to be able to lie down and the hay would keep him somewhat warm, so he nodded to the old farmer. "Thank you, kind sir."

Crowdal moved around to the back of the cart. He pushed some hay aside to make a comfortable and supportive bed, then lifted Sid and laid him down. He covered Sid with his blanket, then piled hay thickly over him, leaving Sid's mouth uncovered just enough for him to breathe. Crowdal hoped the layer of hay would insulate him from the cold. He bent down to Sid and whispered softly, "Hang in there, my friend."

Crowdal removed his coin pouch and took out five copper pieces. He re-tied the pouch and put it back in his shirt, then walked around to the front and handed the old farmer the coins. "Five now. You will get five more when we reach Yisk."

The old farmer took the coins and put them in his shirt pocket, then snapped the reins. The horse immediately began walking, the wheels of the hay wagon creaking as they rolled roughly through the almost frozen mud.

Crowdal walked alongside the wagon. It moved so slowly that he found himself having to take very short steps. It was going to take forever to get to Yisk at this rate, but at least Sid would be warm and comfortable.

As they traveled, the snowflakes grew smaller as the temperature continued dropping. Now that he wasn't running, Crowdal was chilled to his bones. He started to shiver, so he clapped his hands and rubbed them together to stay warm as he walked. His toes were numb and his body ached. He never thought he would feel warm again.

Not long after they started, Crowdal heard horses coming up behind them. He turned tiredly and saw four riders approaching at a fairly quick pace. Soon the horses passed them and Crowdal looked up. He saw three robed figures and an old woman wrapped in a blanket. The old woman glanced at him as she passed, so he smiled up at her. She smiled warmly back, then was past the wagon. He watched the four riders disappear into the snow, then put his head down and forgot about them.

Crowdal checked on Sid regularly, but his condition didn't change, although he did seem to be breathing a little easier. He looked warmer, too.

They traveled the whole day through the gray snow. As they made their way along the road, Crowdal started to see more people and wagons. He smiled and said hello to people but no one smiled back at him. He finally pulled his hood tight around his head and walked with his head down. He was too tired to deal with ignorant people today.

Finally as the light began to fade, they came over a hill and Crowdal saw a beautiful large city spread out below, stretching as far as he could see through the falling snow. A wide river cut through the middle of it.

Finally, Yisk. He never thought they would see it.

The horse seemed to sense they were close to their destination too, because it picked up its pace down the hill. In a short time they came to the city entrance. The farmer stopped his cart. "The end of the line for you two." He held out his hand.

Crowdal pulled out his coin pouch, removed five more copper pieces, and handed them to the farmer. He put the pouch away. The farmer immediately snapped the reins and the cart started forward. Crowdal had to rush to the back of the wagon and lift Sid out while it was moving.

He stood in the middle of the street, holding Sid over his shoulder, and watched the wagon slowly roll away, swaying back and forth from a slightly warped wheel. There were quite a few people about, even on such a cold and snowy evening.

Crowdal carried Sid into Yisk, looking for the House of Healing.

Chapter 19

Crowdal made his way down a wide street filled with people, more people than he had seen in a long time. Buildings lined the street, each one built against the other as if holding each other up. Each building was painted a different color, some bright red, others green and blue. Even this close to evening, many stores were still open. Crowdal saw a combined feed and clothing store, which was a strange combination. As he walked, he looked for the House of Healing, but he didn't see it. That didn't surprise him, it was a large city. He asked a few people but they quickly turned and hurried away from him.

It was getting dark, so he decided to just get a room at a tavern for the night and have them send for a healer. Taverns were not difficult to find, but after asking about a room in several of them, none had any rooms left. On a cold day like this, Crowdal figured travelers would hole up, waiting for it to get warmer. So he continued further into the city.

The people on the streets gave him a wide berth, wanting nothing to do with a Trith. Crowdal ignored them, not in the mood to deal with them. After a short way he saw a tobacco store to his left, its front stained brown with a picture of a tobacco leaf painted on the window. It looked well cared for, and Crowdal could smell the tobacco. He sighed with longing. It had been a long time since he had smoked. If he got time, he would come back to buy some good leaf, perhaps even Uragon leaf if they had it. It was expensive, but worth the price. It was not only the sweetest tobacco leaf you could find, but it gave you an energy boost that lasted quite a while. Crowdal felt he could use some extra energy right now, but he had more important things to do, like find a warm dry tavern.

The wind blew harder and was funneled down the street, making it feel colder than it was. The light from the evening was almost gone and fewer and fewer people were out now, giving the city a desolate feeling in the snowy darkness. Crowdal pulled his hood tightly to ward off most of the cold and soon came to a cross street that was wider than the ones he had passed so far. A wagon pulled by two horses crossed in front of him, so he stopped and looked to his left and right. The street stretched into the snowy darkness, lined with more buildings. To his right, even through the snow he could see a large fortress on a hill. The hill itself was lined with large homes, terraced from top to bottom. 'Probably the city government,' he thought. People liked to build close to the center of power. He didn't want to get caught up in the government area of town so after the wagon passed, he continued down the street he was on.

He checked taverns as he came across them, but found no rooms available. Everyone turned him away and he knew it was probably because they didn't want a Trith in their tavern. He started to get angry, and he was soon short-tempered, which only made people turn him away with threats of calling the Yisk patrol. Crowdal didn't want trouble, so he left the taverns, but not before scowling at the tavern owners, causing them to back away from him. It was at least a little gratifying to do that to such closed-minded people.

He eventually came to a nondescript tavern with the sign 'The Pig n' Griddle' hanging over the door, squeaking miserably in the wind. Crowdal sighed in disgust because the place sounded like it would be filled with criminals or worse, but he knew that Sid needed warmth, so he entered the seedy establishment anyway. He pushed through the door without pausing and stepped into a warm room. It felt wonderful and he just stood there for a few moments taking in the heat.

In the corner, a nice fire burned in a large fireplace. It was dim inside and only a few people were in the main room, quietly drinking and conversing. An old tavern owner stood behind the bar, leaning on his arms talking to a customer. He looked up at Crowdal and walked over. "What can I do for you?" There was no fear in his eyes, in fact he actually smiled at Crowdal. He had gray hair and a kindly face as he eyed Crowdal and Sid.

Crowdal carefully set Sid on a chair, resting his head on the table, then turned to the tavern owner, his voice short. "Do you have a room for rent, or not?"

The old man raised his eyebrows. "Well, I don't for such a rude person."

Crowdal slumped. He was tired and irritable after being turned away from so many places. "I apologize. I've got a very sick friend and every tavern we have checked has turned us away. We've been traveling for days and I'm short-tempered. If you have a room for a few days, I would be grateful."

The tavern owner nodded in understanding. "I can imagine they took one look at you, being a Trith and what-not, and slammed their doors in your face. But I am not racist like most people are." He handed Crowdal a large key. "I have one room left. The previous lodger left just today." He nodded toward the stairs. "Go on up, seventh door on the left." He looked at the young man slumped over the table. "I'll have a healer sent for your friend, along with food and ale."

Crowdal tried to smile but didn't have the energy, so he merely nodded his head and thanked the tavern owner. He picked Sid up and carried him like a baby up the stairs and unlocked and opened the door to his room. He saw two crude straw beds. They weren't much, but they were dry and had thick blankets on them. He removed Sid's wet clothes and laid him in one of the beds, pulling the thick blanket up to his chin.

Crowdal sat down in a chair and hung his head. It had been a long three days. All he wanted to do was sleep, but he couldn't just yet.

He rubbed his eyes and looked over at Sid sleeping under the covers. He looked like he was sleeping normally, but Crowdal knew something was wrong. The fact that Sid had not awakened once during the long run was frightening. The watcher had done something to Sid in that clearing. What it was, Crowdal didn't know. He wished he had killed that thing. He had sworn he would never kill again but he knew that if he ever again met the creature, one of them would die.

Sid moaned on the bed. It was faint, but it was the first sound he had made in over a day. Crowdal stood up and leaned over him, pushing hair from his eyes. They were still closed, but Crowdal saw his pupils moving rapidly behind his eyelids. "Shh... everything will be all right, my friend."

He sat on the floor next to Sid and rested his head on the bed. Without realizing it, he closed his eyes and fell asleep.

In what felt like only moments, he awoke instantly to a loud knocking at the door. Crowdal stood up and wearily opened it part way, leaning his head on the wall as he looked through. He saw a pretty young woman. She held a small bag and had an irritated look on her face. She was thin and dressed in a simple brown robe. He noticed that she had small freckles on her nose, which he found very attractive. He stared at her, completely forgetting to let her in.

She stared back at him, at his size as he filled the opening of the door. His head was above the doorframe, so he had to bend his head slightly to look down at her. She tried pushing past him into the room, but he was so large she couldn't budge him.

When Crowdal didn't move or open the door wider, she sighed irritably. "Great, a Trith. This should be fun. Listen, I hear you have a sick man in here, but I can't heal him with you blocking the doorway."

Crowdal stared at her for a few moments, then stepped back, opening the door wider.

She walked directly over to Sid and set the bag on the floor.

Crowdal closed the door and sat on the chair, rubbing his eyes.

The woman knelt down and put her hand to Sid's forehead. She then lifted each eyelid, peering into his eyes. After that, she put her head to his chest, listening for a few moments. She lifted the covers and examined his body for wounds, not even blinking at his nakedness.

Crowdal started to protest but she glared at him and he held his tongue.

Finally she pulled the blanket up and turned to Crowdal. "I can find nothing wrong with this young man. He has a mild case of hypothermia, but he will be fine. Aside from a couple of small lumps on his head, I see no injuries. And his heartbeat is normal. What exactly do you think is wrong with him? Why am I here?"

She stared at Crowdal with a look of contempt.

Crowdal leaned his head against the wall. With his height, even sitting down his head was higher than hers, so he looked down at her through half-closed eyes. He knew he looked imposing, but this young woman treated him like anyone else. He would have liked that any other time, but not now.

"He's been unconscious since last night. He was attacked by some creature. I was able to save him and carry him here. End of story."

The woman stared icily at him. "I didn't ask you what happened, I asked why you think he needs my help."

Crowdal was tired and he wasn't in the mood to spar with this woman. He raised his voice slightly, although he didn't shout. "I do not know what is wrong with him. I'm not a healer, like you supposedly are."

Her face darkened.

Crowdal continued, ignoring her anger, "But I do know something is wrong. He was unconscious when I found him. I carried him over my shoulder and ran an entire night and morning. I think that if there was nothing wrong with him, he would probably have woken up at some point, especially with his head bouncing on my shoulder all night. So your job is to find out what is wrong with him."

He crossed his arms on his chest and glared at her.

The healer looked steadily at him for a few moments. Crowdal could see anger in her eyes. Finally she let out her breath. "I can find nothing physically wrong with him. So apparently whatever happened affected his mind. I need to know the whole story. And if you speak to me that way again, I will walk out this door. You can find yourself another healer."

Crowdal stared at her, then uncrossed his arms. He had no right treating her this way. She was only trying to help. Despite her lack of personality, he knew he needed her. He softened his voice, "I am sorry, Miss..."

She glared at him, then said, "Melinda."

Crowdal smiled at her, trying to stop the situation from escalating. "I'm sorry, Melinda. It has been a long three days and I'm worried for my friend. I had no right to treat you like I did. I know you are here to help."

Melinda glared for a bit longer, then she, too, relaxed and smiled slightly up at him, although it looked forced, almost as if she never smiled and had forgotten how. "I am sorry, too. I shouldn't have been so brusque with you. So, tell me the whole story of what happened. Maybe I can help."

Crowdal stuck out his hand. "I think we should start over. I'm Crowdal and this is my friend Sid."

Melinda took his hand. Her hand was so small that it disappeared in his. But he only squeezed her hand gently, used to being careful with his strength.

Crowdal let go of her hand and sat back. "I just met Sid three days ago, but this young man has already saved my life. I owe him."

She raised her eyebrows, looking surprised they had only known each other for such a short time. "Perhaps you could tell me the whole story of what happened."

Crowdal sat back with a sigh, running his hands through his long, black hair. He looked at the floor for a few moments, then up at Melinda. He wasn't really in the mood to tell the whole story, but this young woman was there to help them. She deserved to hear what happened.

"All right, although I warn you it will be a difficult story to believe."

Melinda waved her hand. "Let me be the judge of that."

Crowdal looked at her for a few more moments before beginning the story. When he started, he told it as it happened, of the flood, the Niyrreeben tearing the forest apart, but when he got to the attack of the watcher, he paused.

Crowdal was hesitant to tell her about the encounter. He wouldn't have believed it himself if he hadn't lived through it. But looking at her and how calmly she listened to him, he decided to just say everything, uncensored. If she didn't believe him, that was her problem. So he told her about the entire encounter with the beast, leaving out only the state in which he found Sid in the clearing. She didn't need to know that.

As he finished the story, she stood up and walked toward him. She stopped in front of him, her hands on her hips, her face suddenly angry. She was barely half his height, but she looked up at him fearlessly.

"Why do you lie to me? You are wasting my time."

Crowdal raised one eyebrow. So much for the truce they had made. He replied calmly though, trying to keep the peace, "I've told you the truth."

She didn't blink as she glared at him. "You are telling me this young man was attacked by the Korpor, a creature so mythically powerful and frightening that the name alone strikes fear in even the largest of men, and that you fought the Korpor, saved your friend *and* escaped, carrying him all night and day?"

Crowdal nodded, starting to get angry. He had never been called a liar before. He was exhausted and hungry. He stood up to his full height, having to tilt his head slightly to avoid hitting the ceiling, and scowled down at her. "I have told you exactly what happened. No lies. No embellishments. The watcher... or Korpor as you call it, took him; I got him back and here we are." He motioned over to Sid on the bed. "And that boy needs your help. What is a Korpor, by the way?"

Melinda studied Crowdal's face for a few moments, then finally sighed, stepping back a pace. "You're telling the truth. I find it hard to believe, though. There are stories of the Korpor visiting young people and it is said that no one is able to even look at the creature without falling unconscious from pain. Yet here you are, saying this boy was taken by one, and that you fought it. Pardon me if I am a bit skeptical."

Crowdal huffed and sat back down in the chair. "Well it happened. Accept it, lady. Now can you help him or not?"

She shook her head. "I might be able to help him." She looked sternly at him. "But you have to tell me the part you left out."

Crowdal shook his head. "Nothing else happened. I've told you everything."

Melinda crossed her arms and glared at him.

Crowdal stared back for a few moments, then finally sighed. "Well, there is one other thing." He paused, unsure how to tell her.

Melinda let out her breath in exasperation. "Would you just tell me? I don't have all night!"

Crowdal glared at her. "Fine, when I found Sid and the Korpor in the clearing, I didn't describe everything. Sid was... he was on his back and unconscious. His trousers were down to his knees." Crowdal paused for a moment before continuing. "And he and the Korpor did... it."

Melinda's eyes grew wide as he spoke and she stumbled back and sat heavily in the other chair.

Crowdal was embarrassed. "I'm sorry to say such sexual things to you."

Melinda looked up at Crowdal with a scowl. 'It seemed to be her standard expression,' he thought.

"I could care less about sex." She blushed slightly, as if realizing that it came out wrong. She spoke sharply, "You really have no idea what a Korpor is, do you?"

Crowdal shook his head. "I know it is some kind of beast and I know it wants Sid for some reason."

Melinda shook her head. "No, I mean you have no idea what it is, what it does."

"I have a feeling you are about to tell me," Crowdal said with a sigh.

Melinda got up and walked over to Sid, pulling the chair along with her. She sat down and pulled the blanket back, exposing his groin area.

Crowdal started to stand up. "What are you doing?"

She put her hand up to stop him. "I'm checking for something, so if you can keep quiet for a few moments, I would appreciate it."

She bent down and looked at Sid from different angles. She then grabbed his penis and moved it around, looking at it carefully. It didn't grow hard or react to her touch in any way. Suddenly she gasped and bent down to look more closely at the base of the shaft. She studied it for a few moments, not breathing. Finally she let go of it and pulled the covers up to his neck again. She sat back in the chair, an incredulous expression on her face.

Crowdal couldn't take it anymore and asked her what was wrong.

She turned to him. "I don't believe it. He's been *Ringed*."

"What are you talking about?"

Melinda looked lost in thought as she spoke, "The Korpor is supposed to be nothing but myth. People claim to see it every so often in the forest at night, but these are just stories. No evidence has ever been collected to prove its existence."

She looked up at Crowdal and she actually looked nervous. "I personally never believed it existed, but now that I've heard your account and seen the evidence myself, I have to go against everything I believe and say this boy is the Aleph Null and he has been *Ringed*." She pushed hair from her eyes and scratched her nose distractedly.

"Why do you keep saying he has been *Ringed* and he is the Aleph Null? What does that mean?"

Melinda sighed. "It is difficult quoting lore, as it always sounds a bit trivial when spoken out loud." She coughed lightly. "Now mind you, this is all just mythology. It is not based in fact. It is said there will be a time when a person will come who can control the power of both regular and Black Numbers. I think this boy here could be that person."

Crowdal looked at her strangely.

She sighed again. "I can't explain the power of numbers, as I know nothing about it. The power of numbers is a myth created long ago. All I know is there is supposedly a concept called regular and Black Numbers, opposites of each other that allow the wielder of them to control incredible energies. The Korpor is said to be a creature who can awaken these Black Numbers in one special person called the Aleph Null. But it is also said that if the Korpor *Rings* the Aleph Null, the power of Black Numbers can be expanded exponentially. The power that results is beyond comprehension."

She looked down at Sid. "To *Ring* a male means the Korpor cuts around the base of the penis and pulls the skin off before having sex with him." Melinda glanced fearfully up at Crowdal and nodded her head in Sid's direction. "He has the scar on him."

Crowdal stared at her in horror, unable to believe anything she was telling him. It sounded like a story made up by fearful men long ago. But he got up and pulled back the covers to see for himself, anyway. He bent over and saw the puckered scar around the base of Sid's penis. He shivered as he remembered seeing the Korpor on top of Sid's naked body. Maybe something of what Melinda said was true, as strange as it sounded. He stood up and pulled the covers back to Sid's chin, then turned to look at Melinda. "So only men can be *Ringed*, then?"

Melinda shook her head. "No, I believe if a woman had been born as the Aleph Null, then her..." she paused, embarrassed. Crowdal raised an eyebrow, which infuriated her. She gritted her teeth. "The Korpor would have skinned the clitoris and mixed its own semen with the blood of the woman while simultaneously inflicting pain and pleasure. It is the same effect as the skinning of the penis on a man. It is the mixing of blood and pain, of lust, pleasure, and sexual intercourse that completely puts the victim in thrall to the Korpor. The theory is that the blood and pain opens up the receptors in the brain that are normally dormant and the sexual orgasm briefly dulls the defense mechanism in the brain, allowing a clear path for the Korpor to enter the mind, take control, and find the path to the Black Numbers hidden within the Aleph Null."

Crowdal was confused. "But, the Korpor... how?"

Melinda looked to be enjoying his discomfort and confusion. She spoke in a tone he suspected she used on old patients who couldn't understand her very well, "The Korpor is a hermaphrodite."

"What in the name of the gods is a hermaphrodite?"

Melinda pointed to them both as she spoke. "It means the creature has both male and female body parts."

Crowdal's eyes widened briefly before his sarcasm returned. "Of course, why wouldn't it be a... hermaphrodite?" When he saw Melinda about to retort, he shook his head in acceptance. "I'm not making fun of you. It sounds crazy, but I've seen too many things in this world that defy logic, so I can't dismiss this. What do we do now then?"

She sighed and shrugged her shoulders slightly, still a bit weary of his sarcasm. "I have no idea. I'm sorry, I know he is your friend, but I don't know anything more about this. I've studied the lore, but not in depth. You should let me bring him to the House of Healing. If anyone will know about this, it will be Father Mansico."

Crowdal shook his head. He wasn't sure he wanted what happened to Sid to be common knowledge. So he nodded toward Sid lying on the bed. "I don't want to move him just yet." He looked in Melinda's eyes. They were a beautiful brown and Crowdal was surprised to find that he found her very attractive. He softened his voice, "He needs to stay here and I would appreciate if you didn't tell anyone of this."

Melinda shook her head. "I have to. This is important."

Crowdal stood up. "I can't stop you, but we don't want a lot of attention here. My friend has been through a lot. He needs some rest. I've only known him for a few days, but there are things happening here that I don't understand. And until I do, I don't trust anyone."

Melinda shrugged. "I'm sorry, this is too important. We need to know more about what happened. We need to take him to the House of Healing. Father Mansico will know what to do." She grimaced. "Plus, how do you know the Korpor won't come for Sid here? He will be safer in the House of Healing."

Crowdal snorted in disgust. "Haven't you heard a word I've said? I've encountered this thing twice. The first time it got within a few paces of me without my ever knowing it was there. This Korpor could sneak into the House of Healing unseen and nothing would stop it from taking Sid. I kicked it hard enough to kill any normal living creature, yet I am positive that I only stunned it. Look at me." He motioned to the door. "If I kicked that door, it would be nothing but splinters." He looked directly into her eyes and spoke softly, "The Korpor cannot be stopped by large numbers of people. You will only get Sid killed. I don't know if I can stop it, but I've done it once and I'll die trying to do it again."

Melinda studied his face as he spoke. "You really care for this young man, don't you?"

Crowdal's shoulders slumped slightly. He was surprised to realize she was right. He had only known Sid for a few days, but he found that he really cared about what happened to the boy.

Crowdal didn't make friends easily because everyone hated the Trith as a race. He had never considered anyone a true friend. Yet here was this skinny kid, a royal pain in the ass to be around sometimes, who was difficult to speak to without wanting to wring his neck, yet Crowdal found himself caring about him. He also had the feeling that Sid had never had a true friend, either. But they had saved each other from certain death. There was a bond growing between them and Crowdal wasn't going to let anything happen to Sid. He nodded to Melinda. "Yes, I really do. He is difficult to take sometimes, but I consider him a friend. And I don't say that lightly."

Melinda nodded. "I think he is lucky. You take care of him and don't let him out of your sight for the next few weeks. Against my better judgment, I won't tell anyone."

She stood up and picked up her bag, getting ready to leave. Crowdal stood up too. She looked up at him. "I'll stop by tomorrow to check on him. In the meantime, try to get him to drink some water and keep him warm. If he wakes up, have the tavern owner send for me."

They looked at each other for a few moments.

Crowdal felt an attraction between them, but he was exhausted. Maybe they would have the chance to get to know each other, or maybe not.

Melinda opened the door and walked out without another word.

Crowdal shut the door and smiled slightly, despite his tiredness and worry for Sid.

She was quite a woman.

Chapter 20

The whisper in Sid's head became more intense and a void opened up in his mind. He hovered above it and knew he couldn't let himself fall into it or he would be lost. He had nothing left of himself anymore with which to fight.

He whimpered as he started to drift into the void. Then from somewhere inside him, he thought of his numbers. Numbers?

He drifted down. The void was right below him, dark and swirling.

With sudden hope, he remembered his numbers. They brought him peace. He anxiously reached for them, to bring them into the darkness. But he couldn't see them. A barrier pushed against him every time he felt for them. What had always been easy for him was now out of his reach.

For as long as he could remember, his numbers had been a constant in his life, always there for him, a part of him, popping into his mind anytime he wanted them. He could sense them now, but they were blocked, he couldn't touch them.

He heard his name whispered, the voice raspy and intoxicating. The Korpor called to him from the void. He could sink downward into it so easily. All he had to do was let go.

In a panic, Sid concentrated, pushing against the barrier that blocked his numbers. He tried to pull at it, but nothing happened.

He needed his numbers!

He stopped. He had to fight the panic. The void was closer to him. It felt so comforting just to fall into it. He remembered his father saying that if he had a problem that he couldn't solve, he should break it down into its parts and work on them separately, that sometimes the whole problem was too complex to solve.

With the Korpor whispering to him, Sid felt along the barrier to his numbers. It was solid but wasn't physical, it was in his mind. He knew that if it was in his mind, he could manipulate it. Break it. Sid reached for his center, calming himself.

"Come to me my pet. Let go..."

The voice was soft and Sid fought hard to ignore it. A barrier was nothing more than a mathematical equation. In the darkness, he struggled to make a simple line appear, straight and clear.

He needed to pull the numbers from beyond the line. They weren't on the other side, like a barrier in real life, where dimensions were solid. Sid had to think beyond physical dimensions. He studied the line, looking at it from different angles. He studied it for what seemed like an eternity, growing so tired that he wanted nothing more than to just give up. He began to drift into the warmth of the void, so inviting. But as he did, a thought popped into his mind from seemingly nowhere and he suddenly knew what he had to do. He didn't need to reach past the line, he needed to reach inside of it.

The Korpor's voice became more insistent, angrier, "*Come to me now. You are mine. Your blood and semen are a part of me now, as I am a part of you. Let go, come to me. We can be one.*"

Sid ignored the voice, even though it was so hard to do so.

He felt the void below him, very close. He ignored that, too. He concentrated on the line and made it wider. Without even thinking of how to do it, he split it down the middle, a little at a time. He then mentally reached out and pulled the line apart until the whole thing was shaped like a circle. It was exhausting, and he felt so tired he wanted to quit, but he pushed himself on. When the circle felt stable enough, he let go and studying it, realized it was actually a semi-circle, like one would make by splitting a roll of bread dough down the middle and pulling it apart. He stared at it, unsure what to do with it.

Then he got an idea. He concentrated on the semi-circle, looking into it. With a nudge of his mind, he started to spin it.

The voice grew louder and he felt pain build in his head until it felt like it was going to explode.

"*If you come to me, the pain will stop.*"

Sid started to cry from the pain but he pushed against it and concentrated on the circle. It spun slowly at first, almost like it was moving through thick, muddy water. Sid pushed it harder and it spun faster until it started to glow. He pushed harder, fighting the pain in his head, until the circle became a solid circle of light. Then with a huge mental thrust, he punched through the middle.

Light shards blew out in all directions.

Sid slumped in exhaustion but kept it spinning. Inside the hole of light, he could see numbers, letters, and symbols tumbling up and over each other. He pulled on the ends of the spinning hole of light, grunting with effort, expanding it. It stretched wider and wider. And like bread dough, the wider he made it, the easier it became to stretch. He pulled until the circle of light became too thin to support itself and blew out, exploding with a bang. Sid turned away. When he looked back, the numbers, letters, and symbols had turned bright white and were floating, spinning in all directions in the darkness.

He cried out in joy. He had done it! The pain in his head also disappeared.

He heard the raspy voice fading away. "*You are Ringed. You are mine...*"

Sid looked everywhere at once, pulling numbers out of the spinning mass. Within a moment he had lined up random numbers in the darkness. He grabbed letters and symbols and added them to the line. He felt the void shrinking away. He gained strength.

Sid rotated the line of numbers, letters, and symbols until he was looking at them from the back. He spun them around in circles, faster and faster until they were a blur, like a stick taken from the coals of a fire and twirled it in the night air would look, making one solid circle of orange light. Only this circle of light was different from the one he had burst to release the numbers. This circle of numbered light was his to control with ease. He slowed the spin until they settled into the original line. With a little nudge, he made them disappear.

In the darkness, Sid realized there were no more whispers of the Korpor. He felt free and the numbness was gone. He couldn't feel the void anymore. He sighed in exhaustion.

Then he heard voices. It was a man and woman arguing. He thought he recognized the man's voice, but the woman was a stranger. He floated in the darkness, resting and at peace, no longer having to listen to the whisper of the Korpor pull at him. He brought some numbers back and lazily played with them, spinning them, making simple equations, erasing them and melting them.

He heard a door close.

Chapter 21

Crowdal was about to sit down when another knock sounded at the door. 'What now,' he thought in exasperation. He just wanted to get some sleep. But he opened the door anyway. A young boy held out a large tray filled with food and drink, the tray rattling slightly as the boy's hands trembled.

Crowdal's eyes lit up and he smiled.

"Ah... come in." He leaned forward and smelled the food. "Hmm, smells delicious. And is that ale I see? Perfect. Set it down on the table over there."

The boy hesitantly entered the room and set the tray down, keeping a wary eye on the Trith. Crowdal flicked a copper coin in the air and the boy grabbed it in a smooth motion, his demeanor instantly changing. "Thank you, sir. If you need anything, just come downstairs and ask. Good night, sir." The boy left the room, shutting the door softly behind him.

Crowdal was incredibly hungry and the food smelled delicious. There was a pitcher of ale and two large mugs. Next to them were two plates heaped with food. He sat down and picked up a wooden fork. Then the smile left his face. The meal was roast pork with roasted potatoes and carrots. 'Meat,' he thought to himself. 'Always meat.' He sighed and shrugged his shoulders.

He quickly ate the potatoes and carrots. They were very tasty, but he was still hungry after he finished. So he brought his plate with him and left the room, going downstairs.

In the main tavern he saw the boy turn a corner into the kitchen, so Crowdal followed him. He entered the kitchen, where a portly, middle-aged man was stirring a steaming pot. He looked up at Crowdal, taking in his size briefly before looking back down into the pot. "Yes?"

Crowdal gave him a sad smile, hoping he didn't scare him. All he wanted was some more food. He spoke in a gentle voice, "I was hoping I could get another plate of those delicious potatoes and carrots. I couldn't get enough of them. I am a big man, as you can see."

The cook nodded and motioned him closer.

Crowdal stepped over to him. The cook took his plate and heaped it with three large steamed potatoes and two large ladles of steamed carrots. Crowdal was about to say thank you when the man started to place a large slab of pork on the plate. Crowdal held up his hand. "Please, no more meat. Just potatoes and carrots, please."

The cook looked questioningly at him, holding the meat in mid air, dripping grease. He raised an eyebrow. "A Trith that doesn't eat meat? I always thought you people ate anything that moved."

Crowdal grinned. "In general, you would be correct, but I am a little different."

The cook shrugged his shoulders, dropped the meat back in the pan, and handed the plate back to Crowdal. "Hmm... learn something new every day, I do."

Crowdal sniffed the air in an exaggerated motion. "That wouldn't be apple pie I smell, would it?"

The cook beamed and nodded. "Just came out of the oven." He looked around, then whispered, "Dessert is not part of the menu, usually costing extra. But you aren't eating the meat so I think it is fair to give you a piece for free."

He lifted a towel that covered the massive pie and cut a large piece, lifting it over to Crowdal's plate. It was still steaming.

Crowdal smiled in anticipation. He bent down, took a large sniff, and sighed. "That, my friend, is the nicest pie I have ever smelled."

The cook's eyes sparkled and he waved dismissively, although he flushed slightly, obviously not used to getting compliments on his cooking.

Crowdal tapped the cook on the back, causing him to stumble forward a little bit. "You are a good man mister..."

The cook waved dismissively. "Carl. Just Carl, please. I'm only a cook. Mister sounds funny in front of my name."

Crowdal held his hand out. "Nice to meet you, good sir, Carl. My name is Crowdal."

They shook hands, the man a little awed. But Crowdal had an infectious smile and the man grinned at him.

Crowdal hooked a large finger into the pie and brought it to his mouth, sucking the sticky mess with a loud noise. His face lit up. "This is the best pie I've ever tasted."

Carl squared his shoulders proudly. "Thank you. You are welcome here any time. Now, I think you should go before Mr. Richards sees you with a piece of my pie. I'll say a mouse ate the piece if he asks me about it."

Crowdal nodded, a crumb from the pie stuck in his wispy beard. He winked at Carl and left the kitchen, carrying his plate like it was gold, careful not to trip and drop it.

Back in the room, he put the plate on the table and looked over at Sid. He almost jumped back. Sid was lying on his side, staring at the room. His eyes were dark blue but he didn't seem to see anything or even be awake.

Crowdal knelt down and passed his hand in front of Sid's eyes. Sid didn't blink or react. He put his hand to Sid's forehead, pushing his hair out of the way. "Sid, can you hear me?"

He gently shook him and saw Sid blink twice. The blue in his eyes slowly faded and changed to their normal brown color. He looked up at Crowdal in confusion.

Crowdal smiled down at him, putting his hand on his shoulder. "How are you feeling?"

Sid just looked at Crowdal, not comprehending him at first. Then Crowdal saw his eyes clear and he seemed to wake up. He smiled weakly, then licked his dry lips. Crowdal immediately rose and got a mug of ale from the tray. He lifted it to Sid's lips and let him slowly drink, pulling it away after a few sips.

Sid smacked his lips together and whispered hoarsely that he wanted more.

Crowdal tipped the cup again, letting Sid have two more sips. He took the cup away. "Enough for now. I'll give you more in a bit. Lay back and rest now."

Sid put his head down and closed his eyes. He was asleep in moments, but this time it seemed like normal sleep compared to earlier.

Crowdal sighed in relief. He pulled the blanket up tightly around Sid, then sat back down at the table and just watched Sid for a few moments. He knew the fact that Sid had awakened was very important. Whatever battle Sid had endured seemed to be over for the moment. From what Melinda had told him, Sid was either very lucky to have awakened, or he was very strong. Crowdal had a feeling it was the latter.

Crowdal picked up his fork and ate his meal slowly, enjoying it much more now that he knew his friend was going to recover. When he got to the piece of pie, he put each bite into his mouth and let it sit there, enjoying the sticky sweetness and chunks of apple for a few moments before chewing and swallowing. It wasn't often he got a treat like this and he wanted to enjoy every bite. The Trith did not usually eat for enjoyment, they ate for sustenance only. Therefore the food they ate was bland but filling. So Crowdal was learning to enjoy all kinds of new foods now that he was on his own and he loved almost everything he tried. But apple pie was his favorite food so far. He scooped the last piece of pie onto his fork, using his giant fingers to nudge a bit of buttery crust from the edge of the plate. He put it to his mouth, chewing it with pure joy, his eyes closed, before swallowing.

He took a sip of ale and sat back with a satisfied sigh, letting the food digest. He was more tired than he had been in a long time, so he took off his wet shirt and trousers and crawled into the second bed. It creaked mightily as he settled in, his legs hanging over the end of the bed with his feet resting on the floor like he was sitting on a chair. He was used to beds that were too small for him; he adapted and made do with whatever he found at each inn. Just as he closed his eyes, the bed groaned and then collapsed to the floor with a crash, its wooden legs unable to hold his great weight. Dust rose up around him and he sighed.

He could have done without that.

But he was so tired he just stretched his legs out fully across the floor, which was actually more comfortable for him, and closed his eyes and fell instantly asleep.

The room filled with the sound of twin snores, almost like they were in tune with each other.

Chapter 22

Sid woke up to the sound of snoring. He opened his eyes and lazily stretched his arms over his head. He looked across the small room and saw Crowdal sleeping on his back on a straw bed that looked to have smashed to the floor, bits and pieces of wood lying all over the place. His friend was snoring very loudly and was so tall that with his legs stretched fully out, his feet touched the far wall.

He tried sitting up in bed but found he had to struggle, his arms trembling with effort. He couldn't believe how weak he was. How long had he slept?

He slowly swung his legs over the bed and sat for a few moments. Soon the trembling in his arms stopped.

On the table was a tray of food and he realized he was beyond hungry. He stood up a little shakily, but soon he got his balance, made his way to the table, and sat down on a chair. On a plate was a pile of roast pork, potatoes, and some carrots. There was also a bowl with two towels inside. Sid picked up the fork and knife and cut a slice from the pork. Grease had congealed on the edges, but he didn't care as he put it into his mouth. It was cold, but it tasted better than anything he had ever eaten. He quickly ate everything on the plate and sat back with a satisfied sigh. He saw a mug of ale on the table and he drank it all.

Suddenly his stomach started to hurt, bubbling up inside. Sharp pains raced through him and he turned his head and vomited everything he had just eaten against the wall and floor.

Crowdal jumped up from his bed on the floor and lifted Sid's hair away from his face as he heaved. He soon finished and just sat there, letting his head hang low, feeling miserable. Crowdal stood beside him, a hand on his shoulder in support.

"Sid, are you all right?"

Sid sat back, wiping his mouth with the back of his hand. He looked glumly up at Crowdal and tried to smile, but it looked more like a grimace. "I've been better," he whispered. His throat burned and he felt like he had broken all the blood vessels around his eyes from throwing up all that food.

Crowdal squeezed his shoulder lightly. "Just sit back and get your breath." He reached over and poured more ale from the pitcher into a mug. He held the back of Sid's head and lifted the mug to his lips. "Drink slowly."

Sid tentatively sipped the ale. It soothed his throat and he felt a little better.

Crowdal put the mug on the table and picked up a small towel from the bowl and wiped Sid's face.

Sid just sat there, unable to help himself. He was so weak that when he threw up, it took every bit of energy he had left. He slumped in the chair. "I'm fine, Crowdal. Honestly, I just ate a little too fast I think."

Crowdal looked down at the empty plate. "Yeah, you could say that. There were two portions of meat on your plate, along with potatoes and carrots. You haven't eaten for three days. Your stomach can't take that much rich food." He looked at Sid compassionately. "Stay here. I'll go down and get you some soup and bread."

Sid could only nod weakly as he watched his friend quickly leave the room.

* * *

Crowdal went directly to the kitchen, where he found Carl cutting up onions, tears streaming down his cheeks. He looked up and saw Crowdal and smiled broadly, waving him in with a knife. "Welcome, my meatless friend. What can I get for you today?"

Crowdal smiled back. "Hello Carl, how's it going?"

Carl waved the knife as he spoke, "Apart from these stinking onions, it's a wonderful morning, so I can't complain." He winked at Crowdal. "Back for more apple pie, per chance?"

Crowdal laughed sincerely. "No, although maybe later I will take you up on that." He turned serious. "I have a sick friend upstairs who hasn't eaten in three days. Do you have some chicken soup and fresh bread by chance?"

The cook shook his head. "No, sorry, no chicken soup. But I do have some vegetable soup." He hurried over to a giant pot hanging over an open fire and lifted the lid.

The aroma of soup wafted over to Crowdal who smiled. "If you don't mind, could I grab a bowl of that too?"

Carl nodded as he picked up two large, wooden bowls. "Of course." He filled up the two bowls, steam rising up with each ladle he poured in. He took a tray from a stack against the wall and put the bowls on it. He then walked over to another table and picked up a round loaf of black, crusty bread. He broke it in half and put both halves on the tray. He added two wooden spoons and carried the tray over to Crowdal with a beaming smile on his face. "If you want more, come down for a refill."

Crowdal thanked him and left the kitchen with the tray. When he opened the door, he saw that Sid was sleeping, slumped over on the table. Crowdal pushed the door gently closed and walked over to the table, setting the tray down. The smell of soup caused Sid to sleepily open his eyes. He lifted his head from the table.

"I must have dozed a bit. Strange." He leaned forward and sniffed the steaming bowl. He grimaced. "I don't know if I can eat anything."

Crowdal sat down. "I know nothing looks good right now, but try and eat a few bites. It will do you good."

Sid picked up the spoon and dipped it into the bowl, blowing on the steaming broth. He carefully took a sip and swallowed. He sat for a few moments as if deciding whether he was going to be sick again, but the soup must have gone down well because Sid sipped the rest of the spoonful. "Hmm, good," he mumbled as he broke off a piece of bread and dipped it eagerly into the soup.

Crowdal put a hand on his arm. "Slow down. Eat slowly or you will throw this up, too."

Sid nodded and carefully put the small piece of dripping bread into his mouth. A drop of soup ran down his chin, which he wiped off with his hand.

Crowdal picked up his own spoon and they both ate soup and bread in silence except for the sounds of slurping and chewing. When they finished, Sid sat back and looked at Crowdal. "I'm beat. If you don't mind, I'm going to lay down for a bit."

Crowdal nodded, still concerned for his friend.

Sid stumbled wearily to the bed and lay back down. He was asleep almost immediately.

It was still early morning so Crowdal cleaned up the vomit with a towel, then brought the tray of dishes and dirty towel downstairs.

He then decided to step outside for some fresh air.

It was a beautiful, sunny day and almost warm. Crowdal couldn't believe that it had snowed just the night before. The streets were muddy and the snow was already mostly melted. He even felt comfortable in just his light tunic as he stood under 'The Pig n' Griddle' sign, watching all of the people going about their business. Every single person glared at him as they passed. Most walked out of their way to avoid him.

Crowdal ignored their stares and scowls. He was used to it.

He noticed that most of the people were dressed in ordinary clothing, lots of browns and blacks. But occasionally Crowdal saw a woman in a brightly colored dress being carried in a Kritle. On a warm day like this, their curtains were pulled back to let in the sun and fresh air. Crowdal stared openly at them and the beautiful women glared back at him as they passed by. Crowdal was bemused by their self-importance. He had no use for people like that. If they couldn't walk on their own two feet, then they shouldn't be outside.

Crowdal looked down the street the way he had come the day before. He remembered that the tobacco shop was only a few streets away. He looked back inside the tavern, debating if he should leave Sid alone, even for the short time it would take to get some tobacco. To be safe, he walked back inside and got Mr. Richards attention.

Mr. Richards walked over to Crowdal with a smile on his face, asking how he could help him.

"My friend is sleeping in our room. I would appreciate it if you kept him safe."

Mr. Richards nodded soberly. "Of course, sir, you have my guarantee." He reached into his pocket and pulled out a large key. "This is the only key to all of my rooms." He handed it to Crowdal. "Bring it back when you are done with it."

Crowdal was shocked. Few people trusted him and he didn't blame them. He was a Trith. So he held out his hand and accepted the key with a half bow of respect. "Thank you very much."

Mr. Richards nodded. "I have met a few Trith before and I must say I didn't like them much. But you, I like. Just keep the key safe and I'm happy to let you keep it."

Crowdal raised an eyebrow. "I have only met two other people who treated me with kindness and respect. One is in your kitchen and the other is upstairs right now. You are a rare man, Mr. Richards."

The old tavern owner just waved Crowdal away, although he had a twinkle in his eyes. "I'm just an old man who runs a tavern."

Crowdal smiled at him. "I think not, my friend."

He turned and went up the stairs to check on Sid. He was still sleeping, so he quietly shut the door and locked it again, testing the strength of the door. It was solid oak. He figured it would be fine to leave Sid alone for a short time during the middle of the day and he had the only two keys to the room. He walked back downstairs and nodded at Mr. Richards as he left the building.

Crowdal walked slowly down the street, enjoying the warm sun on his face and the fresh air in his lungs. It was great to be alive on days like this. He saw many stalls out this morning. Some sold cooked meats on sticks, most unrecognizable to Crowdal. Some sold ale, others cloth and footwear. He stopped at a stall that sold cloth.

A toothless old man sat in a chair, soaking in the sun and watching people walk by. When Crowdal stopped in front of him, he looked up, putting his hand up to block the sun.

The old man craned his neck slowly back to take in his height and whistled lightly. "My, my, you're a big'un."

Crowdal knelt down on one knee so the old man didn't have to strain his neck back so far.

The old man followed him with his head. "Thank ye, my neck is not used to moving that way. What can I do for ye?"

Crowdal pointed to his ripped tunic where the sword had connected. "I was wondering if you could repair this." He pointed to the other side, where the tunic was also ripped from the axe, "And this, also?"

The old man narrowed his eyes. "Come closer, my eyes aren't so good anymore." He leaned forward slightly.

Crowdal shuffled forward a little, holding his tunic out from his body slightly.

The old man peered at the rips. Then he looked suspiciously up at Crowdal. "How did you get these tears? They look like they were made from a bladed weapon. The edges are cut, not torn."

Crowdal sighed. The last thing he wanted was to frighten an old man because he was a Trith.

The old man quickly picked up a knife and brandished it, hissing, "Get out of here, Trith scum."

Crowdal sadly shook his head and stood up. He looked down on the old man. Even though he got this reaction from almost every person he saw, it bothered him sometimes still, especially from such an old man. Turning, Crowdal walked away from the stall, his back slightly stooped, his eyes to the ground. He walked like this until he smelled tobacco. He lifted his head and saw the tobacco store on his right. He breathed in deeply, enjoying the sweet scent, then turned and entered. A bell rang lightly.

The store was small and Crowdal had to bend his head slightly to avoid hitting the ceiling. A small desk stood in front of a curtained hallway. On three of the walls were clay jars of tobacco, each one labeled. On the last wall was a display of pipes. Some were plain wood, while others were ivory and carved with intricate designs.

Crowdal walked over to the jars on the wall to his left and started looking at the labels, hoping he could find some Uragon leaf. He had to bend at the waist to get low enough to read them. He saw many of good quality, like Yathentia, Rielen, Brassengrub, and Paigonian. They were certainly acceptable, but they weren't Uragon leaf. Crowdal scanned the second wall, with no luck. He saw a large barrel of leaf in the corner. That would be Pig leaf, the most common and inexpensive tobacco available. It tasted terrible, but was easy to get and cheap to buy.

He looked around, thinking maybe they kept the Uragon leaf, if they had it, locked away. He heard the curtains swish open and looked down to see a young woman in the doorway, holding the curtains with both hands. She stared at him, her eyes large and frightened. Her face turned splotchy and she started to tremble.

Crowdal started to smile when she yelped and let go of the curtains. He heard her feet as she ran screaming down a short hallway, and then slammed a door. He sighed, shook his head sadly, and left the store. So far the day was not one of his best. He might as well just go back to the tavern and spend time with his friend.

Outside, he turned and started back to the tavern, but only got about halfway down the street before a group of ten men came around the corner and stopped in front of him, legs apart, weapons in hand. They wore thick black leathers and black metal helmets that covered their entire faces except for their eyes. They all held huge swords with black-gloved hands. Crowdal saw no fear in their eyes. These were battle-hardened men, and Crowdal was now angry. He was tired of being treated like a criminal.

He rested his hand on his sword. "What can I do for you… gentlemen?" The last word came out sarcastically.

Nine hands gripped swords a little tighter, the eyes of the guards narrowed in anger.

But one man stepped forward. He was short, only coming up to Crowdal's waist. Crowdal stared down and in surprise realized the man was a Vringe, a race of people who were very short, but known to be very intelligent and gifted academics. But this man was heavily muscled and carried himself confidently and calmly. He stood with his legs apart, hand on his sword as he looked up fearlessly at Crowdal.

"We have received reports that you are threatening people and stealing from them."

Crowdal sighed, his anger disappearing. It was the same everywhere he went, and he didn't want a fight. Things would get too complicated. So he raised his hands and smiled. "You know I am a Trith?"

The small man nodded.

Crowdal went on. "Then you know that people are frightened of me just for what I am. They can't help it, it is their nature. I have not threatened anyone, nor have I stolen from anyone. I just wanted to get my tunic repaired and buy some tobacco and be on my way. Unfortunately, people did not take kindly to my presence, and for that I am sad."

The small man stared up at Crowdal in silence for a few moments, his gaze hard.

One of the men spoke harshly behind the Vringe, "What are you waiting for? Let's just kill the Trith."

The little man turned his head slightly and spat, then lowered his hand from his sword and spoke harshly. "No, we are not killers, and this Trith speaks the truth." He turned to the guard who spoke. "Trith do not lie. They don't have to because, in general, they can do anything they want." He raised his hand, signaling his men to be at ease. He then lifted his helmet from his head and held it under his left arm.

Crowdal held back his surprise. This Vringe was not an ordinary Vringe. His long hair was thin on top but hung to his shoulders. Whereas Vringe usually took care of themselves, and were even known to be vain, this man was the opposite. He had bad skin, his nose looked to have been broken many times, he had scars on his left cheek and chin that were long and white, and one eye was glazed over with milky whiteness.

The Vringe looked confidently up at Crowdal, daring him to say anything. When Crowdal didn't react in any way, the man finally spoke, his voice deep and gravely. "My name is Writhgarth, grid four captain, Yisk City Patrol."

Crowdal nodded to him in greeting and told him his name.

The captain motioned around him. "I know the people of this city and they are generally law abiding, good people. But as a people, they are sometimes thick-headed. A Trith in our city is rare and not something we like, but I also know that the people can overreact," he motioned his head to the side, "like my second-in-command. Now go about your business."

Crowdal knew a good man when he met one and this one was a strong leader who knew people well. One didn't rise to be captain of the city patrol on strength alone. He held out his hand and Writhgarth shook it, two intelligent men who respected each other. "Thank you, Captain, you are a good man. I'll be on my way and I give you my word that I will be no trouble to anyone, at least of my choosing."

Captain Writhgarth nodded and turned to his men. "Move out."

They all turned to leave except for the man who had spoken earlier. He was a large, good-looking man whose eyes were narrowed in anger as he stood his ground. Captain Writhgarth stopped and turned to him. "Willem, you heard my order."

Willem stared at Crowdal. "We can't just let this *Trith* go."

The captain of the city patrol walked back to Willem, his voice controlled anger. "You will obey my order or you will be relieved of duty."

Willem seethed, and Crowdal could see that he wanted a fight more than anything. The instability in the man's eyes told Crowdal that he was going to disobey his captain. Crowdal waited calmly. He didn't want a fight, but he also knew it could very well happen. He breathed slowly and deeply and watched Willem's eyes, waiting for the moment when the man committed to violence. It was a moment that Crowdal was trained to look for when he faced a man who wanted to kill. The eyes always gave a man away no matter how well trained they were.

Willem trembled with rage, his hands shaking with anticipation. Captain Writhgarth leaned toward the man, his eyes icy calm. "Willem, you make one move and you will never work in the patrol again. I will see to it personally; that is, if you live." He glanced at Crowdal, who stood calmly, acting bored so as not to incite the instable man to violence.

The Captain spit tobacco to his side. "Then again, I don't think there is much chance of that anyway. But I will have no fighting in my sector."

A drop of tobacco juice from Captain Writhgarth accidentally flew up and landed on Willem's cheek as he said the word 'sector'. It was unintentional but Willem pulled back like he had been struck. His face contorted in rage and he roared, quickly striking his captain across the jaw with a powerful right hook.

Captain Writhgarth, surprised by the sudden attack, took the hit full on the jaw and went down on his back. He wasn't hurt badly, but he was stunned.

Willem raised his sword, his eyes wild, and stabbed down at the captain's stomach with all his might, but his sword flew out of his hands with a loud clang. He stared down in confusion, then saw Crowdal's sword point next to his throat. It happened in the blink of an eye. He looked slowly up to Crowdal, his eyes smoldering with anger.

Captain Writhgarth stood up, pushing mud from his pants with one hand and rubbing his jaw with the other. He motioned with his head and two members of his patrol hurried forward and pinned Willem's arms behind his back.

Crowdal lowered his sword and in a smooth circular motion, returned it to the scabbard on his back. He sighed. "Well, that could have gone better."

Willem glared at Crowdal and Captain Writhgarth. "Let me go or I will have you killed Writhgarth. You have no idea what I'm capable..."

Captain Writhgarth punched Willem in the stomach so hard that the air rushed out of his lungs and he doubled over, his arms still pinned to his back.

"Now, that'll be enough of that. Take him back to headquarters and lock him up. I'll be back shortly."

The two men yanked Willem up and dragged him away, his feet making two marks in the mud, followed by the rest of his patrol.

Crowdal raised an eyebrow at the captain and smiled sadly. "You have made an enemy in that man."

Writhgarth chuckled and then turned serious. "Oh, don't worry, he won't be on the patrol again. He'll likely not see the light of day for a long time." He looked Crowdal directly in the eyes and raised his hand.

"Thank you. I've never seen anyone draw a sword as quickly as you did. I'm sure Willem will not soon forget this day."

Crowdal waved off the thank you. "Don't worry about it. I couldn't let him kill you."

Captain Writhgarth laughed. "Oh, I'm not thanking you for saving my life. I'm thanking you for not killing Willem."

Crowdal looked at the captain in confusion. "I'm not sure I understand."

Captain Writhgarth rubbed his jaw lightly as he spoke. "His mother is a powerful woman in the Council Of Eight. You saved me the trouble of explaining his death by a Trith, and why I didn't have you hung immediately. Now I can bring him up on charges of attacking the Captain of the guard with no provocation. It will be difficult, but we have witnesses." He looked up at Crowdal with a half smile. "But if I were you, I would leave town sooner rather than later. There are people on the patrol who like Willem. They may cause you trouble."

Crowdal nodded. "This is exactly what I wanted to avoid. I have a sick friend who is recuperating and needs a few more days rest. You have my word that we'll leave as soon as we can."

Captain Writhgarth grimaced and put his helmet back on. "Please do. Take care and keep that sword in the scabbard while you are here. I don't like dead bodies in my sector."

Crowdal put his head back and laughed.

It was an easy laugh and Captain Writhgarth smiled as he turned to go. But after a step, he turned back around. "Remember to keep your eyes open. If you have any trouble, don't hesitate to ask for me." He turned back and walked down the muddy street, mud still clinging to his back.

Crowdal sighed, the smile gone from his face. Not only did he not get any tobacco leaf, he had made an enemy. He looked down at his hands and clenched them into fists, then looked up and saw that people were staring at him. He scowled at them and they quickly turned away. He was so tired of people.

Crowdal started back to the tavern. It was warm out, yet the sounds of the city filled him with sadness.

The sign for The Pig n' Griddle swung back and forth in a light breeze as Crowdal approached. It felt like home to him, even after just one day. He walked through the door. Quite a few people were drinking in the room, even though it was only late morning. All conversation stopped and everyone turned to look at him as he stood in the doorway. He wasn't in the mood for this and yelled out, "What?"

As one, they all quickly turned back to their tables, although no one started talking again. Mr. Richards gave him an understanding look but didn't say anything.

Feeling stupid for losing his temper, he dropped the master key on the counter in front of Mr. Richards as he passed by, then put his head down and walked through the common room and climbed the stairs. When he got to his room he took out the room key and opened the door. He reached for his sword but didn't draw it when he saw Melinda sitting next to Sid, who was still asleep on the bed.

He stepped inside, bending his head to keep from bumping it on the doorframe, and shut the door.

Melinda looked calmly up at him but didn't stand up or move from the bed.

Chapter 23

Mrs. Wessmank lay on a cot in a small room and stared up at the rough stone ceiling. The light from the small fireplace was comforting and the warmth felt good on her old bones. She had been stuck in this chamber for the past two days and during that time she had received food and water but had no contact with anyone. Father Mansico was letting her know he was in full control. But she didn't care about being imprisoned. She had played this game her whole life and at this point she didn't really care what happened to her. Sidoro was all that mattered to her and by now he should be safely with the Anderom.

She suddenly sat up in the bed as the hairs on her arms stood up. It was time.

She stood up and walked slowly over to the same chair on which she had been carried in and sat down, back straight, hands in her lap, facing the door.

Father Mansico was coming, she could sense him. She also expected to see her sister Ailinora very soon. Mrs. Wessmank shivered from anticipation and trepidation. After almost a lifetime of sparring secretly and remotely with her sister, they were finally going to meet again. She had seen images of her sister through Maelon's eyes. But they were in black and white, as the Tulgin didn't see colors. She looked forward to seeing Ailinora again in person.

Mrs. Wessmank looked down at herself, then lifted her hands and turned them as she looked at the age spots and heavy wrinkles. She remembered a time when she had been young and full of energy. She sighed. That was a long time ago. It was unfortunate she had to fight her final battle at such an old age.

She looked up as the door opened. She saw a Haissan step in first, look around, and then hold the door open.

Father Mansico strode confidently into the room, smiling at her.

"Ah, Elenora, thank you for coming to see me. I am so glad that we finally get to meet." His eyes sparkled in the light of the fire as he stopped in front of her and smiled down at her. "I hope your time here has been comfortable."

Mrs. Wessmank looked up at Father Mansico. She had also seen his image many times through Maelon's eyes, many of those times as he beat the Tulgin almost to death. Father Mansico was a handsome man and the laugh lines along his eyes made him look kind. But she knew what kind of man he really was. While the act was convincing, through Maelon's eyes she had seen how he truly was. After so many years of playing the cat and mouse game with this man and Ailinora, she was in no mood to play any longer. So she scowled up at him. "Oh stop it, Mansico. Let's get this over with."

Father Mansico's smile faltered as he looked down at her. His eyes turned hard instantly. "If that is the way you want it, who am I to disappoint you?" He snapped his fingers and two Haissen immediately came through the door. Their brown robes made them look like they floated across the room. Father Mansico spoke without turning toward them, "Take her to my quarters." He turned without waiting for an answer and left the room.

The two Haissen came forward and picked up the chair. They carried her and the chair as easily as if it were empty. She held on to the arms and looked back at her coat and blanket lying on the small bed. She would be sorry to lose that coat. Her husband had made it for her shortly before he had died. She smiled as she thought of her husband's kind smile and mischievous eyes. She would join him soon.

Harry Wessmank had been a complex, intelligent man, and they'd had a good life together for more than sixty years. They had both endeavored against the Oblate and when she had a vision that the Aleph Null would be born in a small village named Orm-Mina, he had not hesitated to pick up and move there with her. They had started the simple tobacco shop, as was customary as an agent of Anderom, and they had lived in Orm-Mina for fifty years. They had a daughter very late in life, who they named Lorielle. Then Harry had been killed by lightning one summer evening, long before Sidoro had been born. He had never gotten the chance to meet his grandson. Mrs. Wessmank had lived with her daughter after that, carrying on without her Harry. But she could see his easy smile and mischievous eyes within her mind as clearly now as she could when he had been alive.

That was the problem with her visions. They had no timeframe. When she had seen the vision of Orm-Mina, and of the Aleph Null wielding Black Numbers, she had no idea how long she would have to wait before she found him. She could have found him in Orm-Mina as a young adult. But instead she had to wait sixty four years for him to be born. The fact that it was her daughter Lorielle who gave birth to him had been a shock to her. At the age of 35, Lorielle had met and married a man named Danicu and within a year she had given birth to a son, whom she named Sidoro. They had been so happy those first six years of his life but then one day Danicu had come to her with the news that Lorielle had died from an accidental fall and he had burned her body to ashes per her final wishes.

She had never been able to say goodbye to her daughter. But to make matters worse, Danicu, with whom she had never had a friendly relationship, had quickly cut her out of their lives, letting Sidoro see her only when they shopped in her store. Her eyes brimmed with tears at the memories she held of her grandson. After Lorielle had died, Sidoro had been so traumatized by his mother's death, and so young, that he had forgotten that Mrs. Wessmank was his grandmother; and per Danicu's demand, she was to never reveal to Sidoro that she was his grandmother. If she did, then Danicu would take him away and she would never see Sidoro again. So she had stayed silent, enjoying what little time she had gotten to spend with Sidoro as just the old woman who owned the tobacco shop.

Sidoro had been a happy young boy but when he was about eight years old, during the span of one summer, he had become pensive and angry at life. She had never been able to find out why or what had happened to him. Now he was a young man and the numbers were awakening inside of him more and more each day. She had tried her best to ensure he walked the right path, but she worried about the darkness inside of him. She wished she could be with him now to help guide him.

She wiped a small tear from her eye as she turned back forward. They passed through the door of the room and she was carried down the passageway. She was ready to face whatever would happen. She hoped that Sidoro was safe with the Anderom or would be with them soon. She knew the Anderom would help him. She had done her part. There was nothing more she could do for him. She could deal with her sister and Mansico. Even if she died tonight, she was satisfied she had done all she could have to keep her grandson safe.

She was carried back through the main hall of the House of Healing and saw the large double doors that led outside. Four Haissen guarded the doors from the inside.

The Haissen that carried her immediately turned down a white, marble-floored corridor. The Yisk House of Healing was a beautiful building befitting the fact that it was the center of all the Houses throughout the land.

The House of Healing had been around for thousands of years, an institution dedicated to humanity. A House existed in every large city and the healers were welcomed in every village, town, and city across the land. And Father Mansico was the Father of the House of Healing. As the highest-ranking member, only he held the title of Father.

Mrs. Wessmank shook her head sadly. It bothered her more than anything that he was seen as the Father of humanity throughout the land. He was the benefactor, the one man whom people held above all else. He was the representation of all that was good and no one knew how evil the man truly was.

They passed by one of the main guard rooms and she caught a brief glimpse of at least a dozen more Haissen inside, training in different methods of combat. They moved quickly on to a stairwell leading downward and descended to the next level. At the landing, she saw that the stairwell kept going downward and she was thankful they didn't continue in that direction. It smelled cold and musty down there. Instead, she was carried down a long hallway that had holding cells on each side. She grew angry. These rooms used to be healing rooms for patients but had now been converted to prison cells. She didn't look inside of them as she passed by. She couldn't bear it.

They soon entered another small guard room with a Haissan standing next to the opposite door. As they approached, the Haissan opened the door and Mrs. Wessmank found herself inside Father Mansico's private chambers. Why he took chambers down here, close by the cells, was a mystery to her. She had expected him to occupy the top floor. But she had no more time to ponder the question. Father Mansico sat at a desk directly in front of her. At his feet lay the Tulgin. It stared at her with bright eyes but didn't make a move. She cast her thoughts to him.

"*Soon, my child. Soon.*"

"*Of course, Mother.*"

Father Mansico looked up and motioned the Haissen to set her down and leave. After they closed the door behind her, Father Mansico casually slid something Mrs. Wessmank couldn't see into the drawer of his desk and locked it with a leaf key that dangled from a chain around his neck. He smiled and sat back in his chair, spreading his hands wide. "Welcome to my private chambers, Elenora."

Mrs. Wessmank ignored the usage of her first name. She instead looked around the room in curiosity. So this was where one of the most powerful men in the land spent his time. The room was perhaps twenty-five paces across and decorated simply but comfortably. A fireplace was nestled into the wall to her left and a large comfortable-looking bed was to her right. Other than Father Mansico's desk and the extra chair across from it, there was no other furniture in the room. Torches burned along the wall and cast the room in a warm, orange glow.

Mrs. Wessmank turned back to Father Mansico. "I've warned the boy about you, Mansico." She left off his title on purpose and as Father Mansico's eyes darkened, she went on with satisfaction. "You will not get him."

Father Mansico calmed himself and studied her wrinkled face, the two moles above her eyes, her plump body and her hands full of age spots. He spoke almost to himself, "It is hard to believe that you are the twin to Ailinora. Where she is beautiful, you are... ugly." He lifted his eyes to her face and shook his head in mock sadness. "Elenora, you poor thing. Do you really believe that the boy is safe from me? Why right now, at this very moment, he is lying in a tavern room not far from here. In fact, I am going to see him shortly."

Mrs. Wessmank eyed him coldly. He sat behind his desk, completely calm. She cast her senses out, letting them surround him.

She gasped and closed her eyes.

She had expected him to lie, but she knew without a doubt he told the truth. She could feel it. It was one of her talents, something she had always been able to do. No matter whom she spoke with, she could always tell when a lie was told. Father Mansico was telling the truth now. She sunk into her chair and hung her head. It was over. There was no way Sidoro could fight off Father Mansico and his Haissen. He didn't have that much control over his numbers yet.

Father Mansico chuckled, enjoying her defeat. "Yes, you know the truth Elenora, don't you? You are like your sister that way."

Mrs. Wessmank snapped her head up and the Father laughed outright. "Before I leave, perhaps you and your sister would like to spend some time together. It is the least I can do for you."

Mrs. Wessmank sat up straight in her chair. She would not let them know her defeat before she died. "You may find the boy to be stronger than you think, Mansico. I've known him his entire life. He is tough and I've prepared him for sixteen years to be everything you are not."

Father Mansico's laugh settled to a soft chuckle again. "Oh, Elenora, I know you think that, which is really precious." He calmly gazed at her then clucked his tongue. "It is amazing how, after twenty-five years of quietly sparring with you, of appreciating your intelligence, of watching you, of waiting to finally meet you, that I am really quite bored with you already."

He stood up. "I am going to see the boy now. When I return, I may even let you see him one last time before you and I have our final conversation." His voice turned hard and he whispered, "As it will be your final one, please try and think of something intelligent to say."

Mrs. Wessmank glared at him as he walked around the desk and approached her. She wanted nothing more than to slap that condescending smile off his face.

Father Mansico stopped next to her, put a hand on her shoulder, and smiled down at her. "You are on the wrong side of history. You always have been."

Mrs. Wessmank shrugged his hand from her shoulder. "Do not harm that boy."

He chuckled. "Oh, I have no intention of harming him. In fact, I will try my hardest to get him to see the folly of your misguided wisdom. He will join with me voluntarily my dear. It is much better that way."

Mrs. Wessmank grimaced up at him. "You may find that harder than you think."

They glared at each other for a few moments, neither one blinking. Finally a knock at the door broke the moment. Father Mansico called out, "Come." without looking away. He leaned down until his mouth was right next to her ear. He spoke so softly that the puff of his breath against her ear was as loud as his voice, "He has been *Ringed*."

Mrs. Wessmank pulled away and looked wildly up at him. "You lie!"

He smiled at her and stood up as the door opened. "Ah, my dear, just in time. I will leave you two now." He walked out of the room without another word.

Mrs. Wessmank's heart beat quickly and her breathing came in short gasps. It couldn't be true. They wouldn't have dared to *Ring* Sidoro. They would risk turning him into a monster. They risked his sanity. But deep inside, she knew Father Mansico told the truth. Oh poor Sidoro. If he were *Ringed*, that could only mean he had consummated the bond with the Korpor and all was lost. The Korpor owned him by now. She hung her head and closed her eyes. There was no use fighting them now. She looked forward to death. But before she died, she would confront her sister one last time.

Mrs. Wessmank turned in her chair and saw that her sister Ailinora stood by the door. They stared at each other for a long time, neither one speaking. Mrs. Wessmank saw that her sister's hair was white, but she had kept her figure amazingly well. They were not identical twins and it showed. Where Mrs. Wessmank had a mole over each eye, was plump, and walked slowly, Ailinora was thin and quite beautiful for her advanced age. At more than a hundred years old, she was still elegant where Mrs. Wessmank was grandmotherly. Ailinora always did have the looks.

"Hello, Ailinora."

"Hello, sister. You look old."

Mrs. Wessmank laughed. She motioned her head. "Please, Ailinora, come closer. My eyes aren't what they once were."

Ailinora glided across the room and pulled the chair out from Father Mansico's desk and sat down opposite her sister.

They looked at each other carefully for a few moments, each one captivated by the other.

Mrs. Wessmank smiled. "Has it really been eighty years since you left me?"

"I never left you. You abandoned me, Elenora, you and that man."

"Harry."

"I don't care what his name was. You left me."

Mrs. Wessmank looked down for a moment, then back up at her sister. "He was a good man."

Ailinora laughed sarcastically. "He was weak and stupid and followed you around like a little puppy dog."

"Let it go ,Ailinora. You chose your life, I chose mine."

Ailinora sat back and scowled. "Yes, I did. You and your husband foolishly joined with the Anderom."

Mrs. Wessmank shook her head. "And you joined with the Oblate. I could not follow you there."

Ailinora's eyes blazed. "Because you were weak, too, sister. The Oblate is power. Without it, the world would turn to chaos, society would fall apart."

"It pains me that you really believe in that rubbish. You have been brainwashed, Ailinora. Can't you see the truth? The Oblate will use the Aleph Null's powers for their own gain. The people of the land will suffer."

Ailinora looked at her sister with sympathy and barely-controlled contempt. "You always were the idealistic one. You believe that the Anderom is the key to saving people, when all they are is a group of misguided idiots. They make our society weak."

Mrs. Wessmank sighed. It was no use arguing with her sister. No matter what she said, no matter the argument she made, her sister would see her as weak. She rested her hands in her lap and shook her head. "I don't want to argue with you anymore."

Ailinora snorted. "Of course you don't. That is conflict and you hate conflict don't you? Well how about this. Father Mansico is going to take the boy this afternoon and bring him here."

Mrs. Wessmank rolled her eyes. "What good is he going to be to Mansico? His power of numbers is uncontrollable."

Ailinora's eyes glinted and she leaned forward. "He won't be Mansico's. He is mine. I am the Black Robe now."

Mrs. Wessmank's eyes widened slightly and she said in a bored voice. "So you got what you always wanted. Congratulations, I guess."

Angry her sister wasn't more impressed, Ailinora slapped her. "Show me some respect."

"Why? You are only the Black Robe. It means nothing to me."

Ailinora smirked. "We have the Black Numbers manuscript."

Mrs. Wessmank shrugged, already having been told this fact by her Tulgin. "So what, it won't do you any good. Sidoro will not be corrupted by you."

Ailinora sat back in her chair. "Think what you want Sister, but we have it and with it I will train the Aleph Null to fully manipulate Black

Numbers and he will obey my orders." Her eyes took on a feverish light.

Mrs. Wessmank cast out her senses but her sister was a void in front of her. She had never been able to read her, probably because they were twins. But she didn't need to read her now. She could see that her sister believed in her own sense of self-importance. She took a breath and calmed herself. "Do you really think you can control the Aleph Null? You are but a spark compared to the raging fire inside of that boy."

Ailinora shook her head. "You never could appreciate my power, or any power, for that matter. You only care about yourself, you selfish bitch. Well, unfortunately, people die. It is a sad fact. And if many people have to die before we learn to control the Aleph Null, so be it. It is a small price to pay for what that future will bring to us."

Mrs. Wessmank realized without a doubt that her sister was insane. The Oblate had warped her mind, destroyed who she once had been. A tear fell from her right eye. She wiped it away. She had been crying a lot lately.

Well she wouldn't cry for her sister. She had made her choices. There was nothing that could be done for her now. She reached around behind her and untied the blue apron. She bunched it up and tossed it to Ailinora. "You can have this back now. I wore it every day so we could be connected, even though we were enemies. While you thought you were watching me, I was also able to keep track of where you were."

Ailinora caught the blue apron and stared at her sister. "I should have known that you knew the apron was from me. I guess we spied on each other... call it a draw."

Mrs. Wessmank sighed. "Whatever the case, that is all in the past. Unfortunately, I have no further use for you now."

Her sister threw the apron to the floor in anger and shouted at her sister. "You have no use for me? You have it backwards, you twit. It is I who have no use for such a shriveled up shrew of a woman as yourself."

Mrs. Wessmank shook her head sadly.

Ailinora's face turned red and she screamed so loudly that spittle flew from her mouth, "I wield power greater than anyone in the entire land. I create and destroy kings. I control the House of Healing." She stopped, breathing hard. After a few moments, she was again in control of herself. "Yes. Me. Your sister is now the most powerful person in the land. And what has become of you? You are nothing more than a tobacco shop owner."

Mrs. Wessmank casually waved her hand. "Yes, you really are the most powerful person in the land. I grant you that. Congratulations again."

Her sister rolled her eyes. "Go ahead. Be sarcastic. I don't care. Mansico will bring your grandson to me today and soon I will control power beyond anything the world has ever seen." Her voice became silky smooth as she looked at her sister. "You could join with me. You are my sister. I will share the power with you."

Mrs. Wessmank lowered her head. After eighty years, she had hoped that things would go differently between her and her sister. But deep down, she was not surprised at how far Ailinora had fallen. It was time to end this.

"Now, Mother?"

"Yes, my child. It is time."

Mrs. Wessmank looked up at her sister. "I cannot tell you how saddened I am. But I know there is no saving you and I really must go." A tear fell from her eye. "Goodbye, Ailinora."

Ailinora looked at her sister quizzically. Then she felt a presence behind her and she slowly turned her head. Her eyes widened as the Tulgin gently clamped down on her neck with powerful jaws.

Maelon squeezed slowly until her neck snapped in his jaws.

The Black Robe died without making a sound.

Maelon slowly let go of the dead woman. She slumped against the chair, her eyes opened wide. The Tulgin padded over to Mrs. Wessmank, put his head into her lap, and looked up at her with sad eyes. Mrs. Wessmank's heart broke and she wrapped her arms around him and held him close. Maelon whined softly and leaned into her body.

The two of them held each other for a few moments longer until finally Mrs. Wessmank pulled away and kissed him gently between the eyes. She whispered out loud and it was the first time that she had spoken to him in her real voice since he had been a pup, "I am so sorry you had to do that, my child. It pained me to ask that of you."

Maelon whimpered again out loud, then spoke telepathically, his voice soft and full of love, *"Do not feel saddened, Mother. She would have enjoyed watching you die. I could see it in her mind."*

Mrs. Wessmank gently stroked the fur on his head. "Just the same, I am sorry."

Maelon leaned against her hand, his eyes closed. Finally he pulled away and looked up at her. *"You must leave this place now. Mansico will be back soon and he will kill you. I know a secret way out of here."*

Chapter 24

The Red Robe had just closed the door to his chambers when he felt a sharp jab of pain in his head. He closed his eyes and summoned his numbers. They immediately hovered in his mind, comforting him. Then he saw the rogue equation wrapped around his brain, pulsing white. He pulled the equation carefully away and forced it to hover directly in front of him. It was an easy task for him.

He smiled. Exactly as he had foreseen. It was the Black Robe's Modus Ponens, or Law of Detachment. The Modus Ponens affirmed the Black Robe's death. He had placed it secretly into her mind during the Fractional Ascension when she had been weakened by the ceremony. It had been simple to attach the equation to her psyche. She was not that gifted when it came to mathematics; she had ascended because the previous Black Robe had been so weak he was almost a walking dead man.

Tris studied the equation. It had an attractive point that pulled the last negative inputs from the Black Robe's vision and stuck them to the equation, showing him the last few moments of the Black Robe's life. He quickly separated the negative inputs and reassembled them into their own equations. In a matter of moments he clicked the last variable into the equation and it turned green.

A wavy image appeared in his mind, through which he could see an old, red-headed woman. Her voice seemed to come through a distorted spectrum of sound but he could make it out. He listened, then smiled. So the Aleph Null was in Yisk for sure, and would soon be within the hands of Father Mansico. Good. Then his smile faltered. He hadn't expected the Black Robe to die from the bite of the Tulgin. He had foreseen she would die at the hands of her sister. Strange. As he watched the vision go dim, he let the equation fade away.

Things were slightly off-center here, but he didn't let it worry him. He would just alter his plan a little bit. First, he would take the Black Robe position for himself, then he would have the Korpor take Sid from Mansico and bring him directly here.

"*Yes, I will bring him to you.*"

Tris nodded absently. "And don't mess it up this time."

The Korpor stepped forward from a dark corner of the room. "*As you wish. But I don't think you properly fear this boy. He... is trouble. I will have to incapacitate him for the whole journey.*"

"I don't care what you do with him, as long as he is still alive. That's all that matters. He has escaped you three times now. Once in his own room, once in the clearing when you *Ringed* him and should have had him under control, and now he has resisted your mind grab even though he has been *Ringed*. I will not tolerate failure like that again. Do I make myself clear?"

The Korpor cocked its head at the Red Robe, its massive blue eyes blinking in an odd staggered blink. "*Yes. I understand. But I wouldn't be quite so quick to order me around. You may have passed the Proofing last month, but you do not have the power of Black Numbers inside of you. You are not the Aleph Null. I let you look upon me out of professional respect.*"

Tris turned fully toward the Korpor. He casually sent numbers spinning into the Korpor's head and watched in satisfaction as the creature fell and writhed in pain on the stone floor.

"There is no professional respect, you are merely a tool that I use for my own purposes. Do I make myself understood?" He pulled his spinning numbers back.

The Korpor stopped writhing and slowly stood up, fear mixed with anger in its eyes. "*Yes... Master.*"

Tris nodded, already forgetting about the creature. "Now go and bring me Sid."

The Korpor disappeared into the darkness of the room. It used a secret passageway and was gone in moments.

Tris opened the main door to his chamber. His one Haissan stood at attention. As Red Robe, he was entitled to one Haissan. An honor that the Blue Robes did not get, but an insult to him. As Black Robe, he would control them all.

"Gather the Blue Robes."

The Haissan immediately did his bidding.

Tris closed the door and removed a black robe from his desk, then left the room.

It was time to become the Black Robe.

Chapter 25

Crowdal sat wearily down on a chair. He bent his head and stretched his neck before looking up at Melinda. "So, I'm wondering why you broke into my room. Normally, a locked door means stay out."

Melinda stood up and walked behind Crowdal. "I came to check on Sid. I knocked on the door but no one answered so I opened it to see if you two were all right." She reached under his hair and started rubbing his shoulders.

Crowdal sighed with pleasure and spoke quietly, "Well you could have asked Mr. Richards where I was. Ouch." He flinched when she pushed on a tight knot in his neck. "Not so hard, are you trying to hurt me?"

Melinda chuckled. "That depends on whether you like it." She moved her hands down his back, squeezing as she worked her way down. "I didn't want to bother Mr. Richards."

Crowdal leaned forward slightly, his eyes closed. "Gods, that feels good."

Melinda worked at a knot in his lower back. "I didn't know you worshipped. You don't seem the type."

Crowdal chuckled. "I don't worship anyone or anything. It's just a saying."

She worked her hands up his back to his neck again, her touch getting softer as she moved up closer behind him and pressed her breasts against his back. She moved her fingers up through his hair, massaging his scalp. She spoke in a low throaty voice, "Have you given any more thought to letting me take Sid to the House of Healing?"

Crowdal straightened up and pulled quickly away from her. He turned his head in an accusatory glare. "I can't believe I fell for that. You are good." He walked over to Sid and knelt down next to him to see how he was doing.

Melinda sighed. "Just my being in this room proves he isn't safe here. I told you not to leave him alone, yet less than a day later I come up here and find him by himself, sleeping. I think you have just proven that he needs to be at the House of Healing, not here."

Crowdal was about to retort when he realized she was right. He had let Sid down. But it wouldn't happen again. "I appreciate your concern for my friend's safety. But he will not be left alone again. I'll make sure of that."

Melinda started to protest, but he put his hand up. "I know you mean well, but that is the end of it."

She put her hands up in a placating gesture. "All right, if you won't let me take him to the House of Healing, then let me bring someone here."

"Absolutely not. I told you, I don't want him being examined by anyone else."

"Now you're just being stubborn. We're not going to hurt him. We just want to help."

Crowdal sighed, and after a few moments of silence said, "All right, fine, bring someone here. I'm sick and tired of people at the moment, so don't expect me to be civil to whomever you drag over here." He picked up a mug of water from the table and drank it in one long pull, wiping his mouth with the back of his hand.

Melinda studied him out of the corners of her eyes. Finally she walked over to him and put her hand on his arm. "I'm sorry, Crowdal. This is just really important to me. No one will harm Sid, I promise you that."

Crowdal saw the sincerity in her eyes. Despite her poor methods, he knew she meant well. She was a strong woman. He couldn't fault her. He nodded, a small smile on his lips. "You are a dangerous woman, miss Melinda. I have a feeling you could make a blind man give you his cane if you asked." He sat down again. "Just who do you plan to bring here, anyway?"

"My superior, Father Mansico Grigor. He is the head of the House of Healing." She saw his look of distrust. "What?"

Crowdal sniffed loudly. "I've not yet met anyone in a position of power that I trust."

Melinda angrily shot back, "Well you haven't met Father Mansico. He is a great man and I trust him with my life."

"Yeah, well I don't. I will be here the whole time and if he makes a wrong move, I will not be responsible for my actions."

Melinda crossed her arms and glared at him. "Why? Why do you hate a man you have not even met?"

Crowdal looked away for a moment, then looked directly into her eyes. "I've heard stories of how powerful men from one religion or another came to save the poor who have nothing in their lives but work and family." He waved his hand in disgust. "In the end, all they ever want is to enslave people with their morals and false ethics. Entire villages are torn apart, people fight each other in the name of this god or that god, whichever one happens to be popular at the time."

Melinda tapped her foot, her arms crossed as she listened to him. When he finished, she shook her head angrily. "You may be right about heathen religions, but the House of Healing has only one mission, and that is to help people, both physically and spiritually. Without us, the world would be a dark place."

Crowdal snorted. "Is that what you want to do for Sid? Heal him spiritually? Heal him with your god?" Melinda started to speak, but he put his hand up to stop her from talking. "Because if that is your game, we are not playing."

She glared at him for a few moments, then uncrossed her arms and paced across the room. "I'm not here to argue spirituality with you. I really don't care. I am a healer, that is my calling. To tell you the truth, the only way that I could be a healer was to join the House of Healing, which is run by the Father. He took me in. And I trust him."

The room was silent as they looked at each other for a long time. Finally Melinda walked over to Crowdal and took his hands. "Please, just trust me in this. I promise you, I will not let anything happen to Sid."

Crowdal looked into her dark eyes which were partially covered with her sandy brown hair, and he couldn't help himself from reaching out and pushing it away from her eyes.

She pulled away immediately and walked over to the bed.

Crowdal let his hand drop to his side. He watched her body sway inside the light cloth of the robe, the outline of her buttocks causing him to breathe shallowly.

Melinda felt Sid's forehead and spoke softly. "He is still slightly feverish. I am going to try and lower his temperature some." She reached into her bag, brought out a few leaves of spearmint, turned back to the table for the water pitcher and saw Crowdal staring at her. Embarrassed, Crowdal looked quickly away. She shook her head. "If you have nothing better to do than stare at my backside, then bring me that pitcher of water and bowl of towels."

Crowdal stood up and brought her the bowl with the towels in it, along with the pitcher of water.

She turned to him and removed the towels, then started crushing the spearmint leaves into the bowl. Then she took the pitcher of water and filled the bowl. The cool, refreshing scent of spearmint filled the room. She dipped the towel into the bowl and squeezed some of the water out before folding it and putting it on Sid's forehead.

She looked up at Crowdal. "Wet this towel at least five more times today. It will help to reduce the fever. I'll be back later with Father Mansico. Sid should be awake by then." She picked up her bag and left the room without another word, closing the door roughly behind her.

Crowdal looked at the door for a few moments, then down at his friend. He already looked like he was resting easier since she put the towel on his forehead. Crowdal walked over to the table, set the water and bowl down, then walked over to the door and locked it from the inside. He ran his fingers through his hair. The bed looked comfortable, even though it was nothing more than straw on the floor after it had collapsed under him earlier. He figured a nap would do him good, so he lay down on the straw and stared at the cracked ceiling.

He wasn't sure what he was getting himself into here. Sid was walking trouble. He could feel it. But Sid was also a friend, someone he trusted with his life. What Sid did in the flooded river was amazing, and not something Crowdal would ever forget. Not many people would try and save a Trith's life, much less risk their own life in the process. He was a good kid in some serious trouble. Crowdal would stick with him, there was no question.

His thoughts wandered to Melinda. He had never had feelings like this for a simple human woman. In the Trith circle he came from, he was an outcast simply because he liked to laugh. He liked to have fun, to explore. And mainly, he didn't like to fight, even though he was one of the best warriors the Trith elders had seen in generations. No proper Trith woman wanted anything to do with him. For the past year, as he traveled he had seen human women, but he had never spoken to one other than to get a room in a tavern or a meal. Most avoided him completely. But Melinda, she was different. She wasn't frightened of him. In fact, she treated him like an equal, not afraid to tell him he was wrong or to stand up to him. And she was beautiful, at least in his eyes. Those freckles on her nose, those dark eyes, and that wonderful behind. Who was he kidding, though? She was a healer, she was used to helping people. Why would she want anything to do with him, a Trith?

He didn't even realize his eyes were closed as thoughts and images of the healer faded away. Soon his breathing slowed and he started to snore.

Crowdal heard a loud knock on the door and jumped up from the floor before he even realized what he was doing, hitting his head on the ceiling. Rubbing his head, he looked over at Sid and was surprised to see him awake, smiling tiredly.

The knock came again, louder. Crowdal grumbled and walked over to unlock the door and open it. Outside he saw Melinda. Next to her stood an older man in a white robe.

Melinda nodded at Crowdal. "Crowdal, this is Father Mansico Grigor."

She stepped aside and Father Mansico stepped forward, raising his hand in greeting.

Crowdal looked at his hand and reluctantly shook it. "You are welcome here... Father."

Mansico smiled and the laugh lines in his face crinkled in genuine humor. "Thank you, Crowdal. Melinda here has told me of your reservations with men of healing."

Crowdal looked angrily at Melinda.

Mansico put up a hand. "Please don't be angry with Melinda. She only wants us to be friendly." He motioned his head toward the bed where Sid rested. "It is your friend who needs our help most, though."

Crowdal looked back at Sid and saw him rubbing his face and eyes, trying to wake up fully. The Father was right. He had to put aside his prejudices for now. It couldn't hurt to have the head healer look at his friend.

He turned back to Father Mansico and smiled slightly, then held the door open wider. "Of course, you are right. Please, come in."

Father Mansico and Melinda entered the room and Crowdal shut the door behind them. He then walked over to Sid and knelt down.

"Sid, these people are here to help you." He motioned to Melinda. "This is Melinda, a healer who helped you get better over the past two days. And this is Father Mansico Grigor, head of the House of Healing here in Yisk." Sid's eyes widened slightly and Crowdal looked at him questioningly, but Sid shook his head slightly for him to not ask any questions.

* * *

When Sid had first heard Father Mansico being introduced, he panicked. Father Mansico was the person whom his father had told him to find in Yisk. This man was an agent of the Oblate, like his father. Sid's heart started to beat faster. He had to get away from here! He shook his head slightly at Crowdal, hoping he would not ask any questions and was relieved when his friend nodded slightly in understanding.

Sid knew that he had to calm himself down. He couldn't let Father Mansico know that he knew who he was. So he made his face neutral and pretended he was sleepy. As the older man and young woman stepped to his bed, Crowdal turned and told the Father that Sid was still recovering and may not be of much help. Sid silently thanked his friend.

The woman looked familiar to him but he didn't know why. He seemed to remember her from somewhere. Images flashed quickly through his mind, images of a forest clearing, of floating, and of great pain and intense pleasure. He seemed to remember a woman taking care of him, of her soft touch on his forehead. But these images flashed too quickly for him to fully understand what had happened to him. All he knew was he was tired of being tired.

Melinda looked down at Sid. "Hello, Sid. It is good to see you awake. You've been asleep for two days. How do you feel?" She reached out and felt his forehead with the back of her hand. "Your fever is gone, which is good."

Sid looked into her dark eyes and couldn't help staring into them.

Melinda smiled, apparently used to men reacting this way around her. "Sid, do you feel well enough to talk for a bit? I have a friend who would like to speak with you for a while."

Sid nodded, a little embarrassed. "Sure, but could I have some water first?"

Crowdal poured a mug of water and gave it to Sid, who quickly drank all of it. He wiped his mouth and handed the mug back to Crowdal. "Thank you."

Father Mansico stepped forward, an easy-going smile on his face. He was short, shorter even than the woman Melinda. His hair was pure black, but the laugh lines on his face showed he was of middle age. His eyes glinted with good humor.

Father Mansico held out his hand and Sid weakly reached up to take it. "Hello, Sid, I appreciate you letting me visit with you like this." He looked deeply into Sid's eyes as he spoke.

Melinda pulled a chair over from the table so Father Mansico could sit.

Sid let go of his hand as Father Mansico sat down. He started to sit up and Crowdal hurried over to help him. Sid looked up at Crowdal and smiled in gratitude. He situated himself for a few moments. He was sore all over, probably from lying in bed for so long. Finally he felt about as comfortable as he was going to get and had avoided Father Mansico for as long as he could, so he looked up at the man. "Why are you here, exactly? I'm doing much better now. I don't need a healer."

Father Mansico smiled gently. "I'm not here to heal you Sid. Melinda did an excellent job of that. She is my best healer and you are lucky that she was here for you."

Melinda looked away, clearly happy with the remark.

Sid looked over at her and nodded. "Thank you, Melinda. I am not even sure what is wrong with me, but I'm grateful for your help."

She nodded back and told him he was welcome.

Sid scratched his scalp and his hair felt dirty and greasy. He could really use a bath. That could come later. First he had to get Father Mansico out of here without raising suspicion, then he needed to get dressed and out of the city as fast as he could before the Father found out who he was. So he continued trying to look confused as he asked, "So why are you here, then?"

Father Mansico sat back in his chair and crossed his legs, cupping his knee with both hands. "I'm here because you are a very special person, Sid. And I would like to chat with you for a bit, ask you some questions, get to know you."

Sid got a bad feeling. If Father Mansico already knew who he was, he was in big trouble.

Father Mansico narrowed his eyes, as if he knew that Sid was playing a game with him, so Sid quickly looked down at his hands and realized they were shaking, so he put them under the covers. He needed to buy some time to tell Crowdal about the Father and his own situation. He didn't have the strength to get out of here on his own. So he took a couple of quick breaths and called his numbers. They floated in his mind and calmed him down.

Only a few short moments passed before Sid looked back up at the Father, but he was already much calmer. He made his face look innocent and he shook his head. "I'm afraid you have me confused with someone else, sir. I'm just a kid from the country. I'm not special."

"Call me 'Father,' please." Father Mansico pointed to the edges of the sleeves of his robe, which were Red. "This means I am the head of the House of Healing. The head of the House of Healing is called 'Father.'" He smiled at Sid. "But you can call me 'Mansico' if you feel more comfortable."

"Thank you, Mansico. I'm afraid I am not familiar with city ways."

"That is quite all right, my boy." Father Mansico sat back and smiled. "Now, Melinda asked me to come here because you... hmm, how should I say this." He looked up at the ceiling as if thinking of the proper words, then looked down at Sid and shrugged his shoulders. "There is no easy way to say it so I'll just come out with it. You've had an encounter with the Korpor, yes?"

Sid opened his eyes wider, unable to keep himself from reacting. Angry with himself, he clamped down on his emotions. He was still tired from his ordeal and not in full control. He shook his head no again, hoping that Mansico would believe that he was really an ignorant country kid. "I'm sorry. I've no idea what you're talking about."

Father Mansico studied Sid, his eyes briefly narrowing again before he nodded reassuringly. "Of course, I understand. It is a difficult thing to talk about. Please understand I only want to help you. But I know already that you have had an encounter with the Korpor." He motioned to Crowdal and then to Melinda. "Your friend has seen it. In fact, he saved your life. If it weren't for him, you would be dead right now."

Sid looked up at Crowdal questioningly.

Crowdal nodded to him. "It's true, Sid. The Korpor captured you on the road. I was barely able to get you away from it, but not before it did something to you." He fell silent, not able to go on.

In a flash, Sid remembered everything that had happened, including the attack in the clearing, his mutilation, and the long battle he had in his mind. He had beaten the Korpor mentally, but if it weren't for Crowdal, he wouldn't be physically here now. He took a shaking breath. "Thank you, Crowdal. Again, I owe you, it seems."

Crowdal knelt next to his friend and put a hand on his shoulder. "Nonsense, we are even."

Sid took a deep breath to calm himself. They were far from even.

Crowdal smiled at him. "You are a tough kid, you know that?"

"Yeah right. I'm sitting here in bed after how many days unconscious. I'm really tough."

Crowdal winked. "More than you know, my friend." He motioned toward Father Mansico. "You don't have to answer this man's questions if you don't want to."

Sid shook his head. He had to play the next few moments very carefully. So he smiled at Crowdal. "No, that's all right. I don't mind the Father being here. What happened, exactly? I don't remember anything. Just... images." He paused, then continued, "Images that I don't really understand."

Sid glanced at Father Mansico, but Melinda cleared her throat. "It is fine Sid, I already told the Father everything I know."

Father Mansico nodded. "I think it's best if you try and tell us anything you know about the Korpor, anything you can remember about the past few days."

Sid looked down. He didn't want to say anything, but he knew he had to at least pretend that he trusted Mansico. He glanced up and saw Mansico waiting calmly, as if he had all the time in the world. Outwardly the man seemed kind and sincere about helping him. If Sid hadn't been warned by Mrs. Wessmank, he would have completely trusted the man.

He said a silent thank you to the old woman. She was probably making a pot of tea and sitting at her small table right now. He smiled slightly at the thought. He missed her.

He let out a slow breath and looked up at Father Mansico. "What do you want to know?"

Father Mansico gave him a friendly smile. "Good boy. I really just want to hear your story. For instance, had you seen the Korpor before two days ago?" He waited for Sid's answer.

Sid didn't say anything for a long time. No one said a word or made a sound. Finally he nodded that he had.

Father Mansico whispered, "Aleph Null" quietly to himself.

Sid's eyes grew wide momentarily and he pulled back slightly.

Father Mansico's face showed that he hadn't intended to whisper the words out loud. He quickly looked over at Melinda and Crowdal who looked at him quizzically. The Father coughed and then spoke in soft voice, "I'm sorry, please forgive me. I find this all very interesting, Sid."

Sid wanted nothing more than to be as far from this man as possible. He had to get the man out of here, even briefly. So he faked a long yawn, putting his hand to his mouth. "I'm sorry. I guess I'm still a little tired. Would you mind if we talked about this at another time?"

* * *

Father Mansico studied the young man in front of him, trying to decide how much he knew about what was happening. Of course, he had just been *Ringed*. He had a right to be exhausted. The young man looked directly at him with sleepy eyes, but he was too calm. He was hiding information. But now was not the time to try and take the boy. He needed to get back and gather a Murder, a killing group of thirteen Haissen, to accompany him back here, as he had not anticipated finding a Trith accompanying the boy. He had miscalculated, but he was not worried. He would be back quickly, his Haissen would dispatch the Trith, and the boy would be his—and then he would not be quite so polite.

Father Mansico smiled kindly at Sid and shook his head in understanding. "Of course. I'm sorry for keeping you for so long. Maybe we can talk again tomorrow?"

The boy nodded sleepily. "Sure, I would like that. I'm sorry, I just feel so tired."

Father Mansico stood up and smiled kindly down at him. "You get some rest and I'll stop by tomorrow morning. If you need anything, just ask Melinda and she will help you. Now I will take my leave. Rest easy, my son."

The boy smiled weakly, then closed his eyes, falling asleep almost instantly.

Father Mansico turned to Crowdal. "You take care of your friend. He has been through quite an ordeal."

Crowdal nodded and stuck out his hand. "Thank you, Father. Your kindness is appreciated."

Father Mansico smiled back then disengaged his hand and turned to Melinda. "Could I have a word with you in the hall?"

Melinda looked at him strangely for a moment, then nodded and followed him out of the room.

He changed his demeanor instantly, looking intensely at her. "It is important they stay here until I return. Do not let the boy leave and do not let anyone into the room until I return. Do you understand?"

Melinda looked down briefly, then nodded that she understood. Father Mansico continued. "I have a friend out by the front door who will follow them if you can't keep them here." He stared directly into her eyes. "Melinda, I am going to bring the boy to the House of Healing for his own safety, even if he doesn't understand why yet. He is in danger and only we can protect him." He took her hand in his. "I will not forget your service to me."

Melinda nodded, keeping her head down. "Yes, Father. Thank you."

Father Mansico turned and left quickly, his robes flowing behind him, softly berating himself for not bring a Murder of Haissen with him from the beginning. Even one Haissan would have been enough. But he hadn't, because he had not wanted to scare the boy and risk him using his power of numbers.

He almost ran back to the House of Healing.

* * *

Melinda watched Father Mansico until he disappeared down the stairs, then she re-entered the room.

Crowdal glanced at her as she entered and they stared at each other in silence for a few moments. Finally Crowdal said what he couldn't ignore, "Melinda, I honestly don't trust that man."

Melinda looked down. She had spent the past five years with Father Mansico at the House of Healing. She had dedicated her life to the House of Healing and before this moment she would have given her own life for the Father. But now she wasn't so sure.

Father Mansico was normally a quiet man, a man who always had a ready smile for everyone. But he had seemed anxious and intense while he had been here and she could feel that he had been lying to everyone. She glanced at Crowdal and then looked down. She trusted the Trith at this moment more than she did the Father and that scared her more than anything.

She mumbled quietly, "I don't know what to say. I have never seen Father Mansico act like this before. I don't know what is going on."

They both jumped when Sid opened his eyes and spoke in a calm voice, "I do. He is the highest-level agent for an evil and secret organization called the Oblate. He is in league with the Korpor and wants to bring me as a prisoner to their headquarters in Undaluag." He swung his legs over the edge of the bed. "I am not going to give him the chance because I'm getting out of here right now."

Chapter 26

Crowdal and Melinda stared at Sid in alarm, then Crowdal chuckled softly. "You never cease to surprise me Sid." He looked at Melinda. "And he is right. I think it is best we leave right now."

Melinda's voice shook slightly, "I can't believe I'm saying this, but you really do need to leave here immediately. I've never seen the Father act like that before and he frightens me. He will be back soon and he won't be alone. Lately he has been surrounding himself with evil creatures called Haissen. He is going to force you to go to the House of Healing."

Sid nodded respectfully to her. "Thank you for the warning, it means a lot to me." He quickly swung the blankets back, lifted his legs from the bed, and stood up. He swayed for a moment, then steadied himself. He looked down and realized he was naked. He blushed and quickly reached for his trousers, covering himself.

Melinda scowled at him. "Oh stop it. I've seen more naked men than I can count and I've seen you already."

Sid turned around just the same as he got dressed.

Crowdal chuckled, and Sid shot him a look over his shoulder, daring him to say anything.

Melinda just sighed.

Sid tied his trousers, then found his tunic and pulled it on, followed by his socks and boots. He stretched his back, hearing the bones crack. Spending so much time in bed was not something he wanted to do again. He turned to Crowdal. "I'm ready to go now."

Crowdal smiled at Sid. "I believe you. But I have to get us some food, settle the bill, and get rid of this woman before we can go."

Melinda stepped back. "Did you just say 'get rid of this woman'?"

Crowdal smiled innocently at her. "That is what you are, isn't it?"

Melinda shot him an angry look and raised her hands in frustration. "Just hurry, you only have a short amount of time before Father Mansico returns."

Crowdal nodded, all trace of joking gone.

Pushing hair behind her ear, Melinda squared her shoulders and jutted her chin out. "When you leave, don't exit the front door. Father Mansico has someone just outside the tavern to keep you here until he returns. You must find a secret way out of here."

Crowdal sighed. "Great. This just keeps getting better." He turned to Sid. "Get your pack ready. I'll be right back." He then glanced at Melinda. "Thank you Melinda, I'll see if there is another way out of here."

Crowdal quickly left the room and went downstairs. He got Mr. Richard's attention and settled the bill, including extra for food from the kitchen. The tavern owner was sorry to see him leave, but didn't ask any questions. It was none of his business.

As Crowdal turned to leave, he turned back to the tavern owner. "Mr. Richards, if anyone asks about us after we leave, can you tell them that we skipped out without paying for the room and you never saw us leave?"

Mr. Richards looked quizzically at Crowdal, but quickly shook his head. "Of course, sir. I never saw you leave."

Crowdal smiled. No sense in getting him caught up in any of this. "Thank you."

Crowdal stopped by the kitchen next.

Carl looked up as he entered the room and smiled broadly at him. "Good timing, I have a vegetable pie I made just for you. It just came out of the oven."

Crowdal sniffed the air. "Ah, my friend, you make it hard to leave, but alas, I have to go now."

Carl's face fell. "I'll be sad to see you go. Please tell me you have time to eat my pie though. You need a good hot meal in your belly before traveling."

Looking at the pie steaming on the table, Crowdal shook his head sorrowfully. "I'm sorry, Carl, but we have to leave now. And believe me, it pains me more than you can know that I will be leaving that pie behind." He eyed it hungrily. "But I have another favor to ask."

Carl wiped his hands on a white apron. "Of course, anything."

Crowdal smiled. "First, could you prepare a sack of travel food for two people?"

Carl nodded and immediately started gathering food as Crowdal continued. "Second, is there a way out of here where no one will see us leave?"

Carl smiled as he wrapped a fresh loaf of bread into a towel. "Ah, one of those kinds of departures. I like those kind." He motioned toward the back of the kitchen. "Use the delivery entrance. It exits to a small alley. No one is ever out there."

Crowdal quickly went to the door and opened it a crack to peer out. The way was clear. He came back to Carl and shook his hand. "Thank you, Carl. You are a good man."

"Any time."

Crowdal nodded, "I will be right back," then turned and left the kitchen, running up the stairs five at a time and entered their room in a hurry. Sid was rearranging some items in his bag and Melinda was sitting at the table, looking troubled and tapping her fingers. She looked up as Crowdal entered but didn't say anything.

Crowdal smiled sadly at her, but quickly turned his attention to Sid. "Are you sure you have the strength to travel? You've been in bed for days."

Sid finished pushing his winter coat deeper into the pack. "I will likely be a bit slow, but I'll feel better out on the road." He pushed hard on the coat and pulled the ties tightly until the pack was closed, then tied it shut and set it on the floor.

Crowdal quickly got his own pack ready, which didn't take long. He had never really unpacked.

Soon they were finished, looking around the room to make sure they had everything.

Melinda stood up and looked at them both. "I will stall Father Mansico for as long as I can, but don't expect more than a few moments head start."

Crowdal crossed to her and took her hands, but she pulled them from his grasp immediately. He stood there, not sure what to say. Finally he just said the only thing he could think of, "Come with us."

Melinda looked at him, astonished. "Are you kidding?" She shook her head. "Number one, I barely know you. And number two, this is my life here. I didn't work five years at the House of Healing, killing myself to be the number one healer, just to walk away from it all." She saw that he was sincere and embarrassed, so she quieted her voice, "It was... nice of you to ask, but no thanks."

Crowdal nodded and turned to Sid. "Time we got going." He turned back to Melinda, unsure what to say to her.

She saw his hesitation, so she crossed to him and reached up on her tippy toes. Crowdal bent down until she was able to wrap her arms around his neck. She kissed him lightly on the lips, then let go.

Crowdal was stunned as he stood back up to his full height, his head spinning slightly. He heard Sid chuckle next to him and quickly composed himself.

Sid nodded to Melinda and walked to the door.

Crowdal winked at her, then turned and followed Sid out of the room. They walked down the stairs, Crowdal holding Sid lightly as he unsteadily took the steps one at a time. They entered the kitchen, where Carl had two large sacks sitting on the floor.

Carl smiled at the two of them. "I packed a variety of food." He looked up at Crowdal, "and I left the meat out of your sack. Come back sometime and I'll gladly make another vegetable pie for you."

Crowdal stepped forward and clasped the cook on the shoulder. "That, I can promise you. I look forward to it." He picked up both sacks and was able to fit them into his own large pack. He didn't want

Sid to carry any more than he had to for now. "Thank you, Carl. And please do me a favor. You never saw us leave here, all right?"

The cook smiled and winked, then turned away and started whistling as he carved a hunk of meat from a fully-skinned cow hanging from a large hook attached to the ceiling.

Sid and Crowdal carefully opened the door and found themselves in a small alley, wet with mud and stinking like garbage and rotting food. It was filled with shadows even though it was the middle of the day. To the left they saw the busy street at the front of the building and to their right the alley stretched away, fading into darkness.

Sid looked into the darkness and shuddered. "I say we take the street."

Crowdal shook his head and whispered. "I wish we could, but you know we can't, not with the spy out there." He turned toward the darkness of the alley. "Come on, you're not afraid of the dark, are you?"

Sid punched him in the arm and started down the alley.

They followed the narrow, twisting alley for a few hundred paces until they came to a busy street quite far from the tavern. The sunlight hurt their eyes after the darkness of the alley. Sid inhaled deeply, lifting his face to the sun and closing his eyes. He sighed. "It feels like a long time since I felt warm sunlight on my face."

Crowdal waited patiently for a few moments until Sid lowered his head and looked up apologetically at him. "So which way do we go? I have no idea how we even got here."

Crowdal pointed. "We came from that way." He leaned his head to their left. "So I think we should go that way." He looked down at Sid as they started walking along the street. "You know, you never told me why you are traveling east."

Sid's remained quiet for a few paces and Crowdal looked down at the young man. "Listen, you don't have to tell me. I was just curious. Where a man goes is his own business."

Sid scratched behind his ear and looked earnestly up at Crowdal. "I'll tell you, but I just realized I never really thanked you."

Crowdal raised a bushy eyebrow. "For what?"

Sid looked down. "For everything. For being my... friend."

Crowdal realized Sid probably didn't say something like that lightly. 'They were two strange people,' he thought. Neither one of them had probably had a real friend before. He put his hand on Sid's shoulder and spoke seriously for once, "You are the first person who has ever said that to me, you know that?"

Sid angrily pushed his hand away. "You don't have to make fun of me. I'm sorry I said anything." He walked faster to get ahead of Crowdal.

Crowdal hurried to catch up.

Sid looked up at Crowdal out of the corner of his eye but didn't stop.

"Sid, I will tell you this now. I don't know anyone right now I would call a friend."

Sid laughed sarcastically. "Yeah, right. You are the most outgoing person I've ever met. Everyone likes you."

It was Crowdal's turn to laugh. He glanced around before looking back at Sid. "Do you know what I am?"

Sid shook his head. "I've no idea what you are talking about."

Crowdal stood up tall. "I am a Trith."

When Sid didn't react, Crowdal raised an eyebrow. In disbelief he asked, "You've never heard of the Trith before?"

Sid shook his head. "No, why? Should I have?"

Crowdal didn't know what to say. That explained why Sid didn't treat him like everyone else treated him. "Sid, look around you." He spread his hand out.

Sid looked around at all the people on the street then back up at Crowdal questioningly. "So? What?"

"Look closely at the people."

Sid turned his head as he walked and after a few moments he stiffened as he looked about him. In a quiet voice, he said, "They are all either angry or afraid when they look at you." He stopped and looked up at Crowdal. "Why? Why do they all act that way?"

"Because I am a Trith. It is that simple."

"I don't get it. What is a Trith?"

"Ah, now that is the big question." Crowdal took a deep breath. "We are a war race. Plain and simple. We do nothing well except fight and kill. Every single Trith is the same. We don't laugh, we don't cry, and we don't back away from a fight. We fight and kill, fight and kill..." He trailed off, looking into the distance at nothing in particular.

Sid looked confused. "Crowdal, you are the nicest person I've ever met. I don't get it. Why do you talk like that about your people?"

Crowdal spun angrily on Sid. "They are not my people. I am no longer Trith." He softened his voice, ashamed for reacting that way to Sid. "Remember a few days ago I told you I was cast out of my Circle? Well, as I travelled, I came to realize I was sent out into society so I would know there is no place for me here and I would come back home a true Trith." He looked at Sid, his eyes haunted. "I am ashamed of being Trith."

They came to a busy cross street and had to stop for a large team of horses pulling a massive hay wagon. The people that waited next to them stepped a few paces away, looking at Crowdal out of the corners of their eyes.

Sid reached up and touched Crowdal on the arm. "I'm sorry, I didn't know." He looked around at the hate and fear on the people's faces and pointed at them. "Who cares what these idiots think? They are worthless and don't deserve your kindness or sadness." Some of the people glared at him, but none dared say anything. Sid glared back at them.

Crowdal smiled down at Sid. He had never known how important it was to hear someone say that until just now. "Thank you, Sid."

Sid punched him in the arm. "What are friends for?"

Crowdal laughed, rubbing his arm.

They walked in silence for a while. Sid glanced at Crowdal a few times, and finally said, "I have to go to Undaluag."

"Hmm... I've never been there before. Do you mind if I tag along?"

Sid looked at him. "I would love to have you go with me, but why would you do that for me?"

Crowdal glanced down at him. "Well, I guess because I've got nowhere I need to be. I'm just traveling. I don't have a home to go back to so who knows, maybe someday I'll find somewhere worth staying for more than a few days. And who's going to look out for you when you stub a toe or something?" He smiled down at Sid.

Sid opened his mouth to reply when he suddenly turned his head and went pale, slowing down his pace. Crowdal immediately looked around for the threat.

"Sid, what is the matter?"

* * *

Out of the corner of his eye, Sid saw a flash of color and heard a tinkling sound. He immediately focused on a woman walking toward them, her coat shifting colors in the sunlight. Sid's heart started to beat quickly at the sight of the Fahrin Druin.

Crowdal asked him what the matter was, but Sid didn't answer. He had half turned his head away and was trying to shrink into himself, hoping that the assassin didn't notice him.

The Fahrin Druin whistled as she approached and Sid began to hope she would just pass by, but the woman stopped abruptly a few paces in front of him and cocked her head to stare at him, her whistle fading away. She held up a small piece of parchment and looked at it briefly, then back up at him.

Sid picked up his pace and put his head down, but as he approached her, the Fahrin Druin grabbed his arm, spinning him around to face her. She then grabbed his hair and pulled hard, forcing him to look directly at her.

Crowdal grabbed the Fahrin Druin's arm and when she turned to glare at him, he started squeezing. "Why don't you let my friend go and we will be on our way."

The woman grimaced from the pain and finally released Sid's hair. She pulled her arm from Crowdal's grip and rasped at him, "Stay out of this, Trith, it is between the boy and me."

"I can't do that."

The Fahrin Druin narrowed her eyes and put up her hands in a conciliatory gesture, but as she did, she released a cloud of powder into Crowdal's eyes.

Crowdal's eyes immediately began watering. He stepped back and tried to wipe the powder away. He swayed and fell to his knees, then to his side, unconscious.

Sid watched Crowdal fall and fear gripped him as he turned to the Fahrin Druin, who smiled and patted her hand against her coat to wipe away any traces of the powder.

"Hmm... not so big now is he?" She stepped forward and grabbed Sid's collar. "How fortuitous to find you just walking down the street like this."

Sid tried to pull away but couldn't. "Why are you doing this? I've never done anything to you."

The Fahrin Druin dragged Sid by the collar into a side alley where they wouldn't be seen and threw him against the wet, stone wall of a building. She had short, blonde hair and brown eyes and was very beautiful, which only added to Sid's confusion. She was nothing like the first Fahrin Druin he had run into back at Mistress Riana's tavern.

She leaned in close to his face. "This isn't personal, it's just business." She looked him up and down, disappointment on her face. "So you are the Aleph Null?" She snorted. "All this work to find you, hundreds of us combing the cities and countryside, all my anxiety over the idea of being the one to actually come up against you, and what do I find? A skinny little kid."

Sid struggled but she pinned him securely against the wall by his throat. She was much stronger than he expected. He heard the tinkling sound come from within the her coat, loud to him now that they were so close. He gave up struggling and gasped, "What do you... want from... me?"

"Want? Why, I want nothing from you. I am just going to kill you."

Sid breathed out the name 'Fahrin Druin.'

The woman cocked her head and smiled, enjoying the look of fear in his eyes. "Yes, that is what I am."

"But why are you doing this to me?"

"We are hunters, pure and simple. It is our belief that the Aleph Null will destroy the world, for no one can control so much power and not use it for evil. Believe me, you will not be the first to die from my hand, so don't feel badly."

Sid closed his eyes. The woman's breath stunk like dried fish, and the skin on her hands was rough and dry where she gripped Sid's throat. He grew angry. Everyone seemed to want him dead or enslaved. He had done nothing to anyone. His anger intensified, and almost without thinking, he closed his eyes and let his numbers appear in his mind. He concentrated on the hand that gripped his neck and built a wall of numbers as close to his body as he could. He had no idea what would happen, but it was the only thing he could think to do.

Sid heard a scream and opened his eyes. The woman stood in front of him holding her left hand to her right elbow, which was spurting blood that ran thickly down the wall of numbers to the ground.

Sid widened his eyes as he looked down at his own neck. The woman's hand still gripped him, but the arm was severed cleanly at the elbow. He pried the fingers from his neck and dropped the hand and forearm to the ground.

The Fahrin Druin's face turned white as she fell to her knees, holding her bloody stump.

Sid released his wall of numbers, but he didn't give the woman a chance to do anything else. With a scream of anger, he kicked her in the face as hard as he could.

The Fahrin Druin flew backward, hitting her head against the opposite wall of the alley, then slid to the ground unconscious.

Breathing hard, Sid looked down at the woman. He didn't know if she was dead and he wasn't going to wait around to find out. But as he turned to leave, he stopped and faced her again, curiosity getting the better of him. He walked forward and pulled the colorful jacket open. Inside, tied together, were dozens of small glass jars, each closed with cork stoppers. Contained within the jars were different colored liquids and powders. Sid shook them gently and they made a tinkling sound. It all made perfect sense to him now. The Fahrin Druin used chemistry as their main weapon. Quite ingenious.

He heard Crowdal yell his name, so he quickly ran to the end of the alley.

His friend was sitting up and wiping his eyes with his shirt. "Sid. Sid, where are you? Are you all right?"

Sid touched Crowdal's shoulder. "I'm fine." The people on the street had crossed to the other side, anxious to avoid an angry Trith.

Crowdal blinked up at Sid, his face streaked with the white powder. "What happened? Where is the woman who attacked you?"

"I took care of her. She won't bother us again. Hold on a moment." Sid pulled his flask of water out and removed the stopper. "I'm going to splash water into your eyes. It will get rid of the powder. Ready? One, two, three!" He flung water into Crowdal's eyes until the powder looked to be washed away.

Crowdal used the inside of his shirt to dry them and struggled to his feet, a little uncertain at first with his balance. But soon he was stable and looked around, blinking his eyes. "Thank you." He studied Sid. "What do you mean you took care of her? Where is she?"

Sid pointed. "In the alley."

Crowdal immediately lurched around the corner and came to an abrupt halt at the sight in front of him. The woman leaned unconscious against the wall, her right arm missing at the elbow and still pumping blood onto the ground. "Good gods, Sid. What did you do?"

Sid came up behind him. "I'm not sure. I can't explain it."

Crowdal looked down at Sid, a strange look on his face. "Remind me to never get on your bad side. Come on, let's wrap her arm up before she bleeds to death."

They ripped a part of the woman's colorful jacket and tied a knot around her arm, stopping the flow of blood.

Crowdal stood up and looked down at the unconscious form. He still couldn't believe that Sid had done that to the woman. "That's all we can do for her. Come on, let's go before someone finds us with her. We don't want to get picked up by the city patrol."

Sid took one last look at the woman and then followed Crowdal out of the alley.

Crowdal leaned down to Sid and spoke quietly, "Go up ahead and tell someone you saw an injured woman in that alley. It will be easier without me there."

Sid nodded and sped up. He saw a respectable looking man walking toward him, so he stopped him and told him about the injured woman. The man tried to ask questions, but Sid continued on.

Crowdal caught up with Sid. "Good man. With luck, that woman will live."

Almost in tears, Sid looked up at Crowdal. "She tried to kill me, Crowdal. I had to fight back. I had no choice."

Crowdal put a hand on Sid's shoulder. "Don't feel bad for what you did. It's a tough world. You did what you had to do. And remember, you didn't kill her."

Sid nodded, although he still felt badly for what he had done.

They walked on in silence for a few city blocks when they saw a large building loom up on their right. Where before the street was lined with two-story buildings and small stalls, now the street opened up to a large courtyard filled with trees and bushes and a path winding through them. The building was at least four stories tall and had a round roof. Two large doors marked the entrance, guarded by two figures dressed in simple robes. Sid didn't see any weapons on them, but he instinctively knew that they were deadly. He saw Crowdal speed up slightly. Sid caught up to him. "What is it? What's wrong?"

Crowdal just shook his head, not talking. Soon they were past the building and Crowdal slowed his walk. "That was the House of Healing. Although I've never seen a House of Healing guarded before. We got very lucky."

Sid looked back over his shoulder and could just make out the two robed guards standing by the door. He noticed that no people went in and out of the building. He was just about to turn back when he saw a group of robed guards with Father Mansico in the lead, heading for the House of Healing. Two of the robed guards were dragging someone. Sid squinted, then gasped. It was Melinda! She was struggling but it did no good. One guard struck her with the back of his hand and she went limp.

Sid turned away quickly and pulled Crowdal into a side alley, hoping they hadn't been seen.

Catching his balance, Crowdal asked, "What's wrong?"

Sid pointed back behind them.

Crowdal peeked around the corner and then turned back to Sid. "What? Is someone following us?"

Sid looked up at Crowdal, his eyes fearful. "I just saw Melinda being dragged by two of those guards, with Father Mansico leading them."

Crowdal looked sharply at him. "Are you sure it was Melinda?"

Sid nodded. "It was her. She was struggling, but one of those guys hit her and she went limp." He carefully peeked around the corner. "They must have brought her inside the House of Healing already. What are we going to do? We can't let them harm her. It is our fault she was taken."

Crowdal slammed his hand against the brick wall. "I can't believe they took her. This is not good."

"What are they going to do to her?"

"I don't know, but I don't think it will be anything good. I have to get her out of there."

Sid nodded. "So, what are we going to do?"

Crowdal shook his head. "Sorry Sid, but you are too weak to be of any good in this. And don't forget, you are the one they want. If you walk in there, it would be like walking into a nest of Ryppers."

Sid started to protest but Crowdal just looked at him with a sad look. "I know you would go into that nest. But I can't look after you and still find Melinda." He knelt down so they were eye-to-eye. "Stay here. I'll be back as soon as I can."

Sid wanted to help, but he knew Crowdal was right. In his weakened condition, he was no good to anyone, even if he did have his numbers. What good would building a numbered wall do, like he had done so often? He couldn't fight Father Mansico with a wall of numbers. He finally nodded. "All right, I'll stay here. But be careful."

Crowdal stood up and smiled. "This is just a bit of fun. I've been a little bored lately."

Sid chuckled. "You have the strangest sense of fun." He then turned serious. "Good luck and be careful."

Crowdal nodded and quickly stepped out of the alleyway and disappeared around the corner.

Chapter 27

Crowdal slowed his pace and whistled, acting like he was just out for a nice day's walk. He soon came to the House of Healing and saw the two robed guards standing at the doors. He kept walking, not looking directly at them, until he had fully passed the building. There was no way to get in the front doors but he knew there was always another way into a building. One just had to find it.

He casually glanced at the rooftops of the buildings next to the House of Healing. They were some distance away and of no help. He looked between them and saw that there was nothing but open space for at least twenty paces all the way around the building. There were five large windows in the front and five more along the side that he could see. He soon came to a narrow alleyway and looked casually around before turning into it.

The alley was similar to the one behind the tavern: narrow, dirty, and damp. He walked down it, the shadows getting thicker the further he went. He came to an even smaller cross alleyway and looked to his left. He saw a shaft of light not far away where it opened up facing the House of Healing. Crowdal crept down the narrow space until he could get a good look at the building. The windows were high up on the building, ornately carved, and contained multi-colored glass. He saw no way in unless he climbed the wall. It was brick so it was possible, but it would leave him unarmed and in plain view. He would come back here if he found no better way in. He turned and walked back to the main alleyway and turned left, continuing down it.

After what seemed like a long way, he came to another cross alleyway identical to the last one he had checked out. He could see it opened to the back of the House of Healing. He heard a soft squeak and looked down at a large rat that was poking around some rotting food at his feet. Crowdal smiled down at it. "Hey there, little guy. Food around here sucks, doesn't it?" The rat looked up at him and rose up on its hind legs, twitching its nose and whiskers, smelling the air. Crowdal reached into his pack and took out a small chunk of hard bread. He bent down and held it in front of the rat. It shuffled forward and gently grabbed the bread from Crowdal with its little front paws and immediately started nibbling at it.

Crowdal smiled as he stood up. "You're welcome, my little friend."

He stepped over the rat and crept down the narrow alley until he was able to get a good view of the back of the House of Healing. He saw a single door guarded by two more robed guards.

He looked up and saw a small landing and a large double door about halfway up the building. If he could get up there, it would be the perfect way in but glancing again at the guards, he knew there was no way he could trick them into leaving long enough for him to even get close to the building. There was no way he was going to get inside unseen.

He shrugged his shoulders. Well, sometimes going straight in was the only way, so he took a deep breath, stepped out of the alleyway, and walked leisurely toward the door. The guards didn't move when they saw him coming toward them. He imagined a Trith was the last thing they expected to see, so he smiled broadly and nodded to them. "Hello, gentlemen."

They didn't move or respond to him. He was impressed and a little worried. Normally a Trith would be enough to make anyone nervous.

He approached the bottom of the steps and looked up at the guards. He couldn't see their faces behind their hoods, which was slightly unnerving. He smiled. "I need to see Father Mansico. If you would be so kind to fetch him, I would appreciate it."

They ignored him.

This was going to be tougher than he thought. He put one foot on the bottom step and immediately one of the guards leaped at him. The man's robe fluttered and a sword appeared in his hands.

Crowdal froze. He knew if he moved, he would be dead. The figure landed on the step above him, the cold steel of the sword touching his neck. Crowdal didn't even breathe.

The man spoke quietly, his voice cold and menacing, "Do not move... Trith."

Crowdal nodded slightly, feeling a warm trickle of blood run down his neck. He had been to two Houses of Healing before and they had always been open to the public. He had never been threatened before. Something was happening here he didn't understand.

But first, he needed to not die. "I'm sorry, sir. I thought the House of Healing was open to the public. My apologies. I will leave now."

The robed figure glided down the final steps and hissed at him, "You will come with me." Without taking the blade from his neck, the figure moved around behind him. "Move."

They didn't ask for his sword, which surprised him.

They must be very confident.

He decided to play along to see where they took him. 'Not that he had a choice,' he thought bitterly. But at least he was getting inside. He ascended the steps slowly. The robed guard at the top of the stairs had not moved during the whole encounter, but now he stepped back and opened the door with one hand. Crowdal walked past him into a small, dark room just large enough for three people. Crowdal's head grazed the ceiling.

He saw a door directly to his right, covered with iron straps to increase its strength. The door behind him closed and he noticed the other robed figure hadn't entered with them. It was just the two of them. The sword at his neck felt cold and he could feel the razor sharp edge, although it no longer cut his skin. The guard knew how to use it. It wasn't an easy thing to walk with someone while holding a sword on them without cutting them. Even the slightest movement could severely cut Crowdal's neck.

The robed figure rapped on the door three times. It opened instantly and light filled the little room. Crowdal saw an ornate room beyond. As they stepped through, he casually glanced around. The room was large, perhaps a hundred paces across. The floor was made from white marble, as were the walls. Where Crowdal expected to find beds and sick people, he instead found the room was empty except for two more robed figures on this side of the door they had just walked through.

The figure holding the sword to his neck spoke softly, "Walk very slowly, Trith, and you may live for a while longer yet." He pushed against the back of his neck with the sword and Crowdal immediately started walking to keep from being cut. His heeled boots echoed on the marble floor, clacking from his heavy steps. He noticed the robed figure didn't make a sound as it followed him.

He tried to talk, to get some information. "So why are you taking me here by force? What have I done?"

The figure didn't answer.

Crowdal tried a different tactic. He knew from experience that those who used a sword were usually filled with pride at their skill level. "Where did you learn to use that sword? I've never seen your equal."

Still no response.

He sighed. "You're quite the conversationalist aren't you?"

The sword pressed down slightly and he felt a small drop of blood run down the back of his neck. He took the hint. "I guess not."

They reached the other side of the room and Crowdal saw a narrow door cut so precisely in the marble wall that it was almost invisible. He stopped and the sword left his neck, so he turned his head slightly to look behind him.

The robed guard had taken two steps back, the sword no longer visible. It motioned its hooded head toward the door. "You may enter."

Crowdal felt the back of his neck and looked at his fingers. The blood was already dried. He smiled at the robed figure. "Thank you for the escort. You do your job well. Do I tip?"

The robed figure hissed at him, but otherwise didn't move or reply.

Crowdal chuckled and pushed against the door. It swung easily in, opening on silent hinges. He saw a narrow stairway. Torches smoked as they burned, filling the air with an acrid smell. He looked back at the robed guard, then shrugged and started down the stairs. He had only taken two steps when he heard the door quietly shut behind him. He stopped and looked around.

The flickering light showed rough stone walls covered in cobwebs where the flames of the torches didn't burn them away. His head barely cleared the ceiling, which was covered in black soot. He bent his head slightly to avoid hitting it and descended the steps carefully. They were rough and worn from years of use, some of them angling downward, making it treacherous for him because of his very large feet. But soon he was to the bottom.

He had to stoop slightly to avoid hitting his head on the ceiling as he looked around. He saw a long passageway lined with torches next to doors that were spaced randomly. He had no idea what this place was, but it sure didn't smell good, which was a sure sign that it wasn't a nice place to find oneself. He listened and heard dripping water, then looked up and saw that the ceiling was damp. He bent even lower, not wanted to get slime in his hair. The floor was stone but it was so old that it was chipped and cracked, making it more like a dirt floor.

He started slowly down the passageway. It was the only way to go. Before he got to the first door, he saw it open and another robed figure stepped out, blocking the passageway. As Crowdal approached, it nodded its hooded head toward the room.

Crowdal tipped his head casually as he turned into the room, but stopped immediately. The room was well-lit and about thirty paces across. He saw a large fireplace on the far wall, as well as comfortable-looking chairs that were arranged around a bloody and bruised person who hung with arms shackled to the ceiling. He didn't have time to look closely at the person because he caught sight of two more guards standing at attention next to a man seated in one of the chairs facing away from him. Crowdal immediately recognized the red cuffs on his robe.

"Father Mansico, why am I not surprised to find you down here?"

Father Mansico turned and smiled gently at him, then frowned. "I was expecting you and your friend."

"I'm sorry to disappoint you, then."

"He will be found. My Haissen are quite capable."

Crowdal looked again at the robed figures standing in the room. They pushed their hoods back from their heads and their white, alien-looking faces became visible.

Haissen!

He had heard of them but had never seen one before. They were completely hairless, with smooth skin so white that blue veins showed through. Their eyes were almost square and bright green with no pupils, and they had small noses that came to a sharp point. But their mouths were the strangest of all. They had no teeth, the mouth opening looking like that of a sea anemone he had seen in the tide pools one time by the Paigonian Sea.

They were legendary amongst the Trith. The Haissen were the only race the Trith elders spoke about with respect and perhaps even a little fear. Every generation, a few Trith, bored because they couldn't find a challenging opponent with which to battle, went out and searched the land for a Haissan to fight, for they were the only known race that could match a Trith with the sword. Many Trith never returned from their journeys, and those that did never found a Haissan, adding to the legend.

He heard shackles jingle and turned to look at the person hanging there for the first time. He drew in his breath with a gasp.

Father Mansico chuckled. "I thought you would like to be here for the final confession." He rose, walked over to the person, and grabbed bloody hair to lift her head.

Melinda opened swollen black-and-blue eyes and looked at Crowdal. She tried to sigh, but bloody spittle bubbled out of her mouth instead. She spit out a glob and whispered, "You idiot." She coughed and spit out more blood. "Don't tell me you came here to rescue me? Such an idiot." She whispered the last word as she glared at him.

Crowdal shook with rage. She was naked and she had been beaten with a switch. Bloody lines crisscrossed her body. Her breasts were especially mutilated and bleeding, one nipple cleanly sliced in two. Her lips were cut and bleeding in multiple places.

Crowdal tried to control his rage. All he wanted to do was kill Mansico, but with so many Haissen in the room, he knew he wouldn't get two steps before he was cut down. He tried to lighten his voice for Melinda's benefit. "Don't worry, I wouldn't think of coming to your rescue. You look like you have them right where you want them."

She chuckled weakly and spit out more blood.

Father Mansico hit her across the cheek with his fist, his ring cutting a wide gash that gushed blood

The door opened behind Crowdal and Father Mansico nodded. "Ah, there you are. Hello, my boy, so kind of you to join us."

Crowdal turned.

Sid stood in the doorway.

Chapter 28

Mrs. Wessmank rose from the chair and lifted Ailinora's chin. She looked at her sister for a long time, at her finely-wrinkled skin and white hair that hung over her shoulders. How beautiful she was. It had been eighty years since she had last seen her sister and now she looked at her dead face. She had known it would end like this. She had seen it in a vision before she had left Orm-Mina. What would be would be.

She carefully lowered the chin and as she did, Ailinora's body slid from the chair and fell to the floor. Her sister's dead eyes stared up at her.

Mrs. Wessmank gazed sadly down at her. "May the gods bring you peace."

"*I'm sorry, Mother.*"

Mrs. Wessmank looked down at Maelon. "Do not apologize. It had to be done. Do you know where the Manuscript is?"

"*It is in his writing desk.*"

Mrs. Wessmank walked quickly over to the desk and found it locked. She had expected it to be. But she was surprised to see it was secured with a leaf lock. A leaf lock was an amazing mechanism. It was magnetic, with the two poles synchronized to activate another magnet in the slot in which it was placed. She had only read about such locking systems. They were impossible to bypass.

Mrs. Wessmank sighed. Father Mansico must carry it on his person. There was no way she was going to get into the drawer without the leaf key.

"*Yes, Mother. He keeps it around his neck on a chain. It is the only copy.*"

"And if I know Mansico, the drawer is reinforced with solid steel, too. He would take no chances with that manuscript. There is nothing we can do about that." She stood up and looked around the room. "Now, where is that secret passageway?"

Maelon looked at Mrs. Wessmank, his dark eyes alive with intelligence. "*This way.*" He padded across the room and stopped next to the wall by the bed. "*Push the seventh stone up, fourth over from the bed.*"

Mrs. Wessmank did as he said and the wall swung inward. She couldn't see into the darkness, but the air was dry. She lifted two torches from sconces in the wall, putting out one to keep as a backup. She entered the passage without pausing, shutting the door once Maelon was through.

Chapter 29

Sid was escorted into the room by a Haissan. He looked at Crowdal and shook his head. "I'm sorry. They found me hiding in the alley. I tried to fight them, but..." he trailed off when he saw Melinda hanging by the shackles, covered in blood. He glared at Father Mansico and screamed at him. "Why? Why did you do that to her? It's me you want, not her!" He tried to run at Mansico, but the Haissan held him easily back.

Father Mansico chuckled lightly. "My, my, everyone seems to be so shocked by little Melinda here. It is just blood." He reached out a finger and scooped a fingernail across her cheek and brought the blood to his lips, delicately sipping it. He licked his lips. "Hmm, nothing like the taste of blood." He looked at Crowdal and Sid and motioned to the chairs. "Now, if you please, sit down here and we'll chat."

Sid was pushed forward and he stumbled into Crowdal, who caught him. They looked at each other and Crowdal nodded slightly, whispering very quietly, "Don't worry, we'll get her out of here."

Sid nodded, his eyes becoming lidded and hard.

They both walked to the chairs and sat down. Crowdal looked up at Melinda. She hung in front of him, within reach, but he couldn't do anything yet. It wasn't time. He looked back at Father Mansico. "We are here. Take her down and let her rest."

Father Mansico clucked his tongue. "Now that would just take away from the effect. You see, I want you to see what will happen to you if you decide not to cooperate with me." He motioned to one of the Haissan, who came forward. In one smooth motion, it whipped the sword out of its robes and sliced across Melinda's stomach. It put its sword away in the same movement and returned to where it was standing. The whole movement took place in the blink of an eye.

Crowdal was afraid to look at Melinda, expecting her to be cut in half, but he forced himself to look anyway. A small red line, leaking a small amount of blood, ran across Melinda's stomach. The blade had just broken the surface of her skin. Even a little deeper and her intestines would have spilled to the floor. He had never seen such control of a sword before. He wasn't even sure he could have done that.

Melinda looked down at her stomach, then up at Crowdal. He saw fear in her eyes but she controlled it well. She sneered at Father Mansico. "Is that supposed to scare me?"

Father Mansico shook his head and turned back to the Haissan. It walked forward and Crowdal knew it was going to kill her this time. He stood up and yelled. "Wait! We'll tell you anything you want to know."

The Haissan continued to walk forward and took out its sword. It slowly raised it, preparing to cut her in half lengthwise. Just as the blade started to descend, Father Mansico held up a hand. The Haissan stopped the sword just above Melinda's head. It casually returned the sword to its scabbard and stepped back.

Father Mansico looked at Crowdal and Sid. "I appreciate your willingness to talk with me. Thank you, that is very kind of you." He held his hand out for Crowdal to sit down again.

Crowdal slowly sat back down and Mansico sat also, crossing his legs and putting one arm behind the chair next to him.

"But I really don't want to talk to you, you see." He looked at Sid. "You, young man, are to blame for all of this."

Sid looked up at Melinda and tears fell from his eyes.

Melinda saw the pain in his eyes and she shook her head. "Sid, it isn't your fault, don't listen to this monster."

Sid closed his eyes and when he opened them, the tears were gone and the hardness was back. He glared at Father Mansico. "You will pay for what you have done to her. I will see to it personally."

Father Mansico chuckled again. "That has to be the saddest threat I've ever heard." He crossed his legs the other way. "Now, let's get down to business. You, young man, will be staying here with me for a while. We have some things to work out." He glanced down at Sid's waist. "But first, take off your trousers."

Sid looked at the man like he was insane. Indignation rose in him. "I won't."

Father Mansico motioned to the Haissan behind Sid.

Sid turned and saw the robed figure approach him.

"Now stand up and disrobe or I will have my Haissan do it for you," Father Mansico said softly.

Sid looked at Crowdal, silently asking him what he should do.

Crowdal nodded slightly.

His face ashen, Sid slowly stood up and looked back at the Haissan as he slowly unbuckled his trousers and pushed them down, facing Father Mansico.

Mansico stood up and glided over to Sid, staring at his penis.

Crowdal didn't move. He knew the timing was critical. He had to let Father Mansico get engrossed in whatever it was he was going to do.

Father Mansico stopped next to Sid and knelt down until his face was next to Sid's penis.

Sid tensed and Crowdal hoped that he wouldn't do anything stupid like knee the man in the face. If he did, they would all be dead in the time it took him to take his next breath. Crowdal tensed, ready to draw his sword just in case.

Father Mansico took Sid's soft penis in one hand like it was nothing more than a piece of sausage and held it up so he could look at it. He leaned forward and examined the scar running all the way around the base. He smiled and touched it. The scar was puckered slightly but was fully healed. He let go of Sid's penis and stood up. "You can pull your trousers up, boy."

He looked into Sid's eyes for a few moments. "You are very special. I've been waiting for many years for you to come along." He looked at Sid's trousers. "By the way, I believe you have something for me?"

Sid looked at Father Mansico with a blank stare as he pulled up his trousers. He had no idea what the man was referring to.

Father Mansico motioned down to Sid's trousers. "Your father gave you a very special blade. A Rissen blade, to be exact. It is mine."

Sid backed up a step, shaking his head. "I won't. My father gave it to me."

Father Mansico laughed outright. It would have sounded genial and comforting in any other setting. "Your father gave you the blade because he knew you were coming to me. You are merely the carrier." His voice turned hard. "Now take the blade from your trousers and hand it to me, or I will have my lovely Haissan do it for you and they don't like to do menial tasks like that. They may hurt you in the process."

Sid untied the sheath from around his waist and pulled the Rissen blade from inside his trousers. He looked at the beautiful but simple handle, turning it in his hand, then threw it on the floor. It slid in circles as it came to a stop at Father Mansico's feet. "Take it. I don't want it anyway."

* * *

Father Mansico slowly bent down, staring at Sid the whole time with a smile on his face. He picked up the blade and finally looked down at it. His heart skipped a beat. He had the final piece of the equation. He owned the Aleph Null, the Black Numbers manuscript, and now the Rissen blade. He couldn't believe how easy it had been. After decades of searching, of endless nights planning, to have everything just fall into place so easily was a bit anti-climactic. He had expected a bit more drama, to tell the truth. A little sadly, he put the knife on the table and motioned toward the chairs. "Thank you, please, sit down."

Sid sat down in the chair and looked over at Crowdal with uncertainty in his eyes.

Father Mansico paced in front of them, his head down as he thought of what to say. It would make things quicker if he got the kid to cooperate with him. But if the boy didn't cooperate, he was willing to go the more difficult route. In fact, he hoped the kid didn't cooperate. The problem was the Trith. He was obviously close to the boy, so he didn't want to kill the giant quite yet and risk having the boy fall completely apart. He stopped pacing and looked up at the boy with his kindest smile. "My son, I…"

Sid lashed out. "I'm not your son!"

Father Mansico smiled indulgently. "Of course. My apologies. It is just a common way for a Father to address his people. I meant no offense."

Sid scowled at him.

Father Mansico saw that even though Sid was young, the boy was strong-willed. He pulled a chair over so he could sit opposite the boy. He sat down and crossed his legs, leaning back with his arms in his lap, acting like an innocent man who was unfairly accused of a terrible act. "I am sorry about Melinda. I thought she was an enemy of the House of Healing."

Sid crossed his arms. "Then take her down. She has done no one any harm."

Chuckling lightly, Father Mansico shook his head. "I'm so sorry, but I can't do that. Not until I know for sure which side you are on."

"What do you mean?" Sid said angrily, but also looking slightly confused.

Father Mansico spread his hands at the room. "All of this, this room, the entire House of Healing, and this whole land is at risk of being destroyed. All that we know, everything that is good and just, all people could be destroyed if we don't stop the…" He paused for effect, making sure he had the boy's full attention.

Sid leaned forward slightly. "Stop the what?"

Leaning forward himself so their faces were very close, he whispered, "The Oblate."

The breath rushed out of Sid's lungs as he sat quickly back in the chair.

Father Mansico saw the reaction on the boy's face. He was the Aleph Null, there was no doubt about it. "Yes, my son, the Oblate. It is real and has sent its agents out to find you."

Sid breathed out, "The Korpor."

Father Mansico nodded gravely. "Yes, the Korpor. And your father, too. He was placed by the Oblate to train you until it was time for the Proofing." He leaned forward slightly and said kindly, "But he loves you Sidoro and doesn't want any harm to come to you. So he has joined with me instead and sent you to me. If we don't stop the Oblate, the world as we know it will end. You are the key, young Sidoro. Help us."

Crowdal sat forward. "This Korpor, it is nothing but some wild creature. And the Oblate is nothing but an old farmer's tale. It's not going to end the world." He laughed, as if the Father were a child.

Father Mansico scowled at Crowdal. "You, Trith, know nothing about the world. You and your people are nothing but criminals. So don't talk to me about what is or is not true."

Crowdal's eyes became hard but he spoke calmly, "Even though I dislike my people and they are singular of purpose in their love for battle, they are not criminals. They only fight fully-armed men. And they never harm innocent people, like you do."

Father Mansico raised an eyebrow. "Interesting." He turned back to Sid. "Now, my son, don't listen to your friend. While he might mean well, he doesn't know the first thing about the world." He put his hand on his chest. "I, on the other hand, am a healer and a protector. I am the reason why there is peace, prosperity, and freedom for everyone."

Crowdal snickered sarcastically and pointed up at Melinda. "Is that what you mean by peace and freedom for everyone?"

"That... was a mistake. I only did what I had to do for the good of everyone. I took no pleasure in it."

Sid sighed. "I don't care about any of this. About the Korpor, about the Oblate, about anything. You have the wrong person."

Father Mansico chuckled. "Oh no, of that I am sure. You are the Aleph Null. You have the mark of the Korpor on you."

Sid looked down at his crotch despite himself, then spoke in a trembling voice, "What is it you think I have to do with the Korpor?"

Father Mansico stood up and put his hands on the arms of Sid's chair, leaning forward and speaking in a hiss, "It has *Ringed* you." He saw the confusion in the boy's eyes. "Do you know what that means?"

Sid shook his head.

Father Mansico leaned even closer. "It means that the Korpor has bound you to it through the sharing of blood and sexual fluids. Your essences have mixed. You now have the Korpor in your blood. It is a part of you and you are a part of it. You can hear its whispers in your head, can't you?"

Sid's eyes became unfocused and he whispered to himself, "Stay out of my head, go away, I don't accept you." Sid put his hand to his head and slid to the floor.

Father Mansico knew that the Korpor was in the boy's head, weakening him. He stepped back and looked down at the boy. He was weak but he was the Aleph Null. He noticed the Trith start to stand up, so he turned toward him and wagged a finger. "Now, now, let the boy be. You are like an old hen the way you cluck over him."

Crowdal sat back in his chair when he saw a Haissan move forward slightly.

Sid lay on the floor, writhing as he pressed his hands to his head. Finally he stopped and focused on Father Mansico standing above him.

Father Mansico nodded to him. "The Korpor was supposed to bring you here to me, but it failed somehow. That is a shame. But fear not, the Korpor is not only with you in here." He tapped his temple. "But it is on its way here. You two will be together again. We have unfinished business that you need to do for us."

Sid looked over to Crowdal, then back to Father Mansico and whispered angrily, "Whatever it is, I won't do it."

Father Mansico walked over to the table and picked up a piece of parchment. He brought it back and unrolled it as he stared down at the boy. "I copied this from a very special manuscript. You may find it... interesting." He started reading.

> *The union of the Aleph Null with the Korpor*
> *A circle binding both brings forth a birth of power*
> *A union taking and giving*
> *The Aleph Null living but not giving life*
> *Numbers floating in darkness providing light*
> *Numbers floating in light providing darkness*
> *The Korpor shall be the iniquity and the Aleph Null will be the probity*
> *Breathing in one, and out the other*
> *They will be two, bringing Black Numbers from none.*

As the boy listened, his face became calm and his eyes calculating as he glared up at and the Father. "You have no idea what that means, do you?"

Father Mansico looked down at the boy. It wasn't the response he had expected. After all of this, he had expected the boy to either be so overwhelmed that he would crumble, or if he had enough intelligence, maybe he would be swayed and join Father Mansico voluntarily. But this response literally surprised him. And made him angry. He pulled the boy to his feet and punched him in the gut as hard as he could.

The air exploded out of the boy's lungs and he bent forward in pain, then fell to his knees and vomited all over the floor, a sight that warmed Mansico's heart. He loved nothing more than inflicting pain and he was tired of this boy's games. It was time to do this the way he had always wanted. Through pain and fear.

* * *

As much as it pained him to see Sid fall to the floor after being punched, it was the moment Crowdal had been waiting for, when the focus would be entirely on Sid and Father Mansico. Hopefully it would give him the time he would need to stand and pull his sword before the Haissen could react. Taking a deep breath, he leapt to his feet, pulling his sword out at the same time. The closest Haissan turned to him, a sword already in its hands. Crowdal knew he had to put this one down quickly if he were to have any chance at all. The second one would be on him in a matter of moments.

He started to stab at the Haissan, but at the last moment, swung his blade to the left and in a circular motion brought it around his head and back down from his right. He was fast and the blade was a blur as it moved. But the Haissan was quick and able to block it. The jarring of steel on steel went through Crowdal's wrist but he ignored it. He expected the Haissan to have a chance at blocking it, so as their swords impacted, he kicked out with a long muscular leg at the Haissan's chest. He felt his boot crush bones and the Haissan's breath whooshed out. It dropped its sword and crumpled to the ground, not moving. Crowdal knew the bones had probably shredded its heart. He felt a stab of regret. He had never wanted to kill again.

But he had no time to think any more about it.

He sensed movement from behind him, so he dove forward, rolled, and came to his feet facing the second Haissan. Time slowed down, as it always did for him during the key moment of a sword fight. The Haissan's robe seemed to absorb light, making it look like a shadow as it moved toward him, fearless and deadly. A bead of sweat ran down Crowdal's nose. He could feel the warm wetness as it reached the tip, dangling for a moment before falling. He heard the splash on the floor.

The Haissan glided toward him, holding its sword with both hands, the blade angled up at a forty-five degree angle. It was the strongest attack position, allowing a person to deliver an incredibly quick and powerful downward stroke that was very difficult to block or avoid.

But Crowdal also knew it allowed a person to change their attack and strike from multiple angles with little effort. So he waited calmly for the Haissan to commit, holding his sword up with two hands in an identical manner.

The Haissan lunged forward, its blade a blur as it moved. It was too fast for Crowdal to see, but he knew that sight could deceive him, so he let his instincts react. Without thinking, he brought his sword to his right, flicking it in a circle just as he made contact with the Haissan's blade. He pulled with his immense strength and threw the Haissan off balance, at the same time slicing upward with his own blade. He felt the subtle resistance of steel slicing through flesh and the Haissan stumbled backward. Before it got its balance, Crowdal lunged forward and flicked his blade left and right in quick succession at the Haissan's body.

The robe of the Haissan parted from the two powerful cuts and its pale, white intestines slipped from the opening and fell to the floor. The Haissan looked down, then up at Crowdal. They stared at each other for a moment, then the Haissan nodded and with a jerking motion, knelt on the floor and set its sword carefully down in front of it. The Haissan nodded slightly again and there was no anger or fear in its eyes, just acceptance of its fate and respect for Crowdal for defeating it in a fair fight.

Crowdal stepped forward and sliced off the Haissan's head with such a smooth cut that the head stayed on the body for a moment before toppling forward and landing on the floor with a soft, wet thunk. It was an amazing strike not even many sword masters could have performed. If the blade were even slightly off its mark, it would have hit the skull or shoulder bones, causing a huge mess.

Crowdal felt sick to his stomach as he watched the Haissan's body collapse. But then he turned and looked at Melinda hanging from the shackles, all bloody and bruised, and quickly hardened his feelings. He would kill anyone or anything to protect her and Sid. All of the training he had endured as a Trith came rushing back to him. He had to learn back then to compartmentalize his emotions or he would have gone insane. He did that again now.

Crowdal turned and glared at Mansico. He saw that Mansico's expression was stuck in a state of shock, as if the man had never even considered the possibility that anyone could defeat a Haissen, much less two of them. Mansico looked at the head lying on the floor, then up at Crowdal in fear, realizing for the first time that he was alone in the room now. He spun around and ran for the door, but he tripped over Sid's outstretched leg and fell to his stomach. His head smacked hard on the floor and blood gushed from his nose. He struggled to his knees and looked at Sid, who smiled at him with an icy look in his eyes.

Crowdal watched Sid run up behind the Father and quickly kick the man in the head as hard as he could. The Father's head snapped back and he fell backward to the floor, unconscious. Sid was about to kick him again when Crowdal stepped forward and put a hand on his shoulder.

"No, my friend. We may need him to get out of here."

Sid shrugged off Crowdal's hand and stepped forward again to kick Mansico, but Crowdal pulled him back. Sid spun on his friend, his face red with rage. "Let go of me."

"No. Sid, look at me." He lifted Sid's head. "Look at me."

Sid focused his eyes and finally saw Crowdal through the rage. He slowed his breathing and eventually nodded.

"I know you want to kill him, but I have no idea how many Haissen are outside that door. I got lucky with these two. I don't think I will be so lucky against the rest."

Sid nodded, his face slowly relaxing. He wiped his eyes and pushed his hair back before looking back at Crowdal. "I understand. Sorry. I don't know what is going on anymore. I just wanted to kill him." He looked down at Mansico, who was lying unmoving on the floor. "Should we tie him up?"

Crowdal smiled. "Yeah, that is a good idea. Can you do that? I need to get Melinda down from those chains."

Sid nodded.

While Crowdal worked on releasing Melinda from the chains he watched Sid walk resolutely to his pack, digging in it until he found his rope. Sid looked down at the Rissen blade on the table next to it and hesitated briefly, then picked it up and removed it from the sheath. He cut at the rope and Crowdal was amazed how it parted the thick strands as if there was nothing there. Crowdal watched Sid look at the blade in wonder before he put it back in the sheath and retied it to his leg. The boy then ran back to Mansico and grunted as he struggled to flip the man over to his stomach. Sid pulled the man's arms behind his back and tied them together, perhaps a little tighter than he needed to. He tied the man's feet together then rolled him onto his back again. Finally he looked back at Crowdal to see if he needed any help, suddenly looking very tired.

Crowdal could only imagine how exhausted his friend must have been. "Sid, why don't you go sit down and get some rest?" Sid nodded without complaining, walked over to a chair, and sat heavily down in it. He closed his eyes and Crowdal could tell he had fallen instantly to sleep.

Crowdal caressed Melinda's brow as he released the final shackle and lowered her to the floor. She was thankfully unconscious again, not having to deal with the pain. He stood up, brought her bloody robe back, and covered her to keep her warm. He then bent down and examined her wounds. There were cuts from the switch all over her legs, stomach, back, and breasts, but none of them seemed to be life-threatening. The cut across her nipple was still bleeding lightly. Her eyes were black-and-blue and swollen almost completely shut.

He knew he probably didn't have much time, but since she was unconscious, he got up and got a towel from his pack and his water skin, along with his medical kit. He returned and started cleaning her as best he could, paying special attention to her wounds. Melinda moaned but didn't regain consciousness, which was just as well. What he was doing was very painful and he was glad she didn't have to suffer through this at least.

After he was done cleaning her wounds, he dug in his medical kit and took out some bandages and string. He cut them to the appropriate length and tied them to the worst wounds. The cut to her nipple required stitches and he couldn't wait until later to do it. So he dug out his needle and thread and carefully stitched the two sides together, using as small and close stitches as he could. Melinda moaned louder as he worked but he didn't let that slow him down. He worked quickly and was done in a short time. He then put bandages on her breasts and tied them with a strip of cloth around her back to keep them on.

He looked down at her and knew he had done about all he could right now, so he rolled her to her side and slid the robe underneath her. He then rolled her back, pulled the robe over her, and tied it securely. He hated to move her but he knew he had to.

Crowdal stood up and looked around the room. If they left through the main door, he would need Mansico as a hostage. But he wouldn't be able to carry both Melinda and Mansico and be able to use his sword. He looked over at Sid and saw him still sitting in a chair, his head to his chest, asleep. He was going to be no help, either, poor kid.

So Crowdal walked quickly around the room. He didn't know if there was another exit, but he had to look. He moved slowly, sliding his hands along the rough-hewn rock walls. He was almost half-way around the room when he came to a portion of the wall that had a very tiny crack in it. He leaned closer and saw that it ran upwards, so he ran his fingers along it until he felt it turn to his right.

It was a hidden door, he was sure of it. He felt for a latch but couldn't find one. He stood back and looked at the faint outline of the door. It was difficult to see, but now that he knew where it was, he could see it more clearly. If there was no latch, it must be a pressure-sensitive door. So he stepped forward and started pushing all along the edges, but it was solid all the way around.

Frustrated, Crowdal stood back again. There had to be a mechanism to open it. He looked around the immediate area but in the shadows, he couldn't see anything. He bent closer and felt around the whole door, not just the cracks, and that is when he found it. His fingers came to an indentation near the center of the door. He felt closely. It seemed to be about the size of half his hand and was shaped like a leaf.

Then a thought came to him and he knew how to open it. He looked back at Father Mansico lying on the floor and walked quickly over to him. He knelt down and started feeling his robes. When he got to his chest he immediately felt something hard. Anxiously he reached inside it and pulled out a piece of steel on a chain that was around his neck.

He yanked hard at it and it broke. He stood up and examined it briefly. It was a piece of steel shaped like a leaf, with the image of two hands holding each other inset into it. It was the symbol of the House of Healing. Smiling, he rushed over to the door and pushed the leaf into the opening. He heard it snap into place and a clicking sound started inside the door until there was another snap and the door swung inward a short ways.

Crowdal drew his sword and carefully pushed the door open with its tip. He didn't want to be surprised by any Haissen. But the narrow hallway on the other side was empty and lit by torches. Crowdal sighed and put his sword back into the scabbard.

He turned, rushed back to Sid, and shook him gently. "Sid, Sid wake up."

Sid sleepily opened his eyes.

"Sid, we have to go now. Can you walk?"

Sid slowly focused his eyes and shook his head. "Yeah, sorry, I must have dozed off." He struggled to get to his feet and Crowdal steadied him. "Thanks, I'll be all right now."

Crowdal nodded. "Gather your things. We have to leave now. I'll get Melinda." He moved quickly over to Melinda.

Sid went to his pack and looked through it to make sure everything was there, then swung it around his back and secured it before joining Crowdal.

Crowdal pushed Melinda's hair from her swollen eyes. "Melinda, you are safe now. I'm going to pick you up and carry you. We'll be safe soon." She didn't respond but he thought she started breathing easier. He carefully lifted her and carried her in his arms, her head against his shoulder. He was so large that it was like carrying a small child. He turned to Sid. "Are you ready?"

Sid nodded over his shoulder. "What about Father Mansico?"

Crowdal glanced over. He had forgotten about him. "We don't need him anymore, but we will not kill a defenseless man, even someone as worthless as that one. Just leave him."

Sid frowned at Crowdal and hardened his eyes. He turned and walked over to the unconscious man. He stared down for a few moments, then stomped down on Father Mansico's crotch as hard as he could, grinding his foot back and forth. The unconscious figure bucked from the impact but didn't awaken. Sid rejoined Crowdal and casually asked, "Where are we going, anyway?"

Crowdal looked at his friend closely. Sid seemed to have a cruel streak and a lot of anger. Crowdal would have to have a talk with him if they got out of this. But now wasn't the time, so he nodded toward the dark part of the room. "There's a door back there. I'm not sure where it goes, but it is better than going out the main door and saying hi to the rest of the Haissen." He turned and led the way to the back of the room.

They reached the door and Crowdal listened carefully. He couldn't hear anything so he removed the leaf key from the door and entered the passageway. Sid followed right behind him. He turned his head back and whispered, "Can you close the door?"

Sid turned and pulled at the door. It was difficult, as there was no handle, but he was able to grab the edge of the door and pull. The door moved easily and he had barely pulled his fingers away before the door shut with a soft thunk. They heard some kind of mechanism clicking inside the door as it sealed tightly.

Crowdal sighed. "Here is to hoping this passageway doesn't end in a room full of our lovely Haissen friends."

Chapter 30

The passageway sloped downward slightly and was very narrow, but the ceiling was tall, at least tall enough that Crowdal didn't have to bend his head. The walls looked like they were gouged directly into the ground. Burning torches were set so far apart that the spaces in between were almost pitch black.

Crowdal and Sid moved forward slowly, trying to be as quiet as possible. In the dark stretches Crowdal felt himself walking through spider webs because of his height. He wished he had a free hand to wipe them from his face but he didn't want to set Melinda down and disturb her any more than he was already. So he walked on, then almost choked as a spider entered his mouth. It was bulbous and hairy and he felt its legs moving against the roof of his mouth as he quickly spit it out. A shiver ran down his body. Gods, he hated spiders. He kept his mouth closed as they passed torch after torch until they came to a sharp turn to their right.

Peering around the corner, Crowdal saw the passageway ended with a door. He crept up to it and put his ear to the wood. He couldn't hear anything. The door looked identical to the one through which they had entered the passageway. There was a leaf key indentation on this side, so he carefully laid Melinda on the floor a ways back. He pulled his sword from his scabbard, then dug the key from his pocket and placed it into the indentation in the door. He heard the familiar whirling of the mechanism. The door quietly clicked open and swung toward him slightly before coming to a stop.

Crowdal pushed Sid behind him and pulled the door open. The brightness of the room beyond blinded him for a few moments but no Haissen came through. His eyes adjusted to the light and he stepped forward into the room. It was a private bedchamber, simply decorated. A fire burned in a small fireplace on the wall across from the bed. The only other piece of furniture was a simple writing table and two chairs. But he immediately knew it was no simple bedchamber. Only the rich had writing tables, since paper was almost impossible to come by. This could only be Father Mansico's room.

It seemed empty, so Crowdal went back and carefully scooped up Melinda. He caught Sid's eyes and nodded toward the door. "The room is empty. Let's go." He let Sid by, then grabbed the leaf key from the indentation. As he passed through the door he pulled it shut with the toe of his boot.

Sid looked around the room in awe, then walked over the bed and lifted the covers and felt the mattress. It was filled with feathers. He turned to Crowdal and whispered, "These are feathers. Who could afford such a bed?"

Crowdal chuckled. "That, my friend, is a bed fit for a king. My guess is that Father Mansico sleeps in it now. Come on, we have to keep moving." As he stepped around the desk though, he stopped. On the floor next to one of the chairs lay an old woman. He bent down a little and saw that she was dead. Her throat looked like it had been crushed by an animal. Her eyes were open wide, as if in surprise.

"This is strange."

Sid walked over and stared down at the old woman, cocking his head slightly as if troubled by something. Crowdal came up beside him. "Do you know her, Sid?"

His friend studied the body for another moment before glancing up at Crowdal. "No, I've never seen her before. But for some reason, she reminds me of someone I know. I... don't know why, though. What do you think happened?"

Crowdal motioned at her throat. "Looks like she was attacked by a wild animal."

"I don't see any other wounds though, other than her throat."

Crowdal saw that Sid was right. It looked like she had been deliberately killed. Murdered by an animal? He shook his head. It was a mystery he didn't have time to solve, so he stood up straight. "It doesn't matter. We have to keep moving." He angled toward the door on the other side of the room.

* * *

Sid started to follow Crowdal across the room, but as he passed by the writing desk, he felt warmth infuse him and his fingers started to tingle. He stopped and looked at the desk. On the top was a pile of blank paper, worth a small fortune. He felt the warmth pulling at him so he reached down and put his hand on the desk. As he made contact with the surface, the warmth intensified. He heard a wordless whisper in his mind, calling to him.

He leaned over and saw that the desk had a drawer in the front. He bent down and saw the imprint of the leaf key. He called to Crowdal in a hoarse voice. "Give me the key."

Crowdal stopped and turned around. "Sid, we don't have time to delay any longer."

Sid looked up briefly. "Please, just bring me the key."

Crowdal sighed and came back, holding the key in his hand. "Do you have to do that now? We are in a bit of a hurry."

Sid didn't respond. He took the key with shaking hands, fit it into the indentation, and pushed. It moved in and the drawer immediately clicked open on springs. Sid removed the key and dropped it absently on the floor. He slowly opened the drawer. It was empty except for a manuscript. It was beautiful. The cover was made of black leather and etched around the corners with strange writing. It was held closed by a finely-worked silver latch.

But it was the title that entranced Sid. In thick block letters, he read 'Black Numbers'.

Incredible warmth radiated outward from the manuscript as he read the title. The words vibrated in his mind, over and over.

Black Numbers... Black Numbers... Black Numbers.

His fingers tingled and his hands shook as he reached out to run his fingers over the title, but as soon as his fingers made contact, a flow of energy coursed into him.

He gasped in ecstasy.

He curled his fingers around the manuscript and lifted it out. Another burst of energy shot through him. He felt power hum through his arms and down through his whole body. The room became tinged with blue light. He got a stiff erection that throbbed with the energy and a sweet, burning sensation grew around the base of his penis. In his mind he pictured the scar ring the Korpor had carved with its claw. It seemed to magnify the power.

He smiled, although it was more of a grimace of ecstasy. He lifted the manuscript close to his face and stared at it. He couldn't think of anything but the power that coursed through him. It was intoxicating. Sexual. Painful.

Crowdal stared at Sid in confusion, then gasped as he looked into Sid's eyes.

Sid saw his own eyes reflecting back, only his eyes were now a bright blue. Crowdal quickly lay Melinda down on the bed and rushed over to him.

"Sid?"

Sid heard his name from a distance.

Crowdal said his name louder, but it was like the buzz of a mosquito that Sid just couldn't worry about.

Crowdal reached out to shake his shoulders. An explosion of energy shot through Sid and Crowdal was thrown all the way across the room, smashing hard against the wall and sliding slowly down, his eyes dazed.

Sid dropped the manuscript and the energy that flowed through him instantly lessened. He ran over to his friend. "Crowdal? Are you all right? Crowdal, please talk to me."

His voice cracked and he felt tears welling up. Crowdal put his hand to the back of his head and moaned as he looked up at Sid.

When Sid saw Crowdal look up at him he sat back and sighed in relief. "Oh, thank the gods, I thought I had killed you."

Crowdal smiled up at his friend. "It would take a lot for that to happen. I'm a Trith."

Sid chuckled weakly. "I'm so sorry, Crowdal. I don't know what happened."

Crowdal sat up straight and felt again behind his head. "It's all right, I have a pretty hard head."

Sid reached out, but then pulled his hand back, remembering what had happened just a few moments earlier, of the intense power, pleasure, and pain that mixed inside of him, of the blue shimmer to everything.

Crowdal pushed himself up the wall and shook his head. "What was that manuscript you were holding?"

Sid stood up and looked behind him. The manuscript lay on the floor next to the desk. It looked completely innocuous but he still felt the power spinning around inside of him, coming from a constant stream from the manuscript. He wanted nothing more than to pick up the manuscript again, to feel the power. He ached to open it up and see what was inside. But he was also frightened. He wasn't ready to try touching it again, at least not just yet.

He looked up at Crowdal. "I'm not sure what just happened. I could feel the manuscript, even when it was inside of the desk. And when I touched it, I felt... I don't know how to describe it. Pleasure, pain, power, all mixed up. It ran through me." A tear ran down his cheek and he angrily wiped it away. "I don't know what is happening to me."

Crowdal reached out and pulled Sid into a hug. "Don't worry Sid, I'm here and I won't let anything happen to you. We'll get through this together."

Sid felt safe in Crowdal's arms and although he let himself be hugged, he didn't return the gesture. He didn't need to. Just knowing that he had a friend right now was enough.

Crowdal finally pulled back and looked down at Sid. "Come on, we need to keep moving."

Sid nodded up at Crowdal then pulled away. He walked over to the manuscript lying on the floor and looked down at it. He could feel the hum of power emanating from it. He felt a connection to it and knew he had to take it with them. But he also didn't dare pick it up again. He turned. "Crowdal?"

Crowdal walked over to him.

"Do you feel anything from that manuscript?"

Crowdal shook his head. "No, nothing."

Sid glanced down at the manuscript, then up at Crowdal. "I don't dare touch it again, but I know it is important. Can you try and pick it up?"

Crowdal nodded and bent down. He reached out and hesitated above the manuscript for a brief moment before scooping it up in his large hand.

Sid sighed in relief. "Could you put it in your pack and carry it for me?"

"Sure, no problem." Crowdal shrugged his pack from his back and carefully put the manuscript in a waterproof pocket. He closed the pack and slipped it on his back again.

Sid thanked Crowdal and motioned toward the door. "Ready?"

Crowdal walked over and leaned his ear against it. "I don't hear anything." He glanced back at Melinda. She was resting on the bed, so he took his sword out. This door also had the leaf lock in it, so he walked back to the desk and searched around the floor until he found where Sid had dropped it. He stepped back to the door and fit the key into the leaf mold. He looked at Sid, nodded, then pushed slowly.

The door swung open violently, pulling Crowdal off balance. He stumbled but straightened up just in time to block a blade as it descended in a blur toward his head.

Chapter 31

The Korpor entered the tunnel system far outside of Yisk. It knew these tunnels well, as it was the best way it could move around unseen, especially within the city itself. As it passed by a cross-passage, it heard a deep and distant growl. The Korpor paused and casually looked into the darkness. The growl grew louder as something large approached. The Korpor merely stood still, curious about what was making the sound.

The side tunnel was long and dark, but the Korpor could see in the darkness as well as it could during the day. Heavy footsteps grew louder until the Korpor saw a large creature stick its head around a corner from about twenty paces down the passageway.

The Korpor had never seen a creature like it and cocked its head in curiosity.

The creature stepped fully into the passageway. It had a snout full of massive teeth, triangular eyes, and a long body that was much larger than the Korpor. It bared its teeth ferociously and growled deeply, saliva hanging to the ground in thick strands. Then it leaped into the air and sprinted toward the Korpor.

The Korpor narrowed its eyes to slits, watching the creature close the distance. At the last moment, the Korpor opened its eyes wide and leaned forward aggressively.

The creature straightened its front legs out and scrabbled its thick claws into the sandy ground to find traction as it slid to a dusty stop only a few paces in front of the Korpor. It lowered its head to the floor and whimpered in pain, its body trembling.

The Korpor stepped forward and ran one of its own long claws lightly down the snout of the creature, almost affectionately. The creature trembled even harder and when the Korpor pulled its arm back, it turned and loped back the way it had come as quickly as it could.

The Korpor listened to the creature's retreat and smiled before turning and continuing on its way. It would have enjoyed having a creature like that for a pet, but now wasn't the time.

The Korpor increased its pace to a comfortable run. It would soon arrive at the House of Healing and even at this distance, it could sense the boy's power. It suddenly stopped. Something was strange. It quested out for the boy and immediately noticed that the power of numbers within the boy had grown since the last time it had been so close to the Aleph Null. Something had changed.

It shivered in anticipation. The boy had been a challenge so far. More of a challenge than it had ever had before, and that excited it.

Chapter 32

Crowdal pushed back against the sword and kicked out at an awkward angle. He connected, although he didn't get much power into the blow.

With a grunt, the Haissan stumbled backward and hit the wall, but immediately started forward again, its sword casually held in one hand.

Crowdal groaned. He had surprised a Haissan guarding the other side of Father Mansico's chamber door. He should have known there would be a guard. The Haissen were incredibly fast, so the moment it had taken the Haissan to realize it wasn't Father Mansico coming out of the room was the only thing that had saved Crowdal from losing his head.

The Haissan approached Crowdal without fear. It changed its grip, holding its sword with both hands, tilted slightly upward. It was a powerful attacking position and Crowdal shifted his own sword while pushing the door shut behind him with his foot. He wanted Sid and Melinda locked inside the room so he could concentrate on the Haissan.

He faced the Haissan, holding his own sword in the Gaiken position, angled slightly downward and held loosely in his hands. He started to take long, slow breaths to center his energy, but only got two in before the Haissan lunged forward, raising its sword up and slicing downward with such speed and force that had Crowdal not been prepared for it, the blade would have sliced him in half lengthwise. He stepped to the side, avoiding the blurring blade. With the strength and speed that could only come from a lifetime of training, he cut the Haissan in half at the waist. At least that is what he had expected to happen. But somehow the Haissan had been able to bring its sword around and block him. It was an impossible move, but he didn't have time to think about it.

The Haissan spun around, the blade whistling as it moved through the air, and Crowdal blocked four quick strikes.

The Haissan attacked methodically and relentlessly.

Crowdal started to sweat as he blocked the strikes, the ring of steel loud in the room. He was facing a master swordsman and if there was one thing he had learned from years of training, it was that when one got into a sword fight, blood would be spilled. A person who dreamed of winning a fight without getting hurt had never been in a real fight.

Crowdal backed up quickly, sliding his feet along the stone floor and blocking three more quick strikes. He could see the dull and lidded eyes of the Haissan behind its hood. In shock, Crowdal realized the

Haissan was bored! The creature knew it was going to win and was methodically wearing him down.

Crowdal was fighting an opponent more skilled than he was, something he had never thought possible. He had always been the best swordsman in his circle, the only one who had beaten the Trith sword master who had trained all of the Trith for six decades. When Crowdal fought, he became connected to his sword in such a way that time seemed to slow down for him, as if his opponents were fighting him at half-speed.

He blocked two more strikes, the Haissan's blade moving so quickly that Crowdal blocked it purely by instinct. He blinked sweat out of his eyes and knew without a doubt that he would not beat this Haissan. In fact, he realized now that he had gotten lucky with the first two Haissen and didn't fool himself into thinking he could get that lucky three times in a row.

He was getting close to the opposite wall of the room as he backed up, blocking strike after strike. Sweat flew from his head as he parried each attack. He knew once his back was against the wall, he would die quickly. Even with his tough skin, a direct thrust would penetrate him, especially when that thrust was from a skilled swordsman. And this Haissan was a master.

He had to do something now or he would soon be lying on the floor watching his own blood pool around his body.

The Haissan moved purposefully forward, flicking its sword left, then up and around in an arc, all the while forcing Crowdal to the wall.

Crowdal parried the last thrust, knocking it aside. He had to stop parrying the Haissan's blade.

It was the only way.

As the Haissan thrust quickly forward, Crowdal moved slightly to the left and stepped into it at the same time. He felt steel penetrate his side. Pain flared brightly through him but he ignored it. Before the Haissan could pull its sword from him, he dropped his own sword, grabbed the Haissan's head in both hands, and twisted as hard as he could. He heard a loud crack and the Haissan jerked briefly before going limp in his hands.

Crowdal held the Haissan up and slowly stepped backward. He felt the blade slide out of his body. The pain was intense and burned his insides, and blood pulsed thickly out of his side until at last he was free of the sword.

He grimaced in pain as he gently lowered the dead Haissan to the floor.

His shirt quickly soaked with blood as reached down and lifted it. The sword had penetrated his right side and passed all the way through his body. 'A master swordsman indeed,' he thought.

He ripped two strips from the Haissan's robe and gritted his teeth as he stuffed them inside both ends of the wound to stop the bleeding. The Trith had an almost otherworldly ability to heal themselves. The sword had not hit any organs so he would fully heal within a day or two.

Right now though, he had to get the three of them out of this place. He could only hope that he wouldn't have to fight another Haissan. Three was enough for one day, even for a Trith. He had had his fun.

He walked across the room and grimaced from the pain as he knocked lightly on the door.

There was no answer and it didn't open. 'Good boy,' he thought. Sid would have no idea who won the fight. It could be the Haissan coming into the room. "Sid. It's all right, it's me."

Sid quickly opened the door and rushed through it to hug Crowdal. "You are alive!"

Crowdal laughed and hissed at the same time as he put his hands on Sid's shoulders and gently pushed him back a step. "I'm glad to see you too."

Sid smiled up at Crowdal, his eyes sparkling as he slapped him in the shoulder. "You scared me there for a moment. I'm glad I didn't have to take care of that Haissan myself."

Crowdal laughed again. "I thought of leaving it for you, but it seemed quite intent on going through me first."

Sid chuckled and then noticed Crowdal's bloody shirt. He looked quickly up at Crowdal with a worried look. "How did that happen? I... I thought you couldn't be cut."

Crowdal looked down and lifted his shirt to make sure the cloth strips were still inside of the wounds, then looked back to Sid, shaking his head. "Oh no, I can be cut, most definitely. A direct thrust, like the one my friend the Haissan just did, will definitely pierce my skin, if done right. And it was a master."

Sid shook his head. "But what about those two guys in the forest? They were huge and struck you hard enough to fell a tree, but you barely bled."

Crowdal made the motion of a sweeping strike. "When hit from this angle, a blade will most likely bounce off of me. It is all in the angle." He looked around and saw Melinda struggling to sit up in the bed, so he walked quickly over to her.

Melinda tried to clear her vision, but then laid back down and closed her eyes. She grimaced then began breathing deeply.

Crowdal lightly caressed her cheek, being careful of her bruises. She was sleeping again, which was good. She needed to heal and he knew from experience that a person healed quicker when they slept. He looked over at Sid, who had walked up and stood beside the bed looking down at Melinda with a worried look on his face.

"Will she be all right?" he asked, looking up at Crowdal through dark hair hanging over his eyes.

"Yes, but she is in bad shape. She needs sleep to heal, which makes me worried because I need to carry her again. But I don't think she will awaken anytime soon." He looked at the door, then back down to Sid. "We need to get going. The longer we stay here, the more likely we will be caught by more than just one Haissan." He grimaced.

Sid nodded, looking worried still. "Fine, but at least let me bandage your wound. You are no good to us dead." He meant it as a joke, but Crowdal only raised his eyebrow. Sid quickly added, "Just kidding."

Sid bandaged his wound, but Crowdal barely let him finish tying the bandage around his waist before he leaned down and gently lifted Melinda from the bed.

Sid frowned, but just shook his head.

Crowdal nodded down at Sid. "Ready when you are."

Sid nodded back and they left Mansico's chambers, pulling the door shut behind them.

Crowdal made sure he had the leaf-key. It had been invaluable so far and they might need it again.

Sid looked around the small room and saw the dead Haissan lying on the floor, its neck twisted at a horrible angle. He quickly bent down and picked up the Haissan's blade. Crowdal whispered to him, "Be very careful with that, Sid. It is a longer blade than any you have ever held before and very sharp. One slip and you could cut off your foot."

Sid looked over his shoulder and nodded. "I'll be careful. It is not like I haven't held a knife before."

Crowdal raised an eyebrow. "A sword is not the same as a knife, so just the same, be very careful. Look inside the Haissan's robes and take its scabbard at least. You don't want to carry a sharp blade around without a scabbard to store it in."

Sid reached down and opened the Haissan's robe. It was dressed in black, skin-tight leather underneath and had a scabbard tied to its waist. Sid quickly removed it and tied it to his own waist. He awkwardly slid the sword into the scabbard, taking four tries before he actually got the blade into it. He looked up at Crowdal. "Feel better?"

Crowdal smiled. "You inspire confidence in your mastery of the blade. Now let's get going. I'm getting nervous just standing here, and I never get nervous."

Sid crossed the room to the only other door and listened. He stepped back after a moment. "I don't hear anything on the other side."

Crowdal gently moved him aside, took his sword from his scabbard, and opened the door quickly, ready to surprise whomever was on the other side, but there was no one there. He released his breath, peeked his head out, and saw a long, darkened passageway lined with doors on each side. At the far end was another door. He stepped fully through the door and turned back to Sid. "You'd better let me lead the way. Even carrying Melinda, I have a better chance of fending off an attack."

Sid looked like he was going to protest, but then just nodded.

Crowdal walked silently down the passageway, Sid following. When they came to the first door, Crowdal noticed that the top half of the door had iron bars running vertically, letting him see inside. He gasped silently. This was a prison block inside of a House of Healing. It made no sense. He had never heard of such a thing. Now he knew why Mansico probably had his private chambers down here. He probably liked to hear the screams of the prisoners.

Crowdal peeked through the bars and saw that a man hung from the wall in shackles. The man didn't move and was probably dead, so he moved on to the next door. The room inside was empty, so he continued on. He looked in each room but didn't find anyone alive. At the last barred door, he glanced inside, ready to move on when he stopped and took a step back.

He grabbed a bar with his free hand and peered intently inside.

It was dark in the room and he smelled blood and feces. But he ignored that as he focused on the figure that hung from the wall. He couldn't see the face, but he saw by the size of the body that it was a Vringe. The odds of there being two Vringe in the entire city were too much of a coincidence.

Crowdal put the leaf-key into the imprint on the door and it clicked open. He turned and carefully set Melinda down against the wall, then whispered to Sid. "Stay out here and watch her. Let me know if you hear or see anyone coming."

Sid nodded and stayed quiet, stepping closer to Melinda protectively.

Crowdal entered the small cell and crossed immediately to the Vringe that hung on the wall, his head hanging to his chest. The man was so small he looked like a doll, but Crowdal immediately recognized him. His naked body was heavily muscled. Not many Vringe were in such top physical shape. They tended to be historians, court scribes, healers, anything that kept them from doing physical labor.

Crowdal gently lifted the man's chin until he could look at his face. 'The poor captain had probably been double-crossed by his own people,' Crowdal thought bitterly. All because of him. He spoke gently, "Captain, can you hear me?"

Captain Writhgarth slowly opened his eyes and they widened when he saw Crowdal. He smiled although his lips were cracked and bleeding. He coughed, spit dribbling down his chin. When it subsided, he laughed softly. "I never thought to see you again, Trith."

Crowdal smiled at him sadly. "Hold on, I'll get you down."

"That would be most appreciated."

Crowdal gritted his teeth as he pulled the shackles apart. He did the same for the feet and then slowly lowered the small man to the floor.

Captain Writhgarth sighed as he slid to the floor. He slowly rubbed his wrists and grimaced as he looked down to see that his skin was raw where the shackles had held him.

Crowdal dug in his pack, pulled out a shirt of his, and ripped strips from it. He gently tied them around Captain Writhgarth's bloody wrists.

While Crowdal was tending to the captain's wounds, Sid peeked into the room and saw that the man's clothing had been thrown in a corner. He quickly retrieved them and handed them to the little man, who looked up and smiled gratefully.

Captain Writhgarth slowly pulled the tunic over his head, groaning slightly in pain. But he continued, obviously used to pain. He stood up and pulled on his trousers, then his boots.

Crowdal whispered, "Who did this to you?"

Captain Writhgarth scowled then spit a globule of blood on the floor. "It was that bastard, Willem. Luckily, the prick had been called away just as he had started in on me."

Writhgarth looked around the room and saw his sword and belt lying in the corner. "Ah, thank the gods!" He hurried over and picked them up, examining the blade to make sure it wasn't damaged. He looked over at Crowdal and Sid and smiled as he buckled the belt and sword around his waist, walking back at the same time. He finished and held out his hand to each of them. "Thank you both. I owe you my life." It was a simple statement, but the sincerity in his voice spoke volumes more.

Crowdal and Sid both nodded as they shook his hand.

Crowdal went back at the door and picked up Melinda. "I wish we had time to chat, but we had better get going. We aren't exactly welcome guests here ourselves."

Writhgarth nodded, immediately understanding their predicament. "I'm ready. Let's go."

Sid pulled out the Haissan sword and held it awkwardly.

Captain Writhgarth eyed Sid warily, noticing that he was not used to holding a sword. He reached out and took Sid's hands in his own. "Here, put your fingers like this and your thumb here." He helped Sid move his fingers into the proper grip. "Now, if you have to use this sword, your grip will be strong. But make sure if you hit anyone or anything with this blade, that you grip the hilt hard as you connect. Otherwise the sword will jump from your hands and you will likely cut yourself."

Sid memorized how his fingers held the hilt then looked at Captain Writhgarth and nodded. "This does feel better. Thank you, sir."

Captain Writhgarth smiled. "Please, call me Writhgarth." He patted Sid's shoulder.

Sid smiled. "I'm Sid." He gestured at Crowdal. "This is Crowdal, and Melinda."

Writhgarth nodded at Crowdal. "We've had the pleasure of meeting already. Good to see you again, Trith." His eyes narrowed as he looked at Melinda and saw how badly injured she was. "Father Mansico did that to her, didn't he?"

Crowdal nodded, unable to speak.

Writhgarth's face turned red. "Mansico. I can't believe he's been doing this right under my own nose and I never knew about it. Some day I'm going to make sure he answers for this."

Crowdal nodded, liking the Vringe more and more. He would be a valuable person to have with them. He stepped out of the cell. The passageway to his right led to the main door. He turned to Writhgarth. "Do you by chance know what is on the other side of that door?"

Writhgarth nodded. "There is a staircase leading both up and down. They brought me in this way. Up leads to the main guard station." He grimaced. "I don't know where down leads."

Crowdal thought for a few moments, then said, "Well, I think anything is better than trying to get through the main guard station. Down it is then."

Chapter 33

Father Mansico took the cool, dampened cloth from the Haissan and hissed in pain as he put it against his swollen testicles. He then felt the cloth that was wrapped around his head. The last thing he remembered was the boy smiling as he kicked him in the head. He grimaced. The boy must have also kicked him in the groin when he had been unconscious.

Father Mansico smiled to himself. The boy was no innocent and had enjoyed the act of inflicting pain. He would be much easier to control that way. He knew from experience that it was much easier to exert influence upon a person who was already full of anger. He touched the lump on his head while caressing his crotch and smiled again through a grimace. And the Aleph Null was definitely full of anger.

His mistake was in not killing the Trith immediately. He looked at the Haissan as it finished tying the bandage. It was quick and certain in its movements. All Haissen were that way. Before today, Father Mansico would have scoffed at the idea of someone killing a Haissan. His eyes darkened. Much less two of them. Yes, he had underestimated the Trith and it had cost him the boy, but only for the moment.

He turned to the Haissan. "Gather a Murder. Meet me in my chambers. And send word out to the patrol to search the city for the boy, the Trith, and Melinda."

The Haissan nodded and left immediately.

Father Mansico walked gingerly to the back of the room and felt for his leaf key to open the door. He patted his chest all over. His key was gone. He went back to the center of the room and looked on the floor, thinking it may have fallen from him during the struggle. But no, it wasn't there either. He cursed. The boy and the Trith had taken it! He turned and left through the main door and made his way down the corridors, cursing the whole way and forgetting the pains in his body.

As he made his way to his chambers, he was joined by the Murder of Haissen, all thirteen of them silently surrounding him as he walked.

He descended the stairwell and noticed the door to his anteroom was open. Two Haissen immediately entered and secured it, motioning him inside. He saw the dead Haissan on the floor, its neck twisted at an unnatural angle. He grimaced. The Trith again.

Ignoring the dead Haissan, Father Mansico hurried into his chambers. As he opened the door, he saw that it was a mess, but he didn't care as he rushed to his desk to secure the manuscript, but before he got there, he stopped and stared down at a body on the floor. Ailinora stared up at him with surprise in her eyes. He knelt and examined her. Her neck had been crushed, and he could see teeth marks. 'His Tulgin must have done this. His Tulgin!' The idea of the creature betraying him made him more angry than he thought possible.

He knelt down by her body and lifted her head, tilting it at different angles to verify that the Tulgin had killed her. Poor Ailinora. Stupid Ailinora. At least he could trust her, even to the death.

He looked up at his desk and dropped Ailinora's head on the stone floor as he quickly stood up and walked around it.

The drawer was open and empty inside. They had taken the Manuscript.

He sat down in his chair, tilted his head back, and stared at the rough ceiling. He couldn't believe it. He had lost the Aleph Null, the Black Numbers manuscript, the Rissen blade, Ailinora, Elenora, his Tulgin, and Melinda, all in the span of a half-day.

He chuckled as he brought his head back forward. He was going to enjoy the next encounter with the boy and his little group of friends. They would not escape him and now he would inflict a little bit extra pain on them for even trying.

Father Mansico gestured to his lead Haissan. "Find where the boy and Trith went. Now!"

The Haissan quickly bowed and left the room.

Father Mansico removed the bandage from his head, then washed his face in a basin. He put on a new robe and combed his hair, wincing at the lump on his head. Somewhat refreshed, he turned as the Haissan came back into the room. It nodded to him, indicating that it had successfully found where the boy had gone.

"All right. When we find them, I want six of you to immobilize the Trith immediately. No hesitation. Same with the Tulgin, the old woman, and Melinda. But I want the boy uninjured. Not a scratch, understand? I will deal with him myself."

None of the Haissen reacted or acknowledged him, but Father Mansico knew they would do exactly what he had ordered.

The lead Haissan immediately turned and left the room and Father Mansico and his Murder of Haissen followed.

Chapter 34

Sid watched Crowdal carefully set Melinda down and fit the leaf-key into the door. He pulled his sword out as he pushed the door open. No Haissen were on the other side, so he put his sword back and picked up Melinda. "Come on, let's go."

They all started down the staircase. It was lit with a few torches but shadows shifted as they descended, making it difficult to see where to place their feet.

They made three full circles down the steps and came to a landing lit with a single torch. A hallway led to the left but it was completely dark. "Sid, would you mind grabbing that torch and leading the way?"

Sid took the torch and nodded at Crowdal with a mischievous grin. "Looks like you have your hands full. Let a real man lead the way."

Writhgarth laughed softly. "I'll follow behind Crowdal and Melinda. Someone has to protect the large man from the rear."

Crowdal chuckled. "Yeah, yeah, keep talking."

Sid led the way, moving slowly. He could only see a short way in front of the meager torchlight. He looked up at the round, yellow light that reflected off the ceiling and saw the stone was shiny and black. Water ran down the walls, making them oily and slick. As he looked down at the floor, he caught movement out of the corner of his eye on the ceiling. He looked back up and at first didn't see anything. But then he saw that the blackness was moving, looking like a slug as it crawled across a rock. He quickly turned back to Crowdal. "Be careful of the ceiling. Don't let your head touch it, something doesn't look right about it."

Crowdal bent lower and looked up, seeing the blackness slowly moving across the ceiling. He nodded to Sid in thanks and crouched down much lower as they walked.

They made their way like this and soon came to a large heavy door. The handle was completely rusted, but still looked strong. Crowdal stepped forward and leaned down to look more closely at it. There was a faint imprint of a leaf. He turned back. "Remind me to thank Mansico some time for his leaf key." He quickly fit it into the lock and the door clicked but didn't move. So he put the key away and pushed on the door with his huge arm. It still didn't move so he turned to Writhgarth. "Give me a hand with this."

Writhgarth stepped forward, putting his sword away. He leaned into the door and both he and Crowdal pushed. The door didn't move at first. They grunted and pushed harder until, finally, it slowly moved, grating loudly as it did. Soon the opening was wide enough for them to get through. They stopped pushing, breathing hard. The air that came through the opening smelled rotten and stale.

Sid put his hand to his nose and looked up at Crowdal. "That's disgusting. I'm not sure I want to go in there."

Crowdal chuckled. "I don't know about you, but I'll deal with a little stink any day over a bunch of Haissen."

Sid looked back the way they had come. "Yeah, I guess you are right." He held the torch out and slipped through the opening. The torchlight seemed to shrink in on itself, hardly reaching into the gloom. Sid could only see a few paces in any direction. He heard a scrabbling sound in the dark to his left, then again to his right. He swung the torch in both directions, the whoosh of air over the flame sounding distant. Then he heard the scrabbling in front of him. He pushed the torch out as far as he could but couldn't see anything in the dark. "What's that sound?" he asked, his voice sounding small.

Writhgarth and Crowdal slipped through the opening and stood behind him.

Writhgarth pulled his blade from his scabbard, the ring of steel sounding muffled. "I don't know. Probably rats. They are usually more scared of us than we are of them. They won't hurt us, so let's keep moving."

Sid took a hesitant step forward and his boot crunched on something. He looked down and noticed a white bone under his boot. He looked across the floor and saw that it was littered with white bones. He held the torch higher. Bones were scattered everywhere in the dim light.

Crowdal spoke in a low voice, "Looks like rat bones."

Sid looked over his shoulder. "Something in here eats rats?"

He heard the scrabbling sound again, this time coming from all around them. He raised his voice, panic starting to set in, "I don't like this, what do we do?"

Crowdal spoke calmly, "Take a deep breath, Sid."

Sid breathed in deeply.

"Good, now another. And another. Better now?"

"Yes." Sid's voice sounded small but it was stronger.

"Good, now keep moving forward. There has to be another door."

Sid held the torch out at arm's length and started forward again, taking care to avoid the bones when he could. He didn't like the crunching sound. He had only taken three steps when he caught movement at the edges of the light. It confused his eyes though. It seemed like the floor was moving, undulating. He took another hesitant step, then another, concentrating on the floor at the edge of the torchlight. After two steps he realized the floor was not moving.

Waves of bugs moved toward them, crawling over each other so thickly that they were as high as his knees. He yelled out, "Bugs!" He turned and bumped into Writhgarth.

Writhgarth saw the panic in Sid's eyes then looked past him and saw the wave of bugs coming toward them. He coolly glanced around the room, looking for any kind of escape, but the torchlight didn't reach far enough for him to see any way out. He turned to Crowdal. "I think we should go back. Quickly."

Crowdal immediately turned and carried Melinda back through the door.

Writhgarth grabbed Sid's shoulder. "Come on, I don't think we will win this battle with swords."

Sid didn't need to be told twice and ran back to the door, Writhgarth right behind him, their boots crunching rat bones as they went. The scrabbling sound grew louder, closing in behind them as they passed through the doorway.

Crowdal had already set Melinda down and was waiting to pull the door shut as soon as Writhgarth passed through. This time, with both hands, he had no trouble pulling the rusty door shut. As it closed, a few roaches passed through the opening and crawled over his boots, but the door sealed tightly, blocking the hoard from getting through. He stamped his boots, crushing the few roaches that had gotten through. He leaned against the door as if the roaches would find a way to open it.

Sid's eyes felt like they were going to bulge out of their sockets, and he was breathing hard.

Writhgarth stood calmly, as if he were on a stroll through the countryside.

'He was not a man that scared easily,' Sid thought. He took a few deep breaths to calm his nerves and pointed at the door. "I think that was the only way out of here. What do we do now?"

Crowdal rubbed his hands through his oily hair and sighed. "Looks like we have to go back the way we came."

Writhgarth was leaning close to the wall opposite the door and spoke gruffly, "Not necessarily. I'm not familiar with this particular passageway but I've been in my share of underground passages chasing all sorts of criminals, and I know from experience there is often a less obvious door in every tunnel. Criminals love them." He lightly traced a finger along the wall, avoiding the black mold that covered portions of it, until he felt a small wisp of air against his palm. "Ah... here it is."

He looked all around the wall. "Unfortunately, I can't see any mechanism with which to open it."

"Let me try," Crowdal said, taking a step forward and feeling along the wall. He noticed the slight coolness of air against his hand where an almost invisible crack ran down it. He smiled at Writhgarth. "You, my friend, are a genius. I can feel the air."

He felt all along the small crack, noticing that it indeed formed the shape of a door. "I don't see any leaf-key indentions anywhere. I guess this type of door was not intended for the holder of the key."

Writhgarth nodded. "The House of Healing was built on top of an even older site. This door most likely leads to the original sub-structure which pre-dates the House of Healing by thousands of years."

When Sid and Crowdal stared at Writhgarth, the small man shrugged unapologetically. "My father was an historian. I heard stories about almost every major building in Yisk since I was a child."

Crowdal rolled his eyes. "No wonder you became a man of the sword, you must have been bored to death as a child."

Crowdal turned back to examine the hidden door and as he moved his hands he accidentally touched the black mold with his left hand and yanked it away, yelping in pain.

He immediately tried to get the black mold off by wiping his hand along the floor. He lifted his hand and where the black mold had touched him, his skin had melted away and was now covered with dirt and mud. He wiped his hand on his trousers to clean it off a little.

Writhgarth stepped forward and lifted Crowdal's hand to examine it. He looked up at Crowdal. "You are lucky, that is fire mold." He saw the uncomprehending look on his friend's face. "I've never seen it before, but I've heard stories of people who ran into it and died a horrible death, their flesh melting to the bone."

Crowdal looked at the wall and shivered, despite his burned hand. "A lovely place down here. Hoards of roaches and now flesh-eating fire mold." He looked down at Writhgarth. "Thank you."

Writhgarth took out his water skin and poured some onto Crowdal's hand, cleaning out the dirt and remaining mold. Crowdal didn't make a sound, although Sid figured the pain must have been terrible.

Writhgarth put the stopper back on the water skin. "That should do it. I'd wrap that up though."

Crowdal shook his head. "Not now. I'm a fast healer and we need to get through this door as quickly as we can." He bent down and examined the wall again, only now from a safe distance. "There must be a hidden trigger somewhere." He took the torch from Sid and held it close to the wall, moving it slowly as he looked for any anomaly. He traced all the way around the crack but didn't find anything and stood back in exasperation.

Writhgarth saw Crowdal's frustration and whispered, "Looks like the builder was quite clever."

Crowdal looked down and grimaced. "There has to be a trigger somewhere but I can't find anything that stands out."

Writhgarth thought for a few moments. "Perhaps you are looking at this from the wrong angle."

"What do you mean?" Crowdal asked, looking puzzled.

Sid immediately understood what Writhgarth meant, so he blurted out, "You have to look for what is not there, not what is there."

Writhgarth smiled at him.

Crowdal hit his forehead lightly with the palm of his hand. "Of course." He leaned back and held the torch slightly away and looked at the wall as a whole, his eyes narrowed in concentration.

Sid wondered if he could use his power of numbers to find the door. He had never tried to use his numbers for anything like this before, but time was short. He had to make the attempt. He felt the power of the manuscript pulse from inside of Crowdal's pack and closed his eyes and pulled the power into himself. It was wonderful. In the darkness he saw the numbers floating around, bouncing off of each other and moving in random directions. Only now with the power of the manuscript, they seemed different, more alive.

He concentrated on the image of the wall as he remembered it before he shut his eyes. The image hung in the darkness as the numbers floated around it. Sid halted the movement of the floating numbers and pulled them into a line underneath the image of the wall. He knew the wall was really a large equation, taking in length, height, and the random rises and pitting of the uneven rock. He pulled numbers from the line and started plugging them into an equation, taking into account all of the factors that he knew. Soon he pushed the last variable into place and heard the snick of the equation as it turned green. He knew it was right.

The wall started to glow and he could see the normal irregularities. They were random yet that randomness matched his equation perfectly. As he studied the image of the wall he saw where a portion didn't glow. It was a blank, an emptiness. The randomness here was forced. He noted where it was in the wall then let the equation fade away. He had committed it to memory and could recall it at any time.

He opened his eyes and saw that Crowdal and Writhgarth were watching him. He felt embarrassed and looked down. "How long were my eyes closed?"

Crowdal looked at him with a strange look. "Only for a few moments. But you were unresponsive. Are you all right?"

Sid nodded, then looked at the wall and pointed. "The trigger is right here under the black mold. Just push it."

Writhgarth and Crowdal stared at Sid, puzzlement showing on their faces. They then looked where he pointed. Writhgarth glanced back at Sid. "Why do you say that?"

Sid shrugged. "I just know."

Crowdal pulled out his sword and turned to the wall. "Where was the trigger again?"

Sid pointed at a spot without hesitating.

Crowdal pushed the tip of his sword where Sid pointed. It looked just like any other spot, but as the sword tip touched the wall, the stone gave way. A click sounded and a mechanism turned in the wall. Crowdal stepped quickly back and they all watched a door appear in the wall and swing inward. Crowdal looked at Sid questioningly. "How did you know the trigger was there?"

Sid didn't know what to say. He didn't entirely understand what had happened. He felt the power of the manuscript calling to him. He knew it was somehow connected to his numbers, but he had no idea what it meant. He had never used his numbers in this way before. Unable to understand it just now, he shrugged. "I just knew."

Crowdal and Writhgarth looked at Sid for a few moments longer, then at each other and shrugged. They didn't have time to spend on this right now, so they both gathered their things.

Crowdal rubbed the sword tip against the floor to get the fire mold off. He noticed that it slid off the steel easily, causing no damage.

As Crowdal picked up Melinda she moaned and opened her eyes. She looked up at him, smiled weakly, and in a raspy voice asked for water. Crowdal took the water flask from his belt, pulled the stopper out with his teeth, and tipped it gently to her lips. She drank greedily, spilling as much water as she drank. Crowdal pulled it away and wiped her mouth with the back of his sleeve. "How are you feeling?"

Melinda looked around. "I've felt better. Where are we?"

"We are still inside the House of Healing, about to enter a secret underground passageway."

She looked at him questioningly. "There is no secret underground area that I know of."

Crowdal looked into her bloodshot eyes. "That's probably why it is a secret. I'll fill you in later but right now we have to get moving again. We need to get out of here before we have the entire Haissen squad down here after us."

Melinda nodded tiredly. "I can walk, there is no reason for you to carry me."

Crowdal looked at her worriedly. "I'm sorry, you would just slow us down right now."

Some of the fire returned to her eyes. "I'll not have you carry me like some helpless woman. Set me down."

Writhgarth stepped forward. "He is right, miss. We have to go now."

Melinda looked at Writhgarth, raising her eyebrows in anger. "I wasn't talking to you."

Writhgarth's face turned red and he glared at her for a few moments before looking up at Crowdal. "You'd best muzzle her if we are going to get out of here unnoticed."

Melinda struggled against Crowdal to get down, but he held her tightly.

"Let me down now."

Crowdal set her down and she immediately collapsed to the floor. He caught her and spoke softly but firmly to her, "Melinda, listen to me. We are in trouble here."

She struggled for another moment, then saw the look in his eyes and stopped.

Crowdal nodded slightly. "There is an entire squad of Haissen upstairs, probably searching for us right now. It is only a matter of time before they come down to this area. We have to get out of here now and you are not strong enough to keep up with us."

He held her stare with his own. "Do you understand?"

Melinda glared at him for a few moments, then nodded curtly. "Fine." She turned to Writhgarth. "We will have some words when we are out of here."

Writhgarth sighed and without a word, he took the torch from Sid and walked through the opening in the wall.

Sid looked at Crowdal and Melinda and followed Writhgarth.

Crowdal was the last one through and pushed the door shut with his foot.

Sid looked around and saw that they were in another narrow passageway. But this one didn't look to have been used for a long time. Cobwebs hung everywhere, some of them completely blocking the passageway. The torch in Writhgarth's hand burned with thick, black smoke, indicating it was close to burning out.

The cobwebs melted quickly as Writhgarth started down the passageway. Crowdal had to hunch over almost in half to avoid hitting his head on the ceiling. Sid could only imagine how uncomfortable it was for him to carry Melinda in this posture, especially after being run through by the Haissan's sword. But Crowdal pushed on, not complaining. Sid marveled at the strength his friend had.

They walked for some time in silence, listening to the quiet dripping of water and the soft shuffle of their feet. They didn't realize the passageway had started to angle upward until it became steeper. Sid started to feel relieved. Going up meant they were going in the right direction. Unfortunately, the torch also started to sputter.

Writhgarth looked at the torch with concern as he led them. "This torch is going to burn out very soon."

Sid took two more steps when the torch sputtered and went out.

They all stopped immediately as they were plunged into pure darkness. Sid couldn't even see his hand in front of him.

Melinda sighed. "Great. Just what we needed. I don't suppose anyone has a spare torch?"

"We didn't have that much time to search for spares," Writhgarth said in a grating voice.

In a calm voice, Crowdal said, "We are in a passageway. We just feel along the wall as we walk. It goes in one direction only."

Sid spoke up. "What about the fire mold?"

Crowdal cursed.

"We can't just stand here either." Writhgarth said in the darkness.

Sid looked around, widening his eyes to try and see anything at all, but he couldn't. It was pitch black. He felt the power of the manuscript reaching out to him, filling him with pleasure. He called his numbers and they immediately appeared in front of him. He knew his eyes were open. Why were his numbers visible?

He saw them clearly, slowly twisting and tumbling against each other. He decided to experiment. He concentrated on them, pulling them into a line, stopping their random floating. He didn't know why he did it, but he formed a simple equation and watched it snick together and turn green. The glow was faint and didn't put off much light, but it gave him an idea.

He started spinning the equation, watching it rotate in front of him, slowly at first, then he forced it to spin faster. The green glow of the equation became a solid circle. He stopped the simple equation and added variables to it, making it more complex. It was an equation he knew well from his years of practicing math with his father, so it was easy. The last number made a snick as it moved into place and the equation glowed almost twice as brightly. He heard a gasp from his friends and realized he could see their dark outlines standing next to him.

"What is that?" Melinda said from the darkness, as she looked at the glowing numbers and letters in front of her.

Crowdal also stared at the green light, mesmerized by it. Then turned to Sid and touched his shoulder. "Sid, are you doing this?"

Sid nodded, still amazed that he had created visible numbers. "Can you see the light, too?"

All three of his friends nodded.

Sid couldn't believe it. They could see his numbers! He never knew that was possible. He always thought they were only in his mind. He concentrated and forced the equation to spin even faster. The green glow increased, lighting the passageway all around them. He could see everyone clearly now and they all stared at him in astonishment.

Writhgarth whispered, "You're really doing this Sid?"

He nodded, not sure what to say.

"How are you doing it?" Melinda asked, awe in her voice.

Embarrassed, Sid shrugged. "It's hard to explain." They all stared at him, so he went on, "They are my numbers. I can manipulate them in my mind. Up until just now, I thought they were only in my mind. I never thought I could manifest them in the physical world." His voice trailed off.

Crowdal was the first to speak. "You are a constant wonder, my friend. I look forward to talking about this in great detail some day, but right now I think we should get moving." He looked up at the green spinning glow. "Can you keep that going permanently?"

Sid nodded. Once he got it spinning he didn't have to concentrate on it any more.

Writhgarth chuckled. "I think I have found my way into a very interesting group of people here. Come, let's find ourselves an exit."

They started walking down the passageway, the spinning green glow leading the way. Sid found that he could send the light on ahead with just a nudge of thought.

They walked quickly and soon came to the end of the passageway. It was a blank rock wall.

Crowdal whispered. "Sid, can you see the trigger here too?"

Sid looked at the door and brought forth the same equation he had used to find the first trigger. As he suspected, it didn't perfectly fit this wall because the makeup of the stone was different. But he was able to use the equation as a base. He concentrated on the wall, noting the numbers that fit the random indentations, raised rock edges, and pits. It was easy now that he had done it once and he quickly pulled the numbers together into an equation. He heard the familiar snick and it turned green. The wall began to glow and he saw the blank spot like before. He pointed at it.

Crowdal saw where he pointed. There was no black mold this time, so he reached out and pressed with his fingers. There was a click and the mechanism sounded inside the wall until a door opened inward. Moonlight came through the door, almost blinding them after the soft green glow amid the darkness. They all blocked their eyes for a few moments and then the three of them looked at Sid with awe.

Writhgarth was the first to break the silence. "Let me go first." He immediately eased through the opening, his sword held out in front of him. He ducked back inside almost immediately. "We are outside the House of Healing, in an alley." He looked at Sid. "Good job, Sid."

Crowdal nodded agreement, smiling. He looked around the group. "All right. Let's stay quiet once we get outside." He looked at Writhgarth. "Do you know exactly where we are?"

Writhgarth nodded. "We are on the east side of the House of Healing."

"Can you get us out of the city unseen?"

Writhgarth smiled. "Of course I can. I was captain of the city patrol. We will need supplies too. I know where we can get some in a very discreet manner. A... friend owes me."

Crowdal nodded. "Excellent. Are we ready then?"

Everyone nodded.

Crowdal looked at Sid. "Can you make the green circle disappear? It will draw attention to us."

Sid immediately stopped the equation from spinning and disassembled it. The light winked out.

Crowdal whistled softly. "That is so amazing." He smiled at Sid. "Time to join the ranks of the civilized world once again."

Sid walked through the hidden door and breathed in deeply, enjoying the fresh night air. After the dank, stale air of the passageway, the city air actually smelled sweet.

Writhgarth shut the door and immediately led them down the alley. The rest of the group followed him closely.

Chapter 35

Father Mansico and his Murder of Haissen descended the stairwell and looked down the dimly lit passageway. If the boy and his friends had come this way, they were probably dead by now. He knew the passageway ended at the roach room. He knew it well. That was where he dumped the bodies of those who happened to die in his House of Healing. The roaches were kept well fed.

They approached the door at the end of the passageway and his Haissen were about to open it when the lead Haissan stopped them. It pointed at the wall opposite the door. "They went this way."

Father Mansico looked at the blank wall. "What do you mean?"

"Tracks lead into the wall. They went this way."

Leaning forward, Father Mansico studied the floor carefully and saw that the Haissan was correct. There were imprints in the sand all around the wall, but some of them clearly led into it. It was a secret door. He stood up in amazement. This building never ceased to amaze him. He motioned to his lead Haissan. "Open it."

The Haissan stepped forward and studied every pockmark in the wall, its hooded head moving quickly. Then it lifted its sword without hesitating and pushed against a patch of black mold that was disturbed. The stone pushed inward and the door clicked open. The Haissan rubbed the tip of its sword on the floor to wipe off the mold and flicked the blade into its sheath.

It was dark inside, so the Haissan motioned its head to a member of the Murder and hissed, "Torches, lots of them."

A Haissan immediately sprinted down the passageway and returned in moments with torches, which it passed around.

Father Mansico spoke softly. "Move. Quickly, now."

The group entered the hidden passageway. Father Mansico pushed away images in his head of torturing an old woman and of cutting open a particular Trith. The boy was most important. But maybe, just maybe, he could have his fun after the boy and the manuscript were secured.

Father Mansico smiled as the door shut behind him.

Chapter 36

Writhgarth held up his hand at the end of the alley and the group stopped. They stood in a shadow of the bright moon, pressed against a wet and slimy wall.

Writhgarth crept forward and peered into the street. He stood perfectly still for a long time. Finally he came back and whispered, "I don't see any patrol around and there are only a few people about. We need to keep to the alleys as much as possible, but my contact is not far away so we should be safe."

Crowdal nodded. "Sounds good. Let's keep tightly together and move as one. Writhgarth, you lead. Sid you stay in the middle and I'll cover the back."

Melinda spoke up, "Crowdal, set me down. You are giving me blisters from carrying me. I need to walk for a bit."

Crowdal looked down at her in his arms and finally nodded. He set her gently down and she swayed slightly for a moment until she got used to standing again.

She looked a mess. Her face was bruised all over, her eyes swollen almost completely shut, and her bloody robe already stiff and crusty. But she was strong-willed and forced herself to take a few steps. As if she were surprised that she had more strength than she expected, she smiled sarcastically up at Crowdal. "'We can't let you slow us down, Melinda. We don't have time for this, Melinda,' you said. Well as you can see, I wouldn't have slowed you down back there."

Crowdal raised an eyebrow and chuckled. "I am so sorry, madam." He half-bowed. "I forgot you are as strong as a man."

She scowled. "And mocking me is going to make me feel bad?" She stood there, arms crossed.

Crowdal looked like he was about to apologize when Melinda put up her hand.

"Oh stop it. Don't apologize like an idiot. Just let me take care of myself. Now, we are wasting time and our little friend here looks anxious to go."

Writhgarth ignored her. He didn't want to play her games.

Crowdal stretched his back and heard it pop. "Actually, I am a little glad to get a break from carrying you in such tight places."

As Melinda passed by Crowdal, she touched his arm. "I know you meant well."

Crowdal nodded. "Don't worry about it. I guess I can be a jerk sometimes." He smiled down at her.

Melinda smiled back, even though her cut mouth must have hurt when she did it.

Writhgarth shook his head. He couldn't see what Crowdal saw in that woman. To each their own. He led the group to the end of the alley and they all crossed the street quickly to the alley directly across from them. They followed this alley, making what seemed like random turns at cross alleys, but Writhgarth never hesitated and they moved quickly.

Sid stepped over a large rat that darted out in front of him. When he looked up he almost ran into Writhgarth's back. He came to an abrupt halt, as did Melinda and Crowdal behind him. Writhgarth peered up at a darkened window, then bent down and picked up a small pebble and threw it at the glass. He then waited calmly.

No light went on, nor was there any indication that anyone was home. Writhgarth threw another small pebble and after a few more moments, the door in front of them opened hesitantly in the dark. Writhgarth stepped forward and whispered something, then turned back and motioned them all to go inside.

Sid entered through the doorway first, followed by Melinda and Crowdal. Writhgarth came last and closed the door silently behind him. He pushed his way past everyone and stood in front of the person who let them in. "I'm here to collect on your debt."

The man swallowed loudly. "I haven't done anything since we last..." he hesitated a moment, then said, "saw each other. I'm clean."

Writhgarth put up a hand to stop him. "I'm not here for that. Last year I told you I may need something from you in return for letting you go, remember?" His voice turned hard and he took a menacing step forward. "Well I'm here now and you will provide me everything I need." He said the last word through gritting teeth.

The man swallowed again loudly, took a small step back, and put up his hands. "All right, all right. Anything for you, Captain. What do you want?"

Writhgarth pointed back to Crowdal, Melinda, and Sid. "We need supplies. I won't notify the patrol and as far as you're concerned, we were never here. We'll soon be gone and you can go on selling on the black market to your heart's content." Writhgarth leaned forward again looking up at the man. "If I find out you say anything to anyone, I will be back here and you won't like me so much then."

The man shrunk back slightly as if he were trying to decide what he should do. He looked to be more scared of Writhgarth than the patrol, so he turned and led them quickly back into another dark room. He didn't light any lanterns and Writhgarth found himself putting his hands out as he walked to make sure he didn't bump into anything. As he entered the second room, he heard a door shut behind him and light flared from a lantern that hung from a hook on the wall. He blinked his eyes quickly, blinded by the light. But he soon became accustomed to it. They were in a windowless room that had shelves stacked from floor to ceiling, all containing a wide variety of items from food to clothing to weapons.

Crowdal whistled quietly. "Nice set up here, my friend."

The man, who was so ordinary that he wouldn't be given a second look on the street, nodded to Crowdal, then looked fearfully at Writhgarth. "Take anything you want. I'll be upstairs in bed." He turned and quickly left the room. His voice echoed back to them. "Lock the door behind you when you leave. There are... a lot of unpleasant people out there."

Writhgarth looked at all the shelves and was amazed again at the man's operation. He saw one whole shelf stacked with dried meats and cheeses and his mouth started to water. He realized he was hungrier than he had ever been. He reached out and grabbed a chunk of hard white cheese and peeled back a layer of wax. The strong smell of cheese filled the room as he took a large bite. The taste was bitter, but he chewed and swallowed quickly, taking another bite right away.

Crowdal smiled. "Now that, my friend, is a good idea. I'm starving." He looked at Melinda. "May I buy you some dinner?"

Melinda laughed. "I don't know, we've only just met."

Crowdal took her arm, pretending he was escorting her to a fancy tavern. He motioned with his arm at the floor. "How about this table, do you find it acceptable?"

Melinda looked down, then up at Crowdal and curtsied, obviously enjoying the little moment of fun after the horrors of the past night. "It's perfect. I'll have the cheese platter please."

Crowdal selected a couple of nice cheeses, some crusty black bread, some raw onions and carrots and they sat down on the floor. He grabbed a small piece of cloth from his pack and set it on the floor, then removed his knife and sliced some cheese for them. Crowdal looked up at Sid and Writhgarth. "Why don't you join us? There is plenty of room at our table."

Writhgarth and Sid laughed, their stress temporarily gone, and they sat down cross-legged.

Crowdal cut up the onions and carrots as they sat in a circle.

Writhgarth grabbed a haunch of dried beef and cut it up for everyone. Soon everyone was eating, although Crowdal passed on the meat, which surprised him. He had never heard of a Trith not eating meat, but he didn't ask about it. He was too hungry.

After a short while Crowdal told them the story of how he had met Sid; of how Sid had fallen asleep against a tree while two men crept up on him, intent on killing him. Crowdal chuckled. "And he must have been having an interesting dream."

He winked at Sid, who blushed and turned away.

Melinda glanced at Writhgarth with an embarrassed smile.

Crowdal finished the story, telling how the last they saw of the two men, they were tripping over each other as they crashed through the brush trying to get away. They all laughed quietly, even Sid, as they enjoyed the moment.

Writhgarth finished chewing a chunk of cheese. "Those poor gentlemen. I think being terrorized by a Trith will make them think twice before doing something like that again."

Melinda nodded in agreement. "You should be ashamed of yourself, Crowdal. You could have just asked them to leave. You didn't have to humiliate them like that."

Crowdal mock bowed. "Next time, my dear."

Writhgarth turned serious. He motioned to Sid with a hunk of bread. "Sid, I think we have a little time. I'd like to know what you did back in that passageway."

* * *

The small room was filled with the sounds of chewing and swallowing as Sid thought back to when he first left home, not even sure how many days ago it was. It seemed like ages ago already.

He looked at Crowdal, then Melinda and Writhgarth. And now here he was sitting in a small room filled with stolen goods, sharing a meal with three people he had only just met, running from the city patrol, the strange creatures called Haissen, and some crazy man who seemed to run the city; and to top things off, he was being pursued by the Korpor.

He shivered, then smiled shyly at his friends. He owed them an explanation, they were all in this together. But where to start? He hesitated, then decided to just tell them everything he knew.

So in a quiet voice, he told them about his numbers. He took a small bite of bread and chewed as he finished speaking. "I always thought the numbers were only in my head." He stopped speaking for a moment, then went on in a whisper, "Until tonight, that is."

They all sat silently for a few moments, as if not knowing what to say. Crowdal was the first to break the silence. "Sid, I didn't understand a word of what you said about your numbers."

Sid looked down, embarrassed. Melinda elbowed Crowdal in the side, glaring up at him through swollen eyes. Crowdal immediately went on, "What I meant was, what do you mean by using numbers?"

Sid knew Crowdal was only being honest. The numbers in his head were real to him, but to others, they were strange. Sid also believed that since he found the manuscript, what he was doing with them was something new, at least as far as he knew. He didn't blame his friends for not understanding.

He looked up at them through the strands of greasy hair that partly covered his eyes. "It isn't really something I can go into in any more detail. It's not that I don't want to, it's just that I don't know how to describe it. The only thing I can think of that is similar is when you try to remember the images in your head when you wake up from a dream. They seem real, don't they, but when you try to think about them, they feel distant, unreal, and then they fade away. My numbers are like those images but they are always with me. They don't fade away." Sid closed his eyes and sighed. He was so tired.

Crowdal leaned back and patted his belly. "Now that meal was a long time coming. I would eat more, but I don't think I could stand up again."

Writhgarth nodded, patted his own belly and belched loudly.

Melinda rolled her eyes. "Men!"

Sid smiled, thankful for Crowdal breaking the tension. He had never felt this much a part of a group before and didn't know how to act around people. He had never really learned or cared about it before now. People just never really interested him much. He preferred to spend time alone. But these were good people and he was glad to have them around. He cleared his throat and everyone looked at him. "I know we all really just met, but we should figure out what we are going to do, and if we are going to do it together or separately."

Writhgarth nodded. "Good point, Sid." He looked fierce with his scars. "I am a hunted man, I cannot stay here in Yisk." He turned his head and spat on the floor. "My patrol has turned their back on me, something I never thought would happen." He rubbed his eyes with his hand, then looked up at them and took a deep breath. "I need to clear my name, but I can't do it here. I need to go to Undaluag. I can present my case there."

Melinda put a hand on his arm. "I'm sorry for the things I said earlier, I had no right to treat you so poorly." She squeezed his arm. "I have had... well let's just say it was a bad day."

Writhgarth looked at her bruised and cut face, and her swollen eyes. "There's no need to apologize."

Melinda smiled at him, then turned to Crowdal and Sid and scowled. "I'm with Writhgarth. I can't stay here either, not with..." she started coughing and shuddered as pain shot through her breast.

Crowdal put a hand on her arm and she looked up and half-smiled. "Thanks. I'm fine." She coughed again and grimaced with the pain.

Writhgarth and Sid politely looked away as she wiped her mouth with the blood-crusted sleeve of her robe. Crowdal hovered over her with worry.

She looked up at him. "I'm all right, honest." She hardened her voice. "I'm not staying here in Yisk, not with that animal Mansico here." She looked at the three of them. "I would like to go with you, wherever you are going."

Writhgarth waved his arm at Crowdal and Sid. "I guess that leaves you two. What are your plans?"

Sid looked up at Crowdal. He didn't even know where Crowdal had been going when they had met on the road. They just seemed to fall in together and after only a few days he already considered him his closest friend in the world. He hated to think of parting ways. And quite honestly, he was scared. Scared of Father Mansico, scared of the Korpor, scared of the Oblate, and most of all, he was scared of losing his friends. Aside from Tris back home, he had never had any his whole life. It felt good but he couldn't risk their lives. What he was mixed up in would likely get them all killed.

He glance at Writhgarth, then Melinda, and finally Crowdal. "I have to face Father Mansico and end this one way or another. I won't let you all come with me, it is too dangerous."

Melinda looked like she was going to interrupt, but Sid spoke over her. "No, it is settled. I am going to make that man pay for what he has done, even if I die while doing it. But I cannot...," his voice cracked, but he continued, "live with myself if any of you died because of me."

He stood up, but before he could step away, Crowdal reached over and took his arm. "Sid, sit down, please."

Sid looked at him for a moment, then reluctantly sat back down, crossing his ankles and wrapping his arms around his knees.

Crowdal looked Sid directly in the eyes. "We've been through a lot in the past few days, right?"

Sid nodded reluctantly, pretty sure where Crowdal was going with this. "Which is exactly why I have to go."

Crowdal talked over him. "You saved my life, Sid."

Sid shook his head. "What does that have to do with anything?"

"What matters is that you did that for me. I can guarantee that until I met you, I had never met a person who would do that for a Trith." He paused, getting a little choked up. "I consider you my friend and that is not something I have called another person in a long time."

So whether you like it or not, I am going to tag along with you for a while longer yet." He chuckled. "Besides, I would enjoy having a bit of fun."

Sid didn't know what to say, so he kept his face perfectly emotionless.

Melinda laughed and punched Crowdal in the leg. "And I need to come along to watch over this idiot. He'll probably trip over his own feet and fall on you."

Crowdal snorted and rolled his eyes and Sid smiled slightly. It wasn't so much a smile as a thinning of his lips actually, but Crowdal silently thanked Melinda.

Melinda nudged Sid's foot with her own. "So where is this place you have to go?"

"Undaluag."

Melinda cocked her head slightly. "Why Undaluag?"

Sid thought of the manuscript. Of the power in it. Then he thought of Father Mansico and the Korpor. He couldn't fight them on his own, he needed the help of the Anderom, so he whispered, "A friend of mine advised me to seek some people who could help me. They are in Undaluag."

Melinda looked over at Writhgarth. "Well if that is the case, it looks like we are all traveling to the same place."

Writhgarth nodded, then cleared his throat. "I won't pry into your reasons for going there, Sid, they are your own. But I am curious where you are going in Undaluag. It is a large city."

Everyone turned to Sid. He hesitated, but finally reached into his pack and carefully took out the map his father had drawn for him and unfolded it on the floor. "I need to find the east gate and look for a tobacco shop."

They shifted closer to look. When Writhgarth saw Undaluag written on the map he leaned in closer and picked it up. "This is a beautiful piece of work and drawn on high quality paper. This map is worth a lot of coin." He looked at Sid with respect, then back down at the map, but as he did, the color drained from his face and he hissed through his teeth and leaned back quickly, dropping the map as if the paper had burned his hand.

Melinda looked at him questioningly. "What's wrong? What is it?"

Sid was surprised and a little confused by Writhgarth's reaction.

Writhgarth rubbed a hand through his thinning black hair and looked at Sid, fear in his eyes. "Please don't tell me you are traveling to the Oblate?"

"Gods, no! My father drew this map, but I found out later..." He got choked up and had to stop for a moment before continuing, suddenly angry. "I found out that he was an agent for the Oblate."

Writhgarth stood up and paced the floor, twisting his hands together, muttering to himself.

Crowdal studied Writhgarth. "Writhgarth what's going on?"

When Writhgarth didn't respond, he said his name louder.

Writhgarth stopped pacing and looked at Crowdal, fear in his eyes. Sid couldn't believe he was seeing Writhgarth show fear. He seemed like a man who wouldn't hesitate to face ten men in battle.

The panic slowly faded from Writhgarth's face and he rubbed his eyes and looked around with an embarrassed smile. "I'm sorry. I just never thought I would hear that name again."

Crowdal put a hand on the little man's shoulder. "Let's sit down and talk about this. I would like to know more about this place. Until today, I had never heard of it either. But it seems that everyone knows about it." He looked over at Sid. "And I'm pretty sure Sid would like to hear what you know. Everything seems to revolve around him and the Oblate."

Sid nodded, although he was nervous. Every time the name Oblate was spoken, it seemed that bad things happened. But when it came down to it, he really didn't know much about it himself, other than it was some sort of ancient and evil organization that wanted him.

Writhgarth sat back down gingerly, obviously a little sore from the beating he had taken in the cell. He looked at Melinda, who nodded comfortingly at him. He tried to smile back but couldn't. He then looked over at Sid, who sat holding his knees in his arms. Writhgarth shifted and then whispered, "The Oblate doesn't exist."

Sid looked at Writhgarth questioningly. That was the last thing he expected to hear and it didn't make any sense. "It does, my father gave me exact directions to find the place." He didn't tell them about the Rissen blade that his father had given to him as introduction. That was not something he wanted to share.

Writhgarth's eyes widened. "You know where it is?"

Sid nodded, not so sure he should be talking about this. He was getting a bad feeling.

Writhgarth looked over at Crowdal and Melinda and chuckled ironically. "This boy is a wonder. First he tells us that he is going to a place that has been nothing but myth for a thousand years, then sits there and tells us that his father gave him exact directions to it. I would be tempted to call him a liar."

Sid glared at Writhgarth.

Writhgarth shook his head. "Oh stop it!"

The anger burst inside of Sid. It had always lingered just under the surface, always ready to jump out. He grabbed his pack and leapt to his feet. "That's it, I am out of here."

Everyone stood up. Crowdal and Melinda started to object, but Writhgarth beat them to it. He stood up and grabbed Sid by the front of his tunic, pulling him down so they were almost touching noses, and hissed through his teeth. "I've been captain of the patrol for sixteen years. I have literally seen hundreds of young men like yourself get killed for the copper pieces in their pockets. You will die before you get halfway through this city in the night. For some reason, and I don't know why, I don't want that to happen." He motioned to Crowdal and Melinda. "And I don't think these people want that to happen either. It's time you grew up and stopped acting like a child." He let go of Sid's tunic and stepped back, glaring at him.

Sid was shocked and unable to move. He looked at Crowdal, who watched him with no expression on his face. He felt ashamed for losing his temper. He was no longer a kid playing in the woods. This was real life and he would have already been dead countless times were it not for these people, his friends. Whether he liked it or not, not only did he need their help, but he was also responsible for them in a way. If he were caught by Mansico and his Haissen, he would be tortured and would give them away. He didn't fool himself into thinking he would be able to resist.

With his cheeks burning red, he sat down. "I'm sorry, I am a fool."

Writhgarth grunted, then patted his shoulder before sitting down himself.

Melinda and Crowdal also settled back to the floor and Melinda motioned with her hand to Writhgarth. "So tell us what you know of the Oblate."

Writhgarth shrugged. "I only know of it because my father was an historian for the University of Yisk. He studied lost myths as a hobby. I remember him reading through hundreds of scrolls in the evenings at the University library."

Sid looked up. "Hundreds of scrolls? I can't believe that many exist in the world."

Writhgarth smiled. "Not many people know about the room of scrolls at the University. It is worth a fortune." He put one knee up and rested his arm on it as he spoke. "One late night, when I was about thirteen, my father and I were in the scrolls room, far underground. I still remember him leaning over a desk, a single candle burning next to him as he carefully read every word of an old scroll. Then he stood up, angry that it wasn't what he was looking for. So he walked over to the wall of scrolls. He tried to remove another scroll but it was stuck. So he carefully reached inside of the cubbyhole to get it loose. Finally it did come, but he kept his hand inside of the hole. Then he reached in further. I remember his brow furrowing as he reached as far back as he could. Then he carefully slid out a manuscript."

Writhgarth glanced at Sid. "It was pure black. I was not interested in such things, so I went back to pretending that I was fighting with a sword, when all of a sudden he came back to the desk and called me over. I had never seen such excitement in his eyes before, so I ran over. I remember he looked up at me and his eyes danced by the light of the torches as he said, 'I've found it! The Black Numbers manuscript. It exists. I can't believe it!'."

Writhgarth took a deep breath and continued. "My father opened a silver clasp and turned to the first page, then the second, and when he came to the third page, he paused for a long time before reading it out loud. I still have those words burned into my brain. I have never been able to forget them.

What is not visible in this world rules supreme. Chaos and absolute power collide with the awakening of the Aleph Null, true wielder of Black Numbers, bringing that which doesn't exist into existence, or erasing existence for all."

Sid shuddered at the words.

Writhgarth continued, not noticing Sid's reaction. "My father had leaned back, a satisfied look on his face. He had been searching for any reference to the Oblate without success for thirty years, but he had never expected to find the mysterious Black Numbers manuscript. He had roughed up my hair with a grin on his face. When he started reading again, his smile had faded to a grimace and he said, 'This is bad. This is very bad.' And then he started to read out loud.

A union of the Aleph Null and the beast, of claws and youth, binding a ring of bloody flesh to burst forth the seed of life. A birth, spawning numbers unknown, here yet there, a worm alive at both ends twisting the world upon itself until only the Oblate rises bringing darkness upon the world. The Aleph Null, falling to infinity holds the Black Numbers in a mind's eye, twisting on an axis."

Writhgarth shifted uncomfortably. "My father had turned the page again but only saw numbers all over them. He quickly flipped through the remaining pages but only saw numbers. He did something that night that I never thought he would do. He stole that manuscript. He silently slid it into his pack. We went home that night and my father never spoke of it again."

Writhgarth was silent for a few moments, his eyes haunted by the memory. Finally he looked up at everyone and shrugged. "Years later, as my father lay dying, he told me where he had hidden the manuscript and begged me to keep it safe. He didn't know what from, but he knew it was important."

Writhgarth looked at Sid. "I think we should risk going to my place to get that manuscript. I think it is something important. It is too much of a coincidence that you are here Sid."

Melinda looked quizzically at Writhgarth. "What about the patrol? Won't they be waiting for you there?"

Writhgarth shook his head. "I think this is important enough for the risk."

Melinda nodded, agreeing with him.

As Sid listened to Writhgarth, he thought of the Black Numbers manuscript. It called to him. Pulled him inward. The hum of power was like music, intoxicating music. Suddenly he started to feel numb all over. Only his fingers tingled. He felt the hum come from Crowdal's pack. The manuscript called to him. Writhgarth's voice started to fade. He faintly heard his name being called and then he heard nothing more.

All he saw was the darkness in his mind.

He couldn't feel his own body anymore, not even the tingling in his fingers. Desperately, he tried to call forth his numbers, but they didn't appear. He panicked, unable to move or do anything. He had no sense of time.

He could have been floating forever when pain flared in his penis and he felt intense burning where the Korpor had cut him with its claw. But the pain was wonderful to him. It was the only thing that was real. He concentrated on it, reveling in the painful sensation. He used that pain to concentrate and from out of nothingness his numbers floated into view, tumbling around the darkness.

He immediately grasped for them and felt them respond to his mental touch. He sighed in relief.

He thought of the darkness in the underground passageway. He had used his numbers to find a way out. He wondered if he could do it again.

He pictured a door in the darkness and let the numbers float past it. He created some dimensions of the door and plugged in the proper numbers into an equation. He then pictured the door opened up, the angle of the opening, the light that would spill through. It was complex and he strained to switch out variables in the equation, trying to create the correct combination that would force the door open.

He grasped one final number and plugged it into the equation and he heard the snick as the equation turned green. The door grew physical dimensions and he nudged it open. Bright light blinded him. He rushed carelessly toward it, just wanting to get out. He felt his head hit something hard and pain shot through him. He hungrily took a deep breath of air. It was sweet and fresh and he cried in delight.

He felt hands touch his face and then he heard Melinda's voice.

"Sid! Can you hear me? Sid!"

He opened his eyes, squinting at the light. Finally he saw Melinda hovering over him, her concerned brown eyes concentrating on him. He nodded and struggled to sit up.

Melinda, with Crowdal's help, assisted Sid to a sitting position. They sighed in relief when he breathed in deeply. Writhgarth had stood up and was watching them from a few paces away, concern on his face also.

Crowdal sat back. "What happened Sid?"

Sid's body trembled. "I don't know. One moment I was listening to Writhgarth, the next I was stuck somewhere dark."

Melinda asked him to watch her finger as she moved it back and forth in front of his eyes. She then looked at the back of his head. "You look fine. A little knock to the head, but no concussion." She looked at him quizzically.

Sid felt the back of his head and looked at his fingers. There was no blood, but his head throbbed. It seemed that he had been knocked in the head every day lately. He looked around and saw everyone staring at him with concern. He shook his head as he thought about the passage. It terrified him. He struggled to put it out of his mind. He couldn't handle that right now.

Crowdal looked at Melinda. "Is he going to be all right?"

Melinda nodded. "He is fine." She looked at Sid, studying him as if she were not sure she was telling the truth.

Crowdal stood up, brushing the back of his trousers, and gave him a questioning look, and Sid knew what he was silently asking. The Black Numbers manuscript. Should he trust this group? He looked at Melinda, then Writhgarth and saw only concern. He knew that he needed to trust them. There was no other way.

Sid nodded to Crowdal and then turned to the Vringe. "We don't need to go to your place Writhgarth. I have the Black Numbers manuscript already."

Writhgarth's eyes widened, then he glared at Sid. "You stole it from me?"

Sid put up his hands. "No. I found it in Father Mansico's chambers when we were escaping the House of Healing."

Writhgarth looked closely at Sid as if trying to verify that he was telling the truth. The little man let out his breath. "I'm sorry." He paced around the room in agitation. "How did Mansico get it from me? I was the only one who knew about it." He paused, as if thinking, then slapped his leg. "Damn, it was Willem. I bet he told Mansico about my scroll collection and my father's interest in the Oblate. I remember now that I casually mentioned it during a dice game with Willem and the other patrol members. Mansico must have had my house raided." He turned to Sid. "Can I see it, just to make sure it is the same one?"

Sid nodded and turned to Crowdal. "Show him."

Crowdal reached into his pack and pulled out the manuscript, holding it out to Writhgarth.

Writhgarth breathed in sharply, then huffed. "Put it away." He sat down and ran a shaking hand through his thinning hair. "So what do we do now? We have to keep Sid and that manuscript out of Mansico's hands. I've looked into that bastard's eyes while I was being beaten by Willem. He enjoyed it. I say we get out of Yisk as soon as possible."

Sid nodded. "If we can get to Undaluag and meet with the Anderom, we will be safe."

Melinda sighed. "But how are we going to get out of Yisk unnoticed?"

Writhgarth grunted. "Leave that to me. I know a way out that only I know about. It is an entrance to a tunnel system beneath an old building on Riouth Street." He looked at each of them. "Do you trust me?"

They all nodded.

"All right, then we leave here and move quickly." The captain walked to a pile of leather packs stacked in the corner. He sorted through them until he found one he liked, then turned to the group. "Fill your packs with anything you want. I think it would be good for each of us to grab at least two torches, too. While it was nice to have the light that Sid created, I would feel more comfortable using torches."

Everyone nodded, remembering the dark passageway they had just been in. If it hadn't been for Sid, they would not have gotten out. Having a backup light source was important.

Sid looked around the room. "We can take anything we want? Won't that guy be angry?"

Writhgarth motioned his head at the room. "He won't care what we take. He knows better than to question me." He smiled a crooked smile and a single spot of red appeared on his cheeks. "I'm really not a bad guy, but sometimes it is good to let others think that I am."

They all just stared at him.

Crowdal looked down innocently at Writhgarth. "Well I, for one, am glad you're a bastard."

Writhgarth smiled. "I seem to remember letting you go, even though you were wanted for accosting people and stealing from them."

Crowdal chuckled. "That may have been your biggest mistake yet."

With that, Crowdal started putting huge amounts of cheese, bread, and vegetables into his pack.

Melinda walked over to the pile of packs in the corner and found one for herself and started putting food into it. She looked at Crowdal as she stuffed a few apples inside her pack. Her eyes danced mischievously behind the deep purple bruises. "You're packing food like the pig you are."

Crowdal looked over his shoulder. "I wouldn't talk, scar face."

Melinda threw an apple, hitting him in the side of the head. The fruit burst apart and juice and bits of apple got stuck in his hair.

Crowdal wiped at it with his hand, and when he looked at her, she lifted her pack as protection, expecting him to retaliate, but he just winked at her and continued stuffing food into his pack.

The amounts that Crowdal shoved into his pack were astounding to Sid, who picked and chose the things he liked best to add to his pack. Sid turned around to examine the other shelves when he caught the smell of tobacco. He narrowed his eyes and scanned the room, then saw the large canvas bags lying in the corner. He crossed over and opened the top bag, sticking his nose inside and inhaling. The sweet smell of tobacco was intoxicating. He smiled and pulled out a handful of browned leaf. 'There was enough tobacco to service an army,' he thought in amazement. He looked around and saw a small bag on a shelf and grabbed it. It was the perfect size, so he stuffed it full of tobacco.

Crowdal stood next to Sid peering over his head and breathed in deeply. "Ah... tobacco." He reached into the sack and pulled out a huge handful of tobacco leaf, pinching it between his fingers as he let if fall back in. He looked down at Sid, a huge grin on his face. "It has been so long since I've had a smoke." He grabbed a bag similar to Sid's and filled it full of tobacco, pulling the drawstrings tight with a sigh. He looked over at Melinda and Writhgarth. "Do you want some? It's pig leaf, but it's tobacco all the same."

Writhgarth walked over and his eyes gleamed when he saw the tobacco. "I could be persuaded."

Crowdal laughed and threw Writhgarth an empty bag. He turned to Melinda and raised an eyebrow. She shook her head. "Sorry, I only smoke Uragon leaf, not that... trash."

Crowdal chuckled. "Good luck with that. I haven't found any Uragon in a long time."

Melinda shrugged. "I'll wait."

"Suit yourself. Just don't come to me asking for a smoke when we are in the middle of nowhere."

Melinda huffed. "I'd rather smoke hay."

They finished packing up their food and tobacco.

Sid tied his pack closed and saw Writhgarth looking at Melinda as she adjusted her pack. The little man moved to the back of the room and soon returned with an armload of clothing. He stopped behind Melinda and when she turned to him, he held out his arms, looking slightly embarrassed. "I saw these earlier and figured you could use a fresh set of clothes."

Melinda touched his face softly and thanked him as she took the clothing from his arms. She set them down and without hesitating, stripped off her robe and stood naked in front of everyone as she put on the new clothes, including undergarments, thick trousers, a warm tunic, and sturdy boots.

Sid and Writhgarth both turned away, but Sid heard Crowdal quip in a light voice, "You know, despite all the bruises and cuts, you have a beautiful body." Sid turned his eyes slightly and saw Melinda wince as she stretched her arms to pull on the tunic.

"Is that all you can think of you sad man?"

Crowdal stepped forward and helped her, tenderly pulling the tunic down. "I'm sorry." He gently pulled it into place. "Is that too tight?" he asked, looking into her dark eyes.

Melinda flushed slightly and her eyes softened briefly before she pushed his hands away. "It is perfect, but I don't need your help."

Crowdal nodded as he turned away and joined his friends by the door.

Melinda finished getting dressed and kicked her old bloody robe into the corner. She picked up her pack and joined everyone by the door.

They all stood there for a few moments, no one moving. This had been a small safe place, even if it was only for such a short time. They hated to leave so soon, but they knew they must. Mansico was probably after them by now. They didn't have any time left.

Crowdal put his hand on Writhgarth's shoulder. "Ready when you are."

Writhgarth nodded. "Everyone, stay close and make no noise. We have to move quickly but quietly."

Crowdal picked up the lantern, looked once at each of them, then cupped his hand and blew it out. The room fell to complete darkness and Writhgarth opened the door.

Chapter 37

The alleyway was dark but Writhgarth saw the sky was starting to turn a lighter shade of blue. He hoped they could get out of the city before the sun rose and made it easier for their enemies to find them. He heard a soft curse and quickly turned his head back and saw Sid had just stepped into a jagged hole in the ground. The boy had barely caught himself from falling, running a few steps to catch his balance. In the process, he accidentally kicked a small rock, which banged against the wall. Even though it was a small rock, the crack of stone on stone echoed in the narrow alleyway. Writhgarth hissed and Sid stopped immediately.

"Sorry," he whispered.

Writhgarth put up his hand for silence.

Writhgarth heard a rat squeaking softly as it foraged for food. It sounded like an old man talking to himself.

They stood still for a few more moments, then Writhgarth put his hand down and turned to Sid and whispered, "I know it is dark, but we have to be very careful to watch where we walk." He gazed intently at the rest of the group before turning and leading them on.

They moved on quietly, crossing streets quickly when they were clear.

Writhgarth put his hand up to stop them at a corner. He peered around it, searching every dark shadow. Finally, he pulled his head back, turned to the group, and whispered, "Something seems wrong here. Be ready for anything."

Crowdal nodded and reached to his back to make sure his sword was loose in the scabbard.

They made it halfway across the street when four figures stepped from the shadows.

Writhgarth stood up straight, putting his hand on his sword hilt. Crowdal stood calmly, but he looked prepared to draw his sword quickly.

One of the figures strode forward, followed by the three others, until he was right in front of Writhgarth.

Writhgarth noticed Crowdal stiffen slightly.

The man turned toward the group and his face became visible by the increasing light of coming dawn. He was handsome, although the easy smile on his face had always made him look like an asshole to Writhgarth.

The man mockingly half-bowed to him and smirked. "What a nice surprise, I didn't expect to find you with this group, Writhgarth. But I really couldn't be happier. Officially, it will be a shame that you resisted arrest and I had to kill you."

Writhgarth spat on the man's boot and smiled up at him. "You can wash your boots with my spit, Willem, because you are a sad piece of shit." He gruffly turned to the other men and nodded a greeting. "Good to see you tonight, Grug, Srittem, Paal."

The three other men nodded, their eyes dancing with humor at what Writhgarth had just done.

Willem's face turned red as he bent down and wiped the globule of spit from his shiny black boot with a white handkerchief. "I will enjoy killing you, little man. And after you," he looked over at Crowdal, "I'll take great pleasure in running my sword into the Trith's gut."

Writhgarth barked a laugh. "Good luck with that. From the rumors, your *sword* is too limp to stick anywhere."

With a roar, Willem pulled his sword and swung down with incredible speed and power at Writhgarth's head, only the sword struck the dirt of the street instead. Writhgarth lightly poked Willem in the buttocks, drawing blood but not seriously hurting him.

With a yelp, Willem jumped away and turned toward him, his eyes wide in rage.

A chuckle came from the three patrol members and Willem turned to them. "I'll deal with you three after this and it won't be pleasant." He then lunged at Writhgarth, his sword moving in quick thrusts.

Writhgarth parried every thrust easily and then sliced Willem's left ear off with a quick flick of his blade.

Willem screamed, putting his hand to his ear in panic. Blood ran through his gloved fingers and his ear lay in the dirt at his feet like a discarded piece of meat. His eyes dilated and he screamed as he attacked Writhgarth.

Writhgarth stood still. As Willem swung down with his sword, he stepped to the side and tripped him. Willem fell flat on his face and his sword flew out of his hands, landing a few paces away. Writhgarth stepped on the back of Willem's head and pushed the good-looking man's face into the dirt.

Willem shoved violently up, throwing Writhgarth back a step. He stood up, spitting dirt out of his mouth, sputtering in rage. He turned to his men. "Kill him, now!"

The three men looked at Writhgarth, who calmly stood in front of them, his hands resting on the hilt of his sword with the point in the dirt. As one, they nodded to Writhgarth with respect, then faded into the darkness.

Willem screamed after them, spittle flying out of his mouth, "You are all dead men!"

Writhgarth motioned to the sword on the ground and spoke in a calm voice, "Pick up your sword Willem. It is time to finish this."

Willem looked down at his sword lying on the ground, then up at Writhgarth. Without hesitation he turned to run away, but instead ran right into Crowdal and fell flat on his back as if he had run into a brick wall. He lay there, staring up at the Trith.

Crowdal crossed his arms. "Now, now, I believe Writhgarth asked you to finish the fight that you started. I think that is only fair."

Willem stared up at the Trith with hatred in his eyes. He slowly got to his feet. He winced and touched his head where his ear had been, then bent down to pick up his sword. He wiped the blade across his black trousers to get the dust off, then turned to Writhgarth. He was suddenly calm. With a small nod he took up the Rouling stance, his left foot in front of his right, both knees bent slightly, his weight balanced perfectly. He lowered his sword until it was directly pointed at Writhgarth. "Come, little man, let's finish this indeed."

Writhgarth stood up straight and lifted his sword, seeing the calmness in Willem's eyes and knowing that he needed to be more careful from this point forward. Willem was a good swordsman, but not an expert. He was the type of man who relied on his good looks and family connections to get what he wanted in life.

Willem lunged forward, then raised his blade and struck down so quickly that the steel whispered as it cut the air. Writhgarth blocked the strike, then two more in succession. Without hesitating, Willem attacked again and again, relentlessly, using every technique he knew. Writhgarth was at a disadvantage with his lack of height and reach.

The unique ring of steel striking steel filled the brightening dawn, along with the grunts and heavy breathing from Writhgarth and Willem as they moved in an elegant dance around the dirt street.

Willem flicked his sword and nicked Writhgarth's arm, drawing blood. He smiled when he saw Writhgarth wince, the smug look on his face showing that he knew he was going to win. He clucked his tongue. "This is pathetic, it's like I'm fighting a child." Willem increased his speed, relentless in his determination to cut the little man in half.

Willem suddenly stumbled, then watched in confusion as his sword slowly slipped to the ground with a clang, not understanding why it had happened. He looked up at Writhgarth, who stood three paces away, leaning on his sword again with crossed arms.

Writhgarth nodded solemnly. "Good bye, Willem. I didn't enjoy killing you."

Willem tried to bend down to pick up his sword, but he couldn't move. He tried again, his face breaking out into a thick sheen of sweat until he finally whined, his voice cracking, "But I'm not even injured." His legs buckled and he fell to his knees. He looked up at Writhgarth uncomprehendingly before falling heavily face down to the dirt.

Writhgarth sadly looked at Willem's body on the road. Blood bubbled up from the man's severed spine. The poor bastard hadn't even known that he had been skewered from front to back.

Writhgarth wiped his blade on a clean part of Willem's shirt and put it back in his scabbard, then turned to the other members of the group who were all watching him in something akin to awe. The little man motioned his head. "Come on, time to get moving. We don't have far to go."

Crowdal looked down at Writhgarth with a raised eyebrow. "You knew the patrol was out there in the darkness, didn't you?"

Writhgarth didn't even hesitate as he replied, "I saw Willem and his small team hiding in the darkness. I've spent many nights in that spot myself, watching over the streets."

Crowdal raised an eyebrow. "And Willem... you wanted that fight didn't you?"

Writhgarth shrugged. "Of course, he is the one who had me shackled in that cell and beat me when I was defenseless. Listen, if we had made a run for it, they would have raised the alarm. But I knew that Willem's self-importance and hatred of me would make him confront me. It was a calculated guess that I knew Willem well enough."

Crowdal nodded and said in a low voice, "That is quite a risk to take with our lives."

Writhgarth was about to speak but Crowdal cut him off, "Well done."

Writhgarth cocked his head and smiled for the first time in a long time, then shook his head and muttered, "Trith," as he turned away.

The sky was getting brighter by the moment and sunrise was not far away as they stepped over Willem's body and hastily made their way down the still mostly shadowed street. They came to another narrow alleyway and Writhgarth peered into the darkness. He spoke softly over his shoulder as he led them, "We still have to avoid the patrol. Grug, Srittem, and Paal are good men, but there are many who are questionable. I don't really feel up to fighting any of my former patrol members."

They soon came to a major street. There was no one about as they stood along the wall looking out. Writhgarth turned to them again. "This is Riouth Street. It is a lesser-known street that runs directly out of the city. Unfortunately, the patrol knows that I know this, so we can't take it."

Melinda sarcastically rolled her eyes. "Then why did you take us here? Just to show us what we can't do?"

Writhgarth chuckled quietly, his voice sounding like gravel sliding over a washboard. "Yes, that is why I brought you here. I thought it was a nice street and didn't want you to miss seeing it before we left."

Melinda laughed lightly before turning quickly serious again. "So I take it you have brought us here for a reason, then."

Writhgarth nodded. "Indeed I have." He pointed his arm at the street. "While this street is the best way out of the city, there is another way that I found years back while chasing a criminal. I was alone when I chased him down a hole. I followed him for half a day through a tunnel system that I never knew existed. It comes out some ways outside of the city. I never told anyone on the patrol about it."

Sid cocked his head to the left. "Why?"

Writhgarth looked directly at Sid and smiled without humor. "Because, I never caught the man I was chasing."

Sid's face reddened. "Oh."

Writhgarth hardened his eyes. "I chased the man for part of a day. He had never been more than a hundred paces ahead of me. I was gaining on him when suddenly I didn't hear him anymore. I immediately came upon a side tunnel. Blood was splattered all over the walls. When I listened, I heard nothing. I was going to go down the side tunnel, but something about it scared me." He looked at them with a challenging stare. "Yes, I was scared. So I continued on down the main tunnel and it eventually led out of a small opening in a cliff outside of the city." He stared at them all with a serious expression. "It isn't a pleasant way to get out of the city and there is something down there that killed that man, but it is the way I recommend we take. If we move quickly and stay on guard, we should be safe. The entrance is in an old abandoned building close by."

Sid, Crowdal, and Melinda looked at each other for a few moments. They all nodded and Crowdal flicked his head nonchalantly toward the street. "Well, let's get going, we're wasting time standing here like a bunch of old women."

Melinda elbowed him in the ribs and he faked being badly hurt. Writhgarth snapped at them. "Stop that."

Crowdal and Melinda immediately stopped smiling and looked contrite.

Writhgarth huffed and said, "kids" under his breath as he motioned them all to kneel down and put their heads together. He whispered, "When we get into the passage, I will light a torch. As each one burns low we'll rotate, each of us lighting a torch. That way we will all have equal amounts of torches at all times." He stopped and asked them if they had any questions.

Sid raised his hand. Writhgarth pushed his hand down. "You don't have to raise your hand, Sid. Just speak."

Sid nodded with an embarrassed smile. "I can create a light equation again for us."

Writhgarth shook his head. "I don't know if that is wise. We don't know if Mansico or the others who are chasing you will sense your... power. I would rather not chance it. We should just use the tried and true torch."

Sid's eyes widened slightly, as if he hadn't thought of that possibility. He started to raise his hand again, but put it down before asking in a quiet voice, "There is no other way out of the city?"

Writhgarth shook his head. "Sorry, Sid. If we want to avoid Mansico and his Haissen, as well as the patrol, and get out of this city alive, this is the only option I know of." He looked at Crowdal and Melinda. "This won't be easy. But I wouldn't suggest this option if I thought we wouldn't make it through."

They all nodded assent and with daybreak not far away, Writhgarth led them across the street to an old abandoned building. They entered through a hole in the bricks. In the sudden darkness, he searched for the mark he had left the previous time had been there. At first he didn't see it, but on the second pass with his eyes, he saw a "W" scratched in a brick. He moved quickly forward until he was next to it. Then he turned and moved fifteen paces to his left.

There was nothing out of the ordinary to mark the spot, but he knew what he was looking for. He bent down and brushed sand away until he saw a board. He found its edge and lifted it up on hinges. Underneath was a black hole. He reached into his pack, removed a torch, and lit it with his flint. The tarred cloth caught fire immediately and he handed the torch to Sid.

"Jump straight down. It is not far to the bottom."

He looked at Melinda's condition. "Crowdal, you go second and reach up and lift Melinda down. I will go last. There is a rope attached to the board. We can pull it back over the hole from inside." He eyed the group, then the rising sun. "Let's go."

Sid looked into the dark hole, took a deep breath, then jumped in, holding the torch above his head. He fell only a short way before he hit the soft, sandy ground. He fell to his side and dust rose into his eyes. Coughing, he stood up quickly and took a few steps away from the hole.

Crowdal quickly landed next to Sid, his head even with the hole above him. Reaching up, Crowdal grabbed Melinda by the waist and lifted her easily down into the hole. He reached back up and offered to lift Writhgarth down, but quickly pulled his arms back at the dark look that he was given. He ducked his head and stepped away from the hole.

Writhgarth grabbed the rope and jumped into the hole, rolling as he hit the ground. He quickly pulled the board down and the tunnel was lit only by the flickering torch. The tunnel led in both directions as he remembered. It was very narrow and roughly carved from the dirt. The ceiling was far above him but when Writhgarth glanced at Crowdal, he saw that the Trith had to stoop his shoulders quite a bit to avoid bumping his head against the ceiling. He was going to be in pain if he had to walk that way for a long time.

Writhgarth took Sid's torch and held it out, but he couldn't see very far beyond the meager torchlight. The darkness seemed to press upon them, almost a physical presence. A musty and unpleasant smell filled his nose.

Sid looked a little fearfully at Writhgarth and whispered, "Which way do we go?"

Writhgarth pointed with the torch, the flame making a whooshing sound as he moved it. "That way. I'll lead."

Writhgarth immediately started down the passageway. Crowdal and Melinda looked at each other, then at Sid. The torchlight faded quickly away and Crowdal and Melinda started following. Sid stood for only a moment, then followed the bobbing light to avoid being left in complete darkness.

Chapter 38

The lead Haissan led Father Mansico and the Murder of Haissen through the underground passage and into a dark alleyway. It sniffed the air and knelt down in the dirt to scan the ground. It quickly stood up and moved slowly, following almost invisible tracks. Father Mansico was impressed. It wasn't easy to track someone in the city. He was thankful again for his Haissen. As they made their way through the city alleyways, he thought back to his first encounter with them, twenty-five years earlier.

He had been brought to the Oblate chambers and faced the Black Robe, the first time he had ever been in the same room with the one who wielded power greater than anyone in the land. For twenty years, Mansico had been an agent for the Oblate, doing their work as Administrator to Cyllyan, the King of Tauben. Mansico had worked his way into the King's confidence, the whole time passing valuable information secretly to the Oblate.

The Black Robe had spoken from the top of a platform, "Mansico Grigor, you have been a loyal agent. The information that you have provided has helped us gain control of the Tauben treasury, but now we need you for a far more important task."

Mansico had felt bewildered, not sure what could be more important than being administrator to a king. But he had spread his hands wide and bowed low. "Whatever you require, I will do."

The Black Robe continued, "We would not expect any less from you." The Black Robe had paused for a long time but Mansico hadn't dared to interrupt him. Finally, the mysterious leader continued in a strong voice, "In one week, you will become the new Father of the House of Healing."

Mansico frowned. It was the last thing he had expected. "But how? The Father is still alive."

The Black Robe shook his head. "Not for long. He will soon get sick and his healers will not be able to save him."

Mansico stared open-mouthed at the black figure in front of him, then quickly shut his mouth. The Father of the House of Healing was the highest rank in the land, next to the kings of the noble houses. Some would say the Father was even more powerful than a king. The House of Healing was an entity all its own. It owed allegiance to no King. In fact, almost every person in the land worshipped at a House of Healing, even Kings and Queens. The possibility ran through Mansico's mind. To be the Father of the House of Healing was almost beyond comprehension.

The Black Robe coughed for a few moments, the sound more of a rumble than a cough. Mansico knew the Oblate was powerful but he wasn't so sure that even they could assassinate an existing Father and choose the successor. Before he could stop himself, he blurted out, "There is no way they would accept me as the Father. It is the highest rank possible in the land, next to a King. And inside of the House of Healing, it is almost as political as inside the royal courts. Healers spend decades positioning themselves to rise up within the House of Healing. You've got to be crazy to think they will let an outsider become the new Father."

The Black Robe remained silent.

Mansico realized his mistake. He quickly lowered his eyes and bowed his head. "Forgive me, I do not mean to question you."

The Black Robe stared at him, then snapped his fingers. A Haissan stepped forward from the door, and with a nod from the Black Robe, kicked Mansico's legs out from under him. Before Mansico hit the ground, the Haissan had punched him three times in the ribs. The Haissan quietly returned to its post by the door.

Mansico had slowly crawled to his knees, gasping for air and holding his side before finally climbing to his feet. He stood, his head bowed to the Black Robe. He knew that with just another nod from the Black Robe, the Haissan would cut him down.

The Black Robe let the silence go on for a few more moments, and then spoke softly, "Everything has been arranged. You will become the new Father of the House of Healing and you will be our eyes, ears, and voice of the land." He hardened his voice, "You are our servant and you will always be our servant. Never forget that."

Mansico had nodded. "I am here only to serve."

Thinking back on that day, Father Mansico smiled. He had been young and foolish back then. But in the last twenty-five years he had never made that mistake again. He never underestimated the Black Robe, and he had never forgotten how ruthless the Haissen were.

But he had his own loyal Haissen now.

The sky was turning light when the lead Haissan put its arm up and they all stopped next to a two-story building. The Haissan pointed at the door and hissed, "They were in there for a time, but their tracks lead away."

Father Mansico motioned his head. "Open it."

The lead Haissan spun around and kicked the door. It blew inward and off of its hinges. Four Haissen immediately glided through the opening before the last piece of shattered wood landed on the floor. Father Mansico waited patiently outside with the remaining nine Haissen.

In only a matter of moments, a nondescript man was dragged outside, eyes wide in terror.

Father Mansico stepped forward until he was face-to-face with the terrified man. "Some of my... friends were here tonight. If you would kindly tell me where they went, I would be most appreciative."

Spittle dripped from the man's chin as he tried to make words come out of his mouth. "Th... they took supplies and left. I d... d... don't know where they went. I swear."

The Haissan that held him did something behind his back and the man screamed. He would have fallen to his knees had the Haissan not held him up.

Father Mansico picked at a fingernail. "Now, I will ask you again. Where did they go?"

Trembling, the man cried, "I heard something about a secret tunnel out of the city, near Riouth Street. That's all I know. The little man led them."

"What little man?"

"Captain Writhgarth. They went with him."

Father Mansico was surprised. He hadn't known that the captain had joined up with the boy. That was interesting. Absently, he nodded to the Haissan. It immediately twisted the man's neck with a crack and dropped him to the ground.

"Take me directly to Riouth Street. It will be quicker than tracking them."

The lead Haissan immediately led them away. It knew exactly where Riouth Street was and they moved at a brisk pace. On the way, they came across a dead man lying on the street.

The lead Haissan flipped the man over. Surprised, dead eyes stared up at Father Mansico. It was Willem.

Father Mansico gritted his teeth. He couldn't care less about the man's death. He was a pompous and spoiled fool, but his family was powerful. There was going to be trouble with that family. Then he smiled, for he realized that he didn't really care anymore. As soon as he got the Aleph Null and the manuscript back, he would have no more need to play politics.

But first he had to find the Aleph Null.

He looked down at the lead Haissan and motioned his head to the ground around the dead body. "Tell me exactly what happened here."

The lead Haissan looked around then stood up. "This man and a group of three patrol members surprised four people right here. A very large man, a small man, a woman, and the Aleph Null. Only the small man and Willem fought. It was a fair fight. Willem lost."

Father Mansico smiled slightly. He loved the directness and precision of the Haissen. No wasted words. He wished more people were like them.

"In which direction did they go?"

The Haissan immediately pointed.

"Good, let's go."

The Haissan led him down the street, then through an alleyway. The sun had just started to peek over the horizon as they came to the end of the alley. People were already out and about, but the street quickly emptied as Father Mansico and his Murder of Haissen crossed to an old abandoned building. The lead Haissan pushed through a small opening in the brick and Father Mansico and the rest of the Haissen followed.

In the semi-darkness the lead Haissan followed tracks in the dust directly to a spot that looked no different from the others. It bent down without pausing and lifted a board, exposing a dark hole. It turned to Mansico.

"The trail leads down here."

Chapter 39

Sid's legs began to ache as he followed behind the group. His feet sunk into deep sand with each step, making it awkward and tiring to walk. In the small light of the torch, the tunnel walls seemed to narrow. Up ahead, he saw rats running in a sideways gate along the edges of the tunnel, frightened by the approaching light.

The tunnel ran level, but twisted and turned constantly. The air seemed to become heavier the further they walked. They passed by many cross tunnels, but Writhgarth led them forward without pause.

At one cross tunnel, Sid heard dripping water so he stopped and looked into the darkness. It was like a wall of black. He couldn't see even a hand span into the tunnel. He sniffed the warm, heavy air and smelled feces, along with something else he couldn't place. He was about to continue past when deep in the darkness he heard slow, heavy steps and the swish of sand against the walls.

He froze, unable to move.

The torchlight bobbed and faded away down the main passageway as his friends continued on, unaware that he had stopped, and darkness quickly surrounded him. Yet he still couldn't move. The darkness of the tunnel pressed down on him.

'Run,' he thought in panic. 'Run, run, run!'

But he couldn't move.

From inside the blackness of the cross tunnel, he heard slow burbling intakes of breath, followed by wet exhalations. Goose bumps rose on his entire body. He was almost in complete darkness. The sound of the heavy footsteps grew louder until from out of the darkness some sand puffed out and the footsteps stopped.

Without thinking, Sid leaned forward slightly and peered into the darkness, when from out of the black, two pinpoints of light appeared. They disappeared for a moment, then reappeared. A low, wet rumble rose. Sid couldn't so much hear it, as feel it. He was more frightened than he had ever been in his whole life, even more than when he had been eight years old and in Rugger's hut. He felt warm urine run down his leg, pooling in his boot.

Wet sniffing came from the darkness, then a long glistening snout slowly pushed forward from the darkest shadows of the cross tunnel. Sid stood still, paralyzed with fear as the snout leaned toward him until it stopped next to his face. He could feel the hairs of long whiskers brush his cheeks. Two large, triangular white eyes blinked at him, the low rumble suddenly threatening in its intensity. Sid felt warm, acrid breath on his face. The mouth opened and Sid saw rows of sharp curved teeth inside. A single droplet of warm spittle landed on his cheek.

He closed his eyes and immediately saw his numbers floating in front of him. But they were different. He studied them quickly, looking for the anomaly and immediately found it. The numbers pushed away from whatever was in front of him, like a magnet turned upside down and pushing against another magnet. It was similar to what he had done when he first put up a wall of numbers to block the Korpor in his room, only now it was much more powerful. The numbers pulsed with energy.

Sid quickly pulled his numbers from all over and forced them against the pressure in front of him. They wanted to fall away, but he pulled them back and forced them against the void in front of him. It was like trying to keep water on a slanted board with just his hands.

He distantly heard a loud snap of teeth on teeth, then an angry howl followed by loud scratching. He felt his numbers being forced away and he pulled them even tighter. Sweat broke out on his forehead. Air puffed against his closed eyes and the pressure that pushed against him was almost unbearable. He opened his eyes and in the last remaining light of the fading torch, he saw teeth snap at him, and paws with long claws swiping at him.

But nothing touched him.

With one massive lunge, the beast ran its claws down Sid's face. Sid could see the rough points of the sharp claws in front of his eyes, but they didn't touch him as they screeched downward. With a howl of frustration, the beast beat against the barrier between them.

Sid felt his numbers start to slip away faster. First one, then a few more. He was having a difficult time pulling them back. He was getting tired.

He felt hot breath on his face. He pulled his numbers tightly against himself as a large black paw swung at him. It bounced off of his barrier and more numbers bounced away, like hitting a bee's nest with a stick. Sid knew he had to do something soon. He wasn't going to be able to hold the barrier together for much longer.

He pictured the beast in front of him, along with his numbers as a wall between them. In a panic, he called forth more numbers and formed them into an undulating ball. It spun as he pulled in more numbers. When he felt he had enough, he gathered his last remaining energy and forced the ball of numbers through the creature's skin and into its body. It howled and tried to pull away, but Sid reversed the polarity of his wall and pulled the creature back.

He was almost completely spent.

From down the hall, light grew and he heard running feet. As his friends got closer, Sid felt the power from the manuscript in his friend's pack. It coursed through him and filled him with energy.

He opened his eyes again.

He and the creature were face to face. The creature became fully visible and it was an image he would never forget. As the power flowed through him, he expanded his ball of numbers until they could no longer be contained, until they finally burst apart.

The creature's eyes grew wide and it screamed in fear and pain, the sound echoing off of the tunnel walls, then the creature burst apart, blood and flesh flying in every direction. The gore slowly dripped down the wall that Sid had built in front of himself.

In exhaustion, Sid released the last of his numbers and sank to the sandy floor. As he did, the blood and gore fell to the ground with a splash.

* * *

Crowdal ran as hard as he could, bent over as he was, toward the darkness from which he had just come. He had looked back and noticed that Sid was no longer behind them, so he stopped Melinda and Writhgarth and was about to turn around when he heard a howl in the distance behind him that sent goose bumps up his arms. Without hesitating, he turned and ran back down the tunnel, with Melinda and Writhgarth not far behind him.

He heard a scream and what sounded like the screech of claws against stone as he ran. Even though Writhgarth was a ways behind him, the light from his torch carried forward in the narrow tunnel enough for Crowdal to see that Sid faced a black hole in the wall. The air shimmered red around him and Crowdal saw the claws of some giant creature swiping viciously at him. Crowdal wasn't sure what he was seeing, because it looked like Sid was untouched, impossible as that was. Those claws should have been tearing his face to bloody pieces.

As he approached, the light from the torch fully lit up the tunnel and Crowdal heard a long howl rise up, only now it was a howl of fear and pain. Then there was a massive change of pressure and the air in the tunnel burst outward.

Crowdal slid to a stop just as Sid collapsed, falling into his arms.

Writhgarth slid to a stop also, followed eventually by Melinda, who had hobbled as fast as she could.

"What was that?" Crowdal angrily asked Writhgarth, staring at the massive amount of blood and flesh that covered the ground and sides of the tunnel.

Writhgarth's face was white and he swallowed hard, twice. Before he could answer, Melinda spoke in a strangely calm voice, between gasping breaths from the run, "I think it was a Kraagiquazz."

"A what?" Crowdal asked, as he looked into the black hole.

Melinda spoke under her breath, "Impossible, it's impossible."

Writhgarth touched her arm. "Melinda?"

Melinda looked up, her eyes haunted and frightened. "I've heard stories of the Kraagiquazz from... my family." She spoke the word 'family' more as an exhalation of breath. "But I never knew they were real. We must go, now. Its mate will be close by. I don't know how Sid survived." She looked into the black hole and swallowed.

Crowdal didn't argue. He picked up Sid and nodded to Writhgarth to start moving.

They started back down the tunnel. As they ran, they heard a distant, inhuman scream that rose in pitch before it fell to silence. The hair on the back of his neck rose and he shivered. It was a sound filled both with rage and sorrow.

They moved as quickly as they could, not willing to stop. The tunnel led steadily downward as they went. Soon Writhgarth's torch started to sputter, so Melinda took out one of her torches and lit it from his. Crowdal was in agony from having to hunch over at the shoulders while carrying Sid. Just as he was about to ask them to stop, Writhgarth came to an abrupt halt.

Crowdal looked up and saw they were at the entrance to a large cavern. The light from Melinda's torch didn't reach all the way across the massive space. Crowdal straightened his back and heard his bones crack. It felt wonderful to stand up straight again.

Sid moaned, opened his eyes, and looked at Crowdal in confusion. "Where are we?"

Crowdal set him to his feet, careful to make sure that he didn't fall from unsteady legs. "We're still in the tunnels. It is probably around midday."

Sid shakily rubbed his hand through his hair and sat down against the wall.

Melinda sat down next to him with a wince and gingerly adjusted herself. She put a hand on his knee and asked in a quiet voice. "How are you doing?"

"I'm all right. Just a little tired."

Melinda nodded and felt his forehead, then his carotid artery, counting to herself. Satisfied, she took her hand away and leaned back. She closed her own eyes and spoke quietly, "You will be fine, physically at least. I think you need some sleep more than anything, though."

Sid looked at her in concern, then put his arm around her shoulder and they both leaned together against the wall.

Crowdal shook his head. They were both in bad shape. He heard his name urgently whispered and turned to Writhgarth, who was a few paces away, craning his neck up and holding the torch as high as he could.

Crowdal looked up and stepped over to him. "What is it?"

Writhgarth nodded silently upward and Crowdal followed his gaze.

Writhgarth spat at the ground out of the corner of his mouth. "The mate has come."

At first Crowdal didn't see anything. The light from the torch barely reached the ceiling, throwing flickering shadows that confused his eyes. Then he saw it and drew in a quick breath.

On a shelf of rock high above, close to the ceiling, a creature crouched and stared at them with white eyes. It was huge, at least the size of a large stallion. It had four legs that ended in long claws, and Crowdal saw a tail lazily whip back and forth behind it, almost like an agitated cat. He shuddered.

This was no cat, though.

It had two triangular white eyes that blinked slowly, the top point of the triangle collapsing down to a flat line. It had a long snout, and its mouth opened in a snarl. The torchlight glinted off row upon row of sharp curved teeth. All along the snout were incredibly long white whiskers that stuck out in every direction, each as long as Crowdal's arms. It probably used them to traverse the tunnels in complete darkness.

But those were not the features that made Crowdal draw in his breath. He had had a difficult time spotting the creature because its skin was translucent. Crowdal could see its organs, its beating heart, and the blood moving through its veins. He looked closely at its head and could see its entire brain, white and gelatinous.

Crowdal and Writhgarth slowly backed up, careful not to make any sudden movements, until they stood next to Melinda and Sid.

Without turning, Crowdal urgently whispered their names. Melinda and Sid immediately opened their eyes, the urgency in his voice bringing them both fully alert.

"Stand up, very slowly, and gather your packs. Don't make any sudden movements."

Sid and Melinda did as they were told and were soon standing next to Crowdal and Writhgarth, looking around. They didn't see anything and Sid started to ask what was wrong, when he suddenly stopped speaking. He was staring at the creature on the shelf of rock high above them and he began to shake.

Melinda touched Crowdal's sleeve and hissed, "Kraagiquazz..."

Crowdal spoke out of the corner of his mouth, "Stay calm. Move slowly across the room. No sudden movements. If it attacks, get behind me. I will handle it."

Melinda hissed again, "No, don't. It will tear you apart."

Crowdal chuckled humorously. "It has never faced a Trith before."

The four of them took a slow step forward, then another.

The Kraagiquazz stood up on its four legs and growled. They couldn't hear the growl, but they felt the vibration and the hairs on their necks stood on end again. They all stopped and stared at the creature.

It stood on the ledge, staring down at them. The blood pumped through its veins and its heart began to beat quicker.

The Kraagiquazz took a step along the ledge, then another, its head hanging down toward them as it walked.

Crowdal saw the muscles in the beast's legs contract and move as it took each step. It would have been fascinating at any other time. But the deadly intensity in its eyes made him shiver.

The group took another step forward, all of them staring upward at the beast.

The Kraagiquazz dropped heavily to a lower ledge. A few pebbles dropped to the ground, landing in a puff of dust. It then crept slowly along the ledge and then dropped down to another.

The group moved forward one step at a time. The Kraagiquazz kept dropping from ledge to ledge. They were only halfway across the chamber and the beast was almost to the ground. They weren't going to make it.

Sid whispered, "What are we going to do? We're still too far away from the other side of the cavern."

Crowdal was thinking the same thing. He stopped and squared his shoulders back. "All right, listen. Everyone keep moving forward. I'll meet it here in the open."

Writhgarth and Melinda both started to protest, but Crowdal put up a hand. "There is no way we can all make it. But if I stop here and have space in which to fight, I might have a chance. But if we all try to outrun it, we will all die. I can't fight it while surrounded by you all."

Writhgarth narrowed his eyes but nodded quickly, then turned to Melinda and Sid and whispered urgently, "Let's go. Move!" As they started away, Writhgarth lit one of his torches and stuck it into the sand.

The Kraagiquazz dropped from the final ledge and landed with a soft thud not more than ten paces behind Crowdal.

Melinda touched Crowdal's sleeve as she passed and whispered, "Don't you dare play around with it."

Crowdal shook his head sadly. "I will do what must be done."

Chapter 40

The passageway made odd curves as Mrs. Wessmank and Maelon made their way down it. After a particularly strange set of curves, the passageway led steeply downward and the air grew cooler. 'They were probably under the city streets now,' she thought. They continued on. She started to slow down by the time she had to light the second torch. Her legs began to ache and her feet throbbed. She hadn't walked this far in ages.

After what felt like half of a day had passed, the passageway angled upward steeply and Mrs. Wessmank had to climb on her hands and knees to make it up the final stretch of steep sandy floor. She occasionally slipped backward a bit, but she was finally able to rest on a small landing.

She stood up, huffing air and put a hand to her back as it cracked. "I'm too old for this, Maelon. I should have just waited for Mansico to return and taken my chances with him."

"*He would have tortured you, Mother. I've seen him do it many times. He... enjoys it. And I would be dead right now.*"

Mrs. Wessmank nodded sadly down at him, knowing that Maelon had been the target of many beatings. "I am sorry, my dear. I have no right to complain." She felt along the walls, looking for the mechanism to open it. She found it almost immediately and pushed inward. The wall creaked open slightly and she strained to push it wide enough for them to fit through.

She opened her eyes wide and gasped.

Maelon growled deeply and bared his teeth.

Mrs. Wessmank and Maelon peered through the stone door and looked upon a large cavern. It should have been dark but there was a flickering torch almost directly in the middle of it. Two figures stood in the light facing each other. She could see that one was a very large man. No, wait, he was a Trith! She narrowed her eyes and recognized him as the same Trith she had seen next to the wagon on the road to Yisk. Then she heard a low growl and slid her gaze to the other figure and she gasped.

It was a Kraagiquazz!

She moaned. Gods, no. She knew that not even a Trith could kill a Kraagiquazz.

Maelon spoke to her. "*Mother, I cannot protect you from the beast. We must turn around and leave this place now.*"

Mrs. Wessmank nodded absently, mesmerized by the scene in front of her. Then she heard a sound and glanced briefly to her left.

She put her hand to her mouth. It couldn't be! She looked closer and a shiver went down her spine.

It was Sidoro!

He was with a small man and a woman. They stood not far from the center of the cavern, watching the scene about to take place. What were they doing just standing there? They would die next when the Kraagiquazz killed the Trith. She was about to cry out his name when she heard a scream and turned her attention back to the center of the cavern. She watched with resigned fate as the creature leapt at the Trith and pinned him to the ground. She watched, mesmerized for a few moments, but then she panicked. She had to get Sidoro's attention now.

She opened her mouth to yell when she heard Maelon's surprised voice in her mind.

Chapter 41

Crowdal shrugged out of his pack and let it drop to the floor. Then he slowly pulled his sword from the scabbard and turned toward the Kraagiquazz. The ring of steel echoed eerily around the chamber. "All right, my friend. I honestly wish we didn't have to play this game, but I guess neither one of us has a choice."

The deep rumble from the Kraagiquazz grew louder as it stepped forward. The blood that coursed through its veins slowed down, moving in a strange stop-start motion, as if it were being pushed and pulled at the same time as it moved in its tracks. Crowdal could see the muscles of its heart contract and expand in a hypnotizing undulation. The blood was bright red as it left the heart, but he could see it was almost black in color as it returned to the heart. Very strange. He realized that he could hear the swish of the blood, almost like the sound he had once heard when he put his ear to a large sea shell. Without realizing it, he lowered his sword.

With a roar, the Kraagiquazz leapt at him, its triangular eyes blazing with fury.

Crowdal jerked his attention back to the moment and dove to his right. The Kraagiquazz lashed out and razor sharp claws just missed him as he rolled and came up in the Tropp stance, kneeling on one knee, the other bent in front at ninety degrees, hands holding his sword upright.

The Kraagiquazz circled around him, teeth bared, saliva dripping slowly to the ground.

Crowdal calmly climbed to both feet and held his sword up, turning slowly as the creature circled him. Sweat beaded on his forehead. He couldn't believe he had let his guard down, even for such a brief moment. That was an error amateurs made, not him, a Trith. He surprised himself with this thought. A Trith. He had tried so hard to stop thinking of himself as a Trith over the past year, but he knew that he was a Trith and always would be. He glared at the Kraagiquazz and forced himself to concentrate only on the beast and nothing else.

The beast stopped circling and it stared at Crowdal with its head cocked to the left. Its triangular eyes became lidded, as if it realized the change in the man in front of it.

For a few moments, they faced each other, staring into each other's eyes. Time no longer existed for those moments. Crowdal heard a swish of sand as one of his friends shifted their feet, perhaps in nervousness. But Crowdal didn't take his eyes from the Kraagiquazz. He stood, motionless, staring into those triangular eyes, waiting, waiting for that moment when the beast committed to violence. It was a decision that he hoped was never reached, because it meant that one of them would die.

The moments stretched out and a droplet of sweat reached Crowdal's chin, hung briefly, then fell, landing with a slight puff in the dry, powdery sand. It was as if a spell had been broken. The pupils inside the creature's triangular eyes widened slightly, just slightly, and the Kraagiquazz started gliding directly toward him, its large paws making dust puff up with each step. Saliva ran from its mouth and hung to the ground.

Crowdal took a step back, which was a mistake.

The Kraagiquazz leaped at him, claws out, teeth bared.

But instead of trying to get out of the way, Crowdal stepped forward and cut twice in an "X" pattern, the blur of his blade almost impossible to see.

The Kraagiquazz slammed into him and they crashed to the sandy ground. Crowdal's sword flew out of his grip and landed somewhere behind him.

The Kraagiquazz straddled him, pinning his arms and feet. It lowered its snout toward his face, its white triangular eyes opened wide. It growled deeply in its chest, the rumble almost beyond hearing, and stringy saliva hung down in ropey strands from its open jaws, filling Crowdal's own mouth.

Crowdal didn't dare move his head and risk the beast's instant attack, so he did the only thing he could and swallowed the warm saliva to keep from choking. The Kraagiquazz's lips pulled back in a snarl and in a panic, Crowdal heaved upward with all of his strength, the blood vessels in his forehead bulging as he pushed, but the beast was too heavy for him. He gave up, knowing there was nothing that he could do, so he let his breath out and stopped struggling. The Kraagiquazz lowered its massive head, teeth glistening in the torchlight, and Crowdal waited for death to come. He wasn't afraid, his training and upbringing ensured that. But he was saddened. His friends would be hunted down and killed by the Kraagiquazz. They would have no chance against it. He had failed them.

But instead of sinking its teeth into Crowdal's face, the Kraagiquazz gently lowered its head sideways and rested it on the ground next to him, its snout touching his cheek. Crowdal turned his head slightly to look at it. They were so close that he could see the beast's pupils dilate and he could feel its warm breath on his face.

The Kraagiquazz slowly licked Crowdal's cheek with its long rough tongue, the coarseness not unpleasant. It blinked its triangular eyes once more and let out a sigh, its weight settling fully on him.

Crowdal looked into the vacant stare of the Kraagiquazz and felt a lump in his throat. He had been prepared to die, but he had not expected this single act of what almost felt like love from the Kraagiquazz. Tears spilled from his eyes and he heard running feet and saw the light grow around him as Sid, Writhgarth, and Melinda came to a stop next to him.

Crowdal grunted, "Can you try and roll this thing off of me?"

All three of them leaned in and pushed against the dead Kraagiquazz and Crowdal lifted at the same time. Slowly, they rolled the beast off of him and Crowdal took a deep breath, then another.

He looked down at himself and saw he was covered in blood and intestines. He sat up and studied the body of the Kraagiquazz. The beast's stomach was cut wide open in the "X" pattern he had made with his sword. He hadn't known for sure if he had connected with the beast before he had been knocked to the ground.

Writhgarth slapped Crowdal's back and laughed. "That was amazing! You didn't even try to get out of its way, you just cut that beast from one end to the other, giving it what it deserved."

Crowdal stood up and glared down at Writhgarth. "That beast was more honorable than any man I have ever faced in battle. Show it some respect."

Writhgarth's smile fell from his face and Crowdal glared at him, as if daring him to say anything but Writhgarth quickly nodded. "Of course, you're right."

Crowdal felt bad for taking out his guilt and anger on Writhgarth, he was a good man. So he softened his expression and put a hand on the little man's shoulder. "I'm sorry, it's just that I've taken a lot of lives before, but that creature was just avenging the death of its mate. It wasn't evil, and it didn't take pleasure in killing. We were in its lair, we were the intruders. It didn't deserve to die, but we had no choice, neither it or me, in choosing to do battle."

Writhgarth nodded and smiled sadly. "You are a strange one."

Crowdal grunted, then looked down at Melinda as she quickly checked over him to make sure he wasn't injured.

She looked like she couldn't believe that he wasn't even scratched. She quickly looked into his eyes to make sure he wasn't in shock. "You should be dead right now."

Crowdal stood up. "Well you aren't rid of me just yet." He went over to his pack and pulled out a fresh set of clothes and quickly changed, then rubbed his bloody clothes in the sand to try and dry the blood as much as possible. He then rolled them tightly and stuck them back into the pack.

He turned to his friends and spoke a bit gruffly, "Come on, let's get out of here." He started walking across the cavern.

Sid, Writhgarth, and Melinda looked at each other and then started to follow him.

Crowdal had just beaten all odds in killing the Kraagiquazz.

He should be happy. But he wasn't.

Chapter 42

"*The Kraagiquazz is dead. The Trith killed it.*"

Mrs. Wessmank had never heard Maelon act surprised before. She looked back to the center of the cavern and, in disbelief, saw that he was right. The Kraagiquazz wasn't moving. She saw Sidoro and the other two people run back to the center of the cavern and roll the creature off of the Trith.

She couldn't believe the Trith had killed a Kraagiquazz, a beast so legendary that even the hardest warriors only spoke the name in hushed whispers. It seemed impossible. Yet he had done it.

The four people, with Sidoro in the middle, soon started across the room to the other side. She came out of her thoughts and yelled out, "Sidoro!"

The group immediately halted and spun toward her, two of the men pulling swords. But Sid broke from the group and ran toward her, a huge grin on his face. Mrs. Wessmank stepped through the door and smiled back.

Sid flew into her arms, almost knocking her over. He hugged her tightly until she tapped his back and laughed.

"Now, now Sidoro, you are crushing me."

He pulled back and looked at her with tears in his eyes. "I can't believe it is you. How did you get here? Why are you here?"

A calm voice answered from across the cavern, "Because my boy, she decided that my hospitality was not to her liking."

Everyone spun around.

Standing just inside the cavern with his Murder of Haissen fanned out to either side of him, Father Mansico half-bowed. "So good to see you all again."

From a ledge far above, the Korpor watched. Its left eye blinked, followed by its right eye.

It smiled.

Chapter 43

Sid's heart fell when he saw Father Mansico and his Haissen standing at the entrance to the cavern. He looked at his friends, then at Mrs. Wessmank and the three-legged animal that accompanied her and felt tears come to his eyes. He angrily rubbed them away. It wasn't fair, they had come so far!

Crowdal and Writhgarth took in all of the Haissen with a glance and their shoulders slumped. They looked at each other and Crowdal grinned. "Looks like we are going to have some fun before we die, at least."

Writhgarth grinned back. "I'll take the seven on the right, you take the six on the left."

"Why do you get seven and I only get six?"

Writhgarth shrugged. "Hey, if you really want seven, then be my guest."

Crowdal smiled, but it was strained. The levity left his eyes as he glanced at the Haissen again.

Father Mansico motioned slightly and his Murder of Haissen fanned out and surrounded the small group.

"My, you've led me on quite a little chase young man, which I really quite enjoyed. But before we retire back to my chambers, I shall have some fun with your friends." He felt his crotch and looked directly at Sid. "And for kicking me when I was unconscious, well for that I have something special reserved for you."

A chill ran down Sid's spine at those words. Sadness and fear filled him at the thought of his friends being in the hands of Mansico. They would all be tortured and killed because of him. All they had wanted to do was help him. Tears welled up again and his vision became cloudy. He angrily wiped them away and glared at Father Mansico.

The look of kindness on the man's face and the laugh lines around his eyes belied the feeling of malevolence that emanated from him.

The knot of fear faded from Sid's stomach. He let it go. He was tired of running and tired of being afraid. In its place, anger welled up. It was familiar to him. The anger had been his friend and had kept him going over the years when the disgust and shame from being raped in the hut threatened to devour him. Now he pulled that anger in and let it build. It was warm and comforting. The power from the manuscript in Crowdal's pack pulsed in quick bursts and filled him with energy. A throbbing erection grew in his pants and his vision cleared completely.

He set his face and glared at Mansico. He was not going to let his friends be taken into this monster's hands.

Father Mansico saw the look of wild anger in the boy's eyes and he suddenly looked uneasy. He quickly motioned to his Haissen and they immediately moved forward to incapacitate the Trith and the little man with the sword.

As the Haissen approached, Crowdal looked down at Writhgarth. "Here we go. Time for some fun."

Writhgarth grinned. "It has been a pleasure knowing you."

Crowdal put a hand on the little man's shoulder. "The feeling is mutual."

Melinda pulled her knife and faced the Haissen, the blade looking small and insignificant.

Mrs. Wessmank merely waited, her Tulgin leaning against her hip, a look of hopelessness filling her face.

Four Haissen each attacked Crowdal and Writhgarth. The remaining five Haissen surrounded Sid, Melinda, and Mrs. Wessmank.

Melinda lunged with her knife but it was immediately slapped out of her hands by a Haissan blade, which then touched her neck.

Crowdal responded with a roar. The four Haissen backed up slightly, even as they surrounded him. He spun, flicking his sword in intricate motions that were too quick to see. His blade was a fantastic blur as he moved in a beautiful dance of death.

The Haissen responded. They faced an adversary whom they respected but they knew they would win. So some took turns moving in at his blind side, while others engaged him directly.

Crowdal spun first one way, then another, moving incredibly fast for such a massive man, slashing up and out, pulling the blade back down and then to the side and up at a Haissan to his left. At the last moment, he stopped the attack, spun his sword and pushed it behind him. A grunt of pain sounded and he immediately pulled his sword and swung up and to the left, blocking two Haissen strikes. His laughter rang out, full of joy and anger, almost maniacal as he danced across the sandy ground. His blade flashed in the torchlight, moving so quickly that it looked to be almost floating in the air.

Writhgarth attacked his four Haissen. He was short, but very fast and powerful.

The angle from which he fought was different from anything the Haissen had faced before and he managed to nick one of the Haissen in the arm, drawing a thin line of blood. He smiled, happy. It was more than he had hoped for. But the victory was short-lived, for within moments a Haissan knocked his sword from his hands. As his sword flew from his grip, the little man stood still as four swords touched his neck. He glared at the four Haissen over their swords, his eyes flashing in defiance.

Two swords impacted Crowdal's side and bounced off. He swung around before the Haissen could recover and cut horizontally into the

Haissan to his left. Unfortunately, he missed the creature's neck, so instead of cutting off its head, his sword cut through the Haissan's shoulder and came to a stop, buried halfway inside of the Haissan's chest. Crowdal yanked hard, but his sword was stuck. Then two blades touched his neck, and with resignation he let go of his sword and stood back.

The Haissan with Crowdal's sword buried in it toppled to the ground, its entire upper body almost cut in half.

"Bravo, Trith. Two Haissen. I'm impressed. Before I met you, I would have scoffed at the idea of anyone defeating a Haissan. If times were different, I would have made you my number one guard."

Crowdal looked at Father Mansico from the corner of his eyes, unable to move because of the blades at his neck. "And I would have accidentally run you through with my sword on the first day."

Father Mansico chuckled, then turned serious. "Perhaps. Well, I am done with the theatrics. It is time to finish this up. The boy and I have some business to attend to. So I must say good bye to you other folks." He motioned to the Haissen.

Sid had only subconsciously watched Crowdal and Writhgarth fight the Haissen. Most of his concentration was on his power of numbers as he sucked in the energy that pulsed from the Black Numbers manuscript hidden inside of Crowdal's pack. He felt the power fill every pore of his body. He felt stronger than he had ever felt in his life. He didn't close his eyes as he pulled his numbers to him. He didn't need to. The power of the manuscript infused him, made his own body hum with energy.

Numbers appeared in front of him, thousands of them. They glowed white as they surrounded him. Enveloped him. Time seemed to slow down. The power from the manuscript flowed into the numbers. They turned from white to gray, then back to white at different intervals, causing the air around him to shimmer and vibrate.

He concentrated on the power emanating from the manuscript. He felt the frequency. It felt like a twisting wave of power, undulating as it hit the numbers.

Sid twisted the wave of power slightly with a nudge of his mind. The numbers shimmered more violently and the air vibrated in an odd rhythm. He grasped at the frequency and with force of will, bent it back against the direction it was twisting. It didn't want to move, so Sid focused every last bit of energy he had on it. Slowly, the twisting frequency emanating from the manuscript slowed down. The vibration in the air changed, becoming more of a hum. He twisted harder and the energy formed a smooth wave. The numbers began to hum, the sound pleasant and intoxicating.

Sid memorized the new frequency. He let go of the twisting and it stayed as it was. He focused on the numbers. Where before they were pure white, now they were a pure black and pulsed with barely-contained power. He looked into their swirling depths, mesmerized by their beauty.

With pure joy, he reached out to manipulate them as he did with his normal numbers.

Only they didn't move.

He focused his energy and pushed and pulled at them, but no matter what he did, they wouldn't move. They were as solid as if they were rooted in stone.

Sweat poured down his face until finally, in frustration, he slumped in defeat. He could not manipulate the Black Numbers.

He looked at the pack on Crowdal's back. He could see the power emanating from the manuscript inside and knew that he needed to read the manuscript to understand the base principles of the Black Number theory before he could manipulate them.

He cried out in frustration.

He needed them now!

He glanced quickly around the room and saw Crowdal forced to his knees. A Haissan stood behind him, ready to execute him. Sid looked over and saw Writhgarth in the same position.

He was out of time.

Sid let the frequency return to normal. The numbers shimmered violently, then returned to white. He pulled at them and they moved easily. His regular numbers were back.

In desperation, he sent his numbers out and formed a wall around Crowdal and Writhgarth just as the two Haissen blades connected with their necks. The blades flew backward and out of the Haissen's hands as they struck the wall of numbers.

Crowdal and Writhgarth looked up, their eyes wide at the realization that they were still alive.

Crowdal dove for his sword. Writhgarth did the same.

The Haissen backed up, surprised.

Even though Sid couldn't control the Black Numbers, he felt more power than he had ever felt before fill him. His regular numbers were his to control and they pulsed with power. He felt his erection throb inside of his trousers and the ring around the base of his penis burned and pulsed in time with the power emanating from the manuscript. Pleasure filled him, built inside of him.

He looked at the flame of the torch in Melinda's hand. He studied it, then pulled his numbers into a complex equation and let it float above the flame. It clicked green as he placed the last variable and the equation itself rippled in time with the flame.

Sid threw the equation at the Haissan to Writhgarth's right. As the equation made contact with the Haissan, it wrapped itself around the creature's waist and when the two ends of the equation touched, the Haissan burst into flame. It burned so hotly that the creature fell to the ground and burned to ash in only moments.

Sid stared wide-eyed at what he had done. Then a gleam entered his eyes and pleasure infused him. His erection pulsed. He was close to orgasm. He wanted to do it again. They all deserved to die! He replicated the equation and sent ten more of them across the room.

Each one wrapped around a Haissan and when each end of the equation touched, a Haissan fell to the ground in a burst of flame. As the last equation connected around the last Haissan, it fell to the floor in a puff of hot ash and Sid had a massive orgasm.

In a few moments, the smoke cleared from the cavern and Crowdal and Writhgarth stared open-mouthed at the ashes of the Haissen they had just been fighting.

Melinda turned in a circle, taking in the ashes of the Haissen around her, her face showing that she had no idea what had just happened.

But Mrs. Wessmank had watched what Sid had done. As she looked into his eyes, she saw they were bright blue and filled with wild and chaotic pleasure. She had to bring him back. He was being consumed by the power.

She spoke softly as she stepped to his side, "Sidoro, don't let the anger consume you. Let it go. Please."

Sid felt the pleasure of the orgasm building, pulsing, his release ongoing. The sexual energy was almost too much for him to contain, but he wanted more, he wanted the orgasm to last forever, he wanted to kill again.

Then he heard Mrs. Wessmank's voice. It was filled with love and urgency, so soft that it caressed him. He turned and focused on her kind eyes. They were filled with love, with strength. The anger slowly melted away and the orgasm subsided. The power from the manuscript faded and became a small stream of energy again. His eyes turned from blue to brown and his erection collapsed, the pleasure subsiding to a dull ache. He slumped his shoulders, exhausted.

Mrs. Wessmank quickly reached out to keep him from falling, slowly settling to the ground with him. "It is all right, Sidoro. I've got you now."

Sid felt safe as she wrapped him in her arms. He thought of his mother, of the warmth he had felt in her embrace. He closed his eyes and leaned his head against her chest. He was so tired.

Mrs. Wessmank caressed Sid's hair. She leaned her head against his and held him tightly. Suddenly she heard a thump and looked up into the eyes of the Korpor as it dropped from a high ledge onto the sand floor not far away.

Pain blinded her and she cried out, falling backward at the same time. All around her cries of pain erupted and Melinda, Crowdal, and Writhgarth all fell to the ground in agony.

Chapter 44

Father Mansico stumbled forward and caught himself. Conditioned as he was against the agony of the Korpor, it still almost incapacitated him. He had cried in rage and frustration as he watched his Haissen burn to ash, but now the Korpor appeared out of nowhere and relief washed through him. He stumbled forward and grabbed Sid, pulling him out of the old woman's grasp and backed away, dragging the boy through the cavern toward the tunnel entrance.

A lilting voice filled his mind. *"No, he is not meant for you."*

Father Mansico looked over at the Korpor and the creature just stared at him with its huge blue eyes. It blinked its left eye, followed by the right, then smiled grotesquely at him.

Through intense pain, Father Mansico's face turned red. "How dare you tell me what to do? I control you, remember? Now finish off that group and join me in my chambers."

The Korpor cocked its head. *"He is not meant for you. Another awaits him."*

In a rage, Father Mansico pulled Sid closer and backed up. "Who wants him?"

The Korpor blinked again. *"Someone who even I fear."*

Pain, more intense than anything Father Mansico had ever felt before, stabbed into him and he stumbled to the sand, dropping Sid at the same time. He looked up at the Korpor through watery eyes and clutched his head with both hands, screaming in pain and frustration.

No! He would not let the Aleph Null go, not when he finally had him. Father Mansico forced himself to his feet, reeling from the pain. He somehow managed to grab the Sid by his arms and staggered for the tunnel entrance, dragging the boy, almost completely blinded by the pain that burned inside his mind. He heard footsteps behind him and tried to quicken his pace, but stumbled and swayed as he tried to keep his balance.

"Drop the Aleph Null. It is over for you."

Father Mansico glanced fearfully over his shoulder and saw the Korpor right behind him, its blue eyes gleaming in the torchlight.

Realization hit him. He would not get the Aleph Null. It truly was over.

Anger filled him. He dropped to his knees and spun around to sit on the ground, pulling the boy into his lap. He removed a knife from his robe and held it to the boy's neck. "I guess the boy dies right here then. It is too bad, I..."

But he never finished. The Korpor lunged forward so quickly that Father Mansico never even saw it move. With one swipe of its claws, the Korpor struck Father Mansico's head and tore his face cleanly off, along with half of his skull and brain.

It happened so quickly that Father Mansico reached up and pushed a finger into his own brain before falling backward into the sand.

Chapter 45

Sid opened his tired eyes and saw the Korpor standing over him. He looked at the creature's beautiful blue eyes as the left one blinked, followed by the right one. He felt himself sigh in relief, a sense of reassurance and love filling him.

"*You are tired. I will keep you safe. Just let yourself go. Sleep.*"

Sid's eyes drooped. He felt warm. Safe. It was over. He felt himself being lifted by strong arms. A distant memory of his mother picking him up and holding him to her bosom filled his mind and he wrapped his arms around the Korpor's neck and nuzzled his face into the soft fur. He saw through lidded eyes that he was being carried through the cavern.

From a distance he heard a scream of rage and he fell to the sand. It felt cool and the jolt brought him out of his lethargy. He lifted his head and his eyes grew wide.

Mrs. Wessmank's companion had loped quickly across the cavern in his three-legged gate and lunged at the tendons of the Korpor's leg, clamping down with sharp teeth. A scream of rage erupted from the Korpor as it fell, releasing Sid at the same time. The Tulgin twisted his head violently back and forth, ripping flesh from the Korpor's leg. As Sid lay on his side, he watched in horror as the Korpor savagely swatted the Tulgin away, sending him tumbling across the sandy chamber floor.

The Korpor turned back to Sid and limped toward him, leaving a trail of blood as it walked.

Sid knew he only had the strength for one attempt to stop the Korpor. He pulled his numbers together and they floated uneasily within his mind, sluggish and unstable. He concentrated harder than he had ever concentrated before and the numbers stabilized. He quickly took in the measurements of the Korpor and created six open-ended equations, similar to the wall of numbers he had used so successfully before. It was the only thing he could do with the little amount of energy he still possessed.

He positioned the equations in the front, back, to both sides, and above and below the Korpor as it advanced on him. Then, taking a deep breath, he bridged them all at once. Light flared out from each equation as they connected together, forming a shimmering diamond of energy around the Korpor.

Sid was just able to lock the equations before he fell back to the sand, unconscious.

Chapter 46

The Korpor advanced upon the unconscious Aleph Null in a rage, the pain in its leg something it had not felt in hundreds of years. The pain fed the blood lust within it, and now the Korpor only wanted to kill the boy, to tear him apart limb from limb. But within just a few steps, it suddenly found itself completely immobilized, as if it had walked into a wall. It tried to push against the wall of energy that surrounded it but it could not break through. It roared, the rage erupting even more violently and it beat at the wall of numbers, losing control of itself for the first time in ages. Pain in its paws finally made it stop hammering against the invisible wall and it stood, its chest heaving to gain oxygen. It hung its head until it finally felt a sense of calm return.

It lifted its eyes to glare at the boy that lay not far in front of it and concentrated, trying to visualize the numbers, the equations around it, but they made no sense. It could control numbers, but *only* the numbers. It couldn't understand mathematics and therefore couldn't undo the equations that made up the wall that imprisoned it.

The Korpor watched as the other humans surrounded the boy. It then glanced to its right and saw the old woman kneel next to the little creature that had been so bold as to bite its leg. It smiled as it looked at the pain in the old woman's eyes, but the smile turned to anger when the little animal stood up shakily on its three legs. The Korpor wanted nothing more than to tear the animal apart.

Soon the Trith carried the unconscious Aleph Null across the cavern, surrounded by the humans and the three-legged animal, and entered one of the tunnels. The Korpor watched the torchlight fade down the passageway until the cavern became dark. Standing in pure darkness, the Korpor slumped its shoulders. It didn't relish what it had to do next, but it knew that it had no choice. It closed its eyes and sent a thought to its master. "*I have failed. The boy sealed me in a number array.*"

A dark voice filled the Korpor's head and it shivered. "*Has Sid gained control of the Black Numbers?*"

The Korpor grimaced. "*No, Master. I do not believe he did. He was carried out of the cavern unconscious.*"

The voice sounded pleased. "*Good. Don't worry, my pet. I will be there shortly.*"

The Korpor shuddered.

Chapter 47

Crowdal grimaced in pain as he warily eyed the Korpor standing only a few paces away. The creature had gone into a rage, thrashing about, but somehow it had been trapped. He bent down and picked Sid up from where he lay crumpled on the sand floor, almost a little afraid to touch the boy who could control such powers. But he knew that they had to get out of the tunnels quickly and away from the Korpor. With Sid unconscious, he didn't know for how long the Korpor would stay immobilized.

Crowdal heard the swish of dry sand and turned. The old woman was stumbling over to the body of the three-legged beast, holding her head in her hands from the pain of the Korpor. She sunk down to the sandy floor and lifted the head of the animal into her lap. He felt badly for her, but they had to hurry, so he trotted over to her, carrying Sid as gently as he could. "I'm sorry, but we have to go."

The old woman looked up at him, tears in her eyes not only from the pain of the Korpor, but also from sadness. She nodded. "I will only be another moment."

Crowdal watched her look down lovingly at the three-legged animal as she held his head in her lap. He didn't know what kind of animal he was, but she obviously loved him. Then, both he and the old woman were startled when the animal opened his eyes and licked her hand.

She cried out joyfully, even through the intense pain from the Korpor and hugged the animal. How he had survived the blow from the Korpor, Crowdal did not know, but it was wonderful that he did. The old woman stood up and the Tulgin struggled for a few moments but eventually stood up also, swaying slightly on his three legs.

Blinking back tears of pain, Melinda stumbled over to them and quickly checked Sid as Crowdal held him. She looked up at Crowdal. "He looks to be uninjured, but his heartbeat is irregular. I think he will be fine, but try not to jostle him around as you carry him."

Crowdal nodded, then turned to examine the many tunnels leading out of the cavern. "Writhgarth, do you know how to get us out of here?"

The little man grimaced in pain. "I can indeed, and the sooner the better." Writhgarth immediately turned and staggered across the cavern to one of the side tunnels and entered it without hesitating. His torch flickered down the dark passageway.

The rest of them followed in silence.

Crowdal carried Sid gently and with each step he took down the passageway, the pain from the Korpor diminished.

Chapter 48

Sid woke up while they were still in the underground passageways and insisted he could walk. Crowdal set him down and he swayed on his feet for a few moments, then stood up straight. He looked around the group and couldn't believe they were all there with him, alive and well. He then realized that no one knew who Mrs. Wessmank was, so he quickly introduced her to Melinda and Writhgarth. But as he introduced her to Crowdal, they smiled warmly at each other.

Mrs. Wessmank patted Crowdal's arm affectionately. "I remember you from the road to Yisk. You had a smile that warmed me on that cold day."

Crowdal nodded. "I thought the same thing about you. But you were with those men, so I am glad you didn't see Sid in the back of the hay wagon."

"Those weren't men, they were Haissen, so I am also glad that I didn't notice Sidoro."

Sid didn't remember any of this and the confusion showed on his face.

Crowdal slapped him lightly on the back. "Someday I will tell you all about that little journey."

Sid nodded and they all continued making their way through the tunnels.

Writhgarth led them unerringly and they had no more troubles. Eventually, they exited the tunnel system through a small cave in a cliff far outside of the city.

They traveled without incident for the rest of the afternoon and Sid found himself recovering quickly. They finally stopped in the fading light of evening and made camp by a small stand of trees that was hidden from the road. The group was in a somber mood, although happy to be alive. Crowdal, Writhgarth, and Melinda talked softly as they set up camp. After a meager meal they all retired to their bedrolls. The day had been a long one for everyone and they were all exhausted.

Mrs. Wessmank sat against a tree, a blanket around her legs, and her Tulgin laid against her thigh. Sid got up and approached them and as he did, the animal lifted his head and followed his every step with intelligent eyes. Sid sat next to the old woman and put a hand on her knee, then hesitantly reached out to the animal and touched his snout. "I wanted to be introduced to your friend and to say thank you to him for distracting the Korpor and saving us all."

Mrs. Wessmank was quiet for some time, as if she were listening to something, then she smiled. "Maelon says that you are welcome, but he only did what he had to do."

Sid raised an eyebrow in surprise. "He can speak? And he has a name?"

She smiled and looked down fondly at Maelon. "Oh yes, he and I have had an unbreakable bond since he was born. He is like a son to me." She unconsciously stroked Maelon's head the whole time she spoke and Maelon seemed to nod toward Sid, the act so human that Sid nodded back and smiled.

"Is Maelon injured? Does he need Melinda to tend to him?"

The old woman shook her head. "He has some bruised ribs and a bit of a headache, but he is fine. He thanks you for your concern."

Sid was glad that Maelon was going to be all right. He stood back up. "Get some rest, both of you. I'll see you in the morning."

"Thank you, Sidoro, and you get some rest, too. You've been through a lot over the past few days."

Nodding, he turned away and made his way to his bedroll, laying down gratefully.

The sounds of the small camp soon quieted down and he heard loud snoring from both Writhgarth and Crowdal. The sound was comforting to him.

He was tired, but after some time, he realized that he couldn't sleep, so he sat back up. He couldn't shake off a sense of greater danger, but couldn't pinpoint what it was. It throbbed inside of him, filling him with a feeling of dread. They had escaped against all odds, so he should have been happy, but he somehow knew that they weren't out of danger yet.

He thought about the Black Numbers manuscript and couldn't wait to look through it, to try and understand how to manipulate the Black Numbers. But he was also afraid of it. He remembered how the power had filled him with such pleasure. It had been intoxicating and that scared him. He still couldn't believe how easily he had burned the Haissen to cinders.

Who was he? What was he?

He closed his eyes and pictured his father's blank stare. The emptiness in those eyes still filled him with pain, mainly because he knew that his father had betrayed him to the Oblate with such dispassion.

Then Sid thought of his mother. Who had she been? Was she a lie too? He squeezed his eyes tightly and shook his head. No, she was not a lie. He angrily opened his eyes. She had loved him, of that he was sure. It was the only thing in his life he was sure about.

He leaned over and pulled his pack closer. He dug inside until he found what he was looking for. Carefully, he removed the rolled up and torn drawing of his mother It was creased across the middle. It must have happened sometime during his journey, he though bitterly. With trembling hands, he untied the string from both ends and slowly unrolled the parchment.

By the flickering light of the small camp fire, he looked at the charcoal drawing of his mother, at how her long hair fell past her shoulders and the way her dark eyes seemed so full of sadness and empathy. His hands stopped trembling and he lightly touched the large gash in the middle of the parchment he had made when he had thrown the piece of firewood across the room, hitting the picture by accident. He remembered how he had accidentally smudged the charcoal across her face and left eye when he had tried to smooth it out. He looked at it now and without thinking, he called forth his numbers.

They instantly appeared, floating in his mind.

Sid examined the portrait, measuring the dimensions, the thickness and consistency of the parchment. He formed these measurements into equations and let them float in front of him. Then he looked at the gash and how it made a half-moon shape across his mother's chest and face, slightly crumpled in the center where the firewood had damaged it the most. He immediately saw the mathematical formula and pulled the numbers and variables into a complex equation. He then studied the area of the smudge across her face and quickly created another equation.

He examined the drawing, trying to see if he had missed anything. No, he had everything. So he brought all of the equations and lined them up. They floated, gently bumping into each other as he studied them. Without hesitating, he pulled the equation for the torn part of the parchment and placed it above the drawing. Then he brought over the equations for the thickness and consistency of the parchment and connected them with the main equation. He nudged the smudge equation to the end and they all formed together with a snick and turned green. It all seemed so easy now.

Sid looked at the equation and knew it was right. He forced it downward until it hung right above the drawing. Then, with a push of energy, he lowered it until the equation made contact with the parchment. A flash of light blinded him for a moment and when his vision cleared, he saw that the parchment was whole again. He reached out and touched the drawing. There was no remainder of the tear. The parchment was as smooth as if it were new.

He smiled when he saw that the smudge across his mother's face and eye was also gone. Sid looked upon his mother's whole image once again. She was beautiful and the sadness in her eyes seemed to draw him in. Tears fell down his cheeks and the image blurred. He put the drawing down and closed his eyes.

Some day he would find out who his mother had really been.

And some day, he would make his father suffer for his betrayal.

Epilogue

The new Black Robe ended contact with the Korpor. He sat in a comfortable chair in his private chamber and smiled.

So Sid really was the Aleph Null.

Tris shook his head and chuckled. After years of pretending to be his friend, he had never thought that much of Sid's abilities. Sid had always seemed rather dull, actually. But Tris had done his duty and befriended him.

Over the years, Tris had passed every piece of information he could to the Black Robe. And the whole while, he had worked on perfecting control of his own numbers.

Last year he had been Proofed and even though he had failed, he had also proven to be an enigma, for the Korpor could not inflict pain upon him.

Yet Tris was not the Aleph Null. What that meant, no one in the Oblate could guess.

Now he was the Black Robe.

Tris smiled again. Soon, the Oblate would no longer be a silent power. It was time. He would take the power of Black Numbers from Sid and with them under his control, the Oblate would come out of hiding. Power was for those who took it. And he would take it from Sid.

But first things first.

He brought his numbers into existence in front of him. He tossed them about with ease. Then he created an equation that was so complex even he had to struggle with it. Finally he got it right and bent the equation into the shape of a door. He clicked the last variable into place and the air hummed inside of the opening. With a smile, he stepped through the shimmering air.

His feet sunk into soft sand. It was dark.

He quickly gathered some numbers and started spinning them until they glowed. The blue light lit up a small circle around him. In the shadows just beyond the light, he saw the grotesque face of the Korpor. He took a few steps forward and the light glowed off of the white fur of the creature.

It just stared at him.

Tris looked at the equations that imprisoned the Korpor. They were pitifully simple. He casually twisted the equations until they blew apart. The air stopped shimmering around the Korpor and it flexed its arms over its head.

"*Thank you.*"

"You failed me again."

The Korpor bowed its head slightly. "*I do what I do. The boy is... powerful.*"

Tris pulled the black hood over his head. "Yes, maybe he is. But he hasn't come against me yet."

* * *

The Korpor trembled as it looked up its master. It had felt the Aleph Null's powers several times now, and while that power was beyond anything it had ever felt before, it had never been painful.

The Korpor shivered as it looked at the man in the black robe. This man it feared.

The power from him was malignant, diseased. The Korpor had felt pain like never before at the hands of this one. It grimaced, never wanting to feel such pain again.

Tris walked back to the shimmering portal of air and held out his arm. "Come, we have work to do. Things have changed, but I prepared for this eventuality, as remote as it seemed. A new plan goes into effect now."

The Korpor followed its master through the shimmering portal.

THE END

Thank you for reading **Black Numbers: The Aleph Null Chronicles: Book One**.

If you purchased this book from a website, I would appreciate it greatly if you would leave an honest review.

Blood Numbers: The Aleph Null Chronicles: Book Two
is now available at all Amazon sites worldwide.

Look for **Broken Numbers: The Aleph Null Chronicles: Book Three** in 2014.

See what's next for Sid in
Blood Numbers:
The Aleph Null Chronicles: Book Two

Sid is the Aleph Null, his power of Black Numbers awakened after the defeat of Father Mansico and the Korpor, but he cannot yet manipulate those numbers. He journeys with his friends Crowdal, Melinda, Mrs. Wessmank, Maelon and Writhgarth to a faraway land that may hold the key to his powers. Along the way he meets a powerful woman who awakens his first feelings of true love, but who may also be the one destined to destroy him.

Sid is pursued by evil forces from all directions. His former childhood friend, Tris, now rules the Oblate and commands a power of numbers equal to, if not greater than his own. He also controls the seductive yet violent Korpor, and together they are weaving a plot to capture Sid and take control of his Black Numbers.

Sid is also hunted by a sadistic and violent warlord and his death squad who has his own plans for Sid. But worst of all, a forgotten and ancient evil has been unintentionally freed from its millennia-long prison, a nightmarish being that has one purpose...

To destroy the wielder of Black Numbers.

About the Author

Dean Frank Lappi was born in Virginia, Minnesota, a place that is part of the well-known Iron Range, where most of the iron ore in the USA is found.

In 1996, he graduated college with a Master of Arts degree in English and has worked in a number of industries since then as an Information Developer and Web Content Manager.

Dean is very active on **Twitter** (@DeanLappi), and you can also find him on **Facebook**.

Made in the USA
San Bernardino, CA
21 September 2014